TO BE AN ISRAELI

All My Love, Detrick
BOOK FOUR

ROBERTA KAGAN

2nd Edition

ISBN (eBook): 978-1-957207-44-5
ISBN (Paperback): 978-1-957207-45-2
ISBN (Hardcover): 978-1-957207-46-9

Title Production by The Book Whisperer

CHAPTER ONE

Tel Aviv, Israel; 1964

Katja Zuckerman sat on the balcony and looked at the full moon that was just beginning to rise—a blood-red moon. Blood-red moons always coincided with significant events for the Israeli people, and Katja wondered what news the moon would bring.

From where she sat, the city of Tel Aviv looked like an ant colony, people moving in all directions. She felt like an outsider as she watched them—a couple walking hand in hand, a group of young girls laughing, an old man hunched over with a cane looking angry and determined to push through the crowds, and a woman carrying a paper bag filled with groceries.

Across the street, a flag danced softly, caressed by the breeze in the starlit night. It was a blue and white flag with a Star of David. This was her home. This was Israel. Almost a year had passed since she'd learned the truth about her birth, and she still could not accept the reality. Six months ago, she'd traveled to Germany, where she met her birth mother for the first and only time.

A tear slipped down her cheek as she looked down at the streets. Anyone who knew her story might say that she did not deserve to call herself a Jew, not only a Jew but also an Israeli. Katja was still filled with shame that stained her like the mark of Cain. The truth had ripped through her life as a box cutter sliced through pieces of cardboard, and Katja, like the cardboard, had fallen in pieces to the ground. The truth was that she was not born of Jewish blood but was born in the Lebensborn to a pure Aryan German mother and a father who was an officer in Hitler's hideous SS.

This girl, who loved her Jewish family with all her heart, had been christened in that home for the Lebensborn when she was just a year old and given the name Katja by one of the most notorious Nazis, Heinrich Himmler. After the naming ceremony, she was adopted by another monster of a man, the abusive Nazi in charge of work details at the Treblinka Extermination Camp, SS Officer Manfred Blau, and his barren wife.

Even the fact that she had served her country for two years in the IDF was not enough to exonerate her, remove the stain, and purify her blood. Maybe if she had actually served in combat, it might have counted. But as a beautiful girl with exotic looks, she was trained to type and take shorthand. Katja was not just beautiful. After training, she could type at the speed of ninety-five words-per-minute. Afterward, she was assigned to the procurement office of the IDF to work as the secretary for Sergeant Greenberg.

In spite of her unfortunate beginnings, God was watching and had other plans for Katja. Although the Nazis had carefully planned her future, God knew Katja was an innocent child. And so, in his powerful wisdom, He arranged the circumstances that had forced Blau and his wife to give Katja away. Then, that little girl born on Hitler's breeding farm was blessed.

Isaac and Zofia Zuckerman, Jews, had taken the child and raised her as their own. Katja grew up Jewish. She grew to love the land of Israel and to call the Jews her people. All of this took place when Katja was too young to remember. The only parents she remembered were Isaac and Zofia. Over the years, they could not find it in their hearts to tell her the truth. She might never have known and might have remained blissfully ignorant if SS officer

Manfred Blau had not escaped from Spandau Prison and been recaptured and tried in Israel.

She had been preparing dinner when she heard her name and her mother's name spoken by Blau at his televised trial. It was the greatest shock of her life. When her fiancé at the time, Elan Amsel, a native of Israel, learned of her bloodlines, he left her. He was heartbroken but could not marry her, knowing that the blood of an SS officer ran through her veins, and if they had a child, the child would be tainted as well.

The stabbing pain in her heart had still not healed, but she was doing better. When Elan first left, it seemed impossible to go on. She had so many questions. Her mind raced in confusion, and she could not sleep or eat. At one point, Katja even considered suicide until her dearest childhood friend Mendel suggested confronting the problem head-on by meeting her birth mother.

Mendel had searched all over Europe and found a Leah Haswell in Switzerland. After meeting with her, she told them that she knew Helga was married to a farmer on the outskirts of Munich. Mendel arranged the entire trip for Katja, her mother, Zofia, and himself to go to Germany, where they would seek out Katja's birth mother, Helga Haswell.

After an extensive search, they'd found her, married, now Helga Hoffman. Katja had spoken to Helga and looked into her eyes. She'd watched her try to explain, and to some degree, Katja had even forgiven her. She had been trying to make sense of it all and to put the pieces of her life back together since she returned home to Israel.

The phone on the table beside the bed rang, startling Katja out of her rambling thoughts. She jumped up and ran to lift the receiver.

"Hello."

"Hi, Kat."

"Hi, Mendel."

"Let me guess, you've probably forgotten to eat again. Am I right?"

She laughed. "I had a late lunch at work."

"Why don't I pick you up, and we can have dinner? You need to eat, Kat. You're getting so thin that soon it will be impossible to see you."

"I'm not that thin, Mendel." She giggled.

He laughed. "Okay, Kat, you're not that thin, but come on, do it for me. Let's go and have dinner."

"All right. Can you give me half an hour?"

"Sure. I'll see you then."

Mendel. God bless Mendel. He was always there to lift her up when her spirits were low. Katja stretched and went to take a quick shower. Perhaps it would be good to get out of the apartment for a while.

Mendel arrived a half hour later carrying a paper bag filled with groceries.

"I thought you wanted to go out and eat?" Katja said.

"I do, and we are going out, but I wanted to put some food in your refrigerator. You never have anything in there." He winked at her and began unloading fruit and vegetables into her empty refrigerator.

"Mendel. You don't have to shop for me. I can take care of myself."

"Of course, you can. But you've been working a lot lately, and I'd just like to make things a little easier. Besides, if you have some food in the house, you might even eat once in a while."

She watched him as he emptied the bags. "Mendel." She shook her head. "You didn't need to do this, but thank you."

He turned to look at her and smiled. "No need to thank me, Kat. You'd do it for me if I needed you to."

"You're right. I would. I'd do it for Rachel, too."

"You know, we should go and see Rachel. It's been a long time. Would you like to make plans to go one weekend?"

"I don't know if I can take time off work. We've been so busy," she said.

"Then let's plan it for later in the year."

"Good idea."

"Are you ready to go out and get something to eat? I'm starving."

"Yes…" Katja grabbed a white sweater off a hook on the wall. Mendel opened the door, and they walked, side-by-side, toward his car.

"It's a beautiful night."

"Isn't it?" she whispered. "Look, Mendel." Katja pointed up to the moon. "It's almost red tonight."

"Yes, I see, and the sky is so clear that you can see the stars."

"Remember, we used to love to look at the stars when we were kids. We'd wonder if there were people living on them."

"I remember," he said and rubbed her shoulder.

Katja smiled at him and sighed. "I wish we were kids again when we were still innocent."

He opened the car door, and she slid inside. They drove for a few minutes with the windows open while a warm breeze stroked their faces.

"You realize, Kat, you have to move forward in your life. I know you still think about all of it, and it still bothers you…"

"You mean my birth mother and everything?"

"Yeah." He nodded. "That's exactly what I mean."

"How did you know that was what I was thinking about? How did you know I still think about it all the time?"

"Because I know you. Sometimes, I think I know you better than I know myself," Mendel said.

"I am glad you went with me to Germany. I don't know what I would have done without you."

"I love you, Kat—you know that. I will always be there for you, no matter what happens."

"Mendel, what am I ever going to do with you?" she said, reaching over and rubbing his shoulder as he drove.

"You could start by telling me what you feel like eating."

She gave a short laugh. "Tonight, I'll leave it up to you."

They rode for several miles until they came to an outdoor café. They got seated, and Mendel opened the menu, but Katja did not. She glanced around the café.

"I used to come here sometimes with Elan," she said.

"You still think about him, too?"

"Yes, of course. How could I not? We were engaged."

"But any man who was a man at all would not have abandoned you because of something out of your control. You may have been born to Nazis but are as Jewish as I am."

"Not to Elan. He wanted his bloodline to be pure. I have the blood of an SS officer inside of me. Sometimes it makes me want to tear off my skin," she said.

"Don't say that, Kat. You are the same person you always were. Finding out that crap about where you were born doesn't change you at all."

"It did, according to Elan. Suddenly, in his eyes, I became a spawn of the enemy. My blood was not pure. I was unclean."

"Hmmm, pure blood, huh? Now, if that doesn't sound like Nazi philosophy, I don't know what does."

The waitress took their order and left them alone with their thoughts. A silence hung over them like a cloud. Neither of them spoke until the salads arrived.

She toyed with her fork for a few moments. "Mendel, how am I ever going to start over? I can't seem to feel at peace within myself."

"You are going to accept that you were born in the home of the Lebensborn and raised by Jews. Then, you will realize that you are exactly where you were meant to be: here in Israel. You, Kat, are one of us. You're an Israeli. You're a Jew. You are just as much a victim of the Nazis as we are."

"Do you really believe that, Mendel? Do you really think I am a Jew?"

"What do you feel in your heart, Kat? Do you feel like a Nazi, or do you feel like one of us? Can you still remember those days when we were onboard that rickety old boat headed for Palestine? I was all alone. You and Rachel and your families were all I had. My parents were taken away from me. They both died in the camps. I never even found out how or where they died. One day, they loaded the kids into a truck. When somebody said we would be gassed, I slipped off the side and escaped.

"Then I wandered around the forests until I heard about the boat the *Exodus*. The Jewish leaders arranging the voyage felt sorry for me and let me on without any money for passage. I was ten years old and on my way to Palestine. You, me, Rachel, and Abe were just kids who were scared to death. We didn't know what the future held for us because we were Jews and trying like hell to get to Palestine before it was even legal, before it was Israel. Poor Abe died when the British attacked the ship."

"Yeah, I can remember. It was so terrifying that I'll never forget it."

"You were one of us then, and you are one of us now. I can still see you, tiny little Katja, with your long, blonde curls and those big, terrified blue eyes. Remember? You sat beside me, Rachel, and your parents—all of us together, hoping to build a Jewish homeland."

"Yes, I remember. But that was before I knew what I really was."

"You knew who you were then, and you are the same person now. Where you were born and whose sperm fertilized the egg that created you mean nothing. You are one of us."

She nodded. He reached across the table and took her hand. "Kat, you have to believe me. You are one of us! If I were Elan, I would never have walked away from you—never! I can't respect a man who could do that to a person he says he loves."

"Mendel." She smiled, but tears filled her eyes.

"Marry me, Kat. Make my life complete." He cleared his throat. "Give me a chance to show you what it means to really be loved. You don't have to love me back. Just give me a chance to make you happy, to bring that beautiful smile back to your face."

"Mendel." She shook her head. "I do love you. I just don't know if it is in the way that you deserve to be loved."

"Can you try, Kat? Can you give me a chance?" He squeezed her hand. "I promise to do everything I can to make you happy. In just a few more months, I'll be finished with law school. Just give me a couple of years to get my practice going. You'll see. I'll be successful. You'll have everything you ever wanted. You won't have to work. We can start a family and have a couple of kids. What do you say, Kat?"

She might have fallen in love with Mendel if Elan had not come along—big, strong, sexy Elan. The minute he'd entered her life, she'd fallen through time and space into a love affair so filled with passion that she hardly knew herself. Mendel had always been a constant, a friend, a companion, someone she could talk to about anything. Could she marry him? After all, she was getting older. She had turned twenty-three in January. Perhaps he was right. Perhaps she might find a way to begin her life over with him by her side. Maybe she could even forgive herself for the Nazi blood that ran through her veins.

Kat looked at him, his eyes glowing deep-green like a forest speckled with gold dandelions at the beginning of summer, so full of hope, so full of love. "Yes. I'll marry you," she said.

"Kat, oh my God! Kat!" He looked at her in joyous disbelief. His throat was dry, and he coughed a little. "You've made me so happy. I promise you that I will devote every day of my life to making sure you always feel loved and cherished."

Katja saw the pure delight in his eyes and decided that she had made the right decision.

His hands trembled as he touched her cheek. His fingers were a little clammy as they caressed her skin as if it were porcelain. Carefully, almost as if afraid to break the spell, he leaned forward and gently touched his warm lips to hers. "I love you. I've always loved you," he said, his voice deep and hoarse with emotion.

"I know, Mendel. I know."

"You will be my world, Kat. I will do anything, anything at all, to make you happy. You'll see. You'll have a good life with me."

"And you don't mind mingling your blood with mine so we can have children?" she asked.

"Elan was a fool. He lost the best woman in the world. To me, you are and always will be a Jew and an Israeli. You are a precious gift, and I will always remember how fortunate I am to have you as my wife. I will never, not for one minute, forget…"

"Mendel," she said. He was handsome in a haphazard way. His clothes could hardly be called high fashion. In fact, most of the time, the colors he wore didn't match, and his maple-brown hair never looked combed. But his features were fine looking, with his emerald eyes flecked with gold, his strong chin and high cheekbones, and his slender but muscular frame. She leaned over and kissed him. She felt his body quiver ever so slightly.

"Let's drive to the kibbutz next week and tell your parents," he said.

"I'll ask my boss if I can have the week off. He won't be happy, but I think if I tell him that I'm going to see my parents to tell them about our engagement, he'll grudgingly understand. Can you take the time off from work and school?" she asked him.

"Of course. For you, anything."

CHAPTER TWO

WHEN KATJA and Mendel arrived at the kibbutz where she and Mendel had grown up, Zofia, her Jewish mother, was reading a story to the younger children. They were all gathered around her in a circle, their tiny faces upturned in wonder and waiting as she slowly brought the storybook to life. Zofia heard the door open, and she looked up from the book. Then, a smile crept over her face, and the lines of life deepened around her eyes. It was her daughter, her sunshine, her life.

"Hi, Mom." Katja walked over and kissed Zofia's cheek. "And how are you, Mendel?"

"Good, very good," he said, his eyes shining as brightly as a harvest moon. Zofia could see something was amiss, and it certainly pleased Mendel. *Could it be? Nah, they grew up as children together.*

"It's good to see you both, but what brings you home? Is everything all right?"

"Yes, yes. Don't worry so much, Mom. I have good news. Where's Papa?"

"I would have to guess he's in the field. It's just after midday, and he should be there," Zofia said.

"Can someone take over for you here with the kids?"

"Sure," Zofia said, and then called out to the rooms in the back, "Yetta? Yetta, do you have a minute, please?" A thick, heavy-set woman with thinning red hair came out of one of the classrooms, breathing heavily as she walked.

"Yes, Zofia, what is it?"

"My daughter, Katja, is here. I think you know her."

"Sure, of course. I've known Katja since she was a tiny *pitzel*. Oy, you were such a pretty little thing. Not that you're not pretty now, you are, but *oy* you were such a beautiful child. Of course, how could I ever forget such a child?"

"Hello, Yetta," Katja said, warmly hugging her mother's friend and coworker.

"So tell me, Nu, why are you here? Just a visit? It's not a holiday. You're all right, I hope. Yes?" Yetta inquired.

"Don't be a yenta, Yetta," Zofia said. "Can you watch the children for a while for me? Katja wants me to go with her to find her father. She needs to speak with us together."

"But of course." Yetta smiled. "I hope everything is all right. You know you can talk to me. I won't tell anyone. You can tell me anything."

"I'll be back soon," Zofia said, shaking her head and smiling. Yetta would love to know all the news.

Katja had been such a small child, but she had grown taller over the years than her mother. She put her arm around Zofia, and the two walked into the fields. Rows and rows of olive trees lined the walkway, their leaves sparkling like silver coins in the sunshine. The smell of fresh garlic permeated the air. Men and women were harvesting apples across the field, carefully piling them into large barrels. All were working together on the land that was their kibbutz, their shared home. This, too, was Israel.

Zofia called out to Isaac, who turned to see them from where he worked. A smile washed over his sun-kissed face, and he began walking over to them while wiping the earth from his hands on the thighs of his pants.

"Katja, sweetheart. What are you doing at home?"

Katja laughed. "That's exactly what Mom asked. I'm here to see you both. Come back to the main house. I have something to tell you."

They started back together.

"Good news, I hope?" Isaac said. "Nothing is wrong?"

"No, nothing is wrong. Yes, good news," Katja said.

Mendel was sitting, leaning forward on a comfortable old sofa in the main living area of the kibbutz, waiting excitedly. Even though Mendel had known Katja's parents since he was ten, he was still anxious about sharing the news. He just wanted everything to go perfectly.

"Mendel is here, too?" Isaac said. "Good to see you, Mendel. How are you?" Isaac hugged him.

"I've never been better, sir." Mendel cleared his throat.

"Mendel and I have something to tell you."

"*Nu*?" Zofia said, "Tell us already. I'm a nervous wreck. What is it?"

"We're getting married," Katja said.

Zofia and Isaac exchanged a smile. Isaac's eyes danced, and Zofia could not help but laugh aloud.

"Oy! Mazel tov," Zofia said, grabbing her daughter and kissing her.

"Mazel tov!" Isaac hugged Mendel. "You're going to be my son-in-law. That's very good news. Very good, indeed."

CHAPTER THREE

THAT NIGHT, Zofia lay curled in Isaac's arms. She ran her fingers over the skin on his chest. So familiar, Isaac, her beloved. Once, his skin had been young and supple. But now, at forty-seven, even though he was still muscular from working in the field, his skin had wrinkled from years of working in the hot sun, and it was no longer as firm. But to Zofia, it didn't matter. She loved him. She had almost lost him all those years ago. Although they'd had their differences over the years, the memory of having come so close to losing him had always reminded her how blessed she was.

"Isaac… Are you asleep?"

"No, my love. I was thinking about Katja and Mendel."

"I am happy. He loves her. He will take care of her. After all, Isaac, we won't live forever. I mean, I realize that we are still young, but it is something I have always been concerned about. After all, Katja is an only child. She has no brothers or sisters to lean on. At least I will know that once we are gone, Katja will have someone in her life who truly cares for her. Isn't that what every parent wants?"

"Of course, and I love Mendel. He has been like a son to us," Isaac said. "We knew him since he was a little boy. He has a good heart."

"Yes, he does. I remember when we met him when we were all on that boat, the *Exodus*. Poor child, he had no one else. His parents, his family—all killed in the camps."

"I know, and he certainly grew up to be a fine, educated man. That was the only thing I regretted in my life, never getting an education," Isaac said. "You deserved a better man than me."

"Isaac, there is no one better than you. You are the best man I have ever known. And I know you would have gone to school, but neither of us ever had the opportunity. Hitler stole that from us. Yes, the Nazis stole that and much more—our families, friends, everything. But at least Isaac, God returned you to me. And for that reason alone, I am forever grateful. Besides, the kibbutzim have built Israel, and you have worked on this with all your heart."

He gently touched the top of her head. "I love you, Zofia."

"I know you do, and I love you too, Isaac."

"I don't know if I should even mention this. I don't want the evil eye to look and suck away their happiness. But do you think that Katja is in love with Mendel? Or do you think she is still in love with Elan, God forbid?" Isaac's voice cracked.

"I don't know. It's hard to say what she really feels. I would never mention Elan to her. She went through hell when he left. But I must admit, I've been worried about the same thing. I didn't want to say it aloud. I was afraid to put a *ke nignehore* (not tempt the evil eye) on the marriage. *Pu, pu, pu,*" Zofia said.

"*Pu, pu, pu,*" he said, gently running his hand over her salt and pepper hair. "I know that we both wish them every happiness."

She smiled. "We've both become so superstitious. It's funny, isn't it?" He laughed. "I know, it's true. The older I get, the more I remember all the superstitious things my parents did to ward off the evil eye. At the time, I was young and thought they were so old-fashioned and silly, but now that I'm getting older, I find that I'm doing the same things."

"Yes, it's funny how life is. The older you get, the more you understand your parents. Why they did the things they did, things that, at the time, seemed so ridiculous."

"I miss them, my mother and father. Sometimes at night, I still dream of being a little boy sitting in the back of my mother's bakery, eating challah with butter. She adored me. I was such a spoiled, pampered little boy. I was her pride and joy, you know. Oy, how different things might have been," he said, his voice almost a whisper. "But who knows, maybe if Hitler had never come into power, you and I would not have been together. I remember before the war, when you used to come into the bakery, you never even noticed me. I was just a fat little boy."

"I was too young, Isaac. I didn't know about boys then. I was just a child myself. But when I saw you again in the forest, after I'd escaped from Treblinka, you were so big and strong and handsome. I'll never forget it. I can't say how long I'd been wandering without food or water. I thought I was going to die for sure. And to this day, I can still remember how I felt. I think the worst part of it all was being thirsty. Thirst is worse than hunger, you know.

"Well, anyway, I'd fallen asleep exhausted, ready to give up. I was lying under a tree. I think maybe it was an oak. It was a heavy tree with thick, leafy branches, and it shielded me from the relentless heat of the sun. My throat was so dry that it hurt, like a bad sore throat. I believe I even tasted blood in the back of my throat. Awakened by movement, I opened my eyes, and there you were. Your form was illuminated by the sun at your back, and I thought you were an angel. Oh, Isaac. At that moment, I felt the presence of God."

"I remember. I remember all of it. Shlomie and I were out hunting to feed the rest of the partisans. We thought we heard a rabbit and followed the sound. Then there you were, lying on the ground alone, half-starved. I looked at you, and you took my breath away. I was thinking, 'Could it be? Am I dreaming? Is that really Zofia Weiss?' And it was. Praise God, it was. And as I've told you a thousand times, I always had a crush on you."

"So you say." She squeezed him a little.

"I still do." He kissed the top of her head.

"Oh, Isaac, you can still make me feel like a young girl in love."

"I hope I will always make you feel that way," Isaac said, and he kissed the top of Zofia's head again. Then he took a deep breath and continued, "If Katja still has feelings for Elan, we can only pray that she will forget in time and learn to love Mendel. He is a fine person and will make her a good husband."

"Yes, I understand what you are saying, and I agree. We must pray for them and wish them all the happiness our marriage has brought to us. And if she still cares for Elan, all we can do is pray that she will forget him. Oh, Isaac, our little sunshine is going to be a bride. You are going to walk her down the aisle and lead her under the chuppah. I'm kvelling." She smiled in the darkness, and he could feel her smile.

"You know, Zofia, even with all we have been through and all the evil we've seen. It is still a very wonderful world."

She moved slowly to kiss him and found his cheeks wet with tears.

"Oh, Isaac, my Isaac. Promise me you will never change."

CHAPTER FOUR

Zofia wanted to make Katja's wedding gown. "Before the war, I was a seamstress. You know that. I learned under one of the finest seamstresses that ever lived. God rest her soul."

"You never told me about her," Katja said as Zofia was draping a measuring tape around Katja's tiny waist.

"Yes, well, she was a good friend to me. She taught me the trade."

"I've seen some of the clothes that you've made. You are so talented."

"Oy, I remember when I was as thin as you are now," Zofia said, pinning the fabric.

"You'll always be beautiful, Mom."

"She was quite a seamstress, that woman who taught me. Her name was Fruma. She was kind, too. She and her friend Gitel took me in after my mother died. Fruma taught me to make beautiful dresses, suits, and wedding gowns. She and Gitel were good friends to me. They both died in Treblinka."

"I'm sorry, Mom. I hate to think about those camps."

"Yes, but it's a memory we must never forget because it could easily happen again if we ever did forget. That's why it's so important that we protect Israel. If there is ever another dictator like Hitler, the Jews will always have a place to go where they will be safe. You see, before Israel, we had nowhere to go," Zofia said, draping a bolt of white satin across Katja's shoulders and pinning it.

"Mother?"

"Yes, my sunshine," Zofia's voice was muffled by the two pins she held between her teeth.

"You don't believe there is anything to genetics, do you? I guess what I mean is, well, do you think I have any of the characteristics of my birth father?"

"You, my sweet Katja, are the kindest, gentlest, and most loving person I've ever known. You have no characteristics of an evil SS officer. You are a child of God, Katja. The people who were involved in your beginnings mean nothing. Right after the moment of conception, God took over."

"Mendel loves me, regardless of where I came from."

"Mendel had always had a good heart and a sound mind. Even as a little boy, he was that way."

"Did you know that he has a very high IQ? They tested him at the University. He graduated from college at the top of his class. It looks like he will do the same in law school."

"It doesn't surprise me. Besides all of that, he is also good and kind. What else could a woman want?"

Katja nodded. Zofia studied her daughter. Zofia knew her child. She may not have given birth to her, but she raised her, nursed her through sickness, cried with her when she was sad, and rejoiced when she was happy. Yes, Zofia knew every expression, every subtle twist of an eyebrow or raise of a shoulder.

And now, by looking into Katja's eyes, Zofia knew that she still loved Elan and that her heart had still not mended. Elan is so self-righteous. How could he have walked away from her when he learned she was not of Jewish blood? He was cold and merciless, and Zofia could never forgive him for the pain he'd caused her daughter. She wanted to tell Katja that Mendel was a better man than Elan, but she knew it would only stir the bitterness in Katja's heart. *Don't mention Elan,* Zofia thought. *Don't bring it up. Let it be. With God's help, Mendel will find a way to win Katja's heart over the years.*

"So we'll have the wedding here?" Zofia asked, strategically placing another pin in the fabric.

"Yes, of course."

"It's all right with Mendel?"

"Yes, we talked about it. Everyone we know and love is here in this kibbutz. This is where we grew up, and this is where we want to be married. I am going to invite some friends from work, and Mendel plans to invite some friends from law school and, of course, Rachel. Rachel will come home for the wedding. I'm sure of it."

"Of course, Rachel. She hardly ever comes to see her sister. I can't believe she doesn't want to be here for the holidays to be with Shana and the baby. It's a terrible shame. Shana misses her so much. Shana tells me that Rachel writes; sometimes she calls but almost never comes. Last year, she sent a present for the baby for Hanukkah, but she didn't come to light the candles with us," Zofia said, shaking her head.

Katja knew why Rachel didn't come back to the kibbutz, but she didn't want to betray her by telling her secret. If Rachel chose to announce her truth, it must be her choice alone.

CHAPTER FIVE

When they returned to Tel Aviv, Mendel was so happy that Katja could not help but be swept up in the whirlwind of his joy. They were to be married in three months, and it seemed they had a continuously growing list of things to do. Immediately after the wedding, Mendel was graduating from law school. The couple spent an afternoon writing invitations to their friends who did not live on the kibbutz. Katja called Rachel to invite her and her female partner to the wedding.

"I'm still not ready to tell everyone I'm a lesbian," Rachel said. "I think it's best that I come alone."

"You can do whatever you want, but Mendel and I would welcome Sandy if you decided to bring her with you," Katja said.

"I don't think I will yet," Rachel said. "Shana would be so ashamed. And when I leave, Shana would face that embarrassment every day. How would she ever explain it to her husband? And as the baby grew up, everyone would whisper that the child's aunt was a lesbian. No, I think I should come alone."

Katja discussed the situation with Mendel. He agreed that he would readily accept Rachel's lover, but he felt they had to accept

Rachel's decision. If she chose to come alone, then they would respect her choice.

The couple found an apartment halfway between Mendel's office and Katja's job. Her lease was up, and he found a tenant to sublet his previous apartment. Right after the wedding, they would move into their new home.

They went to dinner together at night, followed by long walks and heartfelt talks. But they still had not made love. Mendel did not initiate, and Katja was unsure what to do, so she did nothing.

It was not that Mendel didn't want to take Katja in his arms and make passionate love to her—he did. In fact, every night before he fell asleep, he thought about holding her close to him. And it was not that Mendel was a virgin because he wasn't. He'd had a couple of flings with other women he'd met at school when Katja was engaged to Elan. But neither of the other women he'd courted had meant what Katja meant to him. He loved Katja. He wanted everything to be right between them. He was afraid to offend her. He didn't want to make a mistake.

Sometimes, he chastised himself for being too careful. Other times, he felt pangs of fear travel through him when he thought about how she might be offended if he pushed her too fast or hard. So, he decided to have patience. Mendel would wait until their wedding night and be satisfied with the precious kiss she gave him every evening when they said goodbye. Mendel smiled to himself at how ridiculously in love he was. He never told Kat, but Mendel didn't wash his face after Kat kissed him until the next morning. He wanted to sleep through the night, holding on to the warmth of her lips on his.

One afternoon, Katja left her apartment in a rush. She'd gotten up late and forgot to put her reading glasses in her purse. Everything was blurry when she got to work, making it impossible to concentrate on her job. She would have asked her boss for permission to go home and get her glasses. But he was in a meeting until late afternoon and left a pile of work on her desk with a note that said the work must be finished before she left.

Not only had she forgotten her glasses, but also it was her special time of the month, and she was overly emotional. Looking at the papers on her desk and the typewriter beside them, she knew that even with her glasses, she would have to be at work until well after seven that evening to finish everything.

Her lower stomach was cramping, and she felt bloated. Tears began to form in the corners of her eyes. Katja buried her head in her hand. She'd developed a slight headache from trying to focus without her glasses. Then she gazed at the telephone on her desk. Thank God for Mendel. She picked up the receiver and dialed.

"Mendel?"

"Hi, sweetheart."

His kindness, accompanied by her overly sensitive emotions, made her start weeping.

"What's wrong, Kat?" His voice was soft but filled with concern.

She began to tell him about her glasses, the paperwork on her desk, her stomachache, her headache, and how overwhelmed she was feeling.

"Shh, Kat. It's okay. I'll come by the office and get your key. Then I'll pick up your glasses, a couple of aspirins, and some lunch for you so that you don't take the pills on an empty stomach. Do you think you should see a doctor?"

"No, it's just something natural. I get it every month. It's always bad, but this month, with forgetting my glasses, all this work, and the list of things to do for the wedding…"

"You mean, like, your womanly situation?"

"Yes, exactly. I am having my period." Katja blushed, but somehow, she could tell Mendel anything. He knew her so well. She had never been able to talk about things like this with Elan.

"I'm glad that's all it is," he said.

She smiled to herself. God bless Mendel. He understood everything.

"But even with my glasses, I'll never get all this work done. My boss left a whole desk filled with papers that he wants me to type," Katja said, "and he left me here all alone with no one else to help me."

"I can type," Mendel said. "I'll stay and help you."

"Type? Really, Mendel?"

"For you, Kat? Anything—everything—always and forever. I'll be right over."

She hung up the phone and sat back in her chair. What a lucky woman she was to have a man like Mendel. But why the hell couldn't she feel the same passion for him that she felt for Elan? What was it that made her go crazy over Elan? Damn him, damn Elan to hell.

Mendel arrived in less than half an hour with hot tea.

"Drink this, and I'll go pick up your glasses," he said, handing her the paper cup.

She sipped the tea. It warmed her throat, and the sweetness soothed her nerves, gently calming her stomach cramps. Mendel always knew what to do—always.

Mendel arrived at Katja's office half an hour later with a quart of chicken soup, a sleeve of crackers, two aspirins, and Katja's glasses.

While Katja ate, Mendel began typing the documents on her desk. He asked for instructions and then surprised Katja with his efficient typing. Although he was not nearly as fast as she was, his accuracy made up for the time it took him to finish a page. He sat at the desk opposite hers where there was another typewriter. Everyone else was in the meeting. They were alone in the office, and the only sound was the clip-clop of the typewriter.

"I feel bad that you are sitting here doing my work. I feel guilty about you spending your whole afternoon taking care of me."

"I love taking care of you, Kat. I want to spend the rest of my life taking care of you. Now eat, please, and there's no need to rush. We'll finish this work together," Mendel said.

"Shouldn't you be studying for the bar exam?"

"I'll get it all done."

"When?"

"Whenever I get it done. I don't have anything pressing right now. Whatever work I have to do can wait until tomorrow. You know the Yiddish saying, 'If I don't get there tonight, I'll get there tomorrow.'" He smiled and winked at her. She had to laugh.

But Mendel knew that after they had dinner together and Katja was tucked warm and comfortable into her bed, he would return to his apartment and stay up at least half the night to finish his work. He would never say that to Katja. She would have forced him to go home and study. But being around Katja made him happy, and anything he could do to help her gave him greater pleasure than he'd ever experienced. It fulfilled him.

It was six o'clock when Mendel rolled the last piece of paper from the typewriter. "I think we're done?"

"I don't know how I would have gotten through it without you," Katja said.

"How do you feel?"

"A lot better."

"Now, let's get you home. I'll go out and pick up some food. You can take a hot bath while I'm gone. When I get back, we'll have a light dinner, and then it's off to bed with you, my love."

"Mendel…"

"Yes, sweetheart?"

"Thank you."

"You never have to thank me."

CHAPTER SIX

Katja drove to the kibbutz the week before the wedding to ensure everything was in order. It was a warm day at the beginning of February. Of course, she knew that her mother would have taken care of everything. Everything would have been done perfectly, but she wanted to spend extra time with her parents. Her boss was generous and gave her plenty of time off—a whole month. Mendel was to arrive the day before the wedding. After the wedding, they would take a few days and go to the sea to relax and soak up the sun.

For Katja, this precious week of being home at the kibbutz was like being a child again. She loved the familiar smells of the food. She spent time helping Shana and her mother with the children. One evening, she took a long walk with her father, who told her he believed she'd made a good choice in Mendel.

On the outside, everything seemed perfect. But buried deep within her heart, Katja still had so many doubts. The issue of her Nazi birth parents still lingered in her mind. She could not shake off the vision of Helga, the blonde woman she didn't know who had given birth to her. She could not free her thoughts of Helga crying and apologizing to her. And although she'd never met her birth father, in her mind's eye, she saw him as a sadistic Nazi, a killer of Jews.

She had nightmares where she could see her birth father forcing Jews into gas chambers in an extermination camp. In her night terrors, he was wearing a black hat with a death's head symbol and standing over Zofia and Isaac, ordering them to their deaths. Every time she had one of these dreams, she would stay awake the remainder of the night, just trying to catch her breath. When Mendel arrived at the kibbutz, she would ask him again if he was sure he wanted to marry her—sure that he wanted her as the mother of his children.

At one point, she considered sending a letter to Helga Haswell, telling her that she was getting married. She read somewhere that if she could forgive her birth mother, all the bad feelings toward Helga might disappear. Katja was trying. She wanted to forgive Helga, and sometimes she was able to find forgiveness when she prayed, sometimes but not always. She just wished that she could go back to the way she felt when she believed that Zofia and Isaac were her birth parents. Katja had never realized how blessed she was until she lost that security. As of yet, she had not sent any letters to Helga. Maybe someday she would, but not today.

Then, of course, there was Elan. Why did she still think about Elan? He'd hurt her, turned away from her, and forgot every promise he'd ever made. He'd forgotten how he'd vowed to love her until his dying day. When he left, he made her feel as if she did not belong anywhere, that all of her life spent as a Jew was meaningless. She'd felt as if her entire life was a lie.

But Mendel, dear Mendel, he'd tried to make her see that where she was born and who her birth parents were meant nothing. He'd told her over and over that Isaac and Zofia were her parents, Israel was her home, and its people were her people. She had come to believe him. She needed to believe him. But still, in the back of her thoughts, deep within her mind, she could not forget the truth.

Perhaps she needed to do something to make a difference in the world that would somehow prove she deserved to be a Jew and that she deserved to live in Israel. She pondered that thought for a while, but she couldn't come up with any ideas about what to do or how to do it. Katja had never been very ambitious. She'd always assumed she would be a wife and mother, which would be enough. Now, she could not help but feel that she should do something…something to atone for the atrocities committed by her father.

Mendel arrived the day before the wedding carrying a huge bouquet of blush roses and a big smile. He knocked on the door to Katja's room. It was early morning, and she hadn't gotten out of bed yet. The knock awakened her, and she opened the door with her blonde curls strewn about her head and her lovely blue eyes still soft with sleep. Mendel handed her the flowers.

"One more day, and you'll be Katja Zaltstein, my wife!"

"I know. It's exciting." She smiled. "Come in."

"Exciting! It's the most wonderful thing that has ever happened to me." He leaned over and gently kissed her.

"Mendel, sit." Katja motioned to the bed. He sat down, and a worried look came over his face. "I have to ask you one more time. With all that you know about my background, are you sure that this is what you want?"

"I have never been surer of anything in my life," he said, kissing her palm. "I love you, Kat. I've told you a million times. I've loved you since we were kids, and I'll love you with my dying breath. Now, just give me a lifetime to prove it to you."

She looked into those deep green eyes. Today, they did not sparkle with gold. Instead, they looked like deep pools of water.

"I mean it, Kat. Don't change your mind. Please."

She leaned over and kissed him gently and then more passionately. He put his arms around her, and she melted into his arms. They fell back onto her bed, and he began kissing her neck. His lips moved down to the edge of her bra. Katja sighed.

"One more night. Let's wait," he whispered. "I don't want to ruin our wedding night."

She smiled at him and ran her fingers along the side of his cheek.

"I want to make it special. Our wedding night will be the greatest night of our lives," he said.

CHAPTER SEVEN

ONE DAY before the wedding day, the sky opened, and torrents of rain nourished the dry lands of Israel. Katja sat up and gazed out the window of her room. She watched the rainfall in angles cascading down from the sky. Tomorrow, she would get married, and her life would change forever. She would be joined in the eyes of God to her best friend, a man she'd known as long as she could remember. He was good, kind, and caring. So why the hell was she still thinking about Elan?

She thought her broken heart had mended, but it still had a small open sore. Thinking about Elan so close to her wedding day was a sin. Damn him. Could it be possible to hate and love someone at the same time?

There was a soft knock at the door. Katja got up from her bed, her long cotton nightgown trailing over her bare feet as she went to the door.

"Who is it?" Katja whispered.

"It's me, sunshine."

"Mom?"

"Can I come in?"

"Of course, you must be soaked." Katja opened the door, and Zofia entered. "Come sit on my bed."

They sat down on the bed and looked at each other.

"I'm very happy today," Zofia said. "Mendel will be good to you. He loves you."

"I know. He is my best friend."

"You love him, don't you, sunshine?" Zofia asked, rubbing her daughter's shoulder.

"I do, I just…"

"What? Elan?"

"How did you know?"

"A mother always knows her own child. Your heart is as close to me as my own. I feel what you feel."

"I'm scared, Mama. I'm afraid I will never completely get over Elan."

"You won't, believe me. But I have to tell you something I have meant to tell you for a very long time."

"Not more secrets, Mom, please…"

"Only one, my sunshine. Listen… Once, when I was very young, I thought I was in love with a man who was much older than I was. He broke my heart. I had a child with him, but he never knew, not that I think he would have cared. But when the war broke out and we were taken to the ghetto, my little girl was with us. I was living with two friends, two women—lesbians. Those were the women I told you about, the seamstress, Fruma, and her lover, Gitel. They were very kind to me. They loved my daughter as if she were their own."

"I remember you promising to tell me about this when we met my birth mother. Is it true, then? Do I have a sister?"

"Yes, you do. I've been avoiding talking to you about her. But now I want you to know. You have a sister. Her name is Eidel."

"Is she still alive?"

"Yes, she is living with a very good friend of mine. She doesn't know that I am her mother.

"When we were in the ghetto, Eidel was in danger. I was afraid that she would die of disease or be murdered if we were sent to a camp. Fruma and Gitel were distraught as well.

Finally, Fruma found a solution. She found a man who worked in the black market. I still remember his name. Would you believe it? After all these years, I still remember his name, Karl Abdenstern. This man, Karl, worked in the black market. At night, he climbed out of the ghetto to buy and sell goods. People needed extra food and things, and this man got what he could and brought it back to sell in the ghetto.

"One night, Fruma arranged for Karl to sneak Eidel out and bring her to my friend Helen. Helen agreed to take Eidel and raise her as a Gentile, as her own daughter. This man, Karl, did this at great risk to himself, and he saved my daughter's life.

"After the war, I went looking for Eidel. I went to see my friend Helen. When I got there, I saw Eidel. She was living as Helen's child. It was the only home Eidel ever knew. Helen had renamed her. She called her Ellen. It hurt me, but I could not take Eidel away from the life she knew. She was happy, so happy, and she believed that Helen was her birth mother. It was the hardest thing I ever did, but I had to leave her behind. I did it because I loved her, and it was best for her."

"Why, Mom? Why are there so many secrets and lies?"

"The war, the Nazis—we could not always tell the truth. I know it's hard for you to understand."

"Yes, Mother, it is. It's very hard for me."

"I know, and I can't explain it to you. You want to know why I kept the information about your birth from you and why I waited so long to tell you that you have a sister."

"Yes, Mother. I realize you were trying to protect me, but things would have been so much easier if I had known sooner…"

"Would they, Katja? Would they really have been easier? I wanted to tell you. Many times, I wanted to tell you. But I knew it would hurt you. I tried to believe that if I never told you, you would somehow be spared and that somehow you would never find out. But, of course, I couldn't save you from the pain. We escaped from the Nazis with our lives, but we brought with us our memories."

Zofia sighed deeply. "I hope you can find it in your heart to forgive me.

"However, as important as all of this is, it is not the point of my story. It is not the reason I've chosen to tell you about my love affair when I was young. What I want you to know is this: I never thought I would love another man after the man who destroyed me when I was just a girl, and I never thought I would have another child. But then, Katja, the very first time that I looked at you…you filled that empty place in my heart. I loved you from the first moment I saw you. Then, as you now know, when I escaped Treblinka, I could not take you. You did not belong to me yet. I missed you so much.

"I was wandering for days. I thought my life was over. I was sure I was going to die. In fact, I wanted it all to end. I wanted to throw away God's greatest gift to me, my life. I was so tired that I fell asleep under a tree, hoping I would never awaken. And do you know what happened?"

Katja shook her head. Her mother had so many secrets.

"I did awaken, and when I did, your father, Isaac, was standing over me. I didn't know it then, but my new life had begun. I was on the brink of despair, and God sent me the most wonderful man any woman could ever want, the one true love of my life. Then, I became pregnant in the forest and miscarried because of the conditions. After that, I couldn't have any more children, and it seemed as if the need for a child would fester in my heart and eat away at me until there was nothing left. But again, God was good and brought you to me."

Katja nodded. Even with all the secrets, even with all the pain, Zofia had given her everything. "I love you, Mom."

"But the point of my story is this. Right now, you still miss Elan. He was your whole world. My guess is that he was your lover. You are afraid that you still love him. Perhaps you do. But I believe in my heart that God has sent you true love, the same way that he sent Isaac to me. It may take some time for you to see what has happened and to understand it, but I believe that is the truth."

"I do love Mendel. I just don't know why I'm haunted by these crazy thoughts of Elan."

"Because he is gone, and you have no idea what has become of him. The two of you were so close, and then he turned into a different person in a matter of hours. I think it's more of an obsession with the mystery of how he could just walk away without looking back than true love."

Katja shrugged her shoulders and nodded. "Yes, you could be right."

That night, Katja couldn't sleep. Her emotions coiled inside of her like a snake. She got up, went to Mendel's room, and stood outside the door in the moonlight, her bare feet cool against the moist grass. She lifted her hand to knock. She wanted to see him, to talk to him, to be reassured the way that only Mendel could reassure her. But it was the night before the wedding, and it was considered bad luck for the groom to see the bride until she began to walk toward him, holding her father's arm while he waited under the chuppah.

Katja sighed. A soft breeze rustled the leaves of an olive tree only a few feet away. She turned and began to return to her room when Mendel's door creaked open, breaking the stillness of the night. He stood in his boxer shorts, handsome in his shy, disheveled way. His hair was mussed, and his eyes were still glassy with sleep.

"I thought I heard someone out here. Kat, are you all right?"

"Yes, I'm fine. I just wanted to see you."

"Come in."

"Are you sure? It's the night before the wedding. It's bad luck."

"*Bubbe maisse*, nothing but an old grandmother's tale. I don't believe in silly superstitions. Come on in. Look at you—you're chilled and shaking."

She entered his room. The only light in his room was the silver beam of light that the moon cast through the window. Sitting on his bed, Katja looked up at him. "Mendel, I'm scared." She sat down on his bed. He pulled his blanket from his bed, wrapped it around her shoulders, knelt down, and took one of her feet into his hands, gently warming it between his palms.

"You're freezing." He held her feet against his chest to warm them.

"Oh, Mendel," she said with tears in her eyes.

"What is it? What's wrong?"

"I'm afraid that I still love Elan."

He nodded, turning away quickly, and ran his tongue across his lower lip. Then he got up and walked to the window, and she was instantly sorry she'd told him. There was a long silence, and then he cleared his throat. "Do you love me?" He turned to face her. A deep line had formed between his brows.

She was quiet for several minutes, breathing heavily. "I do. I always have. It's just all of these memories. They keep coming back to me…"

He didn't say another word. He walked toward her slowly. Then he stood before her and held her gaze. "I love you, Kat." Mendel bent to reach her, where she sat on the bed, and took her into his arms, kissing her with all the passion and love he felt. This time, Mendel held nothing back. He felt he must win her love. He must take all the love inside of him and pour it into her to fill all the emptiness that Elan had left. Then maybe she would love him, too.

Katja felt a shiver as her body surrendered to his passion. This was a side of Mendel she'd never seen. His lips brushed her neck, her collarbone. He kissed her softly behind her ear. Slowly, he lowered her onto his bed. She trembled with the force of his kisses. And for the first time, Mendel made love to Katja. It was like nothing she'd ever known. She felt the power of his love, and her soul stirred in response.

She lay spent in his arms, out of breath and amazed. He was still her best friend, Mendel, but he was so much more than she'd ever imagined. Mendel was her true *beshert*.

"Do you think we ruined it?" she asked, her voice barely a whisper, but she already knew the answer.

"Ruined what, my sweetheart?" he said in a husky voice.

"Our wedding night?"

He laughed softly. "Never, this is only the beginning. I promise you, Kat, you are going to be happy. I'll see to it."

She did not speak, but a knowing smile crept across her face.

Yes, she may still think of Elan once in a while, but from this night forward, she knew that her feelings for Mendel would grow.

They lay curled up in each other's arms for a long time, drifting in and out of sleep. Then, as the sun began to peek through the darkness of the night, Katja silently slid out of bed and went back to her room to prepare for the wedding.

Zofia brought some pita bread with hummus to Katja's room at around ten the following morning.

"Nervous?" she asked her daughter.

"A little, yes."

"You should eat something. It will settle your stomach."

Katja nodded, breaking off small bits of bread.

"As soon as you're done eating, I want you to try your gown on one last time to ensure it doesn't need any more alterations. My goodness, you've lost more weight."

"Nerves," Katja said, smiling.

"Try to relax. Everything will be fine."

"I know it will," Katja said. After last night, for the first time, she believed it.

While Katja was nibbling, Zofia went to her room and got the gown. She carefully carried the dress back to Katja.

"Mom, when did you sew these beautiful pearls all over the collar of this dress?!"

"I wanted to surprise you. I did them by hand over the last few weeks."

"It's gorgeous," Katja said, running her fingers over the fine needlework.

"It's for my precious daughter."

Katja smiled and shook her head. She knew how hard this intricate work was on Zofia, as her eyes were not as good as they were when she was younger. But for Katja, Zofia had worked tirelessly to make the most beautiful dress she'd ever made. Katja felt the tears well up in her eyes. The love she felt for Zofia was beyond words. Zofia was her mother, the only mother she'd ever known. And even with all the secrets and all the mysteries, she knew and had always known that everything Zofia did was out of love for her.

That strange woman, her birth mother, whom she'd met in Germany, was nothing more than a pitiful creature who'd been another victim of the Nazi terror. It was true that another woman had given birth to her, but Zofia's gentle hand had soothed her when she was ill. It was Zofia that had held her when she cried gut-wrenching tears after Elan left. And now, Zofia stood there smiling, holding this beautiful dress she'd made for her daughter's wedding. Zofia was her mother.

"I'm going to take a bath. Will you help me with my hair?"

"Of course, that's why I'm here. I want to help you with everything," Zofia said. "Oy, what a joyous day this is for your father and me."

CHAPTER EIGHT

THE MUSIC PLAYED as Katja stood at the front of the aisle. She glanced around her at all the heads turned toward the bride. Everyone Katja knew was seated in the main room of the kibbutz, everyone she'd grown up with. Rachel, Shana, and her extended family. Her heart swelled with love for these people, religion, and country. She drew a deep breath and felt God's love rain down upon her.

Then she took Isaac's arm and smiled up at him. There were tears in his eyes. Together, they walked down the white carpet in the main hall of the kibbutz toward the chuppah, a canopy decorated with white roses, pink mums, and pink and white carnations. Katja's heart fluttered with tenderness when she saw the look of love, admiration, and gratitude on Mendel's face. He adored her.

She looked into Isaac's eyes and said, "I love you, Papa." Then Katja glanced at Zofia, who was smiling through her tears—Mama, my mother.

As was tradition, she walked around Mendel seven times and came to stand beside him.

The rabbi began to speak, and all the guests were silent.

I am getting married. I can't believe this is really happening, Katja thought. A flash of Elan's face entered her mind's eye, but Katja pushed it away. Everything seemed to be spinning in a whirlwind, and before she knew it, Mendel had stepped on the glass, and the guests were all yelling, "*Mazel Tov!*"

Gently, Mendel kissed her, and then she took his arm. And together as man and wife, they walked back down the aisle.

In the main dining room, there were long tables covered with white cloths and filled with food that the women of the kibbutz had spent the last several days preparing. A band of musicians who lived in the kibbutz played Israeli folk songs.

Rachel was the first to come up and kiss Katja. "*Mazel Tov*, Kat," she said, hugging Katja tightly. "You made the right choice."

"Thank you, Rach."

"He's wonderful, and no other man could ever love you as much. Trust me. I know Mendel. He's been in love with you since we were thirteen."

Katja laughed. "Why did he tell you and not me?"

"Because he was always afraid of losing your friendship."

Katja nodded. "It makes sense, I guess."

"What's the matter, Kat?" Rachel's eyes narrowed. Katja knew Rachel was studying her.

"I don't know. I am afraid. I still occasionally think about Elan. Does that mean that I still love him?"

"I don't know. Only you know the answer to that question. But it could just be that the relationship between you two ended abruptly, and you still have unresolved feelings. Besides, it's none of my business, but Elan is a real jerk. He's a conceited, self-righteous bastard. If he were any kind of man, he wouldn't have left you for something that you had no control over. And the truth is, I think that if you were ever married to him, you would get to know him and probably realize what a lousy guy he is. You are still thinking about him because he's the one who got away. You've heard that saying?"

Katja nodded. "I love Mendel. I know that there is no one better for me, but I wish these thoughts and memories would disappear."

"Perhaps in time, they will. Does Mendel know how you feel?"

"I told him."

"What did he say?"

"He says he loves me, and I know that he does. He is so understanding."

"And you love him. Give it time."

"I do love him. Rach, I see that you didn't bring your girlfriend."

"I couldn't. I knew how everyone would feel about me being a lesbian. I guess I'm a coward."

"Don't be so hard on yourself. Listen, once we're settled, I want you and your girlfriend to come and visit Mendel and me in Tel Aviv."

"We will. We will."

This was no orthodox reception. Men and women sat and danced together. Katja danced with her father, and he wished her all the happiness in the world. There was no rising of the bride and groom on chairs. Instead, they danced together without kerchiefs between them.

Later that night, Mendel made love to Katja with a sweet, undemanding tenderness that gave her a feeling of safety and security she'd never known. After it was over, she lay in his arms as he gently stroked her hair.

CHAPTER NINE

Mendel was still in law school, and neither of their families were well-to-do. Finances were short, but the newlyweds could stay at a hotel outside Tel Aviv and spend two nights and days lying in the sun and enjoying romantic Mediterranean sunsets.

After the brief honeymoon, the newlyweds moved into their new apartment. Katja brought some of her furnishings, and Mendel happily allowed her to decorate however she chose. Mendel had always lived in a functional bachelor apartment, but now Katja had created a home. She bought a fluffy paisley bedspread with matching curtains. In the bathroom, she had brightly colored bath towels and a shower curtain.

Mendel graduated from law school and passed the bar. He and Chaim, his good friend from law school, opened a practice together. Mendel worked long hours and was not yet earning much money. They were planning to be contract lawyers, but in the beginning, they took any cases offered. Since they had not yet built a reputation, jobs were scarce.

Katja continued working at her job. In the evenings, she prepared dinner and waited for Mendel to come home to eat. Even though it was often late and they were both tired, they always spent at least an hour discussing what had happened during the day. It was a release for both of them.

Although they wanted children, they didn't want to start their family until Mendel had established his practice, so they were careful to use protection. Mendel was not convinced that the newly discovered birth control pill was safe. It had only been on the market a few years, and he was afraid it might have undiscovered side effects. He didn't want Katja to take the risk, even though it would be more convenient than condoms. She agreed with him, and they didn't use the birth control pill. And so they settled into their new lives as man and wife.

Mendel knew how much Katja loved to dance. He was never much of a dancer, but he wanted to make her happy, so he arranged for them to take dancing lessons. Katja was excited about the whole idea. She was not a great dancer, but she was better than Mendel, who tried but was still clumsy. They learned to waltz, cha cha, and tango, and Mendel learned to jitterbug as best he could. Even after several months of lessons, Mendel was never the dancer Elan was, but Kat found that he was a lot of fun, and his awkward attempts made them both laugh.

On the weekends, they went to dance clubs to practice what they'd learned. As time went by, Mendel improved, and they became semi-accomplished dance partners. Because they always danced together, they knew each other's moves. Sometimes, just because they were such an attractive couple, the other dancers would stop to watch them.

One night, two months into their marriage, Katja had prepared a light dinner and was reading while she was awaiting Mendel's return from work when the phone rang. It was Zofia.

"Mama?"

Zofia's voice was cracked but controlled. "Katja, you'd better come home. Your father is very sick. He's had a heart attack."

"Mama, is he all right?"

"I don't know. I am with him at the hospital. Please come."

"I'll leave right away."

Katja's fingers trembled as she dialed Mendel's number on the rotary phone. "Mendel, my father is very sick. He's in the hospital. I have to go."

"I'll be right there. I'm going with you. Wait for me."

She hung up the receiver and went into the bedroom. She was unable to concentrate but still managed to pack a suitcase. Thoughts of her home, father, and mother ran like an unstoppable movie reel through her mind. Her father was too young to have a heart attack. He was only forty-eight. She'd feared the loss or death of her parents even when she was a little girl, but she had no reason to think about losing them. Katja had never felt secure. Now, the pain and shock that had awakened her in nightmares were real, and it was so severe that it numbed her.

Mendel arrived fifteen minutes later. Katja was sitting on the sofa, pale, silent, her knees tucked under her, her arms crossed over her chest. He went to her and wrapped her in his arms like a cloak of safety as if, by sheer will, he could shield her from the world. She was not crying, but her body trembled so hard that he could not steady her.

"Shh, I'm here," he whispered. Her head fell upon his chest.

"I'm afraid, Mendel."

"I know, I know. I'm here. I'm with you," he spoke softly into her hair as he held her tightly to stop her from shaking.

"We should go," she said. "My mother needs me."

He nodded. Neither said the words they feared to hear—would Katja's father survive?

Mendel quickly threw some underclothes and two clean shirts into the bag Katja had packed, and they were on their way.

Katja stared out the car window, and Mendel held her hand, his thumb gently caressing her fingers. Katja's mouth was terribly dry. She realized she was not breathing through her nose. She was panting.

When they arrived at the hospital, Katja asked to be dropped off at the door, but Mendel refused. He didn't want her to go in alone. He wanted to be with her in case things had gone bad or she needed him. In case… It took several frustrating minutes to get a parking place. Sweat trickled down Mendel's brow, and he wiped it away with his forehand. He circled the parking lot until finally, a car pulled out of a spot, and Mendel quickly rushed the car in.

Katja jumped out of the automobile and began running toward the door. Mendel was tall and limber and easily caught up with her.

"Kat, Kat! Slow down, please."

Her pallor was even grayer than before as if her face had turned to ash.

"Come here." He grabbed her arm and turned her toward him, and again, he wrapped her in an embrace. "Let's go in together. All right?"

She nodded.

The hospital smelled of alcohol and disinfectant. The walls were white, sterile, and foreign. Nurses and doctors, clean, detached, and dressed in white, dashed about as Mendel gave Isaac's name to a woman sitting at a circular desk a few yards away from the front door.

The receptionist thumbed through a Rolodex file and said, "To the right, until you come to the corner, then turn right again, and you'll see the waiting room."

"Thank you," Mendel answered. Then, turning to Katja, he put his arm gently around her shoulder. "Come on, Kat, let's go."

Katja felt as if her knees might buckle. She was grateful for Mendel's strong grip on her shoulder. It felt as if he were holding her up. She thought that if he let go, she might fall to the floor.

When they got to the waiting room, Zofia sat alone in a maroon-colored, straight-back chair in the center of a row of identical chairs. Her eyes were red, and her skin was covered in blotches. She looked small, very small.

"Katja, he's gone," Zofia said, appearing shell-shocked, her grief welling up behind her eyes like water behind a dam. "Your papa is gone."

Katja ran to her mother. Mendel followed her. Katja fell to her knees in front of her mother and began to weep. Then Zofia was weeping, too. Mendel stood helpless, waiting to do something—anything, to make this better.

"He was not even fifty. Why? Why did he die so young? Why?" Katja asked.

"The doctor thinks it's because he had such a hard life. He thinks it has something to do with the years of starvation. Oh, Katja, how am I ever going to live without him? How, Katja, how?" Zofia's nose was running, and tears covered her face. "I can't go on. I don't want to go on, not without my Isaac..."

"You'll have to go on for us," Mendel said, "and for your future grandchildren. They will need you..."

"I can't. I can't."

Katja just lay, crying softly, with her head buried in her mother's lap, breathing in the familiar smell of her mother, the smell of harsh, homemade soap.

Mendel walked over to the nurse's station and asked for two glasses of water. He returned carrying two paper cups. Neither mother nor daughter took even a sip.

CHAPTER TEN

Mendel took care of all the funeral arrangements but felt utterly helpless. There was little else he could do for Katja or Zofia. He'd been at Katja's side, held her hand, and kept her steady as she walked to the gravesite.

Immediately following the burial, everyone returned to the main dining room at the kibbutz. A large bottle of water waited outside. The tradition was that anyone returning from the graveyard must wash their hands before entering the house. Each of the mourners and guests poured water from the bottle over their hands before they walked inside. This was an old ritual: the significance was that they would not bring death into the house.

Inside, the mirrors had been covered, and the women of the kibbutz had laid out food. Friends that Isaac and Zofia had made who lived in town and on other kibbutzim came to pay their respects. Zofia and Katja wore no shoes, only their stocking feet. Most of the time, Zofia sat with her arms folded across her chest, breathing deeply and looking out the window. Mendel brought her plates of food, but she did not eat. Katja lay in Mendel's arms. Quietly, with his fingers, he fed her bits and pieces of food between her moments of grief.

One night, after they retired to their rooms, Mendel ran Katja a hot bath. Then, once she was warm and wrapped in her robe, he sat her down on the bed.

"Kat, I was thinking, do you want your mom to come and live with us?"

Katja looked into his eyes, resembling deep-green pools, so kind and sincere. What would she do without Mendel?

"I think it might be good for her, but I don't know if it's what you want."

This might be a good time to tell him what she had meant to tell him before she lost her father. It had been a month since she'd had her last period. "Mendel, before this happened, I wanted to tell you something," she said.

He cocked his head to the side and bit his lower lip. "You can tell me anything, Kat. You know that."

"I've missed my period for a month. I think I might be pregnant. I know we were careful; I don't know how this happened. And now, my father..."

"Kat, sweetheart, I don't know what to say. I'm happy that we are going to have a child."

"I was afraid you'd be upset. We are hardly managing now financially. What will happen when we have a baby?"

"We'll be all right. If I have to get a second job at night, I will. We'll manage. I'm more than happy. I'm thrilled! A baby is a gift from God, Kat."

"Are you sure?"

"Of course. Yes, of course, I'm sure." He held her in his arms.

"I would like my mother to move in. She would be very helpful with the baby. If she lived with us, I wouldn't be worried about her all the time. I would always know that she was all right. But can we afford it?"

"As long as I have you, I am as rich as a king. Don't worry. I'll find a way." He smiled. "Come lie down. You're tired. Get some rest."

"I'm going to miss my papa, Mendel. I loved him so much."

"I know. I'm going to miss him, too. That's why I want to do whatever I can to take care of you and your mom. I want to make sure your mother is all right. It's what he would have wanted."

"Yes, that's true. He loved her so much. She loved him, too. I can't believe he is gone. Losing my parents has always been my greatest fear."

"I know," Mendel whispered as he held her in his arms, rocking her gently. "I know." He remained awake long after Katja's breathing slowed, and knew she had fallen asleep.

CHAPTER ELEVEN

AT FIRST, Zofia was reluctant to move in with Katja and Mendel. "This kibbutz is my home. I've been here for so long. I don't know…" She wrung her hands in the fabric of the apron of her dress.

"Mama, I'm going to have a baby, and Mendel and I would like you to live with us, help me, and be there for your grandchild. Papa would have wanted it."

Zofia nodded and took Katja's hand. "A young couple doesn't need a mother living with them."

"You're my mother, and Mendel loves you, too. Please, Mama, do it for us. Come, move in with us. You'd be such a help to me with the baby. You'd be doing us a big favor. Will you, please?"

Zofia squeezed Katja's hand, and then she nodded. "I will. I'll move in with you."

Until Katja mentioned the baby, it seemed as if the light had left Zofia's eyes. Katja feared that her mother would soon follow her father in death. But with the coming of a grandchild, Zofia seemed to have regenerated a little. She was able to pack her things and say goodbye to her friends. Then, three days after the seven-day shiva period ended, Mendel, Katja, and Zofia drove back to Tel Aviv.

CHAPTER TWELVE

Katja was glad to have her mother with her. During the first trimester of her pregnancy, she experienced terrible morning sickness so severe that sometimes she could not get out of bed. The vomiting was followed by overwhelming heartburn and then exhaustion. She began missing days at work. She missed so many that finally, her boss let her go.

Money was tight, but Mendel got a second job at night at a restaurant. With a smile, he said he didn't mind because he knew that his law practice would soon start picking up, and he would get enough clients to build a good reputation. Zofia offered to work as a seamstress at a bridal shop, but Mendel said it was best she stayed at home with Katja. Times were tough financially, but Mendel was happy that he was going to be a father. The only thing that concerned him was that Katja was unable to keep anything down, and she was not gaining weight.

Zofia was busy trying to stretch their food as much as possible. Katja was exhausted, so she slept a great deal, and Mendel was working. This tight and difficult schedule allowed little time for grieving. However, sometimes, when Katja was asleep, and Zofia was sitting quietly in the kitchen preparing dinner, tears and memories came upon her like a tidal wave.

Zofia missed Isaac and often talked to him when she was alone. He'd been the love of her life. Without him, the light that had guided her through her trials and tribulations had dimmed. Her only true happiness was knowing that Mendel was there to care for Katja when it was time for Zofia to join Isaac. And, of course, the baby. Soon, a wonderful new life would join them. Mendel and Katja had agreed to name the baby after Isaac. If it were a boy, the name would be Isaac. If it were a girl, it would be Ima. Knowing that Isaac would have a "name" here on earth comforted Zofia.

Because Katja was having such a difficult time with her pregnancy, Mendel slept very lightly. As soon as Katja stirred, he would awaken to see if she needed anything. When she was dizzy and vomiting, he stood like a soldier, alert and waiting, right outside the bathroom door. When Mendel returned from work, he tried preparing her favorite foods, but she continued vomiting. Secretly, he blamed himself for causing her to be so ill, and although she seemed happy about her pregnancy, he was riddled with guilt.

Things began to get better during the second trimester of Katja's pregnancy. She was able to keep some food down and gained a modest ten pounds. Although she still had bouts of horrific heartburn, she began to look more like herself. Her color returned, and she was now glowing. Mendel finally allowed himself to breathe a sigh of relief.

As the time to give birth drew nearer, Katja became uncomfortable in a different way. She was not used to being so large, and her body felt cumbersome. But even more challenging were the thoughts that invaded her mind. She'd already come to love this child she'd not yet seen, and this stirred thoughts of Helga, her birth mother. Katja began to understand how hard it must have been for her birth mother when the Nazis took her child away. This pregnancy had forced Katja to look at Helga with new eyes, the eyes of a mother.

When she'd gone to see Helga in Germany, Katja had been

disgusted with her. She'd found it difficult to forgive her birth mother. But now she realized that everything Helga had told her was true. She now understood how Helga must have loved her even though she was forced to give her away. She wondered how she would feel if she knew that the child whose heartbeat under her breast would never grow up to know how much she loved and wanted it. It must have been terrible for Helga, even more terrible than Helga had been able to express.

Several times, Katja sat down at her kitchen table with a pen and paper in hand and tried to compose a letter to Helga. But she'd been unable to write it. She could not express in words what she was feeling. So, she would abandon the paper for a few weeks and then try again later. But still, the letter remained unwritten.

CHAPTER THIRTEEN

IMA ZALTSTEIN WAS BORN on November 13th, 1965, at eleven o'clock in the morning. Katja had labored for sixteen difficult hours while Mendel wrung his hands and wished he could take the pain instead of her.

He'd waited in the maternity waiting room of the hospital with Zofia, who hardly spoke but watched the clock as the lines of her face deepened with concern.

They both stood when the doctor came out wearing his white cotton lab coat. Zofia leaned on Mendel. He could feel how wobbly she was and put an arm around her to hold her up.

"You have a baby girl. Both mother and baby are doing fine."

Zofia sighed aloud, and Mendel felt the tension leave his shoulders.

"Can we see them?" Mendel asked.

"Yes, but don't stay long. Your wife is exhausted. Let her get some rest."

Mendel nodded and took Zofia by the arm. They both entered the hospital room, where Katja lay surrounded by white walls and cotton blankets. When she saw her mother and her husband, Katja smiled. To Mendel, she looked like an angel. Her hair was disheveled, scattered about the pillow in a giant halo of golden curls, and her face was luminescent. In her slender arms, she held a tiny blanket-wrapped bundle. Mendel felt his heart skip a beat as he carefully moved the cover aside so that he could see his daughter's face for the first time.

"She's beautiful, just like her mother," he said, his voice choked with emotion.

Zofia touched the baby's cheek. A tear fell from her eye. "I wish your papa could be here to see her," she said.

"Papa is here, Mama. He's always with us," Katja said, reaching for Zofia's hand and then gently squeezing, her own life force coming through her hand to give her mother strength.

"We have a child," Mendel said, his eyes glistening. "How do you feel?"

"Good, but I'm starving."

"I'll ask the nurse if you can have something to eat," Mendel said. "I'll be right back. I'm going to go to the desk."

Mendel returned with some crackers and a cup of apple juice. "This is all they have, but they will bring you a lunch tray in about an hour."

"I'm exhausted. I'd like to try to get a little rest before lunch."

"We can go," Zofia said, "and let you rest."

Katja chomped on a cracker. "Besides, you two have a nursery to set up." Katja laughed.

Nothing had been done for the baby. It was tradition. The crib could not be purchased, and nothing could be put together until the baby was born. It was done that way so the evil eye would not see that a child was coming and sweep it away before it was born—superstitions. Now, it was up to Mendel, with Zofia's help, to prepare for the day when they would bring little Ima home.

"You get some sleep, and we'll get started on that nursery. We'll be back later tonight," Mendel said to Katja.

"I'll see you then." Katja smiled.

The nurse came in and took the baby to the nursery. After everyone had gone, Katja broke into tears. Why did she feel so terribly sad? Why now, when she should be so happy? The baby was perfect. She'd examined her tiny fingers and toes, and Ima was beautiful. Katja was doing fine. Except for the pain of the stitches, she felt pretty good. So why the sadness? It was a feeling of overwhelming grief. Could it be because her father was not there? Of course, she'd tried to reassure her mother, but the truth was that she missed him terribly. He'd always been her stability, her oak tree. She could always lean on him; now, when she needed him so badly, he was gone.

And besides that, for some odd reason, she could not get Helga out of her mind. She was exhausted. She only had an hour to rest, but she couldn't sleep. The pain of the labor had been terrible, but she could not imagine the pain she would have felt if someone had taken Ima away from her now. A shiver ran up Katja's spine. Suddenly, she felt terrified. She rang the nurse's bell.

The nurse came in almost immediately.

"Please, bring my baby," Katja said. "I want to see her…"

"I thought you wanted to get some rest, Mrs. Zaltstein," the nurse said. "You said you were tired and wanted to sleep a little before lunch."

"Please, I need to see her right away," Katja said.

The nurse eyed Katja suspiciously and then nodded and left the room. Katja knew she was unstable and prayed that this feeling would leave her. It seemed like hours, but it was really only ten minutes before the nurse returned, carrying Ima in her arms.

Katja reached her arms out and took Ima. She held her baby close to her chest. Her heart was pounding. How must Helga have felt? She couldn't get the look of pain that she saw in her birth mother's eyes out of her mind.

CHAPTER FOURTEEN

IMA WAS A DIFFICULT INFANT. When they brought her home, she didn't sleep through the night. She would sleep for an hour or so and then wake up screaming. The constant crying unnerved Katja, and her breast milk never came in. Finally, the doctor decided that it was best that they bottle-feed Ima. The crying continued. The pediatrician was convinced that it was Ima's diet, and he changed the formula several times. Still, he couldn't find a formula that Ima could digest comfortably. So, each time she was fed, she cried. Katja was beside herself.

When Ima was red-faced and screaming, Katja was trembling and crying. Zofia walked up and down the apartment, trying to quiet the baby. Mendel often got up at night to sit in the rocking chair, hold his daughter, and feed her a warm bottle until she finally quieted and fell asleep. It was difficult for him because he had to be at work in the morning, but he wanted to be sure that Katja got enough rest. She was not working, but it seemed that she was always exhausted.

One morning, as the sun rose, Katja awakened to find Mendel's side of the bed empty. She went to the nursery and saw him sitting in the rocking chair with Ima in his arms, singing softly and gently.

The moment was so tender that it touched her heart. She felt as if she might cry. Mendel was such a good father, such a good man. She thought of Isaac, her father—the only real father she'd ever known. Mendel reminded her of Isaac in so many ways.

Then she thought about the Nazi, the SS officer whose sperm had fertilized the egg that created her. She wondered who he was and wondered if any of him had been transferred by genetics into her child. Ima already seemed so difficult. The baby was quick to anger and demanding, too.

As the months went by, Ima's crying lessened. But Ima was still challenging—she had a temper. When she wanted something, she would not be denied. When Katja tried taking Ima to play groups with other mothers and their babies, Katja had seen other children who were not as hard to please. She'd never mentioned it to Zofia or Mendel, but she was secretly afraid that some of her birth father's traits were coming through in her daughter.

One afternoon, when Zofia insisted that Katja relax while taking Ima for a walk, she sat down at her kitchen table. She wrote a letter to her birth mother. These were the first words she'd ever written to Helga.

Dear Helga Hoffman,

This is Katja. I am sure you remember that I visited you last year. I've given birth to a child. You have a granddaughter. I am sorry for all of your pain. Now that I am a mother myself, I can see how hard it must have been for you. I never thought I would say that. But I cannot imagine how I would feel if I knew Ima would be taken away. Your decision to go to the home for the Lebensborn hurt me for a long time. But now I realize that if you had kept me, I would never have been raised by the wonderful parents who loved me so much. So, in a way, I must thank you.

Katja

She'd written it and reread it. She thought of Ima and how much she loved her daughter. It must have been terrible for Helga, all those years, to wonder what had become of her child. When

Katja had been in Germany and met her birth mother, she'd had trouble understanding her. She was angry, so angry. She'd asked Helga how she could have signed herself into a place like the Lebensborn.

But now, strangely, her anger was disappearing. Katja could see that her birth mother had been nothing more than a young girl in trouble who had been alone and afraid. It was true. She'd had an affair with an SS officer, of all people. That was something Katja felt sick about. But Helga was a German and must not have known any better. She'd told Katja she didn't know what the Nazis were doing to the Jews.

To go on living, Katja had to believe her. Even more so, she had to forgive Helga and everyone else involved in her early life. Because if Helga had not given her up and instead had raised her with her birth father, Katja would have grown up as a Nazi. So, in reality, her life had worked out for the best. Katja had been saved twice from her fate, once by Helga and the second time when Christa had given her to Zofia.

Katja sighed. God had blessed her. She'd lived her life with loving parents in a wonderful country as a Jew. She held the letter in her hands. There was so much more to say, and so much she could not say. But for now, she folded the paper and put it into her lingerie drawer underneath her nightgowns. Someday, she would send it—someday, but not today.

CHAPTER FIFTEEN

IMA GREW QUICKLY. No sooner than she was able to crawl, she began lifting herself up on the furniture, attempting to stand. Now, she seldom cried. Instead, she was always moving and always curious. She kept Zofia, Mendel, and Katja busy constantly. Ima was fearless; even if she fell or hurt herself, she got up without a sound and continued exploring the world.

Wherever Katja took her daughter to the park or a shop, people would stop and admire Ima for her incredible beauty. People who saw her would say, "Just look at that head full of thick golden curls and those sea-green eyes."

By the time Ima was a little over a year old, she was a dynamic and relentless force of curious energy. Zofia and Katja took turns watching her while Mendel was busy at work.

It was late December following a modest Hanukkah due to a lack of funds that Mendel was sitting in his office. He was working on a small traffic case when a perfectly groomed gentleman wearing a pressed, charcoal-gray tailored suit entered. Although the man was not tall, he gave the appearance of a powerful presence. Mendel looked up from his paperwork.

"How can I help you?"

"Good Afternoon. My name is Harvey Greenspan. I'm looking for Mendel Zaltstein."

"I'm Mendel Zaltstein," Mendel said, standing up to shake the man's hand.

"Mendel Zaltstein, I've heard plenty of good things about you. I've heard you're honest and not afraid to work hard. And now that I'm sitting across from you, I think it all might be true." Greenspan smiled and cocked his head to the side.

"By trade, I am a chemist. Right now, I am in the process of opening what I believe will be the largest pharmaceutical company in Israel. I need an attorney for my company, someone I can trust, someone to make sure that we stay within the laws. I would like to make you an offer. I'd like for you to be the attorney for my corporation."

Mendel leaned back in his chair and studied Harvey Greenspan. It was difficult not to be instantly caught up in the flattery. But this all seemed far too good to be true. This was a monumental offer to be the lawyer for such a big enterprise. Mendel wondered if he would be the only attorney. He drummed his fingers on his desk. Why him, why Mendel? Could Mendel trust this man? He bit his upper lip as his mind raced.

"You look a bit perplexed. Let me explain. I need someone young and strong who isn't afraid to work long hours. But more importantly, I need someone brilliant. I checked your university records. In fact, that is how I found you. First, I checked your score on the bar exam. Very impressive. Then I checked your grades in law school and your IQ test. You have a very high IQ, genius, in fact. I've also studied your personal life. You need the money. You have a young child, a wife, and a mother-in-law to support. You're working two jobs, wasting your talent, I might add. So, I am going to offer you a nice salary. In exchange, I will be your only client. You will devote all of your time to my enterprise."

Mendel sucked in a deep breath.

Greenspan continued. "But there is a small catch." Harvey

Greenspan focused his eyes directly at Mendel's. "I don't want your partner. I only want you. To take this job, you're going to have to break your partnership."

"I can't do that. My partner is not only my business partner; he is my friend."

"What is a friend? Huh? You answer me. Can he pay your bills? Can he take care of your wife and child?" Greenspan leaned forward in his chair, his eyes glaring at Mendel. "This is business. You need me, and I need you. Take the night and think it over. Here is my card. Call me in the morning and let me know what you decide." Greenspan stood up. He straightened his suit jacket and composed himself, then dropped his card on Mendel's desk and walked out, closing the door softly.

The silence of the room surrounded Mendel, sounding louder than the words that Greenspan had spoken. Mendel picked up the business card and turned it over several times in his fingers. His stomach was unsettled. He didn't trust this man, not at all. But how could he turn an offer like this away? He was struggling just to pay the rent. More importantly, things were hard for Katja. They needed the money.

Mendel thought of his partner. He had never betrayed anyone before. How could he do this now? How could he not? The law practice was barely paying its bills. In fact, there had not been enough money for him to take a salary for the last several weeks. They barely survived on the small salary he brought home from his second job. If he took this offer, it would make life so much easier for Katja. And there was no doubt that everything he did, he did for Katja.

Mendel laid the business card on his desk and tried to continue to work on the case he had been working on before Mr. Greenspan arrived, but he could not concentrate. He had never betrayed anyone in his life, and yet he needed the money so badly. Something was not right. This man was coming to him for a reason, probably not good, but if he turned the offer down, then what? Mendel would have to continue to live the way he'd been living. Every month, he scrambled to pay the bills, and each month, he was delving deeper into his small and dwindling savings, falling further behind.

Katja wanted to return to work, but he wanted her to be at home to raise their daughter. Even though Mendel trusted Zofia, he wanted Ima to grow up with her mother beside her. It was a dilemma. But when it came to Katja, there was no choice. He would do what was best for the woman he loved, no matter the price.

Ima breathed life back into Zofia. Since she'd lost Isaac, she seemed to be waiting to follow him. That was until Ima was born. Ima gave her a reason to get out of bed, and Zofia doted on her grandchild. In response, Ima adored her grandmother and almost preferred her to Katja. When the baby wanted anything, she reached her small, chubby arms up to Zofia, who gladly swept her up into a warm embrace. Although Zofia missed Isaac every day, at least she could relax knowing that Katja had a good husband and a wonderful daughter.

Except for the lack of financial security, Katja had everything she could want. Of course, she still missed her father and often whispered to him quietly at night when she sat awake with a cup of tea while the rest of the family slept. He'd been such a strong man and so wise. And now, when Katja had so many questions about raising her child, she wished that she could consult him.

Quietly, in the stillness of the night, she would speak to him, "Papa, I wish you could see your grandchild. She is your namesake. We named her Ima for you. She is beautiful. I know you would have loved her. Wherever you are, I know you do love her. She is growing so quickly; sometimes, I worry that I won't have the right answers when she is older and needs my guidance. I wish you were here beside me. Mama misses you desperately. I can see it in her eyes. Oh, Papa, why did you have to go so soon, so young?" She would sigh, wishing he could tell her—if anyone could tell her why.

CHAPTER SIXTEEN

MENDEL BEGAN WORKING for H.G. Pharmaceuticals. His friend and business partner, Chaim, resented his leaving, and Mendel felt guilty, but he knew what he must do to take care of his family. He was the exclusive attorney of the company. He quickly found that Greenspan was always searching for loopholes in the law so he could release his innovative drugs to the public.

The scientists had been working diligently to produce a revolutionary weight loss drug that would hit the market and be an instant success. Most of the time, Mendel did what he could to aid Greenspan. However, the weight loss drug posed a lot of risks to potential users. There were serious side effects. The scientists were working to eliminate as many of the problems as possible, but Greenspan wanted to begin selling the drug quickly.

Mendel saw that a drug like this could quite possibly create a financial windfall, and he knew Greenspan would not rest until this master moneymaker was out on the market. Even though the pills were still in the experimental stage and had not been approved, Greenspan was already working on promoting and creating interest among physicians. Greenspan came into Mendel's office early one morning.

"You must find a way to get this medication approved, no matter how we have to do it. Do you understand me, Mendel?" Greenspan asked.

Mendel nodded.

"This is a game changer. This will make us all very rich."

"I think we should make sure it is safe first. There could be a lot of deaths involved if we don't," Mendel said, clearing his throat and tapping his pencil on the desk.

"We have perfected it as much as possible. We can continue working on it after it's been released."

"I don't know, Mr. Greenspan. You are taking people's lives in your hands."

"I didn't hire you for advice." Greenspan glared at Mendel. "I hired you to find legal ways to push things through—at a hell of a good salary, I might add."

"My conscience is telling me we should do more work on this pill before we begin selling it. We haven't ironed out the side effects."

"For God's sake, Zaltstein, I said do it. I didn't ask what you think. If you don't want this job, just say so. I'll get another lawyer. You sons of bitches are a dime a dozen."

Mendel felt anger stir inside of him. Then he thought of Katja and the baby. There had been plenty of money since he'd begun working for Greenspan. They had even purchased an oven. He remembered how excited Katja was when it was installed. He longed to give her everything—to buy her a beautiful home with quality furnishings. He ached to buy her fine clothes and jewelry. His love for her grew with each passing day. Mendel looked at Harvey Greenspan. *What a greedy bastard*, he thought, but he said, "I'll work on it. Give me a week or so."

"Good. I knew you would see my perspective." Greenspan smiled, then got up and left Mendel's office.

For a long time, Mendel stared out the window and tapped his pencil on the wooden desk. Then he began scanning his law books to find a way to give Greenspan the greasy little loophole he wanted.

That night, Mendel sat at home in the overstuffed chair he and

Katja had purchased from a thrift store. He watched Ima playing on the floor with Zofia as Katja prepared dinner. Guilt infested his heart and soul. There was no doubt he could find a loophole. But what about all the people whose lives would be affected by his decision to overlook the dangers they would face? He knew it was unethical to do this to others so he could give his own family a better life. Ima giggled on the floor in front of him as Zofia covered her face with a washcloth and then peeked out the side. "I see you…" Zofia said.

My God, what am I to do? Mendel felt like his intestines were in knots. Before Greenspan, I was sinking. Every month was another challenge just to put food on the table. I don't want Katja going out to work. That's my job. I am supposed to provide for her. She needs to be at home raising Ima, and I would like to be able to afford to have a second child so that Ima won't grow up alone the way Katja and I did. He sighed. This was a dilemma. His morals told him to leave Greenspan and start out on his own again, but his family's needs pressed at him until he felt the bile rise in his throat, causing terrible heartburn.

Zofia looked up for a moment. Mendel forced a smile. Zofia returned the smile, but Mendel could see in her eyes that she suspected he was troubled.

Katja was far too busy during dinner to notice Mendel's mood. She was so distracted by all the tasks she had to do: cooking, cleaning, and caring for a baby. Zofia was a help, but even between them, there was a lot to be done.

That night, like every other night since Ima's birth, Katja fell into bed exhausted. How could he even consider asking her to get a job? She would be willing to do whatever needed to be done—he knew that, but he couldn't and wouldn't ask that of her. Their lovemaking had also slowed down since Ima's birth. It seemed that as soon as Ima fell asleep, all Katja wanted to do was take a hot bath and sleep.

Mendel was worried. He felt that everything he'd built so carefully with the woman he adored was drifting away like steam dissipating into the air from a boiling pot. Before the child, it seemed to him that he'd finally won the love he'd longed for his entire life, and now it felt like he was losing her.

It would make things easier for Katja if he could afford a housekeeper. *She would be less exhausted, more like her old self.* He thought with delight about how happy and excited she would be if he could buy her everything she'd ever wanted. The tiny chip of a diamond engagement ring he'd given her was all he could afford at the time. Money, lots of money, would change their lives.

Mendel got out of bed quietly so as not to wake Katja, made himself a cup of tea, and pulled out some of his law books. He would do whatever he had to do to make them rich. He would ignore his principles. He would work tirelessly until he found all the information he needed. Mendel adored his wife and would do anything to hold on to his marriage.

CHAPTER SEVENTEEN

"I SEE you have what I need." Greenspan came into Mendel's office a week later. "I found these papers on my desk this morning. I'm proud of you, Zaltstein." Harvey Greenspan laid the papers that Mendel had given him on the desk in front of Mendel. "Good work. And good work is well-rewarded around here. When you get your pay envelope on Friday, I think you'll be very pleased with the substantial raise I've given you."

Mendel nodded. "Thank you, sir," he said, but his stomach tightened.

"Hanukkah is coming. Go out and buy your wife a nice gift." Greenspan smiled and winked. "You won't need to worry about earning a living anymore. I can see that I was right about you. You're brilliant, just like I thought."

Mendel smiled a half smile, and then Greenspan left his office.

Neither Katja, Zofia, nor Mendel had ever had a Hanukkah like the one at the Zaltstein home that year. It was hard to believe that only one year ago, a little after Hanukkah, he'd met Greenspan, and

Mendel's life had changed forever. Every night for eight days, Mendel dazzled his wife, child, and mother-in-law with expensive gifts. He bought Katja a new wedding ring with a four-carat diamond. When she saw it, she screamed with delight. "Mendel, are you sure we can afford this?"

"I'm more than sure, Kat. My new job is working out beautifully." That night, they made love. She lay in his arms, telling him how much she admired him. He was exalted. All of his dreams were realized.

He gave Zofia expensive silk pajamas and a matching robe. For Ima, he brought dozens of dolls and toys, which delighted her. They ate meat and potato latkes every night.

Then, on the final day, the eighth day of Hanukkah, Mendel gave Katja an envelope. She cocked her head to the side and looked at him.

"What is this?"

"It's an I owe you."

"What?"

"Open it."

She did. Inside, there was a note.

Let's spend next week shopping for a new home. I am going to buy us a real house, a home of our own, was all the note said.

Katja gasped in surprise. Then she threw her arms around Mendel's neck and kissed him.

Zofia watched. She had no idea why—there was no logical reason, but she was worried.

CHAPTER EIGHTEEN

GREENSPAN WAS RIGHT. The weight loss drug was an enormous success in just a few months. Once it was approved for sale in Israel, Greenspan sent it for approval in Europe and, following that, in the United States.

Mendel was well rewarded. He and Katja bought a home with four bedrooms and three-and-a-half baths. Zofia had her own wing with her bedroom and bath attached. The kitchen was filled with modern appliances. Katja even had her own oven. It was like a dream. They bought brand new, matching linens and towels in the popular avocado green. Katja took Zofia and Ima, and they shopped for days in search of the perfect furnishings.

When Mendel looked into Katja's eyes, he saw admiration and respect. Finally, after longing for it for so long, he believed he even saw love. All of these things made his efforts worthwhile most of the time. However, late one night, when everyone was asleep and the house was as silent as a graveyard, Mendel sat alone in the thick plush chair he'd purchased from an expensive furniture store and began to study his hands. He looked carefully at the lines in his palm and the nails on his fingers. *These hands*, he thought as he held them up to the moonlight, *were meant to do good things*. He'd always believed that.

But he knew deep in his heart that he could not forget his work would eventually cause more harm than good. Mendel knew it was only a matter of time before someone died due to taking the medication he'd gotten approved for by slipping through loopholes and lying. Who would die? A mother? A father? An overweight teenager hoping to lose weight and change his life? Perhaps someone's daughter—he, too, had a daughter.

He ran his trembling hands through his thinning hair. Then silently, like a ghost, he padded slowly, his bare feet cooled by the marble floor, to peek into Ima's room and watch her sleep. Her tiny body rose and fell with each breath. She was such a perfect mixture of her mother and him. When she was born, her hair was as light as a golden delicious apple. But as she grew, her hair became darker and was now not as blonde as her mother's but not as dark as his. It was sort of brushed gold, the color of a mixture of honey and ale.

When Mendel came home and little Ima ran into his arms, his heart swelled with a love he never knew he could feel. Somewhere, there was a father who loved his child the way he loved Ima, and this father had trusted the integrity of the pharmaceutical laboratories not to produce a drug that they knew would be harmful. Mendel bit his lower lip.

Mendel left Ima's room and went to bed. He sat on the bed beside Katja and gazed at her golden curls, lit by the moonlight that shone through the window. She was the most beautiful creature he'd ever laid eyes on. Although she didn't know it and would not have approved if she did, she was the only person for whom he would willingly sell his soul. Tenderly, he touched her shoulder. He didn't want to awaken her, but he wished he had the courage to tell her everything. Even as his fingers caressed her cool porcelain skin, Mendel knew that he would never burden her with the knowledge of what he'd done to relieve his own guilt. It was his decision and his alone, and he would bear that load alone.

CHAPTER NINETEEN

IMA WAS GROWING SO FAST that Zofia could hardly keep up with her. She was a little over a year and a half old and into everything. To Ima, the world was a giant playground, and she was never willing to sit still and be quiet while Zofia told her stories. Between Katja and Zofia, keeping Ima out of trouble was a full day's work. They often took turns when the child was awake, and when she fell asleep, they would brew a pot of tea and try to catch their breath.

One afternoon, after taking Ima to the park and chasing after her for an hour, they were able to put the child down for an afternoon nap. With a sigh of relief for the few minutes of peace, the two women sat together, sipping tea and eating wonderful Israeli chocolate.

"Mendel has done very well for himself. Your father would have been so proud," Zofia said.

"I can't believe how successful he has become. I would never have believed this could be our lives. You know, Mama, I never thought about being rich when I was growing up. I always felt we had so much because we had each other, the kibbutz, and Israel. In those days, I could never have imagined anyone living the way we live now. It's remarkable. Sometimes, I have to sit back and take a deep breath to remind myself that I'm awake and not dreaming."

"I'm glad you're happy. I'm glad that you have everything you need and that you never want for anything. That was all I ever wanted for you."

"I know that. You have always been a good mother to me, Mama."

"Do you ever think about her?" Zofia asked.

Katja instinctively knew who her mother was talking about. "Helga?"

"Yes," Zofia whispered.

"Sometimes I do. I feel sorry for her, but you are my real mother."

"Did you ever write to her and tell her about Ima?"

"I did, but I never sent the letter," Katja said, looking away. "I don't want her to come here. It might be best that she never knows she has a grandchild."

Zofia nodded. "It's your choice. It's not a choice anyone else can make for you."

"I know, and I chose you."

CHAPTER TWENTY

THAT NIGHT, Mendel arrived home from work exhausted. He discarded the tailor-made suit he'd once cherished onto a chair like an old pair of jeans. Now, he had so many handmade suits that they were no longer special to him. He stretched his back and sat on the bed in his boxer shorts. Even though he had not kept up his daily exercise, he was still slender, but his muscles seemed to be going soft. Mendel rubbed his abs and sighed in lament. This job was aging him quickly.

Katja carried a basket of folded laundry into the bedroom to put it away. She smiled at Mendel and rubbed his shoulders for a moment after placing the laundry on the bed.

"Don't you like listening to that comedian Zilberman on the radio? You used to like him. I remember that you used to listen to him all the time," Mendel commented.

"When I have time, I still listen to him. Why?"

"Guess what I've got? I've got a surprise for you."

"What?" She giggled and sat down beside him.

"Zilberman is doing a show here in Tel Aviv, and I have tickets for us. But these are not just any tickets, my darling." He picked up the tickets that he'd laid on the dresser and shuffled them in front of her like cards. He had a big smile. "We have box seats, the best seats in the house."

Katja giggled. "Really? They must have cost a fortune." She reached for the tickets to look at them.

"Now, I have a feeling that your mother would be happy to watch the baby so that we could have a quiet evening to ourselves. We'll go to a nice restaurant, have dinner, and then go to the show."

Her blue eyes lit up like a morning sky, and his heart thumped. When she was happy, his worries faded, if only for a few moments. He wanted to make this night very special. "I insist that you go and buy a new dress and shoes and whatever else you want or need. Have a facial, a professional makeup job, whatever you want..."

"Mendel, this is wonderful. I am sure that Mom would love to babysit." She smiled at him. And again, there it was, that look of love in her eyes, that look that he lived for, that look that made even the worst of things all right.

"So let's ask your mother to babysit, and I suggest you start shopping. Don't worry about the price. Just buy anything you want."

CHAPTER TWENTY-ONE

ZOFIA DRESSED Ima in a white dress embroidered with lemon-yellow daisies and thick, white tights to keep her legs warm. Although it was the middle of May, it was still cool outside, and she didn't want to risk Ima catching a cold. Zofia, Katja, and the baby were heading into town to shop for a dress that Katja would wear the night she and Mendel would see the famous comedian.

Zofia would have loved to make a garment. She had offered if Katja wanted to purchase the fabric. But Katja said it was far too much work, and she'd just buy something ready-made. Zofia had to admit that her vision was not as good as it was in her youth, but even so, she felt a little slighted. She knew Katja had her best interest at heart, but somehow, the situation made her feel useless. There was a time when she'd made all of Katja's clothes. Well, at least she could babysit for Ima, her precious Ima.

"Come on, *Bubbe*, we go now," Ima said, pulling on Zofia's hand. "Mama said we go out for eats."

Zofia touched Ima's cheek. She glanced down at Ima's tiny white saddle shoes, and an overwhelming tenderness overcame her. For a moment, Zofia thought she might cry. She was such a beautiful child, a joy, and a blessing. Although she was active and exhausting, Ima distracted Zofia from dwelling on how much she missed Isaac.

Katja came out of her bedroom and began putting the diaper bag together. They'd gotten used to bringing what looked like a small suitcase whenever they took Ima anywhere. It contained everything that they could possibly need. Katja had recently learned to drive, and Mendel had rewarded her with the safest automobile available.

Katja loaded the car while Zofia took Ima's hand and locked the door to the house. Zofia could find no explanation as to why she felt so uneasy about Mendel's success. She was always afraid that something would go wrong. She should be happy. After all, her daughter had a life that was only a dream for most people. And yet, something wasn't right.

She couldn't put her finger on what it was. Mendel was not the same. He looked strained. He'd aged, his hair was thinning, and he looked so tired. Sometimes, she would notice that he would sit staring into space with a strange look, always distracted. Zofia was positive that he was not interested in another woman. Even with all the changes Mendel seemed to be going through, his love for Katja was still evident.

It had to be his work. Undoubtedly, the overly demanding boss and his long hours were sucking his life out of him. It ate a little more of him every day, like cancer. Zofia realized that it was not possible to earn the kind of money Mendel was bringing home without working very hard.

But somehow, she wished they were all still back on the kibbutz, living without money, without pressure, just for the joy of living. They had plenty of material things now. In fact, there was nothing that could be bought in a store that they did not have, and that was nice, but the price…

Once in town, Katja parked in front of a well-known, posh dress shop. The three of them entered. Discreetly, Zofia examined the workmanship of the seamstresses who'd made the dresses. She turned several of the gowns inside out and looked at the seams. *Not as good as hers,* she thought. These dresses were made in a factory. The pearls were not sewn on by hand the way she'd always done them. "Shoddy workmanship," she whispered under her breath.

"Mom," Katja called from across the dressing room on the other side of the shop, "bring Ima and come and look at this dress. I want your opinion."

Zofia quietly huffed. Then she whispered to Ima, who would not understand what she said, "Your *bubbe* could make much finer garments than these."

Ima smiled and squeezed Zofia's hand as they walked over to Katja.

"So, what do you think?" Katja said, holding up a black dress with a low-cut back draped with French lace.

"It's nice," Zofia said.

"You don't like it?"

"I didn't say that. Try it on. Ima and I will give you our honest opinion. Won't we, Ima?"

"Mama," Ima said, reaching for Katja to pick her up. Katja lifted her and kissed her.

"Stay here with *Bubbe.* I'll be right back. I'm going to try this dress on."

Zofia and Ima stood waiting outside the dressing room.

Ima began playing with the dresses on the rack. A saleswoman with a pinched smile walked over. "I'm sorry. But she can't touch the merchandise. These are very delicate fabrics," the saleswoman said to Zofia.

Zofia nodded and began playing patty cake with Ima to distract her. The child giggled.

Then Katja came out of the dressing room. Zofia had seen many women try on many dresses in her days as a seamstress, but she'd never seen one as striking or as stunning as Katja was as she stood before them.

"Do you like it?"

Zofia nodded. "You are so beautiful, Katja." And she meant it. "When is this comedy show you and Mendel are going to see?"

"June 4th. I have a couple of weeks to find shoes and a matching bag. Do you think I should have my hair done in an updo?"

"No, wear it down. It's like a golden crown," Zofia said, touching the long, blonde curls she had brushed when Katja was just a child.

CHAPTER TWENTY-TWO

THE NIGHT of the Zilberman comedy show, Ima was fussy. She'd been crying all day, her nose was running, and her skin felt hot.

"Either she has a little cold, or she's cutting a tooth," Zofia said.

"I'm worried. Maybe we shouldn't go," Katja said.

"You and Mendel will go. I'll take care of the baby."

Katja looked at Ima and saw that her skin was the color of fresh radishes. Katja picked her up despite her fancy dress and held Ima to her breast. The child felt clammy.

"What's the matter, sweetheart?" Katja asked.

Ima just clutched onto Katja's dress with her tiny fist, her face crunched and stained with tears.

"I don't know what to do. I am afraid to leave her. I think we should call Dr. Katz."

"No need. If she gets worse, I'll call—I promise. You two go and have a good time. You've been looking forward to this show for weeks."

Katja nodded and whispered, "Okay," but her eyes reflected worry. Mendel entered the room wearing a black suit, a crisp white cotton shirt, and a black tie. He looked charming and elegant.

"What's going on here?" Mendel asked.

"Ima's sick," Katja said.

"Let's stay home." Mendel reached for the baby and took her into his arms.

"I insist that you both go. Now, if Ima needs anything, I promise to call Dr. Katz right away."

Mendel looked at Katja. "What do you think?" he asked.

"I don't know. I suppose Mama is right. Your boss and his wife are going to be expecting us. We can't miss it. I suppose we should be there."

"I don't care about them at all," Mendel said.

"I know, but it makes a good impression."

"All right, if you think we should go, then get your purse, and we'll get going," Mendel said to Katja. "Mom," he addressed Zofia, "I'll call you periodically to see how the baby is doing. If you need anything, call the theater. Here is the box number where we will be seated. Just ask them to go and get me, all right?" Mendel wrote the number down.

Zofia took the paper with the box number and put it next to the phone.

"Either way, we'll be home early, Mama," Katja said. She leaned down and kissed Ima's cheek, then gave Zofia a worried look.

"Don't worry. Ima will be fine."

Katja tried to smile as they walked out the door.

CHAPTER TWENTY-THREE

Elan Amsel was exhausted. He had become accustomed to operating the produce stand on Ben Yehuda St. that his father, Giton, had left for him when he died. Elan had even made friends at the market but was unsatisfied, unfulfilled, and, most often, miserable.

The only good thing about the marketplace was Friday night when it closed to reopen on Sunday. And he also liked being his own boss. It gave him the opportunity to get out of his house, go to work early, and then stay late when there were problems between his wife and mother. Of course, everything in Jerusalem closed on Friday night for the Sabbath, not just the market. In this city, everyone observed the holy days.

Elan often pondered the tragedy his life had become. He had never been the same since his breakup with Katja. He'd tried to start over, tried very hard. In fact, he'd even allowed himself to believe that if he married Janice, she would help him to forget the past. She was such a strong woman.

When they first met, Elan had been so broken that it was easy to step back and let her lead the way, at least for a short while. Then, as time passed, the very thing that had attracted him to his wife now repelled him.

Janice, an American girl, had grown up spoiled by an overindulgent father, who always gave in to her tantrums. Elan's mother, Jerusha, who lived with the two of them, was also a stubborn woman. She and Janice fought bitter battles daily, always putting Elan in the middle. He tried to avoid them whenever possible. But when he was at home in the evening trying to relax, the two women were constantly agitating him. He needed his rest but was unable to get enough sleep.

As soon as he and his wife retired to their room for the night, Janice complained about something his mother had done earlier in the day. She would ramble on, even when he told her he'd had enough and wanted to rest. Most of the time, Janice's constant nagging resulted in an argument. His cute little redheaded American wife was a true firebrand. Elan had a strong will, and although he was trying to keep a level head, Elan was afraid that one day he might strike her.

Instead of going home after work, he would sometimes go to a nightclub to have a few drinks and listen to American rock and roll. That had been something he and Katja, his ex-fiancé, had done together. So when he went to the clubs, he felt closer to the memory of Katja. Out of guilt, he had tried to share his love for American music with Janice. But as he'd expected, they left the club in a heated argument. She'd accused him of eyeing some other girl and drinking too much.

So he went back to going to the clubs alone. Sometimes, on one of his darker, lonelier nights, he would find a willing woman and have a brief sexual encounter with her. He did this to remind himself that he was still the desirable man he'd once been.

Marrying Janice had seemed like a good idea when they'd first met, but now Elan was beginning to feel trapped, suffocated—something he'd never felt with Katja. She had been a freer spirit. She had not tried to control his every move. Besides that, he missed his work in the IAF—the Israeli Air Force branch of the IDF—the Israel Defense Forces. He missed his freedom. Elan resented his mother and wife for their constant fight for power and blamed them for his miserable life.

That night, when he opened the door to the small, stifling rooms he shared with the two women in his life, Elan found his mother sitting at the kitchen table. Her small dark face was red as oxblood, drawn in on itself and angry. He laid his jacket on the back of a chair, and as he walked by, she gave him a snort like a bull. *Another night in hell*, Elan thought. He walked to his bedroom to change his clothes, anticipating his wife would be just as angry as his mother. Elan found the door to his room locked.

"Janice, open the door." He wanted to beat the hell out of her. He'd had enough of her childish whims. He would have liked to take a swing at his mother, too. God help him. If his father only knew the man he was becoming.

"I don't feel like seeing anyone right now," Janice said. Elan could hear in her voice that she'd been crying.

"I need to get into my room. I'm tired and hungry. I don't feel like having this bullshit fight again. Open the door now, Janice!"

He twisted the handle to find the door still locked. Fueled by frustration, he shouted, "I said open the door!" He began banging his fist on the door. Pain shot through his wrist, but he continued to pound.

When she didn't answer, his anger grew stronger. "Fuck you, Janice! Open the fucking door!" He kicked the door and hurt his ankle. This only served to fuel his rage.

"I told you to tell your mother that it's none of her fucking business where I go when I go out. Every time I go to the store, she expects an itinerary. Who the hell does that woman think she is? She has no right to tell me what I can and can't do. I asked you to tell her that. But you didn't talk to her, did you, Elan? You're a coward and a loser, too. You barely make enough money to keep us in this shithole of a house, and I'm supposed to put up with your bitch of a mother, too?"

"Open the fucking door!" he shouted, pounding on the wood. His hand ached, but he couldn't stop hammering.

She opened the door. Elan restrained himself. He wanted to slap her so hard that she'd hit the wall and punch her until she would be quiet forever.

"Get out of my way," he said. "I want to get out of these clothes and shower."

"I don't care what you want. Your mother is on my nerves."

He pushed her out of his way and grabbed the old stretched-out jeans he wore around the house and a black tee shirt. He then turned and entered the bathroom with his hand still balled up in a fist.

The hot water from the shower relaxed him. He began to feel his muscles loosen.

As soon as Elan pulled out the chair at the kitchen table, he felt the tension begin again. He had come home from work hungry, but the atmosphere in the dilapidated house was killing his appetite.

As she always did, his mother was putting on her act. She was pretending to be a caring, loving mother whose only concern was the welfare of her son. But Elan saw right through her, and he knew her motives were anything but warm. His mother did small things that she knew would irritate his wife. Tonight, his mother had purposely prepared boiled fish, which she knew Janice despised. Although if he asked his mother, Elan knew she would never admit that she had any idea how repelled Janice was by this meal.

The thick, black skin was hanging loosely from the white flesh of the whole fish in the dish in front of him. Its dull, golden eyes stared out at nothing. Elan dared not look at Janice's face because he figured she was probably gagging. She'd told him how nauseating the black fish was to her. So, instead of giving Janice the opportunity to react, Elan kept his head down and ate quietly. No one spoke. The only sounds were the sounds of silverware clicking against the glass dishes.

Janice had her arms folded over her chest. She had not touched a single morsel on the table and finally got up and walked out of the room.

"She doesn't even help me clean up," Elan's mother told him. "This is how a daughter-in-law should treat her mother-in-law?"

"You know she hates this fish. You did this on purpose, Mother."

"How could you accuse me of that? Why would I do something like that?"

"Because you two don't get along, you're constantly looking for ways to aggravate each other." Elan threw his fork on the table. "It's driving me crazy. I'm trying to keep peace here. I go to work every day. I pay the rent and all the bills, and then I come home every night to this."

"This what?"

"You know what you're doing, Mother. Janice is as stubborn as you are, and to tell you the truth, I've had it with all of this."

"So you're going to divorce her?"

"That's what you want, isn't it? You want me all to yourself."

"That's terrible that you should think of me like that. I want you to have a wife and children."

"Of course you do, Ma."

"Elan!"

"Just like you want Aryeh and Brenda to be happy. You're always causing trouble between them, too. But they don't live with you, so you can't get to them as much. Janice and I live here, and you're right in the middle, causing all of our troubles."

"I feel sick. My own son, my flesh and blood, the child whom I sacrificed everything for, thinks of me as his enemy. All I ever wanted was what was best for you."

"You never liked any of the women I brought home."

"Are you talking about that Katja? Elan, please, how could you bring such a girl home to me? She was not for you, Elan. She didn't even look Jewish."

"But she was Jewish, Mama."

"Not from what Aryeh told me. He said she was adopted, and her birth parents…"

"She was raised in a kibbutz. She knows nothing else but Judaism."

"Her parents were Nazis. That makes her not Jewish, in my book."

"And what book is that, Mama? It's not the Torah, that's for sure."

"Hmmm," she grumbled. "I've had enough. I never thought you would talk to me this way. You've turned on me. I feel like I have a serpent living in my own house. If your father were still alive, you would never show me disrespect."

"I'm not being disrespectful. I just know how you think."

"What did I ever do to anyone that I should have such a terrible son?" She crossed her arms in front of her chest and glared at him.

Elan left the room and went to his bedroom, where Janice waited, sitting propped up against the headboard on the bed with her arms crossed over her chest.

"All day long, she treats me like shit. I want you to get us our own place. I want to move out of here, Elan."

"We can't. I can't afford to pay two rents. I can hardly afford to pay for this place."

"I don't understand why you have to take care of your mother. Didn't your father leave any money for her? My God, Elan. I can't stand it anymore."

He shook his head. "I don't know what to do, Janice. She has no place else to go and no money."

"Why doesn't your brother take her for a while?"

"Because this is her home. She was living here with me before I married you. How can I just put her out on the street?"

"So you choose your mother instead of your wife? That's it, isn't it, Elan? That's all there is to it? I don't really count as anything important in your life."

"I can't choose between you and my mother. I just wish you would try to get along with her. Can't you just let her have her way for a while? She's older and set in her ways. Try a little harder to make her like you. She'll get used to you if you do that, and then she won't be so difficult."

"Fuck you, Elan. Why don't you tell her to kiss my ass instead of telling me to kiss hers?" she yelled at him. "I'll tell you why: it's because she is more important to you than I am; that's why."

"That's not it at all. It's because she's a lonely, old woman. You're young. If you could just see her for what she is."

"And what is that, Elan? What is she?"

"My mother has nothing left but her sons, two boys who have grown up and no longer need her. My sister has married and moved to America. She never even calls, not even on my mother's birthday. Don't you see how sad my mother is? She is a woman whose husband is gone. Be gentle with her, Janice. She has it harder than you know."

"She's a bitch. She does everything she can to make my life a living hell. I wanted a dog. She says she's allergic. Of course, she is. How convenient. If I had wanted a bird, she would have been allergic to that.

"Every time I leave the house, she wants to know where I'm going. She watches the clock and times when I leave and when I get back. Elan, she has the nerve to time me to see how long I'm gone. Can't you understand? I can't take her anymore. Whenever I cook something and put it in the refrigerator, I find it in the trash. She makes me feel like I don't belong here. I can't stand her. I can't."

With each passing minute, his head felt like it was swelling and might soon explode. The throbbing was unbearable. If anyone knew how hard his mother was to live with, he did, but Janice was no picnic, either. Even though he had no desire to touch her right now, he knew what he had to do to settle Janice down. "Come here," he whispered, pulling her close to him. "Shh, I love you," he cooed into her hair, and she melted in his arms. This worked like a charm most of the time. They made love, and for a while, she was quiet. But just as Elan drifted off to sleep, Janice said, "I really would like to get our own place, Elan. I think you should tell Aryeh that it's his turn to take her. You've done your part. Have your mother move in with Aryeh and Brenda."

Elan took a deep breath. His headache was getting so bad he thought he might vomit. "I'm tired. Let's talk in the morning," he grunted at her in exhaustion and disgust and then turned over and fell asleep.

CHAPTER TWENTY-FOUR

Janice adored Elan for the same reasons she hated him. He was strong, sexy, irresistible, and incredibly attractive. Wherever they went, women still turned to admire him. He was the confident Israeli with oversized muscles and a shirt open to reveal a tanned but hairless chest. Elan was the first person Janice had ever been close to that she could not dominate, which drove her crazy. She kept trying, but he was too strong for her.

On the other hand, Elan felt that he'd lost all of his sex appeal. He felt old and flabby, even though it was not true. His job didn't challenge him. Instead, it gave him an overwhelming feeling of uselessness. His present conditions seemed to have thwarted all of his dreams. Where he had once been so strong, he now felt weak and defeated and began to hate himself. Somehow, he'd found himself burdened with supporting his mother while his brother was off living as he pleased. Although Elan would never admit it to Janice, he resented his mother.

And even worse, any feelings he'd ever had for Janice had dimmed. As time passed, he realized that he really might not have ever loved her. He damned himself for it, but Katja was still the love of his life. He knew that when they were together and still knew it now. A full week never passed that he did not think of her, that he did not remember some small thing they'd shared, the sound of her laughter, or some other haunting memory that drove him to despair.

When he'd broken their engagement, he felt obligated to marry someone of pure Jewish blood. He'd been raised to believe this was his purpose and felt it so strongly that he could not see beyond that obligation. Now that it was over, Katja was gone, and he was married to Janice. All of his days were filled with regret.

The night following the fight with Janice and his mother, Elan stopped at a dance club on his way home from work. He wanted to have a few drinks, listen to music, and unwind before returning to the ever-constant misery that engulfed his life. When he entered the club, the jukebox was playing a song that he loved by the American musician Jerry Lee Lewis. The dance floor was filled with young people jumping and jiving. Elan loved the atmosphere and the life all around him.

He ordered a whiskey, sat down to watch the dancers, and began tapping his fingers on the bar to the rhythm of the music. Elan loved to dance. He couldn't help but remember the night he taught Katja to jitterbug. At first, she was clumsy. Elan smiled to himself. But by the end of the night, she'd moved so gracefully in sync with him that he hardly felt her presence. It was as if they moved as one body.

"Ohhh baby, you drive me crazy…" the voice on the jukebox came blasting through the speakers loud and clear.

Elan poured the whiskey down his throat and ordered another. It burned as it flowed down through his chest like a hot river, soothing all the way to his belly. Tonight, he wanted to leave every memory of his marriage behind. He wanted to find a woman with long, flowing blond hair and pretend she was Katja. Elan wanted to hold her in his arms and make love to her. He wanted to feel alive again, to feel strong, to feel excited about life, and to feel the way that he did when he was still engaged to Katja.

Even though Elan had enough alcohol to ignite his imagination, he could not find anyone in the bar who remotely reminded him of

Katja. He felt disconnected and alone as he watched the others dancing and laughing. The music that had made him feel light-hearted only an hour earlier was now beginning to seem sad and depressing.

He thought about Janice. He'd made a promise to Janice. Elan had stood under the chuppah and promised to love and cherish her for the rest of his life. When he'd made those vows, he'd really believed that he could escape from his past and his feelings. He hoped that his love for Katja would somehow disappear with time. He'd thought his wife would erase his pain and shelter him in the overpowering love she felt for him. In fact, he'd convinced himself that, in time, he would forget Katja and fall in love with Janice. It had not happened. Instead, he felt smothered. When he looked at Janice, all he wanted was to be free of her and his promises to her and his mother.

"Give me another whiskey," Elan told the bartender.

The whiskey no longer burned his throat. Now, it just eased his mind. Soon, he would have to go home and face the same old stuff. Worse, Janice would be mad that he was so late. She would carry on, yelling and stomping her little feet.

It scared him—how much he wanted to slap her, shove her against the wall, and hit her until he saw fear in her eyes. Elan wanted her to know his strength, to be so terrified that she would never dare to anger him again. The drink made it easy for Elan to smile at the thought of using his strength to subdue the spoiled brat he'd married. *One more whiskey, and then I'm going to head home and show both of those women who is the real boss of the house.*

After he finished paying the bar bill, Elan went outside and began to walk home. The night air was cool and sobering enough to make him want to sit down on the curb and weep for his loss and his future in his drunken stupor. Of course, he would never do such a thing. But he felt like it.

"Where have you been?" Janice demanded before Elan had a chance to close the door to the house.

"I went out with a friend for his birthday," Elan said, immediately disgusted with himself for feeling the need to justify himself to her. Who the hell was she to question him?

"Without calling me, Elan? What were you thinking?"

"Sorry," he said, shrugging nonchalantly to make sure that she knew he wasn't sorry.

"Elan, you're a married man. You can't come and go as you please. I've been waiting for you, worrying about you, holding dinner for you. Everything is cold. You are impossible. I don't know how I can go on between you and that bitch of a mother of yours…"

"Shut up. You hear me? Shut up," he said, walking toward her like a lion about to attack.

"You stink of alcohol."

"Yeah, you're right. I've been drinking."

"Elan. What the hell are you doing? You listen to me. You can't just go out on the town whenever you please and stay out as late as you want. Are you seeing another woman? Are you cheating on me?" She pushed herself right up close to him, yelling loudly.

He pushed her away from him, pushed her hard. Her eyes flew open wide. He saw the terror on her face and liked how it made him feel. It made him feel strong like he was once again the man in his house. He wanted to push her again, hit and keep hitting her. Elan wanted to shut her up forever.

"Stop accusing me. Stop telling me what to do. I've had it with your bullshit, Janice. Every night, I have to come home to this fighting. I won't put up with it anymore. Do you understand me?" His face was so close to hers that he could see her flinch at the smell of alcohol on his breath.

She didn't answer. He knew she was shocked. He liked that she was shocked. He stood staring at her for a few minutes. Then logic took over. He must not allow himself to lose control. He must stop himself before he let his animal instinct command his behavior before he started to hit her and pound her into the ground until she would never get up again.

Elan took a deep breath. He clenched and unclenched his fists. If he killed her, then what? Elan turned and left the house. He walked for several hours, just wandering the streets. Then he checked into a cheap hotel, spending money he could hardly afford to waste, and without taking off his clothes or shoes, he lay down on the bed. He fell into a deep, dreamless sleep.

The next day, Elan awoke with a terrible headache. His mouth was dry, and he was very late for work. He'd been so angry the night before that he had not even considered bringing fresh clothes or a toothbrush. He took a shower, dressed in the same clothes he'd been wearing the night before, rinsed his mouth with water, and left to go to work.

The market was full when he arrived. The noise and the people accelerated his nauseous headache. He wished he could just go home and sleep it off, but that was impossible. Home was worse than work, especially since he'd been out all night. First, he'd take the tarps off his produce and declare himself open for business. Then, he'd buy some aspirin and get some water. That should help, at least a little.

As soon as he approached his produce stand, he saw Janice waiting. She looked so small that he was suddenly sorry for what he'd done. *Please don't start a fight with me. I'm not feeling well, and my patience is limited.*

"Hi," Janice said as Elan walked behind the stand. Her voice was soft, apologetic.

"Hi," Elan said.

They were both quiet for a few minutes.

"Listen. I'm sorry. I shouldn't have put my hands on you that way," he said, clearing his throat.

She nodded. Again, there was silence.

"Do you remember? This is where we met, right here. I was standing right where I am now, and you were right there. Do you remember, Elan?" she said. There were tears in her eyes.

He nodded. "Yes."

"Elan, I want to try to make our marriage work. I have to try because I know we have something special."

He nodded again. His stomach turned a little. He felt sorry for her. What could he do? He couldn't just walk away. They were married. Somehow, he had to try to make the best of this. Perhaps there were ways that he could try harder. He would talk to his mother and tell her that if she didn't make an effort to treat his wife better, he and Janice would move out of her house.

Until now, he'd resisted Janice's offers to ask her father for money so the couple could buy a home. However, if his mother continued instigating problems, he would accept Janice's offer to ask for help. Elan had never wanted help from anyone. He'd always felt that it was his responsibility to support his family on his own, and it had been a struggle. But so far, he'd been able to keep a roof over their heads and food in their bellies. He'd done what he knew his father would have asked of him. He'd taken care of his mother.

But he was done bowing to either his mother or his wife. He would treat them with kindness. But he would be the man in his house from this day forward. Elan was going to take control of his life again. In fact, he'd hardly recognized himself last night. Elan had almost beaten his wife. How could he have behaved that way? It had dawned on him in this very instant that because he had spent all his time trying to appease both women, he'd become someone he could not respect.

Today, Elan would begin to make the rules. There would be no more arguing, no more vying for his attention. He would demand that they listen to him from now on, and that way, he would keep himself and his life under control.

"Would you like to come and help me here at the market a few days a week?" Elan asked his wife. "I could use your help."

Her face lit up. "You mean it?"

"Yes, I mean it. I think it might be good for you to get out of the house, away from my mother."

"I've had nothing to do all day but sit at home with your mother. I think this would be wonderful for our marriage."

"Then come here to the market. From now on, you will go to work with me every morning. Together, we will work, and then surely we will make a success of our lives." He touched her chin and lifted her face so that he could look into her eyes, which were glassy with tears.

"I love you, Elan. I want this to work."

He felt such terrible guilt. Elan wanted to love her. He wanted to feel everything a husband should feel for his wife. Just looking into her eyes made him sick with pity. She deserved better.

He nodded. "I know. I know."

CHAPTER TWENTY-FIVE

AND SO A YEAR PASSED, and Janice proved to be a great help to Elan at the market. She had a good head for business, and as the days swept by, he found his feelings for her grew warmer. If not love, at least he felt caring. The day following the night of that terrible fight, he'd come home and talked to his mother. Elan threatened to move out and leave her if she didn't stop trying to sabotage his marriage.

When confronted by a strong Elan, his mother backed down. She could see that he was serious. She didn't want to lose him, and she didn't want to be alone. Then, as time passed, and she saw Elan and his wife growing closer, she began to realize that it was in her best interest to treat Janice with less hostility. Elan's mother was a smart woman. She knew when she'd lost and didn't want to be left to fend for herself.

One night, as Elan and Janice lay in bed, Janice turned to look at him. "I have a special surprise for you."

"Oh?" He put his arm around her. She was a good friend and a good wife. Elan should be satisfied with that. *Some men had marriages that were much worse*, he thought.

"I got tickets for the two of us to go and see Menachem Zilberman in Tel Aviv." She smiled at him.

"How did you arrange that?" he asked, propping himself up on one elbow.

"Last week, my father sent me some money for my birthday, so I bought the tickets. Zilberman is coming next month. I got us a hotel room. Why don't we take off for a couple of days? We can make a little getaway of it," she said, smiling at him.

He felt bad that he'd forgotten her birthday the previous week. He made a mental note to bring her flowers tomorrow.

"I hate to leave the business," he said.

"Elan!" she said, disappointed.

He laughed. "Of course, we'll take off. You silly girl, I wouldn't miss this little getaway for anything."

She laughed and reached up to kiss him. He turned her over and began kissing her neck.

"I love you so much," she whispered.

CHAPTER TWENTY-SIX

The Waiting Period

PRESIDENT NASSER of Egypt ordered the UN Emergency Force to withdraw from the buffer zone between Egypt and Israel that had existed since 1956. Without consulting the UN Council, UN Secretary-General U Thant complied. The next day, May 17th, 1967, The Voice of the Arabs Radio boldly proclaimed, "As of today, there no longer exists an international emergency force to protect Israel. We shall exercise patience no more. We shall not complain anymore to the UN about Israel. The sole method we shall apply against Israel is a total war which will result in the extermination of Zionist existence."

Five days later, on May 22, Egypt closed The Straits of Tiran to all Israeli shipping and all ships bound for Eilat. This effectively cut off all shipping from Asia and Israel's oil supply. The United States had its own troubles in Vietnam. After failing to negotiate peace talks, The United States advised that it would remain neutral, and France joined them in a weapons embargo against the region. The Arab nations had no such issue. The Soviet Union supplied them with an abundance of weapons.

President Nasser of Egypt challenged Israel to fight almost daily. "Our basic objective will be the destruction of Israel. The Arab people want to fight," he said on May 27. The following day, he added: "We will not accept any coexistence with Israel. Today, the issue is not the establishment of peace between the Arab states and Israel. The war with Israel is in effect since 1948." The political cartoons that Nasser had the Arab newspapers publish were very similar to the ones the Nazis ran in Germany prior to the Holocaust. Death was looming its ugly head again like a serpent toward the Jews.

On May 30, 1967, after signing an alliance treaty with King Hussein of Jordan, President Nasser of Egypt declared, "The armies of Egypt, Jordan, Syria, and Lebanon are poised on the borders of Israel to face the challenge while standing behind us are the armies of Iraq, Algeria, Kuwait, Sudan, and the whole Arab nation. This act will astound the world. Today, they will know that the Arabs are arranged for battle, the critical hour has arrived. We have reached the stage of serious action and not declarations."

CHAPTER TWENTY-SEVEN

On the way to the comedy show, Janice turned to Elan. "Honey, please pull over. I'm sick to my stomach."

He looked at her, his eyes filled with concern. Then he swerved the car to the side of the road. She got out and vomited.

"You're sick. Let's go back to the hotel," he said.

"No, I'm fine."

"Janice. You just threw up. You're sick. I insist that we go back to the hotel."

"No, we've been looking forward to this evening for almost a month. I want to go."

"I don't care how long we've been looking forward to it. You're sick, and you should be in bed. Now, let's go back to the room so that you can lie down," he said.

"I feel better."

"I'm a little worried. Maybe it is food poisoning from the restaurant where we had dinner."

"Elan."

"Yes?"

"It's not food poisoning," she said with a little smile.

He cocked his head and looked at her.

"I was going to wait to tell you. I wanted to surprise you after the show tonight. But I guess I'll tell you now." She smiled at him and rubbed her belly. "I'm not sick… I'm pregnant."

"Janice!" he exclaimed, smiling. "Oh, my God! I am going to be a father!" He reached across the seat and took her into his arms. "How long have you known?"

"Only a few weeks. I wanted to wait until tonight to tell you."

"Oh, Janice!"

"You're happy?"

"Elated, I'm on top of the world." He laughed and kissed her. "This is a marvelous blessing."

She laughed. "I am happy, too. We'll have to think of names."

"I'd like to give my father a name. I thought Aryeh would have named their daughter after him, but before my father passed away, Aryeh had already promised Brenda to name the child after her mother, who died a year earlier. And well, anyway, he did. So I would be eternally grateful to you if you would agree to name the baby for my father. His name was Gidon."

"Then, if it's a boy, the baby's name will be Gidon."

"You would do that for me?" Elan asked.

"Yes, of course. I love you," she said.

Elan smiled at her. She was a good wife. "And if it's a girl?" he asked.

"I don't know. We'll have to figure it out," she said. "What is the female form of Gidon?"

"It doesn't need to be the same name, only the first letter."

"So her name will begin with a G?"

"Yes. I'm surprised. You don't have this Jewish tradition in America?"

"We do. I just never paid much attention to it. I wasn't having a baby, so I didn't care. Do you like the name Gabby?"

"Gabby, short for Gabrielle?" Elan nodded, raising his eyebrows in thought, and then rubbed his chin. "Yes, I like it very much," he said.

She reached over and squeezed his hand. "We'll figure it out together."

"Well, since it's June, the baby should come in February."

"Yes, the doctor gave me a due date of February 15."

"February 15," he said and smiled. He was going to be a father. He was going to fulfill his purpose in Israel. Since he was a child, he'd been told that every Jew must have children to rebuild the race that Hitler had tried to obliterate.

When Janice and Elan arrived at the theater, it was filled with people. There were lines to get in the doors and then more lines to the seats.

Once they were inside, Janice turned to Elan.

"Elan, I have to go to the bathroom."

"Are you sick again?"

"A little. I guess it's to be expected." She smiled.

"All right. I don't want us to get separated with all these people, so I'll wait right here outside of the bathroom until you come out. Then, when you come out, we'll go and find our seats together."

"All right. That's a good idea. I'll be right back."

She turned and walked through the restroom door with the sign above it that said "women."

Elan waited just outside the bathroom door. It seemed to be taking a long time. He watched the door open and close, women coming out and going in. The lines in the theater were growing by the minute. He was worried about Janice. Perhaps she was really feeling ill.

Then the bathroom door opened. Elan saw a flash of butterscotch curls dripping down slender bare shoulders, cerulean eyes as blue as the Mediterranean Sea. Everything seemed to stop. It was as if the world had gone into slow motion. Elan could not hear the noise around him anymore.

The blonde woman glanced up at the clock overhead, her eyes locked with Elan's. Those eyes, those celestial blue eyes, brought back memories of making love, of looking down and getting lost in their depth as they shined back up at him like stars leading his way through the darkness. Those captivating blue eyes had never stopped haunting him.

"Katja?" Elan said. His mouth was suddenly dry.

"Elan?" Her voice cracked. They had not seen each other since the breakup.

He stood staring at her, stunned and immovable, as if he had turned to stone and could not move a muscle. He wanted to speak, but no sound would come out of his mouth. Katja. She was more beautiful than he remembered. He had to say something—anything before the moment passed, and she was gone forever. Just as Elan was about to speak, Janice walked out of the bathroom. Janice took Elan's arm. "I'm sorry it took so long. There was a heck of a line in there. Let's hurry. The show is about to start." Elan nodded, dumbfounded, as Janice led him away.

As they were walking toward the auditorium, Elan could not help himself. He had to turn back. He had to see her again, even if only for a second. Their eyes met. *Katja, My God, it's Katja.*

Katja froze for a second. Her limbs would not move. She had to will her feet forward, away from Elan, away from the memories, away from the past that had suddenly formed a hole deep in her stomach.

She entered the stairway to the expensive box seats she shared with her husband, Mendel. He stood when she entered, always the gentleman with the impeccable manners. Her muscles felt tense as she sat down beside him. He took her hand in his own and kissed it gently. The four-carat emerald-cut diamond Mendel had given her caught the light and sparkled in a rainbow on the wall. She turned to him, smiled, and thought, *Mendel. God bless Mendel.*

On the other side of the auditorium, at the entrance to the balcony, Janice handed the tickets to the usher, who read them and said, "You're up in row R, straight up the stairs and then to the left."

"Come on, Elan, why are you in a daze? I want to get to our seats before they dim the lights."

Elan nodded, forcing his head to turn back to his wife. Then he followed Janice up the stairs of the theater to their seats, right on the aisle. Janice slid into her chair, and Elan sat down beside her.

"This is going to be fun. I just love Zilberman. I listen to him on the radio all the time." Janice reached over and patted Elan's hand. "What a perfect night this is, isn't it?" she asked.

Elan felt his breath catch in his throat, and a bead of sweat trickled down his cheek.

Before Elan had a chance to respond to his wife's question, the lights in the auditorium mercifully flickered twice, and then the room went dark. Zilberman took the stage. The crowd roared with applause, and the show began.

CHAPTER TWENTY-EIGHT

"Are you all right? You look pale?" Mendel asked. "I called your mother to see about Ima. Mom says she's doing fine."

"Oh, I am so glad." Katja took a deep breath. "I was a little concerned. Do I really look pale?" Katja lifted her hand to her cheek.

"Yes, sweetheart, you do. Do you feel all right?"

"Yes, I'm fine," Katja said.

Mendel reached up to feel Katja's forehead and checked for fever. "Are you sure you're okay?"

"Yes, it must be the lighting in here that's making my color look off. I'm fine."

"Ladies and gentlemen, take your seats, please," said a voice over the loudspeaker.

The auditorium went dark. Zilberman appeared on the stage as the audience roared with approval and applause. The audience stood to honor the famous comedian. Mendel glanced over to see that Katja was not standing. He helped her to her feet. They both began to clap, but Mendel was worried. Katja seemed ill. Zilberman started with several one-liners, but Katja wasn't laughing at the jokes. She seemed distracted. Mendel kept glancing at his beautiful wife, the love of his life. What if both she and Ima were ill? Perhaps they had the same illness.

Again, here it was, that tick in the back of his mind, that guilt about what he'd done. Maybe he was being punished. Someone may have died somewhere, and now God was going to take someone he loved as retribution. Mendel felt a slight pain in his chest. The sweat was dampening the armpits of his shirt. Had it been a mistake to take this job with Harvey? All he had wanted was to give Katja the world, to make her see that marrying him was a good choice. Mendel had wanted to provide for his family and give them a comfortable life. *From rags to riches*, he thought, trembling slightly, *but at what price*?

Mendel couldn't watch the show. He kept glancing over at Katja.

"Are you sure you're all right?" he whispered in her ear.

"Yes, don't worry about me, please. I just have a little headache."

"Do you want to go home? I'll tell Harvey that we have to leave."

"No, no, really. Mendel, I'm fine."

Katja's mind was like a movie reel that she was unable to stop. All of her memories of Elan played over and over on the screen behind her eyes. Seeing him again awakened the pain that Katja had fooled herself into believing was a part of her past. Oh, how she had loved him more than she could ever say. Elan had hurt her so deeply that she thought she might never recover. He had hurt her the way only someone you truly love can hurt you, a slice through the heart that might grow a scab but was never truly healed. That scab was always waiting to be torn off by a memory and start bleeding again.

She thought of his eyes and then of the first time she and Elan had made love. Katja had been so nervous that night. He was her first lover. Elan was the first man who had ever seen her without her clothes. She'd been so afraid and shy, but he was gentle and adoring.

Then her stomach heaved a little as she thought of the day

they'd become engaged. How happy she'd been on that day. Her mind replayed their trips to the sea. The sea breeze blew through his hair as Elan took her hand and led her to the ocean. With the sun shining behind his head, he'd lifted her high in the air, then gently brought her down into the water and kissed her.

Katja longed to be alone. She wished she could leave this auditorium filled with laughing people. If only she could go to her room, lock the door and weep. Weep for what was, what could have been, and most of all, weep for that horrible day, the day that he'd come to the kibbutz and learned the truth. She had wanted to, but she could not lie to him. She'd told him that her father was an SS officer and her mother was a good, solid German. It wasn't her fault. She'd fallen to her knees and begged him to understand. She had pleaded with him to accept her, but in truth, she did not accept herself.

Katja had only learned the truth about her background a day earlier. She'd been preparing dinner when she heard her and her mother's names spoken by someone on the radio. She ran into the living room to find that the station was airing the trial of Manfred Blau, the SS officer. It was being featured all over Israel on every radio station. How could this strange man, this arrested Nazi, know Katja and Zofia by name? Katja felt faint, but she needed to know the truth.

She'd left everything as it was in the kitchen. Then she got into her car and drove to the kibbutz, where she found her mother. When confronted, Zofia admitted that what Katja heard was true. Yes, Zofia confessed. Her head hung low as she told Katja the facts. Manfred Blau and his wife, Christa, had adopted Katja from the home of the Lebensborn. Zofia was a prisoner in the concentration camp where Blau worked. He'd taken her into his house to care for Katja because his wife, Christa, was ill.

"I loved you from the beginning," Zofia said. Then she explained, "When there was an uprising at the camp, Christa helped me escape. Years passed. I thought I would never see you again, and I missed you so much. I never stopped thinking about you, praying for you," Zofia said.

"Later, after the war, I lived in a displaced prisoners' camp. A lawyer came and asked me to testify against Manfred at his trial in Nuremberg. It was there in court that I saw Christa for the first time since my escape from the camp. Christa knew she was dying, and there was no doubt Manfred would be convicted and put in prison.

"That night, Christa came to see me in my hotel room. She asked me if I would take you and raise you as my own child. Oh, Katja, I was so happy to have you. It was like my prayer had been answered. As you grew from a small child to a young woman, I knew I should tell you everything, but I couldn't find the words. I had no doubt that the truth would hurt you, and I couldn't bear to see you in pain.

"So it just seemed like the right time to tell you never came. And if Manfred Blau had not escaped from prison and been brought to trial again, I am ashamed to admit it, but you might never have learned the truth. I know I was wrong. But forgive me, please. It was only because I love you that I kept this from you," Zofia said.

To Katja, the truth was a cannonball that shattered her heart. In just a few moments, her entire life lost all credibility. She was living a lie. Katja knew that Elan must know the truth, or their marriage would also be based on falsehoods. So she'd done the only thing she could do—she told Elan. And then her deepest fears were realized. He broke the engagement.

The devastation of losing the man she loved was unbearable. Katja didn't know where to begin her life again. The only world she'd ever known was crushed. That was when Mendel, her best friend at the time, had blessedly taken over.

Katja felt she would never have closure until she found her birth mother. It would be impossible for her to go on with her life without meeting the woman who'd given her up to the Nazis, so Mendel agreed to help. He took Katja and Zofia first to Switzerland and then to Germany after meeting Helga's sister-in-law. The three of them hunted for Katja's birthmother until they found her. Katja had expected a Nazi, but what she found was a pathetic old woman filled with regrets and guilt.

Her name was Helga Haswell on her Lebensborn birth certificate. It was at a general store outside of Munich that they found someone who knew Helga and gave them directions to the Hoffman farm.

To Katja's surprise, she was an ordinary woman, a farmer's wife. Helga's skin was wrinkled from years of working in the sun. Her blonde hair was now more of a washed-out yellow sprinkled with gray. This plain, commonplace woman was the result of her quest. When she'd begun looking for her birth mother, Katja had no idea what she was expecting to find, perhaps a villain, a horrible Nazi woman with muscles like a man, or a witch from a fairy tale. But in the end, she'd found a person far less dramatic.

At first, it was difficult to speak. There was so much to say and yet so little. Then, as soon as she regained some composure, Katja asked Helga every question that came to mind. Once she'd learned all she could about her past, Katja, Zofia, and Mendel returned to Israel.

Little by little, slowly, carefully, and with an artist's vigilant but loving hands, Mendel took the broken pieces of Katja's life and molded them back together. Katja loved him. She loved him with all her heart. How, then, is it possible that she still had feelings for Elan? Damn Elan. Damn him for being so handsome, tall and dark, so sexy, so Israeli, and so strong.

Katja glanced over at Mendel, at the familiar line of his profile. She had no doubt that he really loved her and was such a good father to Ima. The betrayal Katja felt in her heart sickened her.

Across the auditorium, in less expensive seats, Janice laughed at the comedian and squeezed her husband's hand. She never noticed that he was not laughing or that his hands were clammy. He'd been so excited about the baby that, at this very moment, Janice felt that her life was perfect. Soon, she would be a mother.

Janice laughed again and laid her head on Elan's chest. Distractedly, he patted her hair. What was it about Katja that bewitched him? Was it her beauty? Was it the love they'd once shared? Perhaps it was that, in truth, he'd never stopped loving her. Katja was somewhere in this auditorium. Who was she with, a man? Had she met someone else? Was she married? Katja! He wanted to stand up and call her name loud enough that she would hear him wherever she was. He wanted to cry out, "Katja!" over and over until he found her again. But instead, he just sat beside his wife and gazed at the stage, dazed and unseeing.

CHAPTER TWENTY-NINE

Katja quietly stared out of the window of the car in silence on the drive home. Mendel was afraid her headache might be getting worse. He hoped she was not seriously ill. When they arrived at the house, he ran to open the car door and help her out.

"I'll check on Ima. You go and get ready for bed."

"I just want to make sure she's all right, and then I'll get undressed," Katja said.

"How was she tonight, Mom?" Mendel asked Zofia.

"I think she's fine. She was better after a couple of hours. She ate and had no fever, so whatever bothered her seemed to have passed."

Katja leaned down and gently kissed Ima's soft pink cheek. The baby slept so peacefully that it made Katja's heart swell.

"I'll carry her to bed. You go to sleep, Mom. You need to get some rest," Mendel said to Zofia. "And you go lie down, too, sweetheart. I'll be right in."

Katja went to her room while Zofia straightened up the living room. She put away the storybooks and toys that she and Ima had played with earlier that evening.

Mendel laid Ima on her bed and covered her with a blanket.

She did not awaken but turned over and put her thumb in her mouth. For a few moments, Mendel stood watching her. He knew they should stop her from sucking her thumb, but he secretly loved how she looked with her tiny perfect thumb in her mouth, so peaceful and contented. How he loved his wife and child, how he loved the life he'd made for them. If only he could rid himself of the nagging guilt that always crept into his mind when he remembered what he'd done. It was as if he'd sold his soul to the devil. His throat felt dry, and he swallowed hard. Then, gently, he kissed Ima's cheek. Her eyes half opened slowly.

"Papa," she said in barely a whisper.

"Yes, darling, Mama and I are home. How do you feel?"

Ima smiled and nodded, then put her thumb back in her mouth, closed her eyes, and drifted back into slumber.

"How was the show?" Zofia asked.

"It was good."

"I'm going to bed. I'll see you tomorrow." Zofia stood up and stretched. "Goodnight."

"Goodnight," Mendel said. He took two aspirins from a bottle in the cabinet and put up a pot of water for tea. Then he stared at the pills, the guilt tapping the back of his brain as he waited for the water to boil. He would bring the tea and aspirin to Katja for her headache.

Katja was already in bed when Mendel came in.

"Here, sweetheart, I brought this for your headache."

She smiled. "Thank you." Katja took the aspirin even though she didn't have a headache and sipped the tea. "Your boss seems like a nice man."

"Yes, I suppose." Mendel didn't want to tell her about what he'd done to get the drug approved. He didn't want to alarm her. No need. He would fix this. It was his problem, and he'd find a solution somehow.

"His wife is lovely, too."

"This is the first time I've met her. She seems nice," Mendel said.

Katja put the half-empty china teacup on the night table beside her bed.

Mendel got in beside her. He would have loved to take her into his arms, to hold her and find comfort in their love, but he knew she was not feeling well. So Mendel just reached over and touched Katja's shoulder, and then he turned off the light.

"I love you."

"I love you, too, Mendel." Katja was glad he had not tried to make love tonight. She wanted to be alone with her thoughts about Elan. She needed to sort things out in her mind.

Katja heard Mendel's steady breathing and knew he'd fallen asleep. It was not as easy for her to rest. She watched the tree branches sway in the wind outside her bedroom window and thought of Elan. If anything, he looked even better than the last time she saw him. And when his eyes locked with hers, she felt that same old tingling. Just the idea that he still had that effect on her made her want to vomit. She was so angry with herself. It took several hours before she finally fell asleep.

CHAPTER THIRTY

THE LOUD KNOCK at the door pierced the silence of the night. Mendel got out of bed. He didn't want to awaken Katja, so he didn't turn the light on. In his bare feet and pajamas, he opened the door.

"CPL Mendel Zaltstein?" It was an Israeli soldier dressed in full uniform.

"Yes?"

"Israel is going to war. We need you."

Mendel felt a chill run down his spine. This was the message every Israeli dreaded hearing. Katja came out of their bedroom with a robe wrapped around her, and Zofia opened the door to her room.

"What's going on?" Zofia asked.

Katja stood motionless.

"Israel is going to war," Mendel said in a small voice.

"To war?" Katja said.

"I have to go." Mendel took Katja into his arms.

"Now? You have to leave right now? Where are you going?"

"I don't know. But yes, I have to leave now."

Katja began to cry. Mendel held her, squeezing her in his strong arms and trying to memorize everything he could about her. He had no idea how long he would be gone or if he would ever return. This was what it meant to be an Israeli. He took in the smell of her hair, the warmth of her skin, and the taste of her tears as he kissed her face and lips.

"I'm sorry. But there is no time to lose—you must hurry," the soldier said.

Mendel nodded. Katja nodded.

With trembling, sweaty hands, Mendel grabbed the duffle bag he'd used in the IDF. He packed his toothbrush, underclothes, a pair of pants, two tee shirts, and a picture of Katja smiling and holding Ima. Then he tossed the duffel bag over his shoulder and returned to the living room. Now, all the lights were on in the house. Zofia was holding Katja, who was almost unable to stand on her own.

Ima still slept. Mendel tiptoed into the baby's room and gently touched the top of her head. Then he planted a soft kiss on her cheek. She was so precious. Would he ever see his daughter, his child, again? Ima stirred. Mendel swallowed hard and then went back into the living room where his wife and mother-in-law stood, both looking disoriented.

"I'll be back soon," Mendel said, smiling at Katja as bravely as he could. But the truth was that he didn't know if or when he would return. "I love you. God, how I love you," he said as he took Katja into his arms and held her, again whispering the words into her ear.

"I love you, Mendel. Come back to us. Please, Mendel, come back to us." She shook him hard as if, by shaking him, she could make sure that he promised to return. "Promise me, Mendel. You've never broken a promise to me. Promise me you'll be back."

"Of course, I'll be back," he said, touching her cheek, but inside, his entire being was breaking down.

"Are you ready?" the soldier asked.

Mendel nodded. He squeezed Katja one final time, then turned and followed the soldier out the door to defend Israel.

CHAPTER THIRTY-ONE

The hotel room Janice had booked had a large, round bed with a mirror overhead. When she and Elan returned from the show, she giggled as she undressed.

Elan was still reeling from seeing Katja and was not sure he would be able to achieve an erection. He knew Janice, and he knew that she wanted to make love. Why did all of this happen tonight? Janice was expecting a wonderful second honeymoon, and he felt anything but amorous toward her. She was so sweet and loving. It wasn't her fault. Women are lucky. They could fake their sexual feelings. Men, on the other hand, had to perform, and if they weren't feeling sexually aroused, there was no way to hide their lack of desire. Their own anatomy betrayed them.

Janice came into Elan's arms and kissed him.

"We're going to have a baby," she said in a sweet, singsong voice.

"I know." He smiled.

"You seem unhappy…"

"Not at all. I'm just a little nervous. I'm going to be a father."

"Yes, we will be a real family."

"How are you feeling?"

"I'm fine tonight, but I've had a little morning sickness. Nothing to worry about. It's to be expected." She took his hand and led him to the bed. "Lie down with me, Elan…"

"Maybe we shouldn't have sex. It might be bad for the baby."

"It's fine. I asked the doctor, and he said it won't hurt the baby." She smiled at him and took his hand.

He lay beside her, hoping he would be able to make love to her. Why was he still thinking about Katja? After all, that relationship had ended three years ago. It was a love affair that should never have happened in the first place. Damn those golden curls, those eyes that glittered like blue topaz, that smile that touched and tormented his soul.

Janice leaned over and kissed him, and he put his arms around her. Mechanically, he went through all the motions. Surprising himself, he was able to make love. But once it was over and Janice lay beside him, he listened to her soft breathing in the darkness. In the quiet still of the night, he once again thought of Katja. Janice was lying on Elan's arm, and his arm had gone numb. He was uncomfortable, wishing he could get up and have a drink. But of course, he knew that if he went to the hotel bar, Janice would awaken and badger him with questions.

It was nearly four in the morning when Elan finally drifted off to sleep. Only fifteen minutes later, there was a harsh knock on the hotel room door. Elan woke with a start and sat up in bed. Because of his years of service in the IDF, he was able to awaken from a deep sleep to a state of alertness without any time-lapse.

"Who is it?" he called out in a firm voice.

"IDF. Open the door," a man's voice called from the other side.

Elan went to the door wearing nothing but his white briefs.

"Are you CPT Elan Amsel?" It was a tall, well-built man in an IDF uniform.

"Yes, I'm CPT Amsel. What is it? What do you want? How did you find me here?"

"We went to your house. Your mother sent us here. Israel is going to war. Sir, we need you."

Janice sat up in bed and pulled the sheets over her bare breasts.

"Elan? What's going on?"

"Israel is going to war. I have to go…"

"What? Now? You can't go. You can't just leave me here in a strange hotel room. I need you now. You can't just go. Elan, I'm going to have a baby…"

Elan turned and began to pack the few things he'd brought.

"There will be no time for you to return home to get anything else you might need, sir," the young soldier said.

"Here." Elan emptied his pockets of all the cash he had brought with him and threw the money on the bed. "Take a taxi home. I'll be in touch as soon as I can."

"Elan, are you serious? You can't go. Tell them you can't go, Elan!"

"Israel needs me. I told you when we met that I would be there if Israel called. My country needs me."

"Elan, this is crazy. You could get killed," she said, jumping out of bed with the sheet wrapped around her. Then, turning to the soldier, she pulled on the sleeve of his uniform. "You can't take my husband. He is going to be a father…"

The soldier did not answer. He just stood straight and steady, waiting for Elan.

Elan had finished packing and walked over to kiss Janice goodbye, but she pushed him away.

"I don't want you to go. I forbid you to go."

He shrugged his shoulders. "I'm sorry," he said, then took his bag and nodded to the soldier. Elan and the soldier began walking down the hall. Almost tripping over the sheet she had wrapped around her, she ran after them into the hall and called to Elan. He did not turn around as he walked with the soldier to the elevator.

"If you go, Elan, I swear I won't be here when you get back. I'm not going to go back to that shack of a house to live with your mother without you. I'm pregnant. If you leave me now, I swear I will go home."

Elan stepped into the elevator, and the metal doors swung shut. Janice let out a cry of disbelief, but he was gone. Janice sank to the floor and sat, staring down the hotel hall. Her mind was racing.

How could he just leave like that? She could understand if he was single but not a married man with a child on the way. Hot tears of anger streamed down her cheeks as she got up from the floor. Nothing she could do would change things. With the sheet still draped over her to cover her nakedness, Janice went back into the room, slammed the door behind her, and then picked up the telephone.

"I need a long-distance operator. I want to place a call to the United States."

She gave the operator the number. It seemed like hours before the phone finally began to ring.

"Hello?" a man answered.

"Daddy, it's Janice. I want to come home."

"For a visit?"

"No, forever. I'm done here. I'm done with Elan, with his mother, and with Israel."

Janice's father took a deep breath and smiled to himself. Finally, the call he was waiting for had come at last. He knew it was just a matter of time before his daughter came home. She was an American girl, a spoiled one at that. Living the life she'd chosen was not something her father believed her capable of doing.

"I'll wire you money to buy a plane ticket. It should be there by morning."

"Daddy, I'm so upset. Israel is at war, and Elan left me in a hotel all alone. And... I'm pregnant."

"Listen to me. Settle down. I'm going to take care of everything. Now, what's the name of the hotel? I'll wire the money there. I'll send enough for you to take a taxi to the airport and buy a ticket home."

"Daddy." Janice was weeping now. "He left me here. He wouldn't even try to tell the soldier who came to get him that he needed to be with his wife and unborn child. What kind of man is that?"

"It will all be okay, sweetheart. You're coming home."

CHAPTER THIRTY-TWO

Elan had suspected that war was on the way. He kept track of everything going on around him. He knew that Israel's neighbors had been threatening her for a long time. He'd seen this coming but was just not sure how or when. He realized that his life was in danger, but there had never been a day that he'd not been willing to risk everything for the country he loved.

Israel was not like other countries. Its people, the Israelis, knew their attachment to their land was like a vein to their hearts. It was their lifeline. Now, he sat on a bus to the Hatzor Air Base to defend his first love, Israel, from its enemies. He'd not slept much the night before, and he dozed on and off as the bus ambled over the rocky terrain.

He thought about Janice. She did not understand how he felt about this country. How could she? She was an American. She'd never known real anti-Semitism. Elan had seen it all of his life, not only from his Arab neighbors, but he'd heard the stories from his friends who'd survived the Nazis in Europe and finally found their way to the Jewish homeland. Without Israel, it was only a matter of time before another Hitler rose to power. Once again, the Jews would face annihilation as they had many times throughout history.

He took a deep breath. Every Jew must put Israel first. That was just the way it had to be.

Well, there would be hell to pay with that little red-headed spitfire-of-a-wife when he got home, but it didn't matter. Nothing personal mattered as much as keeping this country safe. Only another Israeli could understand.

If not for his devotion to this land and its people, he would have been married to Katja, the woman he truly loved. How beautiful she looked last night. When their eyes met, he felt a shiver run through his body like an electric shock. It was undeniable that he still loved her and still lusted for her, too. It was strange how life works. It had only been a few hours since he had seen her last, but it was the first time he'd seen her since their breakup. Perhaps he was going to die in battle, and that was God's final gift to him—a glimpse of his one true love.

As much as he would have denied it to anyone who would have ever asked, he was afraid to die or, worse, be permanently disabled. He was a Jew, but he'd never really been religious. Right now, he wished he could grasp something that would make the idea of death and pain easier to bear. *Religion was good for that*, he thought and laughed a little to himself.

Looking around the bus, he saw so many young men, all of them in their IDF uniforms. Most of them were quiet, probably thinking the same things he was thinking. Then, in the front of the bus, two rows back from the driver, in the seat on the aisle, he saw a face he recognized. Wasn't that Mendel Zaltstein? He remembered Mendel from the kibbutz. Mendel was a friend of Katja's and Rachel's. Elan wondered if Mendel knew anything about Katja.

Mendel must be living in Tel Aviv because the bus Elan was riding was filled with men from Tel Aviv. Although Elan lived in Jerusalem, he'd been to Tel Aviv at the show the night before, so he was transported with this group. Elan wondered where Katja lived now. Was she living on the kibbutz near the Golan Heights? After the breakup, he'd not heard any news about her. Perhaps later, when they arrived at their destination, he would talk to Mendel and see if he could casually find out some information about Katja.

CHAPTER THIRTY-THREE

Mendel's head pounded like a drummer was using his brain as a snare drum. He bit his lip so hard that it bled as he sat on the bus, helpless and worried about Katja and his daughter. He was terrified of battle. He was afraid of death and of being captured and tortured. But even more than that, he feared something terrible would happen to those he loved.

Even Zofia, his mother-in-law, who'd always been a dear friend, came to his mind. With his father-in-law dead, there was no man left to protect the women in his life. Mendel trembled at the thought of Katja alone with her mother and the baby. At least he'd left a nice sum of money in the bank and a handsome life insurance policy. His policy did not have a *war clause* in case he was killed in combat. If something happened, Katja would never want for anything. But it was blood money, stained with the blood of trusting Jews who believed the drugs to be safe. Mendel ran his hands through his hair, which had recently begun thinning. His hairline had receded quite noticeably over the past year.

He didn't remember much of his training in the IDF. After all, it had been many years ago. And even as a soldier, he'd only just gotten by but never excelled. Many of the other men were bigger, stronger, and more adapted to military life. For Mendel, boot camp was a struggle followed by two difficult years in the IDF, which he'd been glad to see come to an end. Now, as he rode on this bus, knowing that he would soon go to battle, he tried very hard to remember everything he'd learned. He would need that knowledge to survive.

As he sucked in a deep breath, someone came beside him and tapped him on the shoulder. He looked up into the face of a man he recognized, but he couldn't place him at first. Too much was happening all at once. Then he remembered. It was Elan, Katja's ex-fiancé. Mendel had only met him a few times, and whenever he had seen Elan, he would avoid looking directly into his eyes. That was because Mendel had always been in love with Katja, and seeing her engaged to Elan hurt him so deeply. Then, when Elan had left Katja, Mendel had forgotten him completely until now.

"I'm sorry. I don't remember your name." Elan pretended not to remember Mendel's name. "But you look very familiar to me. I think you might know my ex-fiancé, Katja Zuckerman?" Elan said.

"Yes, I know her." Mendel cleared his throat. As he looked into Elan's eyes, he felt threatened. Katja still had feelings for this man, and the last thing Mendel wanted was for Elan to come back into their lives. "I'm Mendel Zaltstein, and Katja's my wife. We are married with a child."

The color faded from Elan's face. Katja was married? To Mendel? When? How? And they had a baby? Yes, Elan had to admit he was married, but that was different. Or was it? He'd never really allowed himself to believe that Katja would go on without him. Elan held on tightly to the metal bar overhead so that he would not lose his footing as the bus shuffled forward into the dark, unknown future.

CHAPTER THIRTY-FOUR

When the money from her father arrived via wire, Janice took a taxi to the airport and bought a plane ticket home. She'd had enough of Elan, his mother, and certainly enough of Israel and its crazy, overly devoted citizens. Soon, she would return to her comfortable life. No more getting up early, going to the market, or coming home filthy and exhausted at night.

When she'd first met Elan, the idea of being poor and married to a struggling Israeli citizen with his sexy body and penetrating gaze had been romantic for her. She'd embraced the country and the challenge. However, now he had marched off to war, leaving her pregnant, caring more for his ideals than he did for her. And to make matters worse, she had no idea how long she would be alone, stuck with Jerusha, her horrific mother-in-law. Even her name sounded hostile to her.

Janice was tired of Elan's way of life. She wanted things the way they used to be. It would be nice to spend an afternoon getting her hair cut at the beauty salon or to meet her girlfriends for lunch and gossip at a fancy restaurant. She longed to go to expensive department stores where she, with her father's checkbook, would buy lovely clothes and designer handbags. She wanted to travel not only in Israel but all over the world. Elan could never give her that life, and right now, she was quite ready to abandon the life he had given her.

Who did he think he was? He'd told her all this bullshit about his devotion to Israel when they were dating. It all sounded exciting and passionate, but she wasn't pregnant then. How dare he walk out and just leave her alone, pregnant, and not even safe at their home but miles away at a hotel in another city? What kind of man does that?

If he were standing in front of her right now, if she confronted him and told him her feelings, she knew exactly what his answer would be.

"This is what it means to be an Israeli," he would say. She could hear his voice. It infuriated her. Israel! How could a country matter so much to its people? She just couldn't grasp how a man could put a country before his family, before his wife and unborn child. But she learned the hard way that to the Israelis, their homeland came before anyone or anything. Well, Janice was not an Israeli. She was an American, and she was going home: home to her parents, home to the land of plenty, home to a place far away from this war and her inconsiderate, selfish husband and his unbearable mother.

CHAPTER THIRTY-FIVE

THE BUS ROCKED and tipped as it continued north on its path up to the Golan Heights.

"Katja Zuckerman is your wife?" Elan asked, trying to hide his emotions.

"Yes, we're married. Her name is Katja Zaltstein now. We have a little girl," Mendel said, but he wanted to say, "I hope you will respect our family and stay away from my wife."

"So." Elan managed a smile. "Can I sit down?"

Mendel reluctantly moved his duffel bag, and he felt the skin on his legs prickle when Elan sat beside him.

"You live in Tel Aviv?" Elan asked.

"Yes. Yes, we do…"

"I'm married, too. I live in Jerusalem."

Mendel nodded. "That's good." He sucked in a deep breath of air. Maybe he imagined that Elan still had feelings for his wife. After all, Elan was married.

There wasn't much to say. There was too much left unsaid, and that made the conversation stiff and awkward.

"My wife is pregnant," Elan said, nodding.

"*Mazel Tov.*"

"Yes, thank you. I just found out last night. Then, well, the war broke out, and here we are. I suppose it was to be expected if you kept an eye on the news."

"I was watching but hoped it wouldn't come to this," Mendel said.

"Yeah, well, did you really think Israel would be left to live peacefully? Jews have no peace. All we have is Israel. If Israel is destroyed, we will all go down with it."

"Yes, I know. We all know. Still, I hoped."

"An optimist, huh?" Elan laughed bitterly. "I've never had that luxury."

"What good does it do you to think about all the bad things that can happen? Can you stop them from happening by thinking about them over and over?"

"No, but I've lived my whole life waiting for the other shoe to drop."

"Well, you waited, and now it's dropped," Mendel said, giving Elan a look of disgust.

CHAPTER THIRTY-SIX

Mendel felt the sweat drip down the shirt of his uniform as he stepped off the bus into the heat of the Israeli desert. The first sergeant was barking orders, and Mendel followed the other men who'd gotten off the bus into a line. War! Guns! Fighting! Death! Mendel was petrified. His mind was playing tricks on him again. He couldn't help but wonder if this war was nothing more than a punishment from God for what he'd done with that drug. But if he were being punished, why were all of these other poor souls in line beside him, sweating and smelling of perspiration, knowing that soon they could, quite possibly, look death straight in the eyes?

Mendel glanced over at Elan, who looked calm as if he did this sort of thing every day. How could he be so composed with the sound of bombing in the background, the air filling with black smoke, and the uncertainty of the future?

"Zaltstein, wake up. This is no time to be daydreaming," the first sergeant said to Mendel. "You're part of the Golani Brigade. Line up for that bus right there," he said, pointing toward another bus with a line of men getting on board.

The men he was going with were all adults, but some were barely of age. He looked around. In other lines, they looked like boys, children. He took his place at the bus beside a young Sephardic man, who couldn't be more than eighteen, who nodded a welcome without smiling. Mendel felt the sting of the salt from a bead of sweat drip from his eyebrow into his eye. He wiped his eye with the back of his hand.

Again, he thought if he died in battle, what would become of his wife and daughter? Who would take care of them? Would his death be painful or quick? After he died, would he just cease to exist, or was it possible that he would remain on Earth, watching, unable to speak, unable to help those he loved, invisible? Thoughts of his past actions ran through his mind like the tape in a cash register. A dollar for this mistake, fifty cents for that one, adding up the good and bad choices he'd made in his life. Is that the way that God would decide his future? Mendel's breath was shallow.

From across the way, Elan heard the first sergeant say, "CPT Amsel, your bus to Hatzor Air Base is loading up over there."

Elan nodded at the first sergeant, threw his duffel bag over his shoulder, and walked to the bus. Soon, it would all begin. Israel was about to be attacked or would soon attack her enemies. Elan took one more look around at Mendel and the other men. With the sun beating on their heads, these men were getting on their buses. Once they got their orders, they would be in the hands of God, and fate would decide who would live, who would be wounded, and who would never return home.

CHAPTER THIRTY-SEVEN

THE LAST TIME Janice had seen Chicago's O'Hare International Airport, she and Elan were coming into the city for their wedding. Now she was alone, glad to be home but a little sad that her dreams had been shattered. As always, the airport was full of people.

Someone with a shaved head and a long, orange robe handed her a flower. Then he asked her for money, but she dropped the flower and waved him away. Hippies sat on the floor at the airport, barefooted and wearing tie-dyed clothing that had "END THE WAR NOW" written in black marker on the front. Men and women sauntered by her with long, unkempt hair and torn blue jeans. A couple, a man and a woman, both dressed in black robes, their eyes painted with thick black eyeliner and mascara, invited her to take a magazine that said something about the unification of Christ and Satan. Janice shook her head, trembling as she walked away quickly.

When she moved to Israel, the world she'd left behind was a completely different place than it was now. She'd seen the news of America on the TV. She'd heard all about the protests against the Vietnam War, the hippies, the changes in society, and the civil rights movement, but she had never experienced any of it firsthand.

It was hard to believe that people were gathering in protest marches in the streets across the United States. They were fighting against the police. She would have never believed anything like that could happen in the United States. Janice felt like she'd been away a long time, even though it had only been four years. But while she was gone, the world where she grew up had disappeared.

It was a long walk through the crowded airport to the baggage claim, and all around her was evidence of the changes. It reminded her of how different Americans were from Israelis. The Israelis did not question going to war. When called up, they stood behind their country, no matter what the consequences were. She knew that the Israelis disagreed amongst themselves. She had seen the different factions with conflicting ideas of how the country should be run, and she had no doubt that they would fight against each other for control. However, when it came down to the wire, they stood strong and together against foreign enemies.

Now, in America, people were not united like Israelis. From what she'd heard, Americans were openly burning their draft cards in protest against the Vietnam War. Boys refused to go to battle and fled the country, many of them going north to Canada. It was quite different from what she'd come to expect in Israel.

Outside the airport, with her suitcase in hand, she climbed into a yellow cab and gave the driver instructions. Janice was on her way home. She watched the familiar landscape as the taxi weaved through traffic. This was where she belonged, in America: where people could speak freely, the citizens were not blindly devoted to their country, and love and family came first.

Her parents were both waiting for her. They knew what time her flight had landed and were watching out the large picture window in the living room. Her parents rushed outside when the taxi pulled up to the curb in front of the house. They took turns hugging her. Her father pulled a wad of bills out of his pocket, gave the cab driver a generous tip, and then carried Janice's bag into the house.

"We're so glad you're back," Janice's mother said.

Her father put his arm around her shoulder and squeezed. "Welcome home, sweetheart."

Janice's bedroom was the same as she'd left it when she moved to Israel. Even her giant, pink teddy bear with the white bow that everyone had signed at the lavish sweet sixteen party her parents had given her still sat in the middle of her canopy bed. On the mirror above her dressing table was a picture she'd cut out of a magazine and taped there with masking tape. It was from the Beatles' first appearance on the Ed Sullivan Show. Gently, she reached up and touched the photograph.

The baby-pink rotary princess phone sat on the nightstand beside her bed. Janice ran her fingers over the receiver. She wanted to call her best friend Bonnie. Janice longed to tell Bonnie that she had returned and things would be the way they were before she'd gone off to Israel.

However, the truth was that things were not the same, not at all. Janice was pregnant. It was going to be difficult raising a fatherless child. How would she ever resume her old life? A part of her buried deep inside missed Elan terribly. Not that she wanted to return, but the memories were still there. Janice was angry at him. She wanted to punish him for walking out on her when she needed him. So, in haste, she'd left the country. Now, in her childhood home, alone in the room where she'd grown up, she was having second thoughts about that, too.

Janice kicked off her shoes and lay down on her bed. She felt the chiffon of the bedspread against her cheek. Moving it out of the way, she laid her head on the crisp, white cotton pillowcase. Janice was exhausted. Perhaps after she took a nap, she'd be clearer about what to do next. It had been a long, tiresome flight, and she had not slept much the night before leaving. Within minutes after lying down, Janice was fast asleep.

CHAPTER THIRTY-EIGHT

UPON ARRIVING at the Hatzor Air Base, Elan was allowed two hours of sleep, given breakfast, and then ushered into the briefing room.

"I've received orders to activate Operation, the attack on all Egyptian air bases. Twelve aircraft will be kept in reserve to protect Israeli airspace. All the rest of our nearly two hundred planes will be involved in the attack. War is inevitable. If we allow Egypt to have an air force, Israel will perish. They say all clouds have a silver lining. Egypt has been at war with Yemen for five years, and almost half its army is in Yemen. This is good news for us." The Base Commander Beni Pelid paused, pulled a drag on his cigarette, stubbed it out, and continued. "The mission will be on complete radio silence."

A young pilot asked the question they were all thinking. "What happens if there is trouble after takeoff?"

"Set your course for the sea and eject," the commander said.

"But we can't call for help."

"I wish you luck."

Elan thought about that for a moment and raised his hand. "Sir, since the Egyptians have a better recovery plan for their pilots, we'll have to oblige them to use it."

"Very good, Captain, just what I was thinking." Commander Pelid smiled.

"And to continue, the Egyptians are used to Israeli jets flying routine patrols at dawn. We will give them something to look at while the rest of you fly under the radar, flying west and low over the Mediterranean and entering Egyptian airspace from the north. Once the Egyptians conclude that it is business as usual, they will return to their bases, refuel, and have breakfast.

"With God's help, we will destroy their air force while they are at the breakfast table. Seventeen of you will be sent to attack the Egyptian air bases, and four will be held as quick response units to go where they are needed. ABA (Air Base Attack) will be as follows: Shahaks 73, 75, 84, 77, 06 (Madaf 2), 51, 34, 56, 86, 08, 09, 62, 06 (Michtaba 3), 04, 82, 81, & 52. QRA (Quick Response Alert) are as follows: Shahaks 12, 59, 15, & 33."

Elan was excited at the thought of wasting the entire Egyptian Air Force while they were on the ground. *Maybe I might even get an air-to-air kill*, he thought.

"Moked first wave: Cairo West - Shahaks 73, 75, 84, 34, 56, 86, 08, 09, 62, & 06 (Madaf 2). Bir Tamada–Shahaks 77, 06 (Michtaba 3), & 51. Beni Suef–Shahaks 04, 82, 81, & 52. The secondary target is Inchas in the Nile Delta if ordered. Your launch time and order will be posted on the board. May God be with you. Israel is depending on you. Dismissed."

Elan checked the board. His jet was Shahak seventy-three, and his call sign was Vilon (Curtain) 1. His mission target was Cairo West, and he was the third to take off at zero seven hundred seventeen hours Israeli time, an hour ahead of Egyptian time.

In his Shahak (Hebrew "sky blazer," the name the Mirage IIIC jets were given), in addition to his thirty-millimeter cannon, he carried two runway-piercing bombs, which had to be delivered low like a napalm pass. This took a lot of guts on the pilot's part, exposing him to anti-aircraft defenses, but the damage to the runway was much higher than the GP bombs. The runway-piercing bombs deployed a 'chute to make sure they drifted nose-down. They were designed to destroy runways by creating an additional sinkhole, which took considerable effort to repair.

Once the launch started, the planes flew out quickly, nearly back to back. Elan taped his cassette player with an American rock and roll music tape down within reach with black electrical tape. He loved to listen to fast, hard-driving rock and roll during an engagement but didn't want the cassette player to go flying in the cockpit when he did a barrel roll or a hard vertical climb.

Elan flew one hundred feet over the sapphire-blue Mediterranean Sea with Jerry Lee Lewis singing, "We ain't fakin' it, baby. There's a whole lotta shakin' goin' on."

At zero hundred forty-five hours, local Egyptian time, Elan's group of ten bomber interceptors approached the airstrip at Cairo West. Each plane approached from different directions to minimize the danger of being shot down by air defenses. Since they had flown in under the enemy radar, the base was not alerted.

The Israelis ascended to an altitude of four thousand feet before descending on their targets. Not all the planes had runway-piercing bombs, but Elan's did. His squadron had practiced bombing runs like these hundreds of times. Elan was the fourth plane to approach the runway, and he could see thick smoke and flames coming from the first three bombers' handiwork. Using the smoke to conceal his approach, Ethan came in fast, leveled out low, and kept the smoke on the runway between his bird and anti-aircraft guns. He made it to a clear spot on the runway and released his bombs. They hit the ground soon after the release and burrowed themselves into the concrete runway with a deafening blast. Fire and thick, black smoke was all that was left of the runway section Elan bombed.

This wasn't a spur-of-the-moment attack. Operation Moked had been practiced for years. Elan cleared the runway, climbed to four thousand feet again, and dove fast to run the strafing patterns he had practiced many times before. As he approached a spot on the runway that wasn't covered with thick black smoke, he spotted two Tupolev bombers that were a high-priority target and considered a threat to Israel.

Elan waited until he had the right distance from the targets and cut them both in two with his thirty-millimeter cannon. One more strafing run yielded a MiG 17 and a MiG 21.

With the runway and all targets destroyed, Elan and his squadron returned to Hatzor Air Base for a quick reload and refuel, which took only six minutes.

During Operation Focus, 189 enemy planes were destroyed on the first wave, 107 enemy planes on the second wave, and a total of 320 by the end of the third wave. This all occurred within three hours. On the second day of the operation, an Israeli pilot chased a MiG instead of taking an Egyptian transport carrying Egyptian Marshall Ahmed and his staff. This, too, was the hand of God. Marshall Ahmed had seen firsthand the devastation of the Egyptian Air Force and was so affected by the sight that he ordered the Egyptian Army to withdraw from the Sinai.

King Hussein of Jordan received faulty information about the Egyptian defeat and ordered air strikes on Israeli targets. Israel responded by destroying the two air bases in Jordan and five in Syria.

CHAPTER THIRTY-NINE

Elan ran the preflight check on his bird and decided it was a *go*. His flight crew completed their check of his armaments that were loaded last night when he came in and concluded everything was okay. Since one of the Shahak's cannons had blown up in use due to a cleaning rod being left in the barrel, maintenance was double-checking everything. The maintenance crewman closed his hatch and rolled the stairs away from his jet. The maintenance chief backed off from the bird and gave Elan the thumbs-up sign, and Elan responded in kind.

This was the morning of the third day since Operation Moked had begun. Ninety percent of the Egyptian Air Force had been decimated on the first day. Jordan's Air Force had been completely destroyed, and what was left of the Syrian Air Force had been discreetly removed to rear air bases to keep the Israelis from destroying them. The raid on Iraq's air base gave them second thoughts about joining the fight. There were no aerial threats on the northern or eastern Israeli border. Elan's job now was bombing runs on choice targets in the Sinai and within Egypt and combat air patrols to intercept what was left of Egyptian aircraft still offering resistance.

Elan smiled with the anticipation of another day of rock and roll and making mayhem on the Egyptians but was hoping for a chance to paint another kill score on his jet from another air-to-air engagement. He had three kills already, one before the war and two yesterday, but he needed two more to be the second Israeli ace on record. He sighed. Another bombing run. Their mission was to bomb a radar station northeast of Ismailia on the Suez Canal. He and his number two fired up their engines and proceeded on a course, heading to the target.

It was a surreal thing, really. Flying close to the desert with nothing in sight but miles and miles of sand felt peaceful while they were planning to rain fire and destruction on their targets.

Elan glanced at his watch. They should be coming up on the target in about three minutes.

Elan's radio crackled with a message from GCI, Ground Control Intercept. "Vilon 1, abort mission. Vector two seven zero to interdict four MiGs spotted fifty kilometers due west of your position."

"Roger that, Vilon 1 out," replied Elan. As much as he wanted more kills, he saw the radar station just one minute away.

"You heard the man, his number two radioed."

"Not yet. We would have to dump our extra fuel tanks and bombs to chase them, anyway. I have a better place to drop them besides the desert. I'll drop my fuel tanks and bombs on the radar station building, and you drop them on the radar tower. That should light up their life."

"You are one extreme individual, but I like it," he said, laughing.

They climbed to four thousand feet just before arriving at the radar station. They sharply dove upon it, leveling at two hundred feet and dumping their excess weight on the intended targets. The bombs and fuel tanks made a pyrotechnic display that resembled fire falling from heaven with the thunderous voice of God.

"Goodness gracious, great balls of fire," laughed Elan. "Now, let's go kill some MiGs."

"Roger that."

He should be afraid. After all, intellectually, he knew he could be killed in battle, but he felt no fear, for his heart was filled with exhilaration. His fingers trembled as he ran them over the controls. Adrenaline rushed through his veins, and he felt alive in a way that only a combat pilot could understand.

His mind was consumed with the upcoming challenge of battle, so he forgot all of his pain, the loss of Katja, his father's death, his mother's needy pull, and his wife's spoiled demands. They disintegrated like a sun shower on a scorching summer day. Poof, gone, all the pain, all the memories, for the moment they were gone. There was no time or room for thoughts other than the challenge of the present moment. Elan smiled and sucked in a deep breath. He had come into his own, for Elan was a true warrior, and he felt ecstatic.

Elan and his number two broke hard left, excited at the prospect of another air-to-air engagement. Elan turned on his cassette player as the two of them streaked across the desert sky at mach speed toward their intended target. Jerry Lee Lewis sang, "Help me, Mister Fireman, please. You know I'm burning from my head to my knees..."

Elan's number two was a twenty-one-year-old, Daniel Goldstein, with eyes as sharp as an eagle's. He spotted the MiG 21s first. "Four MiGs at two eight fiver, on a course heading of zero two zero at nine o'clock."

There was an unusual amount of cloud cover that day for the desert. Both men hit full afterburner, climbed to five thousand feet, and stayed above the clouds, navigating not by sight but by compass, elapsed time and airspeed. Elan dipped his wing to signal his number two. It was time to drop down. They dove hard to gain as much energy and speed as they could, and Elan caught a visual of the four MiGs flying in tight formation at one thousand feet.

The pair of Mirages dropped down to put themselves behind the MiGs at six o'clock because the MiGs had a blind spot to their rear, which the pilots call *the killing zone*. Elan could see his number two's face plainly through the cockpit bubble, and he gave hand signals to take the outside two, Elan being on the left and Daniel on the right. Both pilots activated their short-range radar lock of four hundred meters and, after four seconds, got tone.

Daniel fired his two thirty-millimeter cannons with their explosive-tip projectiles at his target, and it tore its left wing completely off. The MiG automatically started to turn in a tight circle to the right, dropping from the sky like a stone and exploding. The desert below was charred black where the plane crashed, but the pilot did not live to eject.

At the same time his number two was firing, Elan pulled the trigger on his target, placing his explosive-tip projectiles into the enemy's fuselage. The MiG exploded, broke into two pieces, and fell to the ground. The pilot had punched out in time, and Elan pulled up hard to avoid hitting him as he parachuted to safety. The other two MiGs split right and left in a sharp turn to avoid the same fiery fate of their partners, and the Israelis gave hot pursuit.

Daniel followed close to his target while the Egyptian did a dance of tight turns to try to entice the Mirage into a horizontal fight that favored the MiG. The Mirage was one hundred miles per hour faster but couldn't turn quickly. Daniel's preferred fight was on a vertical plane, where he could take advantage of his fighter's extra speed and energy.

As the MiG made a hard left turn for the third time, Daniel deduced that he was probably right-handed as it was easier for a right-handed person to push the stick to the left. He stuck with him, looping on the vertical plane, and came down on his six again. The Mig did some more breaks and weaved side-to-side to shake his adversary and avoid a radar lock.

Then came the moment the Israeli was waiting for. The Egyptian turned hard left, and Daniel was waiting for him. As soon as the MiG started his turn, the Israeli flew vertically with a slight turn, executed a barrel roll, and came down on his enemy's six, locking his radar and firing his cannons into the MiG's fuel tanks. The MiGs had a design flaw. The oxygen tanks were right next to the fuel tanks. The MiG exploded and fell from the sky in three pieces. The pilot was dead before he had a chance to pull the ejection handle.

Elan's adversary went on full afterburner and initiated a hard climb to get into the cloud cover so he could lose Elan. He wasn't trying to initiate any turns because the MiG would lose energy and speed. The Mirage was already faster than the MiG, but Elan had to engage his afterburners to dump more fuel into the engine to not lose his quarry.

The MiG was weaving just enough to keep Elan from getting tone, and Elan was in danger of flying right past him, so he started a pattern of circular flying to keep his distance behind the Egyptian. They were almost at cloud level. Elan tightened his circle and got dangerously close to the MiG's six. He knew he wouldn't get four seconds to get a tone, so he turned his automatic system with radar off and prepared to fire manually. He fired a one-second burst of cannon fire into the fuselage of the MiG, and Elan rolled left before he got caught in the MiG's wreckage.

Elan rejoined his number two as Daniel reported, "Bingo fuel." Elan checked his fuel gauge. If they left now, they would make it to Hatzor AFB on fumes.

"That makes your fifth, right, Ace?"

"You bet." Elan turned the cassette player up and sang along over the radio with his number two. "I'm gonna keep a shakin'. I'm gonna keep a movin' baby. Don't you cramp my style. I'm a real wild child, whoa."

CHAPTER FORTY

KATJA AND ZOFIA huddled together on the sofa, waiting for news. Neither of them slept that night. Blessedly, Ima did not awaken. Few words were spoken between mother and daughter, but they each felt the other's fear. Mendel was on his way to God knows where, and only God knew what awaited him. Was this the end of Israel? After everything they'd suffered, the Jews had finally come this far, and now? Israel's enemies encircled the tiny country on all sides. Although neither Katja nor Zofia voiced the truth, they knew that every Israeli would fight to the death rather than lose their land. To the death. Mendel would fight beside them, and he, too, would die if he must. But even with all the sacrifices the Israelis would willingly make, would it be enough to save the country?

"Should I put up a pot of coffee?" Zofia asked.

Katja nodded. "Yes, I don't think either of us is going to go back to bed."

Zofia rinsed the coffeepot and began to boil the water. They were easily unnerved. Everything was exaggerated—the water running, the noise of water on steel as it filled the pot, the roar of the steam beginning to rise. Every sound crashed into their ears, interrupting the silent horror of their thoughts.

The time ticked by so slowly that their lives seemed to have come to a stop. Katja would often return her gaze to the old clock on the kitchen wall. She felt as if hours had passed, but it had only been a few minutes.

Ima awakened crying. Her needs distracted them for a while.

Later that afternoon, Zofia fed Ima, but neither she nor Katja were able to eat anything. They sat with their eyes glued to the television, waiting, wondering, worrying, silently praying, but not knowing if Mendel was alive or dead and not knowing the fate of their beloved country.

Israel did not have any TV stations. The only TV stations they could pick up told the war from an Arab viewpoint, complete with all its bias. The newscaster ranted about bombings, fighting, death, and how Israel would be destroyed. Katja and most Israeli citizens did not trust Arab news, so she shut the TV off, turned on the radio, and tuned into KOL, The Voice of Israel. During the day, reports told of a resounding victory over the Egyptian, Lebanese, and Syrian Air Force. This was certainly reason for rejoicing, but the radio said clearly that the ground battle was still to be fought, and Mendel was with the Golani Brigade and fought on the ground.

Zofia understood. Most of the day, they sat glued to the radio, watching for news of the war and waiting for answers.

Somehow, despite the impossible tension that filled the room, day finally gave way to night. Zofia put Ima to bed. It was the first time in Ima's life she had gone to bed without a bath. Ima was restless and unable to sleep. She lay in bed crying, then would seem to fall asleep only to awaken a few minutes later, crying again. The sound was driving Katja mad. Ima's wailing was the unspoken voice she and Zofia felt: tension, uncertainty, and fear. Usually, Katja was calm and able to cope with Ima's moods, but not tonight.

Zofia went into the nursery and sat beside Ima, gently cooing and rocking her crib while she softly rubbed her back until the baby finally let go and fell asleep.

When Zofia returned to the living room, she saw Katja sitting with her arms wrapped around herself.

"Do you think Mendel will come back home? Do you think he'll survive?" Katja asked in a small voice.

"I hope so," Zofia said, biting her lip. She walked over to Katja and put her arm around her daughter. "All we can do is pray."

Like she'd done when she was just a child, Katja laid her head on her mother's lap. Zofia patted her hair. Neither of them said another word. There was nothing else to say. They stayed together, breathing softly in the darkness, the radio playing in the background.

Katja and Zofia were paralyzed with fear. They spent their days going through the motions of taking care of Ima, but their hearts were with Mendel and Israel. They both knew that anything could happen. If Israel lost the war, the Jewish homeland they'd worked so hard to build would face destruction. Mendel, their beloved Mendel, might be maimed or killed. Anything could happen. Zofia wanted to take her daughter and the baby and return to the kibbutz.

No one had any idea how long the war would last, and Zofia felt isolated from her friends and extended family while she was at the house. She longed for the camaraderie at the kibbutz. However, Katja refused.

"When Mendel comes home, he'll come here to our house. I want to be here waiting for him."

CHAPTER FORTY-ONE

June 8, 1967

Israeli intelligence had deduced that the likelihood that the Soviets would intervene had been reduced. Had they wanted to be involved, they would have helped Egypt. The Syrians were no longer advancing into Israeli territory but continued to shell Galilee from the Golan Heights. Many Israelis wanted Syria punished for shelling the kibbutzim in Galilee even before the war. Moshe Dayan had bitterly opposed the taking of the Golan because the estimate of troop losses was 30,000.

A break came when Israeli intelligence intercepted a telegram from Egypt's President Nasser to the president of Syria to immediately accept a cease-fire. Israel needed to take and keep the Golan to secure the kibbutzim in Galilee. Dayan agreed it was time to move before the Syrians sued for a cease-fire and the UN would disapprove of taking any more land. Operation Hammer had begun.

June 9, 1967

Mendel had been assigned to the Golani Brigade. After the previous day of fierce fighting, only twenty-five men were left alive in his unit. His unit was tasked with taking the stronghold at Tel Faher. His brigade commander addressed the men.

"The enemy is dug in at Tel Faher with trenches, bunkers, an extensive minefield, and three belts of two-sided sloping fences and coiled barbwire. They are armed with anti-tank guns, machine guns, and 82 mm mortars. Tel Faher has not seemed affected by aerial bombardment. This stronghold is the key to the Golan. Failure is not an option," concluded LTC Moshe 'Musa' Klein.

Mendel was terrified. He wasn't a warrior. He was a lawyer who fought his battles with books, papers, and arguments in a courtroom. How he had lived through yesterday's fighting was a mystery to him. So many good men had died, all more deserving to live than him. Perhaps it was his time to pay with his life for becoming rich by defending a product that took innocent Israeli lives. Whether he deserved to die or not, God would judge.

Mendel thought of Katja, Ima, and his mother-in-law. I will fight for my family and nation, and perhaps God will forgive me for my trespasses. In any case, I will pour out my life as an offering to keep the Syrians from attacking my wife and family. Still, Mendel was terrified.

"Time to move out," his brigade commander said. The men split into two units, one to attack the southern flank and one to attack the northern flank. Mendel was assigned to the unit led by LTC Klein, attacking the northern flank. If the men made it alive to the trenches, they were to throw down their rifles and use their Uzis for close-in fighting.

Although his surroundings were unnerving, Mendel's thoughts were more about his family than himself. What if the enemies bombed Tel Aviv, his wife, and his baby? Sometimes, a horrific vision would cross his mind, and he'd see Katja or Ima dead. Then, he would shiver with fright and helplessness that would almost throw him into a panic.

The Syrian commander ordered that his men hold their fire until the Israelis made it to the barbwire, *the killing zone.* LTC Klein's group belly-crawled to a place in the fence where there was poor visibility to the entrenched enemy positions. A private that Mendel had ridden with on the bus, Uri Medina, cut the bottom three strands of the fence on both sides to allow the men to belly-crawl past the barbwire perimeter. Mendel hesitated when it was his turn to crawl through but was met with a stern glare from his commander. The Israelis belly-crawled at a snail's pace up the hill and to the trenches.

Just before they reached the trenches, a sniper shot PVT Medina in the forehead, and he sunk silently to the ground, blood running down his face from the hole in his forehead. As the corporal next to him tried to climb into the trench, a mortar round blew off his right arm, and it landed on Mendel's back, its blood staining his uniform shirt and its hand dangling in front of Mendel's face. He opened his mouth to scream, and his commander put a hand over his mouth, gave him a withering look, and threw the bloody limb to the side as they listened to the wounded man screaming in pain. The unit's medic tried to attend to the wounded man and half his face was blown off by a mortar round, and he sank to the ground, his body convulsing in its death throes.

LTC Klein waved to the men to hurry up and get into the trenches. Mendel and his commander ran through the trenches, firing their Uzis. The trench was filled with the smell of damp earth and burned gunpowder. It was confusing to tell who was who, so they had established a password. When a lone gunman stood in front of them, LTC Klein challenged him with a password. He didn't know it, fired at them with a submachine gun, and missed. Mendel and his commander bailed out of the trench, and LTC Klein was shot and killed. His blood poured out on the soil of the land he fought so hard for.

Mendel stood up and found himself face-to-face with a Syrian soldier who couldn't have been more than sixteen. Mendel heard more rifle and Uzi fire in the trenches as he watched the boy frantically struggle to put a new clip in his rifle. Mendel wrestled with his desire to quit, go home, let this boy live, and do his duty and defend his family and country. He sadly shook his head and fired a burst of rounds into the boy's body. The young Syrian fell over backward and died, eyes open, seeing nothing, his mouth agape like a dead fish at the market.

Machine gun fire opened up from the bunker and riddled Mendel's body. He never saw it coming but felt the bullets enter his body. At first, it was like a dream. His mind would not accept the fact that he'd been hit. Everything around him began to move in slow motion. The shock of what had happened dulled all feeling at first, but then it wore off, and he felt intense heat and pain where the bullets had torn his body open. His breath became shallow. He dropped his Uzi, and his hands held the open wounds as if he could force them closed by sheer will.

He fell over the body of the young Syrian boy and choked on the blood from his internal injuries. He looked at the face of the young boy. What made them different, anyway? Would his mother cry when he didn't return home? Why did they have to fight and die here? Was he a traitor for having these thoughts? Why couldn't they live in peace? But he knew why—because they were Israelis, and they would never be granted any measure of peace without blood. Yes, Israel must survive. Otherwise, the Jews as a people would surely perish. But Mendel wished he could understand why there was so much hatred, anger, death, and destruction. Why couldn't people find a way to live together? Why did it have to come to this? He cried for himself, this young Syrian enemy no more than a child, and his family whom he would never see again.

Blood, so much blood… Mendel realized he was dying. And once he accepted it, all the fear he'd felt about death was gone. The pain ceased, and somehow, he felt at peace with death. The only worries on his mind were his family. Who will take care of my family? He saw Katja's smiling face in his mind's eye. She was holding Ima above her head. Ima was laughing and drooling. *Such a beautiful child*, Mendel thought. He knew he was drifting away. He would never grow old with his wife, never see his daughter under the chuppah at her wedding, never…

Then, in his mind, he spoke to Katja. She seemed to be right before him, her lovely face just inches from his. Goodbye, my Katja. You've been my everything—yesterday, today, and forever. Please don't mourn me. The best thing you can do for me is to go on living. Take care of Ima. Take care of yourself. I want you to know that you've given me so much. From the day I first saw you in the *Exodus*, when we were just children, I knew I loved you, Kat. I've always loved you. He spoke the words in his mind but believed he was speaking them aloud. She was there, right there. He felt her kiss gently on his lips. Mendel sighed. "I've had a good life, Kat, because of you," he whispered. Then he took his final breath and left the earth on his way to a place where there were no borders, no differences in people, no hatred or wars, where there was only light and love.

Of the thirteen men who were part of the Golani Brigade who attacked the northern flank, only one man escaped injury, and only two who attacked the southern flank finished uninjured. The southern flank fell, but the northern flank was stubbornly dug in. The brigade's reconnaissance unit was called to reinforce them, and the target was finally taken at dusk. After the fall of Tel Faher, all the other Syrian fortifications fell, and the entire Syrian line fell like dominos. Many of the Syrian commanders deserted.

The war only lasted six days. Never before had one nation fought three nations at once and won so decisive a victory. This could only have been described in words like "providence" or "hand of God." Israel was here to stay.

CHAPTER FORTY-TWO

For Janice, America had changed so much that returning home felt like she'd landed on the moon. It was all new and exciting. Everywhere she went, there were head shops—small stores selling antiwar tee shirts, wall hangings, bongs, papers to roll marijuana cigarettes, love beads, and books on organic farming. She resented being pregnant. She hated that she was gaining weight. There were men everywhere, and she looked like hell.

Grant Park and Lincoln Park were common sites for love-ins and peace-ins. The parks were filled with young people eating, smoking dope, talking, and listening to music. Janice's father forbade her to go to any of these events. But as always, Janice did as she pleased.

She called her best friend, Bonnie, and they went to a love-in at Grant Park together. The park was right next to the Art Institute of Chicago. As they walked by, Janice looked up at the two statues of lions and remembered that she'd been to the Art Institute on a field trip as a child many years ago. The entire area was filled with people sitting on the ground. Music blasted from the bandstand.

"Hey, you two wanna join us? Come on, sit down." A fellow

with long, dirty blond hair beckoned. "I've got some acid. Ever drop acid?"

Janice had no idea what he was talking about. She shook her head. "No, thanks."

"Okay, no acid. Here, have a puff of my joint."

"I don't smoke."

"Have you ever smoked dope?"

Janice shook her head. Bonnie took Janice's arm and led her away.

"Acid is LSD," Bonnie said. "It's a hallucinogen. Dope is another name for marijuana."

"Did you ever take them?"

"Sure."

"What happened?"

"Dope just makes you feel kind of calm and creative. Acid's another story. It can be good or bad, depending…"

"Depending on what?"

"On your state of mind, if you have a good trip guide and lots of stuff."

Janice had no idea what Bonnie was talking about, so she didn't say anything. Although she desperately wanted to be a part of everything she saw going on around her, Janice was afraid to try drugs because of the pregnancy. It was not so much because she cared about the baby but her mother had warned her about how young people were also taking drugs and dying from them. Her mom was always so dramatic.

But her mother had also said that if Janice took any drugs, the baby could be born defective. And even though Janice hardly ever listened to her parents, she couldn't help but believe that taking drugs while carrying a child might be dangerous. It would be far too hard for her to raise a kid with problems. She wanted to be rid of the baby as it was, not to add any extra burden. So, she refrained from trying any illegal substances.

Janice was surprised to find men willing to have quick and casual sexual encounters with her, regardless of her pregnancy. She felt fat and ugly but longed for excitement, so she took advantage of the offers. For Janice, casual sex was a way to break out, break away from her past, from the mistakes that were still weighing her down like an albatross. If she had known of a reputable doctor willing to perform an illegal abortion, she would have had one without thinking twice. But girls were dying from trying to abort babies with the help of medical students or women who just needed some extra cash. Janice wasn't about to take that risk.

Meanwhile, Janice's father, Ronald Lichtenstein, arranged for a lawyer to prepare divorce papers to send to Elan. If necessary, Janice's father was willing to pay Elan to sign them and free Janice of this marriage. On her parent's advice, Janice wrote a letter to Elan explaining why she wanted the divorce.

The lawyer also suggested that she lie in the letter and tell Elan she'd suffered a miscarriage because she'd been so upset when he'd walked out on her. The attorney warned that if Elan knew he had a child in America, the day might come when he would come looking for his offspring. It would be best to sever all ties now. Otherwise, Elan would always be in the background waiting to resurface. After all, Elan knew that Mr. Lichtenstein was a wealthy man. One could not be certain that Elan would not come to America and try to claim some of his father-in-law's good fortune in exchange for any claims Elan might have on the child. Janice took the attorney's advice.

The Six-Day War in Israel played out on television sets all over America. Janice could not help but wonder if Elan had survived. Strangely, she'd once believed she loved him, but now, watching the war in Israel on television, she was glad to be far away. She had no desire to go back, ever. She watched in horror as the bombing continued. She could have been there, could have been killed. What was she thinking? What had once seemed noble and romantic in Elan now seemed overwhelming, horrific, and even annoying.

When she'd first met Elan, she was swept in by his sexy, strong body, determined mind, and passion for his country. But when he told her in no uncertain terms that he would put his country before anyone or anything, she hadn't really understood him or, for that matter, believed him. Janice was a romantic, and she was sure he would fall so deeply in love with her that she would come first in his life, before anyone or anything else.

When he walked out on her in that hotel room, she suddenly realized that he meant what he said about his love for Israel, and like a light switch, her feelings had turned off. Well, maybe not turned off, maybe turned from love to hate. To Janice, a man's family—his wife and unborn child—should be more important to him than an ideal. *Who would want a man like Elan? Certainly not me*, she thought. *Not anymore, anyway.*

It was great to be able to order cheeseburgers and pizza with cheese and sausage. She didn't realize how much she missed them. Her family in America didn't keep kosher and only attended temple on high holy days. God forbid she would have eaten meat and cheese at the same meal in Israel. Her mother-in-law might have dropped dead on the spot. Janice laughed to herself at the thought. Jerusha, that terrible woman. And Janice certainly didn't miss the disgusting black fish that her mother-in-law insisted upon boiling until the skin was so loose that it hung from the flesh. Just the thought of it made her nauseous. She'd had her fill of hummus, shawarma, and falafel. If she never had another bite of an Israeli salad, it would be too soon.

And with this pregnancy, it seemed as if time had almost stopped. She felt as if she might be pregnant forever. The swelling of her body appalled her. If only she could just leave everything about Elan in her past, including this child.

In the divorce papers, the Lichtensteins offered Elan ten thousand dollars to divorce Janice without any problems. Janice and her parents had discussed the situation of her coming child, and they were considering putting the baby up for adoption when it was born. It would be better for Janice. She could go back to school without anything holding her back. When she met someone new, she would not have to explain or tell him anything about her time in Israel or her previous marriage.

Janice agreed with this arrangement. It all sounded perfect. All she had to do was get through the pregnancy, and then she would be free to start over. Now that her belly was big, she decided to stay inside. It was best that no one ever knew she'd had a baby. It would be hell to remain a prisoner in the house, but why give anyone food for gossip?

CHAPTER FORTY-THREE

ISRAEL's speedy and miraculous victory stunned the world. For Elan Amsel, it restored his pride and confidence that he'd lost somewhere along the way. Elan sat in a bar celebrating Israel's triumph. He toasted loudly and joyfully as he drank beer after beer with his fellow pilots.

The door of the tavern closed, and a dejected SGT Benjamin Siemion walked up to the bar to get a drink to fortify himself against the last bit of today's sorrow. The tavern was full of soldiers and citizens celebrating Israel's miraculous victory. Stories were being told, and laughter filled the air.

The bartender approached SGT Siemion, wiping the counter with a cloth as he approached. "What'll you have, soldier?"

"Screwdriver."

"One screwdriver coming up."

Elan took notice of the man and slid over beside him. He pulled out a ten-shekel note and said to the bartender, "I got it."

"Thank you," the man said. "You a pilot?"

"Yes, CPT Elan Amsel of the 101st Squadron."

"Israel is proud of all of you pilots."

"Did you see combat?"

"No." He took a drink and looked at Elan. Elan could see tears forming in his eyes. "In my office, they call me the 'Angel of Death.' I tell the widows and children that their husbands and fathers are not coming home. I broke twelve widow's hearts today, and I have one more before I can go home to my wife and kids." Elan felt sorry for the man and what had to be the war's toughest job. He paid the bartender for the man's next drink.

"Give me the paper. I'll go do it. Go home and hug your wife and kids."

"It is not allowed," but I thank you.

"Why is it not allowed? I am IDF, and so are you. What does it matter which soldier comes to the house to bear the bad news? Give me the paper, and I will do it. Today is the day of celebration for Israel. You go home and tell your family that Israel has defeated her enemies. I'll tell this last widow the bad news."

SGT Siemion thoughtfully considered and retrieved the paper from his pocket with one last name on it and slipped it into Elan's hand. "God bless you," he said, finished his drink, and headed home.

Elan unfolded the paper in his hand and stared. Twelve names were crossed, leaving only one at the bottom of the page—Mendel Zaltstein.

CHAPTER FORTY-FOUR

KATJA WAS PICKING at the chipped pink polish that remained like broken glass in clusters and specks on her fingernails. It was hard to believe that she was at a beauty salon, carefully choosing this color only a week ago. How silly it all seemed now. How important it had been to her then that her nail color complemented the dress she planned to wear to the Zilberman show.

She looked out the window, trying desperately to hold back the terror in her heart that made her want to scream. Ima and Zofia slept. Katja began aggressively tearing the chips of polish off with her thumbnail. She wanted to hurt, to feel physical pain, anything to obliterate this terrible fear that gripped her. Mendel, God, what would she do if something happened to him? He had been there with her for as long as she could remember, first as a friend, later as a husband, lover, and father of her child. All she could think of was Mendel.

Ima had left one of her blankets on the floor. It was a knitted blanket that Zofia had made for her. The blanket was white with ducks made of yellow cotton sewn on the front. Katja picked up the blanket and held it close. Her heart ached, and she began to cry into the comfort of the soft yarn. Oh, Mendel. If only she could see him, talk to him. She tried to reason that at least he'd served in the IDF, so he'd been trained. But Katja knew Mendel, and she knew he didn't have the disposition to be a soldier. He was too gentle, too sensitive. That was what scared her. Her breath was ragged as she tried helplessly to control her fears. Perhaps, she prayed, Mendel had been given office work. Maybe he'd been spared actual combat. But Katja knew better. She knew what it meant to be an Israeli.

It had been four days since she'd eaten anything, and the last food she'd tried to eat had stuck in her throat. The man on the radio said that the war was over. Israel won. In six days, Israel had been victorious. That was good news, but she was still shaken because she had not heard anything from Mendel. Katja had a terrible sensation of being disconnected from him, as if she knew somewhere inside of her that something wasn't right. Her mother, Zofia, told her to relax, that it was just her nerves, but Katja couldn't stop the screams of terror that were silent to the rest of the world but constant in her own head.

Ima awakened before Zofia. For the last six days, Ima had been sleeping in the bed with her grandmother.

Katja heard Ima babbling and knew that Ima was waking her grandmother. Katja decided to take Ima out of the bedroom so that Zofia could get a little extra rest since she had not been sleeping much, either. Katja placed the baby blanket she'd been clutching on the coffee table and wiped the tears from her cheeks with the back of her hand. But it was too late. Zofia was already awake. She heard Zofia's voice softly whispering to Ima. Katja sunk back into the chair. It made her smile to hear Zofia and Ima together. It seemed Ima was the only thing that could still make her smile.

Zofia came out of the bedroom holding Ima's hand.

"I hoped you were resting," Zofia said, her face still swollen with sleep. Katja noticed that puffy circles had formed around her mother's eyes. She knew that as much as Zofia tried to comfort her, she was worried, too.

"Mama!" Ima said, hugging Katja.

"I want the cereal with the chocolate today."

"Yes, my love, the cereal with the chocolate," Zofia repeated, walking toward the kitchen.

"I'll get it, Mom," Katja said.

"It's all right. Sit. I'll take care of Ima," Zofia said, mustering a small smile.

Zofia filled a glass bowl from the cabinet with Ima's favorite cereal and milk. Then, she began to boil water for instant coffee for Katja and herself.

There was a knock on the door, and Katja jumped. Her heart leaped into her throat. It could be Mendel. She wished it was Mendel. She saw the look of panic on Zofia's face. Before the door was even open, they both knew. They both felt the coming disaster like a mudslide in the pit of their stomachs.

"I'll get it," Zofia said.

"Elan? What are you doing here?" Zofia did not even try to contain the disgust and shock in her voice.

"I have to see Katja. I have something…"

"This is a bad time, Elan. Go away, please…"

"I have to tell her something."

Katja came to the door, still dressed in her terry-cloth robe, her hair disheveled. "What do you want, Elan?"

"Katja, I'm sorry to bring you this news." He cleared his throat and looked at her. She could see the pity in his eyes. "I am truly sorry. Mendel was killed in battle."

Both of Katja's hands flew to her face. Even though, in her soul, she'd already known, hearing the words spoken hit her so hard that she lost her breath. She covered her mouth with her fists. It all felt like a dream, a terrible dream, and a nightmare. She shook her head. "No… no…"

Zofia put her arms around Katja. Katja began to scream. Ima saw her mother screaming, and she began to cry, too. The child ran over and pulled at Zofia's nightgown.

"Up, Bubbe, pick me up."

But Zofia was holding Katja. Ima kept pulling at Zofia and crying.

"Let me help you. I'll make all the arrangements," Elan said. "You need not worry about anything. I'll take care of everything."

Zofia glared at him.

"I don't want anything from you in return. We are old friends. I just want to be here for you. To help you, to make things right. I treated you badly. Let me do this to make it up to you."

Katja was too weak to resist. She left him standing in the open doorway, ran to the bathroom, and vomited.

CHAPTER FORTY-FIVE

KATJA HAD PASSED OUT, and when she came, she heard Ima crying and Elan on the phone with her family doctor, telling him to come immediately. Elan had considered carrying her to bed, but one icy glance from Zofia changed his destination to the couch in the living room.

Zofia informed Elan that Katja had not eaten in four days and was not sleeping much. Doctor Ben-Zvi arrived twenty minutes later. Elan took him aside and explained that Katja was not eating or sleeping and fainted when she heard the news of her husband's death.

The doctor took out his penlight and stethoscope. He examined her eyes, listened to her heart, and checked her pulse with gentle, knowing hands. Then he exhaled and looked at her and spoke tenderly to her. "Mrs. Zaltstein, all Israel shares in your loss. Your husband was an honorable and good man." He glanced at Elan and Zofia. "See to it that she has a bowl of broth, and she takes two of these pills afterward," he said, handing the bottle to her mother. Here is my card. Call me anytime. He patted Katja's hand and said, "Shalom, my dear." With that, he arose and left.

Zofia quickly moved to make the broth, and Elan was now

feeling out of place. Ima climbed up on the couch and wrapped her arms around her mother, and they both cried some more. Zofia brought the bowl of broth and a spoon, set it on the coffee table next to the couch, and knelt beside Zofia.

"It's all right," Zofia was whispering. "Shh… It's all right."

"It's not all right, Mama. It will never be all right again."

"Life goes on, my precious sunshine. I know how hard this is. I've lost many people whom I loved. I know heartbreak, and I'm no stranger to loss and tragedy. But you have to go on for Ima," Zofia said. "Ima, please help Bubbe feed your mama some soup."

The child nodded and slid over to give Zofia access to spoon-feed the soup to Katja. "Eat, my sunshine. Do it for Ima. I had to make a decision once to live for my child's sake. You must decide that right now."

Katja nodded, and Zofia tenderly spooned the bowl of soup into her mouth, then fetched a glass of water and two sleeping pills. "The doctor said to take these," Zofia said, and Katja complied.

Elan was on the phone in the living room, making funeral arrangements and notifying friends and family. The body would arrive later that afternoon. The burial would take place two days later. Zofia gave Elan the name of the rabbi who had married Katja and Mendel. She asked that Elan request that this rabbi speak at the funeral. Next, Elan telephoned the kibbutz and informed the member who answered the phone about Mendel's passing and the funeral. He asked them to inform everyone on the kibbutz.

All of Zofia's old friends planned to come and help to arrange the *shiva* for the mourners. They all knew Katja and Mendel. Within the hour, one of the members of the kibbutz called and said that several people would be arriving in Tel Aviv that night.

Katja faded in and out of sleep due to the medications the doctor had given her to dull her senses.

She awakened to hear voices in the kitchen, strange voices. Then she saw the mirror in her room covered, and she remembered she was *sitting shiva*, the Jewish mourning ritual where the family members sit on low stools to receive the guests to the *shiva*, funeral.

A pain shot through her, but then the drugs kicked back in, and she fell into a fitful sleep.

For Katja, the next two days were a blur. Zofia helped her dress for the funeral. Because she was so heavily medicated, Katja could hardly stand on her own. So, with one arm in Zofia's and the other in Elan's, Katja walked slowly into the funeral home. She was seated beside Zofia in the front row. Ima was at home with the women from the kibbutz who had come to prepare the shiva.

People approached Katja to pay their respects. She faintly heard them say that they were sorry for her loss. Katja nodded, her eyes unfocused, her mind dulled. It felt unreal as if she were watching herself in a movie. Katja's consciousness was so detached from the situation that she didn't even recognize many of her old friends. The medication had dulled her feelings to the point of nonexistence. That began to change when Rachel walked over to Katja.

"Kat, I am so sorry," Rachel said as she knelt down and took Katja's hands.

"Rachel…" Katja put her arms around her old friend and hugged her tightly. Seeing Rachel brought everything back. Katja was still in a daze, but all of her pain returned. "I can't believe he is gone. Do you remember when we were children in the *Exodus*? When we all first met, you, me, and Mendel? Remember Abe? I remember Abe," Katja rambled, her mind hazy but filled with thoughts. "Mendel was always the level-headed one. He was my rock, Rach. He was my rock. I didn't realize it, but I've been leaning on Mendel all my life. Now he's gone. Oh, my God… Rachel, I can't go on without him." Katja began crying so hard that the tears spilled down her face. Her nose was running, and her skin was blotchy and red.

"Shh, it's okay, Kat. It's okay," Rachel said. She took the tail of her shirt out of her pants and wiped Katja's face. "Shh…"

Rachel saw Elan sitting behind Katja in the second row and shook her head at him with disdain. She held Katja in her arms and continued to rock Katja like a baby until the rabbi walked onto the podium.

The first row of the memorial chapel was usually reserved for mourners, but Rachel sat beside Katja anyway. Why not? She was a mourner, too. Mendel had been one of her oldest and dearest friends.

After the services, Rachel stayed with Katja through the burial. Then, they returned to the home Katja and Mendel shared with Zofia and Ima. Outside the house, Rachel helped Katja lift the jug of water placed there by the women who set up the shiva. She poured the water over Katja's hands and then her own. This was part of the shiva that was symbolic of not bringing more sorrow into the house.

Ima ran to her grandmother as soon as they walked through the door, and Zofia lifted the child into her arms.

"Are we having a birthday party, Bubbe?" Ima asked. She was too young to understand. The house was filled with people, food…

"No, sweetheart, this is not a party," Zofia said, kissing Ima's head.

Katja took off her shoes. She would walk in her stocking feet for the next seven days. This was another tradition of mourning. The rabbi had torn the lapel of her dress at some point. This was tradition, too, but she could not remember when it happened.

"Can I get you some food?" Rachel asked Katja.

"No, thank you."

"You must eat." Rachel guided her to the table and began making her a plate.

The women who'd set up the shiva prepared tables of food for everyone who had come from the funeral. Visitors would continue coming to the house for the next seven days. They would all bring food for the mourners, and everyone who came to pay their respects would be sure to take nothing from the house with them and to eat something sweet before they left. Katja picked at her plate, but Rachel persisted until she ate some dates, falafel, and hummus.

Katja heard the ten men gathering for the Mourner's Kaddish. It would always begin the same, "*Yit'gadal v'yit'kadash sh'mei raba…*"

The sound of the words of the *kaddish* unnerved Katja.

She ran into her room when the minyan for the dead began and covered her head with a pillow. She could not bear to know that these prayers were being said for her young husband, the husband she would never see again.

Over the next seven days, Katja was aware that the house was filled with people. Harvey, Mendel's boss, and his wife came to pay their respects. All the friends Katja and Mendel had made were in and out of the house while Katja watched them, her mind in a haze. At some point, Elan had sat beside her on her bed. He'd taken her hands in his and turned her head so she could look at him through her swollen eyes.

"Kat, I've never stopped loving you," he said. "I want you to know that."

She nodded. Katja had just taken a pill, and her senses were dulled.

"I know you still love me. I knew it when I saw you and saw the look on your face at the Zilberman show," Elan said.

The Zilberman show… Katja's mind went back to that moment when she came out of the bathroom and saw Elan standing there. Had she really still felt desire for him? Suddenly, she was ashamed, terribly ashamed by that memory. For a single instant, Katja wanted to strike Elan for bringing that moment back.

She realized the truth now when it was all too late. The truth was that she had loved Mendel. He was her one true love. Any feelings she'd once had for Elan were gone. Now, she thought of him as just an old friend. Katja shook her head. Even the anger and hurt he'd once caused her was gone. Everything was gone.

"I want to try again, I mean, with us. Please, Kat. I made a terrible mistake. Now, I've grown up. I've learned a lot of things, and I am willing to face the world and say that I don't care who your birth parents were. I love you. To me, you are and will always be a Jew. I love you, Kat. Marry me…"

"No, Elan. You must go now."

CHAPTER FORTY-SIX

Rachel was the last one to leave Katja's house. She stayed until the end of the shiva. Before she left, Rachel hugged her old friend and told Katja to stay in touch. No one but Katja knew that Rachel was a lesbian and lived with her lover. Other than Katja, only Mendel had known. The three were old friends, and it was hard to believe there were only two.

"Listen, you can call me anytime, Kat. Anytime. Day or night, I mean it. I'm here for you. I'll always be here for you."

Katja nodded.

"Are you going to be all right?"

"As all right as I'll ever be. I don't know what I am going to do with the rest of my life, Rachel. I thought I would spend the rest of my days as Mendel's wife, and we would have another child. I don't know who I am or what I will do without him."

"I'd stay here longer and try to help you, but I can't. My job expects me to be back," Rachel said.

"I know, and Sandy is expecting you, too."

"Yes, and Sandy, too. I wanted to bring her with me, but I knew it would cause everyone to gossip, and I figured you didn't need that."

"How are things going with you and her?"

"We love each other. There are problems for sure. We try to stay as inconspicuous as possible, but people are always watching and talking. Sandy lost her job as a teacher because they said they thought she was living a questionable lifestyle. It's not easy."

"I'm sure it's not."

"Kat, look at me," Rachel said, taking Katja's hands. "You're stronger than you know. You've always been stronger than you realized."

"No, Rach, you were always the strong one. You were the strong one. Mendel was the smart one, and I just tagged along."

"You are strong, Kat. You're strong, you're young, and you're beautiful. I know you've lost someone—the man you love and your best friend. I realize the pain is overwhelming right now, but the pain will lessen as time goes on, and then you will decide what you want to do. You still have a long life ahead of you…"

"If it weren't for Ima, I would take a bottle of pills and end the whole thing."

"Yes, maybe so, but the fact is that you do have Ima to think about. God was good to you and gave you a daughter. Now, you must find a way to go on and give your life purpose. If not for yourself, then for Ima."

Katja hugged Rachel tightly. "Thank you," she whispered, "for everything."

Rachel kissed Katja's forehead, and then she got up and left.

Long after everyone had gone and the house was dark, Katja sat alone with only her thoughts and memories for company. The guilt she felt for thinking about Elan the last night she and Mendel spent together devastated her. How could she have ever allowed herself to think she had feelings for anyone but Mendel? He'd been such a good friend and such a wonderful husband. In fact, it was not until he was gone that she realized just how much she'd really loved him, how much she had always loved him.

What a difference a couple of weeks could make in a person's life. Only two weeks ago, she'd been carefree, getting ready for a show she'd planned to attend with her husband, his boss, and his boss's wife. She'd been busy obsessing over the importance of having just the right dress, perfecting her hair, and getting a manicure. She remembered how smug she felt when she saw her reflection in the mirror and how she'd known that she was beautiful.

Later that night, before the show, she'd walked out of the bathroom with her freshly applied lipstick, and her eyes met Elan's. After so many years, she'd been secretly glad to see the admiration in his eyes. She remembered he'd hurt her once as she looked at him, and now she was rich and beautiful. She'd felt so triumphant. They'd stood there fully, returning his gaze for a few minutes. Then she'd returned to her seat beside Mendel.

None of that even mattered to her anymore. Nothing mattered to her except Mendel. Mendel! God, what she wouldn't give to have Mendel back with her now. But that night, the last night they'd had together when she and Mendel returned home, her heart had betrayed her husband. As they lay in bed together, all she could think about was Elan. How could she ever have done that?

Of course, at that time, she did not know what would happen just a few hours later. How could she know that, on that very night, as she lay beside Mendel with memories of Elan burning in her heart, it would be the last time she would ever feel Mendel beside her? Her hands pressed at her temples as if she could drive that memory right out of her head if she pushed hard enough, and then she tore at her hair. If only she could change the past. She prayed to change the past as tears rushed down her cheeks. *If only. Please, God, if only, please let me change what I did, what I thought, what I felt…*

CHAPTER FORTY-SEVEN

Elan decided that he would change his life from this day forward, this time for good. He no longer had any doubts about where he saw his future. He'd made a mistake moving in with his mother and taking over his father's fruit stand. After fighting in this war, Elan knew his destiny. He was a soldier. He loved Israel, and he loved to be in the company of others who had the same great love for this country.

Two days following Mendel's shiva, Elan Amsel went to the office of the Mossad and asked to join. His record in the IDF was undeniably impressive. They told him to go home and wait for three days while they reviewed his application. During those three days, Elan went home to his mother's house and told her his plans.

"I'm going to join Mossad," he said.

"Are you crazy? What are we going to do with Papa's shop at the market? There is nobody else to run it!" she screamed. "Elan, you can't do this. What am I going to do? What's going to happen to me?" His mother cried and carried on, but Elan paid her no attention.

"Sell Papa's store and take the money. I'll send you whatever I can, but I am never going back to the market. I'm done with that," Elan said.

"Your wife? Where is your wife? If you don't care about me, and I can see that you don't, at least you have to keep the shop open to take care of your wife!" his mother shouted.

"She left me. When I was called up, we were in the hotel in Tel Aviv. She said that if I went to war, she would leave. It was my duty to go, and I did what I knew was right. She went home."

"To America? Was it another man?"

"Yes, to America. There was no other man. It was me, Mama. I want something different from what she wants. It's better this way."

"Elan, you're talking crazy. I'm not saying she was ever good for you, but you stood under the chuppah with her. You're married. Aren't you even going to call her to see if you can work things out?"

"No, if she wants to leave, that's her business. I don't care. In fact, I think it's the best. Like I told you, I'm going to join Mossad if they will have me, and I'm going to work for Israel."

"Elan?" His mother wrung her hands on a dish towel. "You're talking crazy. You're a married man with a wife to take care of and a mother…"

"I'm sorry, Mama. This is the way it is going to be."

For the next three days, while Elan awaited the decision from Mossad, his mother tried everything from guilt to anger to convince him to change his mind. She could see that she'd lost her hold on her son. Even trying to make him feel guilty about leaving her alone after the death of his father no longer had any effect on him. Although Elan's mother hated his wife, Janice, she had tried to call her in America. When Janice's father answered the phone, he told Elan's mother that Janice was ill, that she had suffered a miscarriage because of Elan, and that divorce papers were already on the way.

Elan's mother was frantic. She called his brother, Aryeh, and asked him for help. Aryeh drove to his mother's house that evening and tried to talk to Elan, but Elan was firm in his decision and pushed his brother away.

He wanted quiet. He was nervous and edgy while waiting to hear from Mossad. If they denied him, he still planned to leave his mother's house. He had no idea where he would go or what to do, but he was done with working in the market.

Even now, with everything on his mind, Elan's thoughts would drift to memories of Katja. God, how he missed her. He couldn't believe she would have ever married that skinny runt of a boy, Mendel Zaltstein. Mendel had hardly been man enough for Katja.

She was the woman Elan had always loved, the only woman he'd ever truly loved. Well, there was little he could do about that now. She rejected his marriage proposal at Mendel's shiva. Just the thought of losing her forever felt like his heart had been struck and sliced by a furious bolt of lightning. Somewhere deep inside of him, Elan had always held a secret dream that he would see Katja again. He knew he could never marry her, but the yearning to hold her slender body in his strong arms, touch her skin, kiss her yielding lips, and feel her soft golden curls fall across his naked chest never stopped.

The letter from Mossad arrived on time, precisely three days after the interview. Elan opened the envelope quickly, slicing his skin and causing a painful paper cut on the first finger of his right hand. He cursed as the blood came to the surface and spilled onto the white envelope, but he was too nervous to stop and wash his finger. Instead, he unfolded the letter. When he read it, a sigh of relief left his lips. Elan Amsel was accepted. He would be a member of Mossad.

Elan found the divorce papers waiting for him when he returned to his mother's house to pick up the rest of his things. He opened the envelope that contained the letter from Janice. It said she had miscarried. It was probably best. The child would not have had two parents. But even so, knowing that his child had died in the womb was like a hammer fist to the back of his head. At this moment, Elan wanted nothing to do with any woman ever again.

He'd thrown himself at Katja, bared his heart and soul, and she'd just looked at him blankly and said she loved Mendel. It was hard to believe she'd forgotten everything they'd once shared. Elan had refused to accept that Katja could love Mendel more than she loved him. But when he told her how much he'd regretted their breakup, her response was emotionless.

Women were nothing but pains in the ass. Elan shook his head. At that moment, Elan vowed never to take another woman seriously. Then, without hesitation, he signed the divorce papers. However, he never read them thoroughly. Therefore, he never even noticed that his father-in-law had offered him money to agree to the divorce. It probably would not have mattered anyway. Elan had too much pride to take anything from that man. Elan didn't need his father-in-law's American money. He could take care of himself.

He shoved the letter into his back pocket without looking at it again. He'd throw it into the mail as soon as he saw a box on his way back to Tel Aviv, and for him, it would be like tossing away the trash of his life.

Stuffing the pain in his heart deep into the recesses of his mind where he would bury them for years, Elan packed the remainder of his things. His mother met him as he was bringing his suitcase to the door.

"Where are you going?" she demanded.

"I'm leaving, and I won't be back."

"You are an ungrateful son! I will die if there is no one here to take care of me! If only your father were alive to see how you treat your mother!" Her screams cut the air like a knife and could be heard at the next apartment building. She wailed as mournfully as if she were at a funeral. "Please, Elan, don't leave me!"

"Sorry, Mother, I have to go." And so, with his mother screaming loud enough to wake the dead, Elan Amsel got into his automobile and drove out of Jerusalem, away from his mother and the market on Ben Yehuda Street forever.

There was a bounce in his step as he headed forth. He tossed the duffel bag into the back seat of his car. Then he laughed as he reached his arms up to embrace heaven. Elan had just closed the door on his past and was on his way to report to the office of Mossad in Tel Aviv.

CHAPTER FORTY-EIGHT

"It's a girl," the doctor said as he looked at the tiny, trembling form that had just come into the world.

Janice had been in labor for the last fifteen hours, and they had been the most difficult hours of her life. Her hair was stuck to her head with sweat, and her body was still shaking with the effort.

But once the child was born, some miraculous change took place deep inside Janice. She knew as soon as she laid eyes on the baby that she would never sign the adoption papers. This was her child. The nurse placed the infant wrapped in a white blanket into her arms, and Janice felt her heartbeat quicken. How could she ever have thought she could walk away from this part of herself? Tears fell from Janice's eyes.

"Tell the adoption agency I have changed my mind," she said.

Janice and Elan had planned to name the baby after Elan's father. If it was a girl, they were going to call her Gabby. But Janice wanted nothing to do with Elan or his family. This baby would be named after her maternal grandmother, the middle name would be that of her paternal grandfather, and the child would carry Janice's maiden name.

She would be called Bari for her grandmother Bertha, Lynn for her grandfather Lawrence, and Lichtenstein for her family name.

Bari Lynn Lichtenstein, Janice loved the name, and her parents were honored and joyful that she'd not even considered Elan or his family in any way when naming the baby. It was decided in a conversation between Janice and her parents before Janice even left the hospital that little Bari Lynn would never know her father. The plan was to tell Bari that her father died in Vietnam. Bari Lynn would never know about Janice's life in Israel or that her father was an Israeli. It was best that way. If she never knew about Elan, and Elan believed that Janice had miscarried, there was no chance of him ever interfering in their future.

Ronald Lichtenstein insisted that his daughter have help with the baby, so he hired a nanny. Her name was Violet Davis. She was a tall, slender woman with skin the color of night and eyes that twinkled like the stars. Violet had an apartment in the Lichtenstein's basement, with a bedroom and adjacent bathroom. Her primary job was to help Janice with the baby, but she also did light housekeeping. She stayed with the family from Monday through Saturday. She went home to some mysterious place that Janice knew nothing about on Sunday.

In the first few weeks, when she'd just brought the baby home, Janice had no interest in Violet's life, as she was far too consumed with taking care of her child. But as the weeks slipped by and Bari Lynn began to sleep through the night, Janice and Violet became friends.

Their conversations were short at first. It seemed to Janice that Violet was secretive about her personal life. But Janice began to regard her as more like a friend than a nanny. Having a baby had alienated her from her former friends who were out enjoying their single lives. Because Violet was the one that Janice trusted Bari Lynn with when she went to class, it seemed as if Violet was the only person to whom she could relate. Violet cared for Bari Lynn like she was her own child. Janice told Violet about her feelings of alienation, and Violet was a good listener. Sometimes, she offered small bits of advice, but mostly, she just listened.

One afternoon, Violet was folding the baby's laundry while Janice fed Bari Lynn.

"I don't know much about you," Janice said, testing the bottle to see if the formula was too hot.

"There ain't much to know."

"I don't believe that. Where do you live? Do you have a boyfriend? A husband?"

"I got a boyfriend, and I got a little boy of my own."

"You have a child?" Janice asked, shocked that all these months, she'd had no idea.

"Yes, ma'am."

"Who watches him?"

"My mama. We need the money, so I have to go out and work."

Janice didn't answer. She sat looking out the window for a moment, then gazed down at Bari Lynn's tiny, contented face. "You only see your son on Sunday?"

"Yes, ma'am."

Janice nodded. Her eyes narrowed in thought, and she bit her lower lip. It didn't seem right. Here, she had so much, and this woman, her friend, had so little. "You must miss him all week. How old is he?"

"He'll be two next month."

Janice drew in a sharp breath. For several moments, she was silent. She knew her father would never approve of what she was about to do, but that never stopped her before, and it wouldn't stop her now.

"Violet, why don't you bring your son and your mother here to live with us? There is plenty of room downstairs." It was true. The basement was fixed up beautifully with brown and beige tile floors and blond wood-paneled walls. There were nice wool rugs on the floor, and the bathroom had just been redone a few months before hiring Violet.

Violet shook her head. "No, ma'am, I don't think that would be a good idea."

"Why not?"

"Well, I don't know. I mean, I'd feel like we were imposing."

"You wouldn't be. We have plenty of food and plenty of room. Why don't you think about it?"

"I will, ma'am, and I sure do appreciate the offer."

Janice had been watching the civil rights movement unfolding on the news. She had been made aware of how difficult life was for Black Americans. There was a lack of opportunities for good education. Without education, it was almost impossible to rise out of the ghetto. Janice had seen a speech by the civil rights leader Martin Luther King.

When they were alone, Violet had told her about her admiration for King and his work. There were marches and protests on the news constantly, some against the Vietnam War and others for civil rights or women's rights. The world was changing. Janice felt that the change was necessary. She wanted to do her part, to do something with her life that would make a difference.

When Janice told her mother that she'd asked Violet to bring her mother and son to live with them, Frances Lichtenstein was shocked.

"Are you nuts? We can't have another family moving in here. The last thing we need is another child and an old woman to take care of. Forget it, Janice."

"But don't you think it's hard on Violet never seeing her kid? Can you imagine what that must be like for her?"

"Yes, maybe it is, but that doesn't mean we must support her whole family. Your father would go crazy if you told him you did this. Tell Violet that you made a mistake. We can't have a house full of colored people."

"Mom, that is a sickening term you just used. Black people don't like to be called colored. Do you like to be called a kike or a dirty Jew? We're Jews. For God's sake, have some sympathy. The civil rights movement is not so different from the plight of the Jews."

"Janice, you were always a pain in the ass. First, it was Israel, and now it's this. Why don't you go to college and see if you can't find a husband and settle down? You've done enough damage to your life as it is. You have a fatherless child, which is a *shanda,* for sure. I'm sick when I have to face the neighbors and explain what you've done. I go to the beauty shop, and all the women from the neighborhood ask questions. I tell them you were married to an American who was killed in Vietnam. They say, 'Wasn't she in Israel?' I tell them, yes, but her husband had family there.

"I have to make up stories to try to save us from the shame you've brought upon us all. Who knows what everyone is thinking? I know that, for sure, they are talking, and what they are saying isn't good. You have a reputation to live down, let me tell you. And now you want to get involved in civil rights? Janice? Why don't you just try to find a nice Jewish boy with a good profession, and then if, by the grace of God, he accepts you with a baby, kiss the ground he walks on?"

Janice glared at her mother. "Times are changing, Mom. It's not like it used to be when a woman was defined by her husband. I will go back to school, not to find a husband but to find my own way in this world. I'll have a career of my own. I don't want to be like you, waiting for Daddy to give you an allowance. I want my own money. I want to make my own decisions. And if I want to be a part of the civil rights movement, then by God, I will. But don't you worry. I won't bring any more shame into your house. As soon as I can find a job, I'm going to move out of here." Janice flipped her long, flaming-red hair back over her shoulder and walked out of the room.

Later that afternoon, Janice was giving Bari a bottle, and Violet was ironing. This was their daily quiet time when the baby would drift off to sleep while she was feeding, and the two women could chat. No one else was in the house.

"I'm sorry, Violet. You were right."

"About what?"

"My parents. I don't know how to say this, but you can't move your mother and son here. This is their house, and they won't allow it. I feel terrible."

"Don't feel bad. I expected it. Why should they support my family? It's not their responsibility."

"Yeah, I know..."

"It's all right. I'm glad to have this job. It pays well and..."

Janice put her hand up. "Don't say any more. I just wish I could do something…"

Janice was upset at her own weakness, but she couldn't leave. She didn't have any money of her own. She had no skills, no job, nothing. She was stuck for now, living under her parents' rules, and that really made her angry.

However, she did sign up for more classes at the University. If she planned to make a difference in the world, she would need an education to get a decent job and get out of her parents' house.

CHAPTER FORTY-NINE

The first time Janice attended a civil rights protest march was in early March 1968. Because she had gotten to know Violet over the past month, and Violet had become a good friend, Janice wanted to be a part of this movement toward equality.

Her father was appalled as they watched the news. He couldn't believe that violent uprisings had taken place on peaceful college campuses. Ronald Lichtenstein wanted the war in Vietnam to be over, and his wife agreed with anything he said. Although he gave lip service to believing that black Americans deserved equal rights, they weren't about to step out of their comfortable lives to do anything about the situation.

Janice was different. All of her life, she'd been fearless. Even when she was secretly afraid, she'd pushed forward against the fear until it dissipated. Her parents tried to use what they called *her mistake in Israel* to convince her to control herself, but Janice could not be stopped. When she believed something was right, she was willing to risk everything. And she was vocal about her beliefs.

"You're naïve," her mother had told her. "You have enough trouble as it is, Janice. You have a fatherless child, and now you're going to get involved in this?"

"You never learn your lessons," her father had said, his face red with frustration. "You're going to get into trouble again."

But her inner strength, which her parents and friends called stubbornness, drove her forward, and she would not rest until she did what she believed to be the right thing.

So after her economics class, Janice stood outside the student union building holding her books. She would never admit it to anyone, but she felt uneasy and a little scared. Her heart pounded in her throat, and she wanted to run away. Violet was not with her. Only students from the University were there, and she didn't know anyone. The quiet campus of Northwestern University in Evanston was filled with angry civil rights protesters.

When Janice thought about Violet, guilt and shame came over her. Why was she, Janice, privileged to attend this beautiful school where she would be given the finest education while Violet had no opportunity to better her life? It was not fair, and Janice was a headstrong believer in fairness.

Across the courtyard, she saw a group of men standing together wearing berets. Based on their clothing, she knew that they were not students. They were part of the deeply feared Black Panthers group. With all the words of caution her father had drilled into her, although she would never admit it, Janice was afraid. While watching the news one night, her father had mentioned how Mayor Daley said that the Black Panthers were a menace to the city, and he planned to get rid of them. Her father had agreed with the mayor. "These are dangerous people," he'd said. What if he was right, and she was really in danger?

Janice looked around her. Why should she be so fearful? She believed in this cause. That was why she was here. So she planted her size five feet on the ground and stood as tall as her four-foot-eleven frame would allow. Then, she waited with the other protesters until a speaker got up onto the platform in the center of the courtyard.

CHAPTER FIFTY

It was a cool day in early April. Janice had a bad cold, so she didn't attend classes that day. Instead, she sat in the living room watching a game show on TV with a box of tissues next to her and a cup of hot tea. Bari Lynn was blissfully napping. Together, Janice and Violet had gotten Bari on a regular schedule. At two months old, she slept through the night and took two short naps during the day.

Violet was in the kitchen just a few feet away from the living room, sweeping the tile floor when the program on the television was interrupted.

"Martin Luther King, the civil rights leader, has been shot and killed…" The news anchor continued speaking, but Violet dropped the broom, and the next few words were drowned out by the sound of the wooden handle hitting the tile. Violet rushed into the living room. Janice stared at Violet with her mouth hanging open.

Words were spoken on the television, but Janice did not comprehend them. The next thing she was aware of was a replay of Martin Luther King's famous speech. "I have a dream," Dr. King said in the replay… And now he was dead.

Janice saw the tears fall from Violet's eyes. The old reel of Dr.

King continued. Both women were silent. Violet remained standing with her fist in her mouth.

"We cannot walk alone. And as we walk, we must make the pledge that we shall always march ahead. We cannot turn back." Dr. King's voice rang like a premonition through the airwaves.

"I can't believe he's gone…" Violet whispered, more to herself than to Janice.

"Violet, I am so sorry. All I can say is I'm sorry. I don't know what else I can say or do. I was going to tell you that I attended a civil rights meeting at school the other day."

Violet didn't say a word, but her eyes grew wide as if she was suddenly aware that she was not alone in the room. It was as if she'd been awakened from a nightmare.

"You should think about joining some demonstrations. It's not fair how your people are treated."

Violet shrugged her shoulders and shook her head. More tears threatened to spill from the corners of her eyes.

"Why are you so complacent? I mean, why don't you want to fight?"

Violet shrugged again. Her throat was closed, and she could not bring forth the words.

"Are you afraid? Is that it?"

Violet shrugged, shaking her head. "You don't understand. You can't understand." Her voice was barely a whisper.

"What Dr. King said makes a lot of sense. You have to become an active part of this whole movement for it to happen."

Violet had reached her breaking point. Her eyes, filled with fire, turned to Janice. "I don't want to talk about this, please. Stop now."

"No, we have to talk about it. Nobody else is home. Now, you have to listen to me—"

"It's easy for you to stand there and tell me what you think I should do. You are a pampered white girl. If you make a mistake, it don't mean nothin'. You got money, and you got education. I don't got nobody to help me.

But if I go out and start causin' a ruckus, I'm gonna lose my job. Then I won't have no money to feed my baby, and my mama's too old to work. For you, this is all a game. For me, this ain't no game. It's my life. You have someplace to go back to. We are different, you and me. You sit there lookin' at the TV, and you see a man died.

But I see a dream died along with Dr. King, a dream that is my reason for livin'. A dream that maybe someday my people are gonna have the opportunities to make choices, to get educated, and get good jobs. There's things you don't know nothin' about, and you can't know nothin' about."

"Then why don't you tell me? How can I know if you don't tell me?"

"A few years back, my best girlfriend was goin' around with this man. He was real involved with this here civil rights movement. He was a black man. He talked big stuff. Said he was gonna change things. We was all gonna change things. We was gonna be equals. Then he went with two white boys. They drove down to Mississippi where they was supposed to be doin' some kinda civil rights work to help the southern blacks. You hear about it? You know what happened?"

"No." Janice shook her head, but her face had lost its color.

"He didn't come back. They killed him, him and them two white boys, too. They lynched 'em, yep, they killed them boys, all three of 'em. That's what they do when black folks get outta hand and get too powerful. That's how they put 'em back in their place. When Dr. King was alive, I believed we might've had a chance, but now, well, now, they done killed him, too."

"It's not over, Violet. Dr. King is dead, and it's terrible. But didn't you hear what he said just a few minutes ago in his speech? He would have wanted the civil rights movement to go on. You have to know that. You have to believe it. What about Jesse Jackson? He's still here. He won't let it die."

"You and me be so far apart. Our lives be so different. You can't know what this means to the black folks. You can't understand because you don't live it."

"Is that what you think? Do you really believe that we're different? Because if that's what you believe—if you really think that the color of your skin makes you different from me, then you're never going to be able to rise out of the life you are living. I want to help you. Let me help you. I'm a Jew. Do you have any idea what that means? Do you know what happened to the Jews under Hitler? And even before Hitler. Before Israel, the Jews were persecuted all over the world. My case is not so different from yours." Janice couldn't believe she still felt a certain love for Israel, even though it had broken her heart.

Violet shook her head, and then her shoulders slumped. "I'm sorry. I just can't be talkin' to you about this right now." Then she went downstairs to her room, where she stayed until Janice's parents returned home.

CHAPTER FIFTY-ONE

Janice made friends in the art department at school. Her friends believed, as she did, that the world needed to change. The war in Vietnam must cease. People of all colors should have equal rights, and women must be treated equally.

There was a group of radicals in the art department who Janice began to spend a lot of time with. There were three other women and two men. They attended rallies, love-ins, and peace-ins at Grant and Lincoln parks. She'd seen and heard Abbie Hoffman and Jerry Rubin of the Students for a Democratic Society (SDS) speak. They'd talked about ending the war. She'd seen and heard Fred Hampton talk about equal rights. The world was ablaze with a new consciousness. Janice decided it was her responsibility to make a difference.

The day after King was assassinated, the friendship between Violet and Janice became strained, not because Janice chose it to be that way but because Violet avoided her. Violet got up earlier in the morning to do her ironing to evade Janice's pressing and invasive talks. Janice was hurt, but she was busy. She'd grown close to Debbie, one of the girls in her group of friends, and they spent a great deal of time together. While Janice was out crusading, Violet took care of Bari.

Janice believed in the causes she promoted, but being a part of the excitement also drew her in. At parties with her fellow students, Janice smoked marijuana, listened to folk music, and felt as if she'd finally found a place where she fit in. She practiced tantric yoga and became a vegetarian. Then, she traded her traditional clothes for jeans and tie-dyed tee shirts.

That summer, in the heat of August, a group of Janice's friends planned to take a minibus to a protest that was to take place in front of the International Amphitheater. This was where the Democratic Convention was to be held. The protests were to get the attention of the candidates that would be attending. The artists in her class had painted a beautiful design of graffiti on the side of the little bus, which belonged to one of the boys in their crowd. It read, "LOVE AND PEACE" in neon colors and psychedelic patterns. They'd removed all the seats so that they would be able to accommodate more people.

This was to be a huge event. The president and all the potential Democratic candidates were scheduled to attend. Mayor Daley of Chicago was a Democrat, and it was a great honor for him to be hosting the convention in his city. Chicago was preparing in every way. The restaurants, the hotels, and the nightlife were all making preparations to provide services for the delegates that would be arriving.

However, Daley was aware that there was great dissension in his city and was not going to allow the protesters to embarrass him. He was in control, always. This was the way he ran Chicago. Mayor Daley, also known as "The Boss," refused all permits submitted for peaceful protests during the convention and then imposed an 11:00 p.m. curfew.

On the hot Sunday morning of August 25, 1968, Janice and her fellow college students piled into the back of the hand-painted minibus. They wore flowers in their hair, and most of them were barefoot. As the bus sailed down Lake Shore Drive, with Lake Michigan shining like a sea of diamonds on one side and the city flashing before them on the other, they sang along with the radio as it played the latest antiwar songs. There was an air of optimism and excitement on the little bus.

They planned to camp in Grant Park even though Mayor Daley had denied them permits. The minibus was packed with large signs that they had written with sayings like, "End the War" and "What if they gave a war and nobody came?" They were sure that this demonstration would make a difference. With all the democratic politicians attending this convention, it would be the perfect time to show the world just how serious America's youth was about ending the war and the draft.

Young men were burning their draft cards across the country, but this was illegal. If they were caught, they could serve jail time, but the thought of Vietnam was terrifying. The news showed men being brought home in body bags every day.

When Janice and her friends arrived, they found the park flooded with young people. They sat down and shared food and marijuana joints with a group that invited them to have some wine. People had brought transistor radios, and music was playing everywhere. The hours passed, and the crowd grew larger. The police came and tried to clear the park with tear gas. It was difficult to move. There were too many people. Janice began to feel afraid.

At night, they slept in the park, and it seemed as if there was a blanket of people covering the ground. On the grandstand, Tom Hayden yelled passionately about ending the Vietnam War, followed by Rennie Davis, Abbie Hoffman, and Jerry Rubin. The air was electrified with excitement as the crowd waved signs and began shouting in unison, "Hell, no! We won't go!"

Janice began to feel trapped. It would be hard to get out of the park if she needed to. There were too many people. The crowd was too big and getting louder and more out of control.

Then, on Wednesday morning, the mass of protesters marched down Michigan Avenue, impeding all traffic. There was confusion around her, and Janice was swept up in the stampede down the street. She was too short to see above the heads of the other protesters, and panic began to rise in her at the thought of being trampled underfoot.

Over the loudspeaker, the police began demanding that the marchers disperse or they were going to take serious action. Janice had no idea what that meant, but she was scared, and there was no way out. She pushed, but she couldn't get through the crowds. It was stiflingly hot on that day in August. She felt as if the crowds were sucking all the air out of the atmosphere, and she couldn't breathe.

Angry protesters and furious police officers were shouting obscenities at each other. Then Janice heard someone in the crowd say, "Let's shit in bags and throw it at the pigs." Janice knew that the heads of SDS had given the police the nickname "pigs." Janice wished she'd never come.

Then, a male voice came from somewhere in front of her, "Listen, everyone. The pigs called out the fucking National Guard. The National Guard is here."

Janice was trembling. She'd lost track of her friends and was alone in the midst of this crazed mob. She heard screams and someone saying, "The pigs are beating the shit out of people with their billy clubs."

What? she thought, her mind racing. She felt so short and small and helpless. Then, she saw police officers and armed soldiers coming through the crowd. Some of them had feces dripping from their uniforms. Their faces were beet-red, and their eyes were filled with anger, hatred, and fear. The protesters were not letting up. They, too, were filled with anger and hatred.

Janice saw an officer hit a young girl across the face with a billy club. Blood flew through the air like a red bird, some landing in Janice's hair. Janice couldn't catch her breath and began to panic.

This is what Violet had been warning her would happen. This was why Violet had refused to get involved. Janice never thought she would be afraid of the police. She'd never believed that the police in America could be this violent, but they were, and she was terrified.

Janice looked around frantically for an opening in the crowd. She could see no way out. Her heart raced as she tried unsuccessfully to push through the sea of people. Although she didn't realize it, Janice was crying. She'd never been so frightened in her life, and she'd never felt so out of control. There was nothing to do but keep pushing, trying to steer clear of the billy clubs.

The protesters were still throwing bags of feces, pushing the police and National Guard even harder. Why did she ever come to this? Yes, she believed the war should end, and she thought she was brave, just not this brave.

Then, from behind her, she heard a man's voice. "Do you want to get out of here?" he asked, putting his hand on her shoulder.

She whipped her head around and looked up at him. Then she said, "Yes, oh yes."

A pair of strong arms lifted her and carried her, pushing through the crowd, going against the crowd, and heading back toward the park. He carried her effortlessly deep into the park and away from the war that had broken out in the streets of Chicago. Once they were far from the protesters and the police, the man set her down gently on her feet.

"Who are you?" Janice looked up in disbelief at a man she'd never seen before.

"Hi, I'm Lucas Allen." He smiled. He had a dimple on his left cheek.

She regarded him with a look of surprise, not understanding. "Well, I guess I should say thanks. Things were getting pretty rough."

"Yeah, they were. I saw the look on your face, and I knew you wanted to get out."

"Again, thanks. By the way, I'm Janice Lichtenstein."

He smiled. He was tall, very slender, with long, lean muscles. His hair was long and wavy, almost to his shoulders. Lucas was disheveled but incredibly attractive. His eyes were dark, but his skin was light. There was an easy, relaxed air about him and a strange attractiveness unlike any she'd ever seen.

"So, Janice Lichtenstein, would you like to go and get something to eat? I'm starving."

"Yes…"

"Come on. Let's get out of here. This whole thing has turned from a peaceful demonstration into a war zone."

Lucas led her to his motorcycle, a lean, black Triumph 650. Janice got on behind him, and they headed in the opposite direction of the chaos.

"I know this great pizza place. It's out in the suburbs. Have you ever been to Salvatori's? It's got the best deep-dish pizza I've ever had."

"Sounds great," she said, and for the first time in several hours, she took a deep breath.

CHAPTER FIFTY-TWO

LUCAS AND JANICE sat at a booth in the corner in a quaint little place with a red and white checkered tablecloth.

"I guess I should tell you that I'm a vegetarian," she said.

"Great, so am I." He smiled. "I had to get out of there today. When I went to the march, I went as a peaceful protester. But once it became violent, that was my cue to leave. I don't like violence of any kind, ever."

"Me neither. I was really scared."

"I know, I saw." He smiled, and then he laughed a little. "It's okay to be scared. I was, too."

She smiled bigger than she had in a very long time.

"So tell me a little about you, Janice."

"You first." She giggled.

"Okay, what do you want to know?"

"Well, where do you live? How old are you? Are you in college, or do you have a job? Stuff like that."

"Okay, very well. I think I can furnish the necessary info," Lucas said, clearing his throat and putting on a mock-serious face. "I'm twenty-eight years old. I live on the north side of Chicago. I teach martial arts, and I have my own studio. I've never been married. As you already know, I'm a vegetarian, and although I was raised Catholic, I don't believe in organized religion." He smiled broadly. "So, Ms. Lichtenstein, did I get the job?"

She laughed out loud. "I hope you didn't feel like you were being interviewed."

"But I am. It's okay. I am being interviewed to see if I am someone you might want to see again."

She laughed again. "Martial arts? I thought you were into nonviolence."

"I am." He smiled. "You don't know much about martial arts, do you?"

"No, not really."

"Well, I don't want to sit here and talk about myself all night. I'd rather hear a little about you. So someday, I'll tell you all about what I do and what I believe."

She was surprised. Elan loved to talk about himself. She thought most men did. Lucas was a strange fellow, but she liked this man with his easy smile.

"Now it's your turn," he said, leaning back in his chair.

Janice took a deep breath. She was going to have to tell him that she had a child. She hoped it wouldn't discourage his attention. Most of the men she'd come in contact with were not interested in becoming involved with a woman who already had a child. Oh, they would have sex with her, but then they were gone.

"Well, let's see. I am studying art at Northwestern University. And I love it." She smiled cautiously. Janice was suddenly unsure of what to do with her hands and where to put her gaze. She looked down at the silverware in front of her and toyed with her fork.

He returned the smile. "Go on," Lucas said, trying to catch her eyes.

"I grew up in the Chicago suburbs." She looked up at him and then quickly looked away. "And for the last few years, I lived in Israel."

He nodded. "Israel?"

"Yes." She took a deep breath of courage. This could be the end of the relationship before it even began, but better now than later. "I was married in Israel, and then I was divorced. And I have a child, a daughter, less than a year old."

Lucas was calm, somehow unaffected by the news. "I love kids."

How strange and delightfully different this Lucas Allen was from the other young men she'd met.

"I'd love to come over and meet your daughter maybe sometime in the future?"

The pizza came, and they ate silently for a few minutes. Janice wondered if he was just saying these kind words to get her into bed. She'd learned that men would say anything to get what they wanted. It would be terrible if that were the case.

"So, I have a question for you: How did you ever see me in that huge crowd, and how did you get us out of that mess? There were wall-to-wall people in the streets. I felt so trapped."

"Well, I guess I have a thing for little redheads. I saw you yesterday, and I kept an eye on you. I figured things might get hairy once the march started, and I didn't want you to get hurt."

"But how the heck did you get through the crowd?"

"The truth?"

"Yeah."

"My will, my intention. I willed us through."

"Huh?"

"Let me explain. Like I said before, I've been studying martial arts since I was sixteen. I'm a fourth-degree black belt in karate and a second-degree black belt in judo. Lots of people think that martial arts are only for defense and maybe exercise. But the martial arts are more than just physical. They teach spiritual truths that lead to discovering the strength of the spirit.

"You mean, like your soul?"

"Yes, your soul."

"But I thought you didn't believe in God."

"Ah, Janice. You misunderstood me. I believe in a God that is everywhere, inside all of us. What I don't believe in is organized religion."

"But isn't that the same thing?" she asked.

"Not at all." He winked at her. "Not at all."

CHAPTER FIFTY-THREE

LUCAS DIDN'T HAVE the rugged, sexy masculinity that Elan had, but there was something about him that was incredibly attractive. However, unlike Elan, who revealed his bad qualities as time passed, the more Janice got to know Lucas, the better she liked him and the more attractive he was to her. Lucas was truly kind and grateful for even the smallest of favors. In fact, he seemed to love everyone and everything.

Janice was terrified of spiders. Once, she spotted a spider on the dashboard when they were in her car headed to a restaurant. She'd pulled over screaming and got out of the car, terrified.

"Kill it, Lucas," she'd said, shaking.

He'd taken a leaf from the ground and carefully picked the spider up with it. Then he gently placed it outside in the grass.

"No need to kill it," he'd said, touching her shoulder as they both returned to the automobile.

At least three times a week, Lucas came to Janice's house over the next several weeks to take her out. Whenever he arrived, he always brought her something. Once, it was a book of beautiful, romantic poetry. Another time, it was a tiny silver pendant with a lotus surrounded by slivers of amethyst. They went to the beach, walked along the shore, and explored the Art Institute, but mostly, they talked.

Lucas listened. He really listened. When she spoke, he looked into her eyes, never letting his gaze drift away to things happening around them. She found Lucas to be wise. He was well-read, and although he never flaunted his knowledge or tried to appear intellectual, he seemed to know at least a little about everything. But he was open-minded and always ready to hear new ideas.

One day, as they sat on the shore of Lake Michigan having a picnic, Janice reached into her handbag and brought out a small drawing she'd made for him. She'd worked on it for several weeks and felt it was quite good. It was a charcoal drawing of him rescuing her at the convention.

For a silent moment, he just sat and looked at the paper. She felt nervous, afraid he would be critical, although she had no reason to feel that way: Lucas had never been judgmental. Still, it was her art. It came from deep inside of her. She always felt this way when someone was studying her work. Then, without speaking a single word, he looked into her eyes, slowly leaned over, and kissed her.

"Do you like it?" she asked as he touched her cheek.

He nodded. "I love it because you made it for me. But I also want you to know that you are very talented."

"Do you really think so?"

"I never lie."

She smiled at him. "Thank you."

"Would you like to see my studio?"

"You mean your martial arts studio?"

"Yep."

"Yeah, I would."

They finished lunch and rode over to the studio on Lucas' motorcycle. Lucas unlocked the door. Janice was greeted by a pleasant whiff of sage as they walked inside. It was a quiet place until Lucas turned on the record player. The music of a sitar came through the speaker, soft and unobtrusive. Janice felt strangely at peace.

"I live in the back," Lucas said.

In a way, it reminded her of a ballet school with blond wooden floors and mirrored walls. But unlike a ballet studio, there were large, colorful pillows from India against the walls.

They walked through the front, where the classes took place, and through to the back, where Lucas had his modest apartment. It was clean and minimal, simple but comfortable. There were lots of pillows made of vibrantly woven fabrics and a large woolen rug on the floor, but no bed.

"Where do you sleep?" Janice asked him.

"On the floor. I lay out a mat. I don't believe in mattresses. Not good for your back. Sleeping on the floor strengthens your back muscles."

She nodded. She'd never met anyone quite like him. He certainly was weird, but she couldn't help but like him.

They sat side-by-side on the floor. He lit a candle and dimmed the lights. The album still played softly in the background.

"If you'd like to take classes, I'd be happy to have you," he said.

"How much are classes?"

"For you, they are the price of a single kiss," he whispered.

She giggled. *Damn*, she thought. He really said the strangest things.

"May I kiss you?"

She nodded. No one had ever asked before. Lucas was such an odd man.

His lips touched hers so lightly and tenderly that she almost felt as if she'd imagined the kiss. Then he gently caressed her face. His hand was tender, exploring. It felt more sensuous than making love. Although all he had done was run his hand along the perimeter of her cheek and jawline, she felt vulnerable and exposed.

"Beautiful," he said, his voice soft but hoarse. Lucas stood up and took a bottle of fragrant massage oil from the shelf. Then he put a small amount into his palm and rubbed it between his hands to warm it. He looked into her eyes and slowly began to massage her shoulders, neck, and the lower part of her arms that were not covered by her tee shirt. She felt all the tension leave her body as his gentle but firm hands moved expertly over her muscles. He moved down, and for almost a half hour, he massaged her feet. Slowly, slowly, each toe, until she felt her entire body was limp and at ease.

Now Lucas moved back up to her lips and kissed her. This time, she felt the strength of his growing passion. Lucas took her hands and brought her to her feet. Slowly, he undressed her until she stood before him in nothing but her panties and bra. She'd been naked with men before, but she'd never felt so exposed. It had never felt so real. Next, he pulled his tee shirt over his head and revealed his naked chest to her, and then he removed the rest of his clothes. He smiled at her. His smile was gentle and warm. Now he took her hands again, sat back down on the floor cross-legged, and helped her to sit the same way directly across from him.

He continued to hold her hands and gaze into her eyes. He had rubbed her feet and held her hands but had not touched her intimately so far, yet she felt more intimacy than she'd ever felt. Her body trembled with longing. She wanted him to hold her, to touch her, to take her, but he didn't move. The longer he sat across from her without touching her, the more her desire increased until she thought that she could no longer bear the wanting of him.

After what seemed like an hour, he reached up, took her face into his hands, and brought her head close to his own. Before pressing his lips upon hers, he fixed his gaze on her eyes. Janice felt that she was looking directly into his soul, feelings, and everything he was in the depths of his eyes.

Then, tenderly, he let his lips brush hers. She let out a sigh. Lucas brought her to him closer and kissed her. With one hand, he unclasped her bra. She felt his naked chest pressed against her own. The connection between them was so strong that their breaths coordinated in sequence together. It seemed to Janice that time had stopped as he moved his lips slowly over her body, removing the rest of her clothing. When he finally entered her, she felt she had found something she never knew was missing from her life.

Their bodies moved together. She could not think, only feel. Her body was alive with sensations. He moved slowly, watching until he knew she was ready, and then they climaxed together. It was like nothing Janice had ever felt before. A smile came over her face.

Even though she'd been with many men, she decided that until she'd made love with Lucas, she'd been a virgin.

After they made love, Janice and Lucas lay together. The music had stopped, and all they could hear were the birds chirping outside and the needle skipping on the end of the record album. For the first time in her life, Janice felt at peace.

CHAPTER FIFTY-FOUR

"YOU'RE BRINGING some guy home to meet us, and he's not even Jewish? Janice, your father is going to go crazy. You just got out of a terrible marriage. Now, you've found some guy who is a karate teacher? Come on, Janice. We sent you to an expensive private university so you could meet an accountant, a doctor, a lawyer, and this is what you come up with? *Oy vey*, didn't you have enough trouble with the situation you got yourself into in Israel?"

Frances Lichtenstein was sitting on the sofa glaring at her daughter. Janice had always given them so much trouble. Frances and her husband had hoped that when the marriage to Elan failed in Israel, Janice would finally grow up. However, it seemed as if she'd only gotten worse. To add to the problems, she now had a child to think of. But it didn't seem to Mrs. Lichtenstein that Janice gave much thought to anything.

"Mom, he's a great guy. I want you and Dad to give him a chance," Janice said with her arms folded across her chest. In the other room, Bari Lynn was crying. Violet rushed in to pick her up and give her a bottle.

"You just don't learn. You are so stubborn. This man makes a living teaching karate? How much money can he possibly make? He can't afford to support you. You have a child to think about, you know."

"I am going to talk to Dad about this when he gets home from work tonight. I want to invite Lucas over to the house this weekend."

Frances Lichtenstein shook her head and walked out of the room. Janice sighed with frustration and went into the baby's room to help Violet.

That night, when Janice told her father that she was bringing a man home to meet them, at first, he was interested. But when she told him a little about Lucas, he was furious. "Where did you find this guy? Why didn't you meet someone at school? For God's sake, Janice, this is another potential divorce."

"Did I say I was getting married?"

"Why are you getting involved with a weirdo who has no money, no education? Janice, what the hell is the matter with you?"

"He's not a weirdo. He's a great guy."

"Come on, he has no real profession. He teaches karate, Janice? Karate? Does he know you come from money? Is that maybe why he's so interested in you?"

"Dad, don't you think someone could like me for who I am? Do you think I'm so worthless that nobody could love me for being me?"

"Stop being a child. Money means a lot, especially to a man who has no profession, no education, nothing—a karate teacher. Janice, what am I going to do with you?"

"He's coming on Sunday. And that's all I have to say," Janice said and walked out of the room.

That Sunday was a perfect example of Indian summer. It was late September, and the sky was blue, the weather unusually warm for that time of year. The ground was a blanket of color from the leaves that had begun to fall. Lucas arrived a little before noon with a small book for Janice and a basket of fruit for her mother.

"Mom, this is Lucas."

"It's a pleasure to meet you," she said.

"Dad, Lucas."

Her father nodded.

"It's a pleasure to meet you, Mr. Lichtenstein."

Any conversation was stifled until Bari Lynn got up from her nap, and Violet brought her into the living room to feed her. Bari Lynn was fussy. The family decided that she must be cutting a tooth because she'd been crying for the last several days. As soon as Lucas saw the baby for the first time, he asked if he could hold her. Janice said, "Sure."

He took the child gently from Violet's arms and held her close to his chest. Then he began to rock her and sing softly. Bari Lynn grew quiet, but her eyes were wide. Then she broke into a smile, and Lucas returned one of his own. Janice was surprised to see the ease with which Lucas handled the baby. She caught a glimpse of her mother and knew that her mother could see what she saw in Lucas.

By the end of the day, Janice's parents had, by some miracle, come to accept Lucas, perhaps even like him. He was helpful in every way. In fact, even though he did not eat meat and Janice knew that the very sight of it sickened him, he helped her father with the barbecue. Like Lucas, she was a vegetarian, but Janice wasn't sickened by the sight of meat. She just ate the salad, grilled corn, and baked potatoes.

It was obvious to Janice how different she and Lucas were. She was strong-willed and determined, and he, as he put it, was willing to bend. Once, during a disagreement, when she'd been furious, he'd recited a quote that quieted her down almost immediately.

He said, "In a storm, the oak tree will break because it is rigid, but the palm will sway and bend and therefore will survive the storm."

He never argued. In fact, when she became difficult and wanted her own way, he would just come up very close to her, so close that she could smell the scent of the incense that lingered on his body. Then, even as she pouted or argued, he would take her into his arms and hold her until the anger melted from her like an ice cream cone on a summer day. Then she, too, melted into his arms. And so it was that Janice fell in love with Lucas.

Janice was naturally high-strung. Everything seemed to put her on edge. At Lucas' suggestion, she took classes in meditation at the studio. It helped her to calm her headstrong ways. She learned to listen. She became less abrupt, gentler, understanding, and, in most cases, more honest.

However, Janice was still adamant that Bari Lynn could never know anything about her real father. She insisted that Bari Lynn grew up believing Elan had died in Vietnam. It was best that way. If Bari knew about her father, she might want to meet him when she grew up, and Janice wanted Elan to stay buried in the past. She and her daughter had a new life, and Janice was not about to let Elan make a mess of things again. Lucas didn't agree, but he respected her wishes.

Janice had a strong mind and unwavering opinions and loved long, intellectual discussions with Lucas. They talked about everything from music to politics. In the middle of a heated discussion, Lucas would sometimes get a special look on his face as if he were seeing an angel. Then he would just stop speaking, stare at her, a smile would come over his face, and he would gently kiss her.

Janice brought up marriage several times. However, Lucas said he didn't need a piece of paper to legitimize his feelings. She didn't worry too much about his choice because she was still in school, and it was easier to live at home with her parents and have Violet's help with Bari Lynn. However, when Lucas received his draft notice, and his number was up in the spring, Janice became frantic.

"Oh, my God, they'll send you to 'Nam."

"I'm going to go to Canada. Do you want to come with me?"

"I can't. I have to finish school."

"So you'll come when you've finished?"

Janice wrapped her arms around her shoulders. Perhaps she'd been deluding herself. What had made her believe that Lucas loved her? He'd never even said that he did. She turned away, not wanting him to see the tears welling up in her eyes.

"What is it? You don't want me to go?"

"It will be at least two years before I see you again. That is unless I go and visit you." She huffed. He tried to hug her, but she pushed him away. "You know, Lucas…"

She looked at him, really studied him. Lucas stood there, his hands at his sides, a puzzled look on his face. He seemed like a lost little boy who didn't understand what she was saying.

"I don't even really know how you feel about me. I mean, you've never really said..."

He walked toward her, his arms open to take her inside. She did not come to him as she usually did, so he did not force his embrace upon her.

"I haven't said the words, but I thought you knew." He took her hand in his and kissed it. She let him hold her hand for a minute, then withdrew it. He gently took her chin in his palm and then turned her face to look at him. There was no trace of deception in his eyes. "I love you, Janice. I love you."

He said it so simply, so naturally.

"I love you, too, Lucas."

He smiled and kissed her hand again.

"I know you should be the one to propose. But, well, since you got this draft card... I mean, I know that papers don't mean anything to you, but..."

"Do you want to get married? I'll propose. You don't have to ask me."

"Yes, but I wish it wasn't only because you were being drafted. For God's sake, Lucas, you just don't understand." She started crying.

He looked at her, completely dumbfounded. "What is it, Janice? What's wrong with you? I mean, there is no guarantee that our being married and you having a child will keep me out of 'Nam. It might, and we can try."

"I pray that it does, but you see, I want you to *want* to be my husband. Every little girl has a dream of how her future husband will propose. And let me tell you, this was not how I imagined it."

"Listen, Janice, please listen. The draft is the reason for the official paperwork, okay? But it isn't the reason I want to share my life with you. As soon as I fell in love with you, in my heart, we were married. I was planning to spend the future together whether we had the official papers or not."

She smiled through her tears. "Say it again."

"What?"

"Lucas, don't be clueless. Tell me that you love me."

"I love you. I love you with all my heart. Will you marry me, Janice? Please be my wife."

He loved her. She knew he did, but just hearing the words made her want to jump up and down joyfully. She was trembling in his arms now. "Yes, yes, I'll marry you."

He kissed the top of her head. "I don't know how you could have ever doubted my love for you," he said.

"A simple wedding? Just a few friends and family?" she asked.

"Yes," he said. "Yes, that sounds good."

"Where are you from? You know, I've never even asked you about your family."

"I'm an orphan. I grew up in foster homes. I have no family. But now, I will. I'll have you and Bari. We'll be a family."

CHAPTER FIFTY-FIVE

THEY TOLD her parents that they planned to marry. Her parents stared at them.

"Are you sure you don't want to get to know each other a little better before you jump into this?" her mother said.

"I'm sure, Mom."

"Janice, you're impossible…"

"I know what I'm doing. We are in love. We'll be happy."

Her father didn't say a word. He bit his upper lip, his brow furrowed as he stared out the window and listened to the baby crying in the next room. Arguing with his headstrong daughter was no use, but he had an idea.

One afternoon, a week later, when he was sure Janice would be at school, her father called Lucas at the karate studio.

"I'd like to talk to you. Would you be willing to meet me for lunch? My treat?" Mr. Lichtenstein said.

Lucas cleared his throat. "Yes. Sure, I'll meet you."

They agreed to meet at a coffee shop that served sandwiches and salads and was not far from Lucas' studio.

Ronald Lichtenstein watched Lucas eat his salad. He was quiet for several moments.

"I know you asked me here for a reason. We may as well get started talking about whatever it is that you want to talk about," Lucas said.

"Yes, I did ask you here for a specific reason. I think you know how much Janice means to her mother and me."

"Of course I do. She means a lot to me, too."

"And I'm sure that you can see a lot of things. You know what I mean?"

"Not really."

"Well, by the size of our house and the kinds of cars we drive. I know you're not stupid, so you can see that we have some money."

"Yes, I guess you do."

"Listen, if it's money you're after, I'd rather write you a check right now and have you get out of my daughter's life than for her to be hurt later. She's been through a lot, Lucas. I'd rather just give you some cash and send you on your way. That way, you'd have what you want, and she would never have to know what happened."

"You think I want your money?" Lucas almost choked. Then he shook his head and laughed. "Money means nothing to me. I don't care about it at all. I have all that I need, and I'm a happy man. I love Janice. I don't care where she came from.

"I love that she's short, spunky, and outspoken, and she makes me laugh. I love her fiery red hair that matches her fiery convictions. I love the way that she can make a strong point in a conversation. I love her passion and her artistic sensitivity, but I sure as hell don't love her money. Listen. Don't give us anything—ever. We'll make it on our own. I don't want anything from you except maybe your blessing to give it freely if you can find it in your heart."

"Is this about the draft? Because I have friends. I know people. I can get you out of Vietnam."

"Do you think so little of your daughter that you would believe I couldn't love her for who she is? I don't want anything but her love. And as far as the draft is concerned, I was prepared to go to Canada. I don't want your money or your favors. I'm marrying a woman who I love because I love her and for no other reason at all."

Lucas took two bills from his pocket, threw them on the table, and walked out, leaving Ronald Lichtenstein shocked but reassured in a strange way. At that moment, Ronald Lichtenstein decided that he would go back to his office and pull some strings. Lucas wasn't perfect, but he was good for Janice and truly loved her. And for that reason, Ronald Lichtenstein would see to it that Lucas never set foot in Southeast Asia.

CHAPTER FIFTY-SIX

JANICE'S PARENTS were having dinner alone one night outside on the porch. Violet was caring for the baby, and the house was quiet. Across the road, a dog was barking softly, and there was a cool breeze in the air.

"Janice is hell-bent on getting married again. I think it's too soon," Mrs. Lichtenstein said.

"Yeah, Janice… so headstrong. The only thing I am disappointed about is that he isn't Jewish. Otherwise, truth be told, he's not a bad fellow."

"Her last husband was Jewish, and that didn't end so well," her mother said.

"It's just hard for me to accept that she's marrying a *goy*, that's all. This isn't what I was hoping for. But you know, Frances, I believe that boy really loves her."

"I agree with you, Ron. You've always been a good judge of people."

"Well, I sure knew that Elan was no good right from the beginning."

"Yes, you did know that," Frances said.

"He doesn't have much to offer: no college, no profession, and no money. I don't know," her father said, shaking his head, then he lit a cigar. "Well, you know Janice. She's a lot like me, I guess. And she's going to do what she wants anyway. At least they'll be living here in the U.S. We'll see her and Bari all the time. It could be worse. Elan was Jewish, but he took her to live all the way across the world in a country that was full of constant unrest. Now that was terrible."

"She's going to live in the back of a karate studio. That's pretty bad. I can't believe it," her mother said.

"I know. We always gave her the best of everything, and, for some reason, she always seemed to end up with *dreck*, trash. Remember that sweet sixteen party we threw for her? It cost me a small fortune."

"Yes, how could I forget? She wanted the best of everything at that party: the food, the music, the entertainment. Oy. But still, Ron, don't call Lucas 'dreck.' He's going to be our son-in-law, and you said yourself that he does love her."

"Yes, they act like kids right now, but they'll grow up together, and then, later, with a little help from us, we can make sure that they'll have a good life. We'll wait a couple of years to be sure it's gonna last, and then we'll give them a down payment on a house. It will be all right. At least he treats her well. And I'll make sure Janice and Bari never want for anything, even if I have to do it without Lucas knowing that the help is coming from me."

"Yes, and I guess this Lucas fellow is a pretty nice guy even though he has nothing to offer," she agreed.

Ronald patted Frances' shoulder and then shrugged. "Oh well, we'll make the best of it, even if it isn't what we had hoped for her."

Janice and Lucas were married on a Monday morning in a civil ceremony in the downtown Chicago office of the Justice of the Peace. She wore a simple beige dress, and he wore a pair of black slacks and a white cotton button-down shirt. Afterward, they went to a Chinese restaurant and had lunch. Janice's parents drove all five of them because they didn't feel it was suitable for the couple to ride the motorcycle. Janice's mother sat in the back seat, holding Bari Lynn with Janice beside her, while Lucas sat in the front with Janice's father.

Lucas surprised Janice that night. He told her he had some money saved and asked if she would like to spend a few nights in a cabin up in Wisconsin, in Eagle River. They would have a honeymoon. Janice was elated.

So the next morning, Janice called all of Lucas' students who were on the list to attend classes in the next three days, and she told them that classes were canceled and would resume the following week. Then she and Lucas packed a single backpack between them and drove north to Wisconsin while Violet cared for Bari Lynn at the Lichtenstein's home.

Eagle River was a quiet little town with many trees and ducks swimming in the open water. The cabin was homey and simple, but it had a king-sized bed, and Janice convinced Lucas to make love to her on it. It was the first time they'd ever been in a bed together, and it had been years since Lucas had lain on a bed at all. When they were finished, she rested in his arms, listening to the birds and crickets chirping outside.

"So, how did you like that?"

"The bed?"

"Yes."

He laughed. "I did like it, actually. It was really comfortable. I felt like I was immersed in a cloud."

"Lucas?"

"Yes?"

"Can I ask you a question?"

"Sure, anything."

"I know you told me before. But please just reassure me, you did marry me because you love me and not to avoid the draft, right?"

"Yes, right. I would never have done that to you or to me."

"I'm glad…"

They lay quietly for a few more minutes.

"Lucas?"

"Hmm?"

"You've never asked me about my ex-husband. Why not?"

"Because I thought you would tell me if you wanted me to know."

"Do you want to know?"

"If you want to tell me. I would never pry into your life."

"Even though I'm your wife?"

"Yes, even though you are my wife."

"My ex was an Israeli."

"Yes, you did tell me that much. You also said that you lived in Israel."

"I thought I loved him. I thought he was the most wonderful man in the world, at least, that was until I met you."

"I guess if you want to know the truth, I would like to know more about you and your ex. If you feel comfortable talking about it. If not, I'll understand. But I am wondering why you two broke up."

"Well, when I first went to Israel, I was caught up in the whole romanticism of it all. I mean, it was so different from America. In Israel, the Israelis live for their country. It all seemed so storybook to me. Do you know what I mean?"

"Not exactly."

"Israel is very different from the States. In fact, when you meet a new person in Israel, one of the first things they talk to you about is their country. Now, who the hell does that in America? It's like, to the Israelis, the country is more important than they are. When I first got there, that mystique was so attractive to me.

"My ex, Elan, was a Sephardic Jew. His family originated in Spain, but he was born in Palestine before Israel was even a nation, and so were his parents. And the thing was, Elan was all caught up with the European Jews who had come to Israel after surviving the Holocaust. He was always talking about how important it was that Israel didn't fall and must never lose a single war. He said that if they did, it would be the end of the Jewish race.

"He was strong, a fighter, a powerful man with so much passion that I guess, in the beginning, I was attracted to the excitement of him. Does that make sense?" She shrugged her shoulders and continued. "But I certainly changed my mind later when he walked out the door on me, leaving me in a hotel to fend for myself.

"It was the night that the Six-Day War broke out. This was the way Israel was. A soldier came to our hotel room and told Elan he must prepare to leave to go to war. Can you imagine? No warning, just some guy appears dressed in an IDF uniform at the door to your hotel room in the middle of the night. It was surreal.

"But the thing that really got to me was that earlier that night, I had told him that I was pregnant. I was very sensitive. Maybe it was my hormones because I was pregnant, and when the soldier told us that war had broken out, I was terribly frightened.

"I had to return to Jerusalem, where we lived, from Tel Aviv, where the comedy show was. I told him I could not do it alone, knowing the country was at war. He knew that there could be bombings and that anything might happen. I begged him not to go. I told him how much I needed him, but he went anyway. I ran after him into the hall of the hotel. I saw him get on the elevator. I yelled his name, but he never turned around," she said, gripping Lucas' upper arm, caught up in the memory of how afraid she was.

"I have to tell the truth. The Six-Day War wasn't the beginning of the problems between Elan and me. We'd had a troubled marriage from the start. His mother was very domineering, and she made my life a living hell. The reason we were in the hotel was because I'd purchased tickets for us to go to a show in Tel Aviv, just so that we could be away from his mother, even if it was just for a night.

"And when I first told him I was going to have a baby, he seemed so happy. For a moment, I believed that things were going to get better. But then, after the show, when we got back to the room, he was acting strange, distracted, and very detached. I tried, but I couldn't get him to open up and tell me what was bothering him. It was like all of a sudden, he was so unhappy.

"Finally, I gave up and fell asleep, hoping that whatever this was would pass and he would be better in the morning. I told myself that maybe he was tired. Elan could be like that sometimes—cold, I mean, uncaring, aloof. I don't know what would cause these moods, but sometimes they just came on, and the only thing I could do was ride them out.

"Then, when we heard the loud knock on the door in the middle of the night, Elan jumped out of bed and answered it. That's when the soldier gave him five minutes to get ready to leave. I couldn't believe what was happening. Five minutes? Leave your pregnant wife in a hotel room in a strange city? I'm an American. I had no idea what to expect. I've never been in the middle of a battleground. I reminded him that I was pregnant. He never answered me. I said that if he walked out of that room and left me, I was going home to America and never coming back.

"Then, like I said, he got into the elevator with the other soldiers and never even looked at me crying as I sat on the floor in the hall of that hotel. So the next day, I came home."

"Did you tell him about Bari when you contacted him after the Six-Day War ended?"

"No, I sent him a letter asking for a divorce, and in that letter, I told him that I miscarried."

Lucas didn't say anything.

"You think that's terrible, don't you?"

He sighed. "I don't think it was fair, but I won't judge you. You did what you thought you had to do."

"I told you that I am going to tell Bari that her father died in Vietnam. I don't even want her to know that he was an Israeli."

"Yes, I know."

"You don't think it's right. I can tell."

"More importantly, Janice, do you think it's right?"

"I don't know what's right or wrong anymore. All I know is I want to put that part of my life behind me. The very thing that I thought I loved about Elan, his passion for his country, was the very thing I ended up hating."

Lucas didn't speak. He just ran his fingers gently through her hair.

"Do you still love me?" she asked in an almost childlike voice.

"Janice. Of course, I love you. You're spoiled, and you're as stubborn as can be, but I love you."

"Why?"

"Because you're you, and there is no one else I have ever known who is like you. You're incredibly brave."

"To the point of being stupid sometimes," she said.

He laughed. "But brave nonetheless. And you are kind, and you are open to new ideas. I have never seen you pass judgment on anyone."

"Except maybe Elan."

"Yes, but that's understandable considering what you went through," he said.

"You make me sound so much better than I am."

"That's what love is. Love is seeing the good in someone, and even though you know they have faults, the good things you see far outweigh them."

"I hope you'll always love me. And I have to thank God that you understand that I've made mistakes."

He pulled her close to him and kissed her. "There are no mistakes, Janice. If you hadn't married Elan, you might not be with me now. Everything that happened in your past and mine is what led us both to this moment, so let's just cherish what we have now."

CHAPTER FIFTY-SEVEN

On the west side of Chicago, on the corner of Monroe and Western, nine people slept in a roach-infested apartment that almost never had enough hot water to take a full shower. At four forty-five a.m. on December 4, 1969, the heat was barely working on this bone-chilling morning. Some of the occupants shared twin beds. Others just rolled up with blankets on the floor. This was the headquarters of the Black Panthers.

The race wars between blacks and whites were escalating every day in the city of Chicago, resulting in the deaths of police officers.

Although Mayor Daley refused to admit it, the race riots following the death of Dr. King had brought the city to its knees. Chicago became a battleground filled with fire and violence. Instead of uniting as one people, the races were divided. Dr. King's dream of peace was buried beneath the hatred and anger that clouded perspectives and created mass hysteria and overwhelming fear.

The Black Panthers were growing stronger, and rather than negotiate with them, Daley chose to fight. This was his city, and, by God, he was going to take control.

So a secret attack was planned, and, on that very morning in December, the Chicago police raided the Panther's headquarters. As

Daley expected, the police found nineteen guns and one thousand rounds of ammunition. Chaos ensued, and by the time the raid was over, Fred Hampton and Mark Clark, two of the leaders of the Black Panther party, were dead, and four others were seriously wounded.

That morning, without giving any notice and without offering any reason, Violet packed her things and quit her job working for the Lichtensteins. Janice tried to talk to her, but Violet was not speaking. She was leaving. All Janice could do was thank her for her help with Bari Lynn and wish her the best. Then Janice stood at the big picture window in her parents' living room, watching as Violet walked out of their lives forever.

CHAPTER FIFTY-EIGHT

It was decided that Bari Lynn would live with her grandparents, who hired another full-time nanny to take care of her. Lucas legally adopted Bari Lynn, but the back of a martial arts studio was no place to raise a child. At least Ronald Lichtenstein didn't believe it was. He insisted that Bari stay with him and his wife until Janice finished school.

Janice's parents bought her a used car, and Janice took extra classes in hopes of finishing school early.

Lucas learned that his father-in-law had gotten him an exemption from the draft. At first, he was angry at the interference. However, Janice was elated that Lucas didn't have to leave the country. She didn't care how he had gotten out of going to Canada or, worse, to Vietnam. She was just glad that he could stay with her and be safe. Janice's joy was contagious, and Lucas decided to thank his father-in-law instead of being stupidly prideful.

Now Lucas decided that he needed to earn more income to take care of his family, so he added an after-school karate program for children. He bought a minibus and hired a driver to pick the children up at school and bring them to the studio, where they stayed until their parents finished work each day.

CHAPTER FIFTY-NINE

AND SO A YEAR PASSED. It had been a cold winter, but the spring had finally arrived. Janice and Lucas always had the radio on while sharing their evening meal. On this Monday night, they were both tired. It had been a long weekend. They'd had Bari with them; she was an active, busy child.

Janice and Lucas were worn out and ready for a quiet night at home. She planned to study while he meditated. The radio played softly in the background. They both loved folk music, and Simon and Garfunkel were singing their hit "Bridge Over Troubled Water" when the program was interrupted.

"We interrupt this program to bring you the latest news."

Janice cast a glance at Lucas and cocked her head. They both listened more closely.

"Today, at Kent State University in Ohio, four students were shot and killed by the National Guard during a Vietnam War protest."

"What?" Janice said.

Lucas turned pale. "Students killed by the National Guard? Every day, more and more, it's beginning to feel like we're living in a police state."

"It's really scary, and it's only getting scarier."
"Yeah, it sure is."

CHAPTER SIXTY

Two years later, Janice graduated from college and went to work as an art teacher at a high school that was close enough for her to walk from Lucas' studio. They'd been careful not to get pregnant until Janice finished school, but now they began to talk about possibly renting an apartment and taking Bari Lynn and her nanny, Maria, to live with them.

Ronald Lichtenstein insisted that Janice have a nanny to help her and insisted that he would pay Maria's salary. Janice wanted to spend more time with her daughter. Lucas didn't like taking anything from his father-in-law, but he could hardly afford a live-in nanny, and he knew how much Janice longed to spend more time with Bari Lynn, so he swallowed his pride and agreed. They moved into a small three-bedroom apartment. Maria had her own room, which was adjacent to Bari Lynn's room.

The after-school program became so popular with the local parents that Lucas created a martial arts summer camp. That, too, had a huge enrollment, but Lucas was a terrible businessman. His kindness overran any ambition he might have had to earn money. If a student could not afford to attend his after-school program, he would not refuse the student attendance. He would just tell the parents to pay what they could when they could.

Living a minimalist lifestyle was satisfactory to Lucas, but Ronald Lichtenstein wanted more for his daughter and granddaughter. So, unbeknownst to Lucas, he gave Janice money. Between his help and Janice's salary as a teacher, they were getting by.

Janice's father had grown to like Lucas as he came to know him. He'd never met a man so sincere and honest. Lichtenstein respected Lucas, but he doubted that his son-in-law would ever be a good provider if he were not given some help and guidance. Ronald Lichtenstein wanted to insure his daughter's future, not just through inheritance but also by helping his son-in-law find some measure of success. So he offered to provide the money for Lucas to open another studio on the other side of town. Lucas did not want to take money from his father-in-law, but Ronald insisted. He said that this investment would benefit both of them. And more importantly, it would be good for Janice and Bari.

So, after much convincing, Lucas finally agreed, but only on the terms that Lucas would pay Ronald a percentage of the profits each month. They would be partners. Of course, without Lucas knowing, Ronald Lichtenstein would turn any money Lucas gave him back over to his daughter to help support the family. He didn't need it, so why not use the profits to ensure his daughter and granddaughter would have a comfortable life? Lucas hired one of his best black-belt students to manage the school.

Bari Lynn started kindergarten, and Maria picked her up every day and brought her to Lucas' studio. Bari Lynn sat on the sidelines. She never wanted to participate in the classes. She was overweight and clumsy. Lucas considered pushing her to join in but decided against it. He knew Bari Lynn lacked self-confidence, but forcing anything was not the answer.

Often, Janice thought about Violet. She wondered if there was anything she could have done differently that could have lightened Violet's load in life. She wondered if anything had connected Violet to the Black Panther raid. It could have been a coincidence, but Janice didn't think so. Once, she tried to look Violet up in the phone book. She only wanted to talk to her, to tell her how often she thought about her, but there was no listing. It was as if Violet had disappeared.

The student demonstrations continued. When the soldiers returned from Vietnam, they were treated with disdain and treated like the enemy. Unlike the America that had fought in WW2, and unlike Israel, America was divided, and its division within had weakened the world's view of the country.

On their fifth anniversary, Janice's parents gave Janice and Lucas a gift: a down payment for a house.

"This is too much, but thank you for the thought," Lucas said.

"I want you two to have a nice place to live, a place of your own. Don't do it for yourself or me. Take this money and buy a house for Janice and Bari. It would be selfish if you refused."

Lucas studied his father-in-law. Love complicated things. It made people reconsider their beliefs and principles. What was best for Janice meant more to Lucas than his pride. So finally, Lucas agreed.

No marriage is perfect. As time passed, Lucas found that Janice's stubbornness could be frustrating, and Janice found that Lucas's lack of ambition kept them dependent upon her father. Janice resented the idea of depending on her father all of her life. She'd seen her mother kowtow to his whims and swore she would never be submissive to a husband. And she wasn't. In her mind, the fact that she was the breadwinner made her the head of the house.

When they'd first married, she thought she liked the feeling of control, but now she began to wish that Lucas would take the reins sometimes. She was getting tired of working and paying bills.

He kept the studio and all the classes but gave away more than he earned. Janice was sure that if Lucas had not married, he would have been completely satisfied to live all his days in the back of his studio. Yet even though he drove her mad with his quiet acceptance and lack of ambition, she cared far too much for him to let him know that she was accepting money from her father.

With the gift of a down payment from the Lichtensteins, the couple purchased a small house in Evanston. The following month, they both agreed that Janice should stop her birth control. She wanted a sibling for Bari, so they decided she would have another child. With Maria's help, they would manage. They had been in the house for less than six months when Janice got pregnant.

She said she would be uncomfortable sleeping on a mat on the floor once she began to grow big and demanded that they purchase a bed. Lucas wanted her to be happy, so he agreed. Although Janice did not realize it, Lucas had made as many sacrifices for her as she did for him.

In the second month of her pregnancy, Janice woke up with intense uterine cramping. Lucas helped her to the car and drove white-knuckled to the local hospital. He refused to leave her side, even when the doctors told him he must. Lucas was a powerful man, and the security guards were unable to move him. But several nurses and orderlies gently coaxed Lucas out of the room. He watched as Janice was wheeled down to surgery.

For three intense hours, he sat cross-legged on the floor by the door of her room, waiting for her to return. The doctor finally came to speak to him. Janice had lost the baby, but she was going to be all right. He was sad at the loss but relieved that he would not have to endure a life without the woman he loved.

Lucas was at her side as soon as Janice was brought back to her room. When she awakened and learned the news about the baby, he held her as she cried and told her how much he loved her. She was strong-willed, but when she was hurting, Lucas gave her the strength to keep from breaking.

Bari Lynn was not what would be considered a pretty child. She was overweight with thick, frizzy, auburn hair, a round face, and a shy, self-conscious disposition. Her grandparents gave her everything a child could want materially. Growing up, she had the best clothes and modern bicycles, trips to Disneyland, and even tickets to Bozo's Circus. But Bari was a lonely child except for her friendship with her stepfather, Lucas. What she longed for was acceptance. She started kindergarten as an outcast, and that stigma continued through the first, second, and third grades.

Every day after school, she went to the karate studio and sat on the sidelines watching the classes. She knew she was clumsy and was afraid of looking foolish, so she didn't get up to exercise and practice with the other children. Lucas never forced her. He knew how difficult life was for Bari.

Her grandparents, in their overprotective love for her, had instilled a fear inside her, a fear of everything. Bari was afraid to try anything new, afraid she would get hurt. Her grandparents warned against playing on the slide or the monkey bars. They warned about strangers. They warned about swimming. Bari was crippled with fear.

Although Bari Lynn was eight and no longer needed a nanny, Janice wanted Maria to stay on. Maria, not meaning to hurt Bari, reinforced the child's fears by constantly reminding Bari to be careful and that the world was dangerous. When the other children played on the playground, they teased her because she was heavyset. Unlike her mother, she could not speak up for herself, so she withdrew further.

Her strong mother had been her voice all of her life, so when Bari was alone with children her age, she was awkward and unable to make friends.

One afternoon, after school, Bari arrived at Lucas' studio as she always did. He looked at her swollen eyes and red, blotchy face, and he knew she'd been crying. Class was about to start, but Lucas felt he needed to talk to Bari alone in the back room, away from the others.

"Mike, you take the class through beginning exercises," Lucas said to one of the students. "I'll be back in a few minutes."

"Yes, Sensei." Mike bowed and began instructing the class.

Lucas knelt beside Bari Lynn. "Hey, how ya doin'?" he asked in a Chicago accent meant to get her to crack a smile.

She shrugged, and he sobered.

"Let's go in the back and have a talk."

She shrugged again. "I'm okay," she said.

"Come on."

Bari got up and followed Lucas. When they got into the back room, he pointed to a chair. "Sit down. Let's have a talk."

She sat and looked at him, then began to cry. "All the kids hate me, and everyone makes fun of me, calling me fat and ugly. And they're right: I am fat and ugly. I hate my life. I wish I could die."

Lucas knew it would help if she took up martial arts, but Bari was too self-conscious to try. Every day, Lucas had watched her sit on the sidelines, leaning against the wall and observing the class. His heart went out to his adopted daughter.

"Listen, I have an idea," Lucas said. It was then that he knew she needed to be trained privately. Once trained, she shouldn't feel like anyone would laugh at her and would not be so embarrassed and afraid of failure. If he could convince her, this just might be the answer. Lucas would make the effort. He would help her.

"You know, I was thinking. Why don't I train you in judo or karate? Your choice. I will teach you privately. That way, you won't have to feel uncomfortable with the other kids. What do you think?"

"I don't really want to learn. I'm afraid to spar, even with you. I might get hurt."

"How about if you don't spar? I'll just teach you after the class is done. It will be just us until Mom gets here. What do you think?"

"I'm so scared I'll get hurt or look like a fat cow."

"Bari, you can't spend your life being afraid. And you can't worry about what other people think of you. I won't think you're a fat cow."

"But I don't know how to stop being scared."

"Listen to me," Lucas said, taking her hands in his. "Pull the energy and strength from your chi. Do you know what that is?"

"No," Bari said.

"It's your life energy. It's right here." Lucas pointed to the area of his solar plexus. "You have great inner strength in your chi. It's a strength that you have never known was there. I promise you won't get hurt if you train with me. And I promise you won't make a fool of yourself, and I will never think badly of you. Will you try for me?" he asked.

Eight-year-old Bari Lynn studied her stepfather. He'd always been so kind to her and her mother. His warm and sincere gaze never left hers. He was the only father she had ever known, and she trusted him completely.

"Okay, I'll try," she said.

"Good, then we'll start tomorrow," Lucas said, getting up. He wet a towel in the sink and handed it to Bari. "Here, wash your face. It will make you feel better, and then come on out and watch the class."

Bari Lynn did not excel at her training at first, but Lucas continued to work with her every day. Lucas made it fun instead of work. When Bari messed up, he laughed *with* her rather than *at* her, and soon, she was confident enough to laugh at herself.

Three weeks later, Lucas and Bari Lynn decided she no longer needed a nanny. Bari had become more self-sufficient and appeared to be coming out of her shell and growing up.

She was uncoordinated because she'd never used her muscles, and it took her a long time to accustom her body to the martial arts. However, Lucas was patient.

As they trained, Bari began to open up to Lucas even more than she had before, and he listened to her in a way that no one ever had. She had always loved him, always considered him more than a father. He was a friend and easier to talk to than her mother. But now, she'd begun to tell him her deepest secrets: how her mother made her feel small and worthless and how her grandparents did not see her as having any will. Even though she was only eight, she wanted a voice in her family, a voice in her decisions, and a voice in her life.

Lucas knew that because she was shy, lonely, and tied up in silence, she'd made food her best friend. The other kids had been outside riding their bikes, but Bari had never joined them. Though she had the best bike on the market, no one had ever taught her to ride.

Before she started studying with Lucas, all she did was sit on the sidelines of the class, and as soon as Lucas was finished, she asked to be taken home.

Once she got into the house, she would change into a long tee shirt and sit in front of the television with a bag of potato chips and a Coke. Her unhealthy eating habits had not only put extra weight on her body, but she'd begun to have problems with her complexion, breaking out in pimples, which made her even more self-conscious.

She had to study hard just to be an average student, so even the smart kids shunned her. Until she had begun training with Lucas, Bari was alone most of the time.

Now, every day, Lucas trained Bari after the rest of the students went home. Once they'd finished their work, Lucas and Bari would sit on the floor at the studio and talk.

"Dad, I wish the other kids liked me."

"Before the other kids can like you, you must learn to like you, Bari. How can you expect other people to like you if you don't like yourself?"

"I don't like me. I hate myself."

"I know, and you shouldn't. You are a beautiful girl with so much potential. I can see the potential in you."

"Really, you can?"

"Yep. I sure can. What would you like to do with your life?"

"You mean when I grow up? I don't know."

"If you had a choice of doing anything at all, what would it be?"

"This is going to sound silly, considering I get such lousy grades."

"Nothing is silly. What is it you want to do?"

"I'd like to be a veterinarian."

"I know you love animals."

"Mom doesn't. She won't let me get a dog. I've been begging her, but she says the dog will make a mess of the house."

"Maybe I can talk to her, and we'll see if she might consider letting you have a pet," Lucas smiled.

"Do you think I could be a vet? I mean, really, do you think so? I mean, am I smart enough?"

"Sure. I think you could do anything you want if you put your mind to it."

"Dad…"

"Yes?"

"I'm going to try harder in school."

"Mom and I will help you every step of the way. And I'll talk to Mom about getting a dog."

Janice didn't want the responsibility of a dog. She thought it would be far too much trouble. So Lucas compromised, and they decided to get a kitten. "There is no training with a cat," Lucas told Janice. "They automatically use the litter box, and they don't chew."

"But they scratch, and they claw up the furniture. Oh, Lucas, there you go again. You're always trying to make someone happy." She smiled and shrugged her shoulders. "You know that's one of the things I love about you."

"Well, isn't that what life is all about, Jan? Besides, Bari is a good kid. I know I'm not her birth father, but I've raised her like my own child."

"Yes, you really have. I couldn't have asked for a better father for Bari. You have been wonderful, not only to Bari but to me, too." *He has his faults, but so do I.* "Sometimes, I don't know how you put up with me."

"I don't know how I do, either," Lucas joked.

"Shut up," Janice said, laughing. "You put up with me because you love me."

"I do, Jan. I really do love you. You've given me a home and, a family and a life. Before you, I was searching. I always felt alone."

Janice leaned over and kissed Lucas. Then she closed the door and turned off the light. He walked over to her, kissed her, and unbuttoned her blouse.

"Have I ever told you that you're the best lover?"

"Tell me again. I love to hear it," he said.

Bari was thrilled the following day when Lucas took her to the local animal shelter, where she picked out a kitten. She named the cat Harry. He was a tiny black and white tuxedo cat who adored Bari. This little kitten gave Bari the love, acceptance, and fulfillment she did not receive from children.

The two became the best of friends. Harry followed Bari everywhere. As soon as she got into the house, Harry met her at the door. When Bari did her homework, Harry sat on the edge of the bed and waited. In the evenings, after dinner, Harry played with Bari until they both fell asleep on her bed with his head resting beside Bari's on her pillow.

And so it was that her stepfather, Lucas, and the martial arts changed Bari's life. Over the next nine years, she slimmed down, got her hair straightened, and became best friends with her stepfather.

CHAPTER SIXTY-ONE

THE OFFICES OF MOSSAD
ISRAEL 1972

ELAN AMSEL RETURNED to work after taking a week off to bury his mother in Jerusalem. After he had left Jerusalem to join Mossad, his mother moved in with his brother and sister-in-law. They were polite at the funeral, but Elan knew they resented him for leaving his mother and father's business behind.

He shrugged it off. He was tired of caring. People demanded far too much. They expected him to spend his days living a life that sucked the will to live right out of him.

Five years ago, when he returned from the Six-Day War, he realized where he belonged, and it was not selling tomatoes at the market. As soon as he'd joined Mossad, he felt a rejuvenation. He began to see the world with new eyes. Aryeh had tried to tell him he was turning his back on his responsibilities to his family.

Sometimes, he felt bad about leaving his mother when he was alone at night. But why was it always his duty to care for her? Why not Aryeh? He'd had her for a few years. It was time for his brother to take a turn. When he thought of it all that way, it was easy to rationalize his decision. Besides, guilt was a wasted emotion. It didn't serve any purpose.

Tonight, he'd turn on some music and have a few drinks. In fact, he'd have as many cocktails as it took to forget all about the funeral and the accusing face of his brother, Aryeh.

"Amsel, go home already, it's late," said Zui Zami, the director of Mossad. "Get some rest. I'm sure it's been a long week for you, with your family and all."

"I'm glad to be back, Zui. This is my home. This is where I belong."

Zui nodded. "I feel the same. I know what you mean."

Michael Harari picked up his briefcase. "Good night, you two. I'm exhausted. I'll see you both in the morning."

Elan nodded a silent goodnight. He was the last one to go home, and nothing was waiting for him at his apartment but an empty fridge and an answering machine full of messages to call Marva. Marva—the last of a long line of women he grew tired of as soon as they pressured him to marry.

When Janice divorced him, and then he was rejected by Katja, he decided that he was never getting married again. And the more he dated, the more it seemed to him that was what every woman wanted. So when one of his girlfriends would start to nag about the future, he dropped her cold without any messy explanations and went on to the next one.

Elan knew he was handsome, and there was always another one in line. And quite frankly, he didn't feel that any of the women he had been with were worth the effort. He lit a cigarette and leaned back in his chair.

"I'm going home, Elan. I'll see you tomorrow, yes?"

"Yes, of course, Zui. You have a good night," Elan said.

Now Elan was alone in the office, looking down at the street. He could hear the sounds of the automobiles and people outside, but the room where he sat was peaceful. The sun was painting the sky in varying shades of orange and fuchsia. It had been a hot August day, and the following day was predicted to be just as hot. Elan thought it would be good if they got some rain to cool things off.

In a few minutes, he'd leave and pick up a falafel sandwich from the café down the road, then go home to watch the opening ceremony of the Olympics on television. He hated the fact that Munich had been given the honor of hosting the Olympics. The last time the games were held in Germany, Adolf Hitler, that son of a bitch, had been in power. Elan hated Germans. He could not forgive them for what had happened and blamed every German for not standing up to Hitler.

Over the years, he'd made many friends who'd come to Israel after surviving the torture and death camps the Germans built. And whenever he thought of Germany, it brought back memories of his one true love, Katja, the girl he could not marry because of her German blood. He didn't want to admit that he knew in his heart that she, too, was a victim of Hitler's insanity. And if she was, how many other Germans were victims? It bothered him to be so soft. It was easier to hate than to forgive.

Elan believed that Katja was the only woman he would ever really love. He'd tried to tell her. He'd tried to explain, but things had gone too far. So now he had a steady string of women who moved in and out of his life, like a slow-moving freight train, without too much excitement. They gave him what he needed, but he didn't give much thought to their feelings.

After all, Elan Amsel prided himself in the fact that he never lied to any of them. He never promised any single one of them that he would marry her. Not once had he ever told one of these women that he loved them. The only two women he'd ever said those words to were his wife and Katja. And he'd come to believe that he had been mistaken when he'd said it to Janice.

In his new life, when he dated a woman, he took her out to nice dinners, sometimes dancing because he still loved American rock and roll, and then to bed. That was all there was to the relationship. When she even hinted at wanting more, Elan quite simply disappeared.

This most recent one, Marva, had really begun to care for him. She'd tried to show what a good wife she could be by trying to take charge of his life. He'd had enough of that with his ex-wife, Janice.

He felt a chill run down his spine when he thought about her. She was one controlling pain in the ass. It was strange, but he never, not even for a minute, missed his ex-wife after she left.

He knew that she was going over the line when Marva began showing up at his apartment with food, trying to do his laundry, and telling him he smoked and drank too much. She'd cheerfully insisted on cleaning his kitchen and bathroom. As he watched her on her knees scrubbing, he began to feel smothered.

It was time to say goodbye. He'd let the phone ring, trying to avoid confrontation. But she was not giving up, so the next time she called, he would have to tell her firmly that it was over.

Elan sorted through the papers on his desk. He locked up the top secret ones and put the others in a pile according to their priority for addressing the next day. Then he locked the door to the office and went home.

When he awoke at six o'clock the following morning, his phone was already ringing. He knew it had to be Marva. He was annoyed and quickly losing patience.

"This is Elan Amsel," he said into the heavy black receiver.

"Elan, it's Marva."

"Yeah?"

"I hope you're doing all right after the funeral. Is there anything I can do for you?"

"I'm fine."

"Do you need anything? Can I bring some food to your apartment, maybe?"

"No, I'm fine."

Marva had asked to go with him to his mother's funeral, but he refused, telling her he needed to be with his family. It wasn't true. Elan had grown such a hard shell that he didn't need anyone anymore. In fact, he told himself that if he ever saw Katja again, he wouldn't have any feelings left for her, either.

"Elan, I know this is a hard time for you, so I will not bother you. Why don't you call me when you need me? I'll be here, waiting," Marva said.

Elan heard the tears she was trying to disguise in her voice, and he was eager to get off the phone and away from this clutching, clawing, needy woman. "Yeah, that's a good idea," he said, trying to control the desire to yell at her, to tell her to leave him alone, to go away already, to quit grasping onto him, and to let him breathe.

"I hope I'll hear from you soon. Please, Elan, if you need anything…"

She was still talking when Elan hung up the phone. *Women*! he thought.

Elan went to a nightclub a few blocks from his office that night. He was tired of Marva. It was time to find a new and less demanding woman. As he sat having a drink, Elan glanced across the bar and saw a young Israeli woman. She wore a black dress that fit like a glove and had long, tight ringlets of curly, dark hair that surrounded an arresting face with olive skin and dark eyes. She appeared to be in her early twenties. Even on five-inch heels, she was as graceful as a deer.

"Send that girl over there a drink, whatever she's drinking. Tell her it's from me," Elan told the bartender, tossing a bill on the bar.

The girl looked up at him when she received the drink, and her eyes sparkled like black diamonds. She looked him up and down, then smiled. She stared at him for a moment, and he returned her smile. Then she laughed and turned away. The girl got up and walked out of the club without touching the drink he'd sent.

Elan was shocked, a little angry, but strangely intrigued. This girl's behavior was highly unusual. Women usually fell at his feet. He threw another bill down on the bar to pay for his tab, then got up to follow the girl.

She wasn't hard to find. In fact, she was standing outside with some guy. They were laughing and talking. When he looked at her, Elan felt his back stiffen. Then he chewed on the side of his lower lip. *Fuck her. I don't need this shit. Women are nothing but a waste of time anyway.* Turning around, Elan headed back home to his apartment.

But that night, he dreamed of the girl with the long, dark hair and the piercing, black eyes.

Two days later, Elan was at work. The employees had access to a kitchen in the back of the office. They had a coffee pot that boiled water, a refrigerator, card tables, and folding chairs. Elan was in the kitchen pouring a cup of instant coffee for himself. Harari walked into the room and patted Elan's shoulder.

"Amsel, I want you to meet Nina, our newest agent. She is brilliant. She served one term in the IDF and two years in training. Can you believe she's made it into Mossad, and she's only twenty-two?"

Elan turned around to see the same girl from the club who had spurned him. There was no doubt in his mind that it was her. He'd never seen anyone else with those laughing, diamond eyes.

"Nina, this is Elan Amsel. You won't meet a more devoted agent," Harari said.

"It's a pleasure to meet you, Elan Amsel," Nina said. He thought she sounded like she was mocking him at least a little. Infuriating!

"Nina has been trained for special ops."

"Impressive," Elan said with just a touch of sarcasm, "for such a young girl."

"I've always wanted to be a part of Mossad," Nina said.

Elan nodded. "Well, here you are…"

"Stay away from her, Amsel. She's young and innocent."

Nina laughed. Damn, she was bold and sure of herself. Her confidence annoyed Elan. Her arrogance incensed but intrigued him. In many ways, she reminded him of himself, and that really got under his skin for some reason.

Elan couldn't help but watch Nina as she moved through the office. She wore a colorful cotton skirt and a white sweater over a black camisole. He noticed that she wasn't particularly curvy, and he usually liked his women curvy. She was slender, with muscular legs and thin, strong arms. He knew she'd undergone rigorous training to be accepted into Mossad, and he had to admire that. But most of the other women he'd worked with had not been so damn delicate and feminine-looking, so strangely irresistible.

This Nina appeared to be an odd mixture of opposites, a mix of both strength and frailty. How was that possible? Elan found himself pondering that question as he stared at Nina several times a day. For some reason, she seemed to be unaware of his attention. It was odd.

Most women were flattered if he even looked their way, usually enough to fall into his bed. So, what the hell was wrong with this one? *Maybe she's a lesbian*? This thought soothed his wounded ego.

After she'd ignored him for several days, Elan couldn't stand it anymore. He walked over to her desk.

"I'm sorry if I made a bad first impression. I'm Elan."

"I know who you are. Remember, we were introduced? Besides, your reputation with women precedes you," Nina said, not looking up from her work.

"Listen. I'd like to take you for lunch today. Would you consider it?"

She laughed. "You don't give up easily, do you?"

"Never. I'm an Israeli. We don't give up."

She laughed even louder. "Touché," she said. "That's the truest statement I've ever heard."

"You look Sephardic, are you?"

"Yes, I am a Sephardic Jew of Spanish descent."

"So am I…"

"I can tell. Your dark features sort of give it away," she said.

"Has anyone ever told you that you're beautiful?"

"Only men who want to get into my pants."

He was shocked by the boldness of her answer. Elan was at a loss for words. He just stared at her.

Nina laughed again. "Well, it's true, isn't it? That is what you want."

"I can't say I don't. But it's not all I want. I want to get to know you," Elan said, and he meant it. This girl was different. She was, well, she was fascinating.

"I won't go to lunch with you today."

He looked at her, disappointed.

"But…"

Elan hung on her every word.

"I will allow you to take me to dinner tonight. I expect that if you want to see me again, you will take me somewhere nice and then behave like a perfect gentleman. If you find it too difficult to be on your best behavior, then it will be our first and last date," Nina said, looking up into his eyes.

Was there such a thing as a black star? Her eyes sparkled like the stars but were as black as night. She was mesmerizing.

"I will be on my best behavior. I promise." He bowed slightly in mock servitude.

"Good. I'll give you my address, and you can pick me up at eight."

"Yes, princess," he said, smiling.

"And, Elan, be on time."

He laughed. What a bold woman.

Elan made reservations at the finest restaurant in Tel Aviv. It was above his price range, but he wanted to show this girl that he had class and sophistication.

He arrived at Nina's apartment exactly five minutes before eight. She invited him in. He was surprised to see that she still lived with her parents. It was not a fancy place. In fact, from what he could see, the family was lower-middle class at best. Nina looked lovely. She wore a simple, fitted, black dress, just an inch above her knees, and a single strand of pearls. Her usually wild hair was tamed into a sleek knot at the nape of her slender neck.

"This is Elan," she said to her parents. "He works with me."

"A pleasure to meet you," Elan said.

"Come on, let's go," Nina said. "I won't be too late," she told her mother and bent to kiss her cheek.

Elan wasn't sure what to say as they drove to the restaurant. It wasn't like him to be at such a loss for words. There was an awkward, uncomfortable silence.

"Do you like American music?" he asked, thinking he might turn on the radio.

"Not particularly." Damn, this girl was difficult.

When they arrived at the restaurant, Elan jumped out of the car to open Nina's door. It had been years since he'd done that for any woman. She got out, and he followed her inside. They were seated by a window overlooking the street. She didn't pay any attention to what he ordered, and she didn't ask him to order for her. In fact, she ordered the most expensive dish on the menu.

Hmm, she doesn't like me, Elan thought. She doesn't think much of me at all. He'd heard that if a woman ordered the most expensive thing on the menu, it meant that she didn't care if her date liked her or not. But instead of being discouraged, Nina's inconsiderate behavior only drove Elan's desire to make this woman want him.

"You're a lot older than me. Maybe, something like fifteen years?"

She saw the worried look on his face, and then she laughed again. "Don't worry so much, Elan Amsel. It's okay. I like older men. They know what they want. Not like the boys I've dated who are wishy-washy mama's boys," she said.

"Well, I'm glad you like older men. Then perhaps I might have a chance?" He didn't tell her, but he was actually seventeen years older than she was.

She laughed. "Who knows?" She shrugged her shoulders. "We'll have to see."

She was clever and witty. The banter kept him on his toes. But when the food arrived, and he saw her tiny, delicate hands as she held the fork, his heart ached. What was it about this small-boned, big-haired girl that touched something deep inside of him?

"I'd like to ask you a serious question."

"Already, Elan? You want to get serious already?" She smiled and winked at him.

"No, I mean, yes…"

"Wait a minute. I thought you weren't wishy-washy." She giggled.

"I wanted to know why you, such a pretty young girl, would want to join Mossad? It's such a dangerous job."

"Yes, well," she said, and her face suddenly grew serious. Her eyes met his and held the stare. "I am an Israeli. For me, life is always going to be dangerous."

He nodded. "Yes, but Mossad will only make it more so…"

She sat looking at him silently for several minutes. Then she began to speak:

"Four years ago, my sister and I were supposed to meet at an outdoor café for a quick lunch. She had called me earlier that day to tell me she had a surprise and wanted to tell me in person. We were going to meet at twelve-thirty. The restaurant was in the middle of town and was very busy. She said that if she could, she would try to get there early and get a table so we wouldn't have to wait.

"I had an appointment for physical therapy on my shoulder and arm earlier that morning. I had hurt them when I fell off my bike, and I'd been going to a therapist. My therapist was late that day. It was unusual for her to be late. But because she was not on time, I was running late to meet my sister.

"I was rushing through town, first on a bus, then on foot, trying to get to the restaurant, when I heard all kinds of noise and commotion. There was a loud, thundering roar that filled the street. People were everywhere, running in every direction. I had no idea what was going on. I grabbed the sleeve of a man as he tried to race by me, and I asked him what was happening. He said that there was a bombing at a café right on the main street. I ran as fast as I could toward the café where I knew my sister was waiting, but it was too late. She was blown to pieces, along with over a hundred other people. If I had been ten minutes earlier, I would have been one of those people.

"I stood on the street feeling as if I would faint from the smoke, and I kept calling out my sister's name as if she could hear me. No one stopped to look at me. They were all too terrified. I finally found what was left of her body. I screamed until I fell to my knees and cried. Nobody came to help me, no one at all. There was nothing else I could do, so I picked myself up, and with chills running down my back, I walked to the bus stop and went home.

"The following day, I found out what the surprise was that she had wanted to tell me. Her boyfriend had been notified that she was dead by the police. He called our house. He wanted to help with the shiva. When he told me that they had just gotten engaged, I knew right away that it was the surprise that she was going to tell me."

"My God," Elan said.

"Yes." Nina nodded her head, a sad expression in her dark eyes. "And from that moment, I knew I wanted to be a part of Mossad. I decided then that I was willing to risk my life to protect the people of Israel. I didn't see combat when I was in the IDF, but once I finished my term, I went back and worked hard to pass the special training." She smiled, but the sparkle had left her eyes. "And so that brings me to right now. And here I am, sitting with you and having dinner." She shrugged her shoulders. "That's it. That's my story."

When Elan was with a woman, his mind was always on sex. But here with Nina, he didn't think at all about seducing her. He reached out and took her hand to comfort her, never thinking she might get the wrong idea. "I'm so sorry," he said.

"Yes, so am I. Anyway, let's not talk about sad things." She pulled her hand away. "So tell me, Elan Amsel, what's your story? Why are you in Mossad?"

"I'm not sure what you want to know. After that, I was married to an American girl for a while. It didn't work out, and I joined Mossad."

"That's it?"

"I suppose I always knew I belonged working in service to Israel in some capacity. I love this country, and I love our people. When I was called up to fight in the Six-Day War, it triggered something inside me, and I knew I wanted to join Mossad."

"You had to retrain?"

"Yes, but I didn't mind. It felt good to get back into shape. I served a lot of time in the Air Force. Much more than one term. And even then, I was always interested in special ops. So, for me, Mossad felt like the right choice."

"Fair enough," she said, nodding her head.

When Elan walked Nina to the door of her apartment building, he leaned over to kiss her goodnight. She gently covered his lips with her palm.

"Not on the first date," she whispered, and her voice was so breathy and soft that he felt himself getting an erection. He was embarrassed. It was unlike him, but Elan was afraid she would notice the bulge in his pants and start laughing at him, so he turned and left quickly.

The next day, Nina did not come to work. Elan kept watching the door to the office, wondering where she was. By the end of the day, he was distraught. Had he done something wrong? He wanted to call her, but he didn't have the number. If he asked for her number at the office, everyone would question why he wanted to contact her. Elan wasn't ready to share his feelings for Nina with anyone. These things were best kept to oneself. That way, he wouldn't have to bear the shame if things didn't work out.

Elan went home from work that evening angry with himself for allowing Nina's absence to bother him but discounted the idea of going to her house to check on her. Elan didn't want to screw this up by appearing overly needy. He knew firsthand how that affected him from experience with his former girlfriends. He was too upset to eat, so he poured a drink and then another, hoping it would help him fall asleep. It didn't. He lay awake most of the night and finally drifted off into a fitful but deep sleep at four o'clock in the morning.

It was a little after six o'clock in the morning when Elan's phone rang. The sound of the phone shook him awake. He cleared his throat and took a sip of water from the glass by the bed, not wanting to sound like he just woke up. Then he picked up the receiver.

"Amsel. It's Harari. Get your ass out of bed and get into the office. Some fucking terrorist group has broken into the sleeping quarters of the Israeli athletes at the Olympics in Munich. The terrorists have taken the athletes hostage."

"Holy shit. I'll be right there," Elan said. When Elan served in the IDF, he was taught to respond to any situation in seconds. He didn't wash his face, brush his teeth, or comb his hair. He dressed quickly and got right into the car.

Elan arrived at the office, and only a select few of the Mossad agents, including Nina, were there. Zui Zami slammed his fist on the desk to quiet the others. "Dayan will be here any minute," he said.

Elan looked around at his fellow Mossad agents, who looked

disheveled but alert. This was Israel, and they all knew they must be prepared for anything to happen at any time.

Moshe Dayan, the Minister of Defense, entered at nine o'clock, and everyone grew silent. All eyes were on him, waiting to hear what he had to say.

"Shalom, my brothers and sisters. I have just finished a meeting with Prime Minister Golda Meir. As you already know, Israel has another challenge to meet." He stopped for a moment to look around the room. "I am assuming that you have all been briefed on the main facts of the situation at hand. The terrorist group who broke into the Munich Olympics call themselves Black September. Right now, we are not sure how many of them there are. But we know that they have taken eleven of our athletes hostage.

"We believe the West German police were purposely lax in protecting our people. That comes as no surprise to any of you, I am sure. However, we have no proof of this accusation, so we must act accordingly.

"The terrorists demand that we release more than two hundred political prisoners. If we meet their demands, they say they will release our athletes alive." Dayan took a deep breath, and then he sighed. "As all of you know, Israel does not negotiate with terrorists, so we need to work as quickly as possible to devise a plan to rescue our athletes."

Everyone was silent, alert, ready.

"Director, I suggest we parachute our teams into the Olympic grounds and then take the terrorists by surprise."

"Very well."

Mossad did not have enough time to carry out this plan. A few hours later, Black September took the hostages to the airport. The West German police tried to stop them, but their efforts were small, and it seemed to Israel that they were more gestures than actual efforts.

"Where do you think they are taking them?" Director Zami asked Defense Minister Dayan.

"I don't know. Could be Syria, Lebanon, who knows?"

"How can we plan a rescue if we don't know where they are going?" The Director ran his fingers through his hair.

As they worked on devising a new strategy, the Mossad agents sat in the office and watched the events in Munich unfold in real-time on the television. They sat helplessly and riveted as they saw the plane with the athletes on board blow up and turn into a ball of fire in midair. No one said a word. They just looked around the room at each other. Then Harari spoke, "Do you think they are all dead?"

Minister Dayan shrugged his shoulders. "I don't know."

It was less than five minutes before a newscaster came on the screen. "It is a sad day for all of us," he said. "All the hostages are dead. Two were killed in their rooms this morning. Their bodies have been found. The rest were on board the aircraft that exploded. They are all gone, all gone."

When they heard the news, several of the Mossad agents cried.

The phone rang. Minister Dayan answered it. "Yes, Prime Minister, they are all dead. He listened for a few minutes, then placed the receiver back on the hook."

Minister Dayan cleared his throat and looked around at the faces of the agents. Then he got up to speak again.

"As you all know, the group who call themselves Black September murdered Israeli athletes competing in the Munich Olympics.

"Right at this very moment, the rest of the countries participating in the Olympics are meeting to decide if the games should be stopped out of respect for those who died or if they should continue. I don't see how the games could possibly go on. But the truth is that their decision will make very little difference to us.

"Right now, it is our job to stand strong. We need to show them that Israel cannot be terrorized. We must be sure that terrorists are made aware that Israel is a force to be reckoned with. Our vengeance must be shocking and powerful. However, it is important that, although the world will know the truth, there is no proof that Israel is responsible for retaliation.

"Those of you here today were hand-selected by the Prime

Minister and me. You are probably asking yourself why you were chosen. I will tell you. It is because you are not the most well-known of our agents. If we were to send our most well-known agents, the Palestine Liberation Organization would recognize them immediately. It is important that you can move around undetected to locate and then eliminate anyone responsible for the atrocities that occurred against our people in Munich today. Two days from now, we will bomb ten PLO bases in Syria and Lebanon. This is to be only the beginning."

Dayan looked across the room at Harari and said, "Harari, I am putting you in charge of organizing a team of agents. Your agents will do whatever is necessary to learn the names and locations of everyone involved with Black September. Then, once we have a list of names and places, we will see to it that terrorists know that Israel is a powerful country. They will know that the Jews of today are not the same as the ones who walked into the concentration camps. Israel will not back down. Do you understand what I want you to do, Agent Harari?"

"Yes, sir."

"Amongst ourselves, we name this mission of revenge Operation Wrath of God. And by God, we will unleash a wrath that has never been seen before," Dayan said. His body was shaking with anger.

Michael Harari stood up. "This will be a very dangerous mission, as you all know. Give it some thought before you sign on. Be sure you are willing to commit to all that will be asked of you. If you are at all unsure, then speak now. If you need more time to think, then speak now. There will be no turning back once you agree to take on this mission. You will be required to carry out the tasks assigned to you regardless of the dangers or difficulties involved." Harari stood silent for a few moments. "Since no one has left the room, I am to assume that you are all in." The agents nodded.

Then, slowly and clearly, Michael Harari called out each of the names of the eight agents gathered in the room. He called them one at a time, hesitating before he continued. Amongst the chosen to be in Harari's group were Nina and Elan. The room was silent except for the voice of Harari. "Elan Amsel, are you with us?"

"Yes," Elan said without hesitation.

"Boaz Ben-Shalom, are you with us?"

"Yes."

"Nina Sofer, are you with us?"

"Yes."

He continued until he had confirmed that all eight agents had pledged their willingness to participate. Before they were chosen, the lives of each of these agents had been thoroughly examined, and all of them were deemed trustworthy. Minister Dayan and Prime Minister Meir knew everything about them: their lives, their pasts, their mistakes, their secrets, what they had for breakfast in the morning, and how they took their coffee. Everything about them was carefully scrutinized before they were selected.

"First, we will form two squads of four people each. Then, you will pay a visit to the PLO snitches that we have working for us. Negotiate with them, but pay them whatever you have to pay them to find out as much as you can, and do this as quickly as possible."

CHAPTER SIXTY-TWO

A LITTLE OVER a month following the attacks at the Olympics that had occurred on October 10, 1972, the Operation Wrath of God squad met again.

"From what I have been told, approximately twelve to fifteen people were involved. I have a rough list. Not all the names or locations are on this list," one of the agents reported.

"Good work. Now, we have a starting point. We can begin working with what we have and then continue to gather more information," Harari said. "Meanwhile, I want the rest of you to continue to infiltrate Palestinian organizations and find out whatever else you can about the members of Black September. As we add names to our list, each of you will be given additional assassination assignments," Harari said. "And get ready because we are about to unleash the wrath of God."

CHAPTER SIXTY-THREE

ON THE EVENING of October 16th, Nina sat at the bar in a posh restaurant in Rome. She looked more than fetching in her tight black dress and high black pumps. Her wild curls were tamed into a sleek French twist.

Nina wasn't a drinker. In fact, she didn't really care for the taste of alcohol, but she took small sips from a glass of white wine as she quietly watched the table of men who were eating just a few feet away from her. With thick black eyeliner framing her large almond eyes and light pink lipstick applied perfectly to her full lips, she looked like an Italian model. The bartender made flirtatious comments to her, and she laughed so sweetly that the men at the table began to flirt with her as well.

Nina was in control. She knew what they wanted, and that was okay. It kept them intrigued with her as she charmingly teased and toyed with all of them. She'd studied languages and could speak fluent Italian without an accent. The men at the table finally asked her to join them for a drink, but she refused, saying that it was late and she had to be up early in the morning to meet with a photographer for a shoot. She took a bill from her purse and placed it on the bar beside her drink, but she didn't leave.

One of the men at the table shrugged. "It's a shame. Maybe another time," he said. Then he turned to the others at the table and said in Arabic, "Let's call it a night. I'm tired."

Nina understood as she spoke Arabic as well.

When the man's check arrived, the one who had spoken to her picked it up and took out his wallet. Nina stood, straightened her dress, and then excused herself to go to the ladies' room. When the bathroom door closed, she quickly checked under the stalls to be sure that she was alone. Then she took out her radio and called Elan.

"They're leaving now," she spoke softly into the mouthpiece.

"For God's sake, be careful," he said.

"I will. But you should be ready. I am calculating that he will be there in less than ten minutes." The man whom she was referring to was Wael Zwaiter. Mossad knew that Zwaiter was directly involved in the assassinations in Munich.

"Everything is ready," Elan said.

At a small house in Palestine, a young woman was feeding a baby when the doorbell rang. She wiped her hands and secured the child in his high chair before answering the door.

"I have a flower delivery for the niece of Wael Zwaiter," the delivery boy said. "Is that you?"

The woman nodded. "Yes, I am the niece of Wael Zwaiter."

"Can you please sign here?"

She couldn't write but scribbled an "X" and took the package inside. She had never received flowers before. She opened the paper to find a beautiful bouquet of red, pink, and white roses, surrounded by baby's breath and white orchids cascading down the sides of a tall glass vase. The only person who could have sent the flowers was her husband, but the boy who delivered them had specifically mentioned her uncle, who was out of town. *What a surprise. They must be from my uncle, but why?*

Then she shook her head. Something was very strange. It was a magnificent bouquet. It had to be expensive. She would place a call to her husband because she had no idea where to begin to reach her uncle.

The phone rang, and her husband picked it up. "Thank you for the flowers," she said.

Her husband hated to receive calls at work. He was far too busy to be bothered with women's nonsense. "I didn't send flowers. You are not supposed to call me here," he said and hung up. She swallowed her pain. That was just the way he was. Men were cold. She'd learned that years ago, but sometimes it still hurt.

The delivery boy had mentioned her uncle. Although he was not her blood, he was, in fact, her husband's uncle. They had always had a good relationship. She thought the flowers must be a belated gift for her birthday, which had passed a few weeks ago, although no one ever acknowledged it before. She took the card that came with the flowers, but she couldn't read. However, she knew that her neighbor's husband could.

So she picked up the baby and went to her neighbor's house next door. The husband should be home from work by now. She hoped he would take a minute to tell her what the card said. She knocked on the door with the baby on her hip and the card in her pocket.

"Can your husband please read this for me?" she asked her neighbor. The two women were friendly but not close.

"You can ask him. He's right in the living room. Come in."

The man agreed to read it and took the card and the envelope. "It says on the envelope that this is a condolence card."

"What does that mean?"

"Has someone recently died in your family?" the neighbor asked.

"No." The young woman shook her head. "Not recently."

He took the small folded paper out of the envelope. It was made of fine linen paper, and in beautiful cursive handwriting, it said: "This is just a reminder that we do not forgive, and we never forget," he read it aloud.

What did this mean? She asked herself. A cold chill ran over her.

Perhaps she should call her aunt and get his number, then call her uncle in Rome.

"Thank you so much for reading this for me," she said. The baby had begun to squirm in her arms. He probably needed to be changed. She would change his diaper and then call her uncle. Again, she thought how strange all of this was. But the delivery boy had mentioned her uncle. This must have something to do with him. She would call and tell him what had just happened.

Wael Zwaiter closed the door to his hotel room. He was staying in a suite in a plush establishment. It was a cool night, with just enough of a breeze to refresh the soul. He opened the window and took a deep breath of the sweet air. Then he sat down on the bed to remove his shoes, but three Mossad agents came out of the bathroom before he had a chance to untie the laces.

Between the lazy night air and the alcohol he consumed, Zwaiter was disorientated and caught off guard. It only took a few seconds for him to realize what was happening. He jumped up and tried to run, but it was too late. He never heard the gunshots because he died almost instantly.

After pumping bullets into Zwaiter's body, the Mossad agents checked to ensure Zwaiter was dead. Then they quietly left the room, locking the door behind them. Once they were out, the gloves they'd worn were removed and tossed into a trash incinerator just a few feet down the hall so as not to leave any fingerprints. Elan and the other Mossad agents heard the phone ringing in Zwaiter's room.

"I guess the flowers were delivered," Elan said. "The niece is probably calling to see what's going on."

"Yep. Well, she'll understand soon enough," one of the other two agents answered. "Let's go pick Nina up and get something to eat. I'm starving."

CHAPTER SIXTY-FOUR

December 7, 1972

Mahmoud Hamshari was looking out the window at the beautiful city where he lived in France. It was a cold but picturesque December morning. A group of children was playing with a sled in the snow. They were laughing and calling out to each other. Just watching them, Hamshari had to smile. After all, he had children of his own.

The phone rang on his desk, and he rushed to pick it up. He was expecting a call from a childhood friend who remained in contact with him through the years. The man, like Hamshari, was an activist for Palestine. He was traveling and promised to call him as soon as he returned safely home. Mahmoud assumed that this was the call he'd been waiting for. He could get on with his day once he'd spoken with his friend.

Mahmoud Hamshari picked up the telephone. "Hello?"

"Good morning. Is this Mahmoud Hamshari?"

"Who is this calling?"

"My name is Giovanni Battistelli. I am an Italian journalist. I am looking for Mahmoud Hamshari. I would like to interview him for a magazine article."

Hamshari was flattered. A magazine article was to be written about him. Perhaps it would help educate the world about the evils of Israel—its terrible prime minister and her counterterrorism advisor, Aharon Yariv.

"Is this Mahmoud Hamshari?" the caller asked again.

"Yes, it is he."

"May I come over today?"

"Yes, how would three o'clock in the afternoon do?"

"Ah, *eccellente*."

Mossad agent "Robert," posing as an Italian journalist, interviewed Hamshari for over an hour. Once during the interview, Hamshari's French-born wife Marie-Claude added to the criticism of Israel. Once the *interview* was concluded, Robert had work to do.

"May I use your phone to call my publisher?" he asked.

"Yes," Hamshari said, pointing to the adjacent room where the phone was.

Robert noted the style and color of the phone. He took out a notepad to trace the shape and size of the phone while Hamshari's daughter, Amina, played an upbeat tune on the piano in the next room.

Later, when no one was home, Robert, the bomb maker disguised as a telephone repairman, broke into Hamshari's beautiful home and replaced the phone with one loaded with plastic explosives and a wireless receiver and detonator.

The next day, a Mossad team in a car on the street within transmitting distance of the Hamshari home set up to detonate the bomb. The agents waited until Marie-Claude took her daughter to school to set up the assassination. The Mossad team with the detonator did not have "eyes" on the phone. The phone itself was visible through a window from the street where a spotter was. Another agent would make the phone call, and once the identity was confirmed, the team would detonate the bomb.

Marie-Claude returned unexpectedly to retrieve something she'd forgotten, and the spotter saw her in front of the phone. He raced to the car where the detonation team was, preventing them from making a serious mistake. Once she left, the spotter returned to his position.

With a confirmation that only Hamshari was home, another agent made a call from a payphone to the Hamshari home.

"Hello?"

"Is this Mahmoud Hamshari?"

"It is he."

"Hello, Mahmoud Hamshari," the agent said. "This is just a reminder that we don't forgive, and we never forget."

The caller signaled the spotter, who gave the thumbs-up signal to the detonation team, which activated the bomb. The explosive was detonated through the phone line, fatally wounding Mahmoud Hamshari.

Another one of the terrorists who had been involved in the Munich massacre was dead.

CHAPTER SIXTY-FIVE

Nina and Elan grew closer as they continued to work together on Operation Wrath of God. They traveled to London and New York. It was dangerous work. The agents involved were human, and it was hard for them to execute so many people. They had to remind themselves continually what had happened to the young, innocent athletes at the hands of these men to stay the course.

Nina's hard shell was falling away to reveal a kind and sensitive girl. Although she had trouble admitting it, she was a little frightened. When Elan was in danger, he secretly enjoyed seeing the concern in Nina's eyes. They spent a great deal of time together, but he still had not kissed her.

One night, Avrehm, another agent they were working with, went to bed early, leaving them to have dinner alone. For some reason that Elan could not explain, even with all they'd done together, he was incredibly self-conscious about being alone with Nina.

They brought food into the hotel and sat together on a small sofa while Avrehm and Boaz slept in the other room.

Nina was wearing sweatpants and a tee shirt. Her face was clean of makeup. Her massive, uncontrollable curls were tied back into a low ponytail, but they looked like they might free themselves at any moment.

"This mission is difficult for you," he said.

"I've never been involved in killing anyone before. And even though I hate these horrible people who murdered a group of innocent young Jews, it's still very hard for me. I have to keep remembering my sister and what happened to her in order to go on."

"Would you believe me if I told you it is hard for me, too?"

"No. I would not."

"You're right. I guess you know me better than I thought you did. No, it isn't hard for me. I have so much anger and hatred for them that it is actually easy."

"Elan?"

"Yes…"

"Sometimes, when you go out on an assignment, I am scared for you."

"I am always scared for you, Nina. If anything happened to you…"

She had tears in her eyes. He got up, walked over to her, sat beside her, and put his arms around her. She didn't fight or resist. Nina laid her head on Elan's chest and cried softly. She cried for her sister, for the athletes, for the horror of what she felt she had to do in Operation Wrath of God. And while she wept, Elan held her.

For a long time, they sat silently.

"Nina, can I kiss you?" Elan asked.

She nodded. He kissed her gently, carefully.

"You are so delicate. I can't believe that you are doing a job like this."

She nodded. "I know. Sometimes I can't believe it myself."

"I think I am falling in love with you."

The tears welled up in her eyes again. "I know I am falling in love with you…"

He kissed her again, this time with more passion. "I don't want to be disrespectful, so I don't want to ask you to come to my bed. But Nina, with the life we are living, we can't be sure that we will have tomorrow. So I would like to ask you to marry me as quickly as possible. I want to hold you in my arms. I want to love you. It has been a very long time since I have felt anything like this for another person. Be my wife?"

"Elan, what makes me different from your first wife? You couldn't make it work with her."

"She wasn't the great love of my life. I've grown up, Nina. You are my one true love. I'm not young anymore. I want to be happy with one person…"

"You've never really loved anyone else?"

"I can't say that. I once loved a woman when I was very young, but she wasn't right for me. I wasn't right for her. There were a lot of silly reasons we couldn't be together. I could have tried harder. I might have made it work, but I was stubborn and a little stupid. Anyway, she is a part of my past.

"Nina, you are my future. I know I am a lot older than you, and you are so beautiful you could certainly find a younger, better man. But if you are willing to be mine, I will do everything in my power to make sure that you are always happy. And I promise you that I will never want or need another woman for the rest of our lives. Will you marry me, Nina?"

"Yes. Yes, Elan, I will marry you."

"Tomorrow?"

"Yes."

"Do you want to call your parents and tell them?"

"No, I don't want them to insist we come home and have a wedding. We can tell them when we get back to Israel after it's over. If they want to have a party, then it will be their choice, but we will already be married."

"You don't think they will approve, do you?"

She let her eyes meet his. "Do you really want to know the truth?"

"Of course."

"Will it matter to you?"

"I don't know if you don't tell me what it is…"

"They will think you are too old for me."

"Do you feel that way?" He held his breath, terrified of her answer. It could change everything. With just a few words from Nina, his life could feel like it had ended. Her response to that question he'd asked mattered more to him than anything had ever mattered in his life.

"No. I don't care how old you are."

"Then you will be my wife?"

"Yes. I will."

They planned to fly back from London to Israel in a few days to receive their next assignment. But before they left London, in a quiet, private ceremony, Elan put on his yarmulke and the tallis his father left him when he passed away. Then he and Nina went into the office of a local rabbi.

Elan paid the rabbi to perform the ceremony, and the secretary who worked at the synagogue stood as a witness. Then, under a makeshift chuppah in the temple's auditorium, Elan Amsel, with sweating palms and trembling hands, took a gold ring that he'd purchased earlier that morning from his pocket. And for the first time in his life, he spoke vows of unconditional love from the depths of his heart.

And so it was on that day that Elan Amsel, a former playboy, formerly self-righteous, and an arrogant, pompous ass bowed down to the power of love, a power so strong it could only have come from God.

As he stood trembling in the only suit he owned, he knew for certain that, after this ceremony, everything in his life would change for the love of a woman. All that he was and every possession that he owned, he gave willingly to Nina. All of his dreams and aspirations were elevated because he wanted to be a better man for Nina. His heart fluttered, and he involuntarily closed his eyes because his emotions were too strong for him to look at her when she said, "I do."

His voice cracked as he repeated it, barely a whisper. For the first time in his life, Elan forgot to control himself and felt the pure joy of true love as he married Nina Sofer.

After the ceremony, they went out for dinner and then got a cheap hotel room for the night to celebrate.

For Nina, it was strange to be a married woman. She'd often wondered if she would ever marry. Nina had always been particular, finding fault with every man she met. Elan was older, different, more tolerant, and more understanding. She knew he'd had failed relationships in the past, but he'd explained that that was when he was younger. Now, he was ready. And seeing the way that he behaved toward her, Nina could not help but know that he was telling her the truth.

After they'd each taken a shower, Elan came to Nina as she lay in bed naked with the covers pulled up almost to her face. She was shy and nervous. He got in beside her and felt her shiver.

"Are you cold?"

She shook her head.

"Something is not right. What's wrong? Talk to me," Elan said, leaning over her and lifting her chin so their eyes met.

"I feel like a fool, but there is something I have to tell you," she said, clearing her throat.

He cocked his head to the side. "Go ahead. It's all right. Whatever it is, just tell me. I love you, and it is all right."

"Elan, please don't laugh at me, Elan, but I am a virgin. So please be gentle. I'm a little scared."

He did laugh. She glared at him and turned away from him, crossing her arms over her chest.

"I'm sorry, my love, don't be mad. I didn't mean to laugh, but there is nothing wrong. I didn't expect that, that's all. You know that I love you. I will be gentle. It just came as such a surprise."

"Why is it a surprise? Do you think every woman in Israel is loose? It's not so."

"I don't think that at all. It's just that here you are, this beautiful, amazingly, strikingly, frighteningly beautiful woman." He smiled and turned her over gently to face him again. She did not resist. "And besides all of that, you're a strong and tough Mossad agent." He kissed her gently. "I don't know. I just thought you would be, well, you know, experienced."

She grunted. "Now I wish I never told you."

"Nina, I love you. I am honored to be the first and last man you will ever take to your bed. I love you with all my heart, and you will never need any other man. I promise you that."

She was as light as a child when he took her into his arms. He smoothed the hair from her face.

"My God, you're gorgeous," he said.

"You just think that because I'm so much younger than you. I'll bet all your buddies will be jealous that you have a younger wife."

"I love you. I don't care what anyone thinks—jealous, not jealous, it means nothing to me."

Then he kissed her. He made love to her slowly, carefully, and gently until when it was over, she lay in his arms and said, "If I had known it was going to be so good, I would have made love with you when we first met."

He laughed. "My Nina…"

She laughed.

CHAPTER SIXTY-SIX

IN JANUARY 1973, Golda Meir was speaking in Rome when an attempt was made to assassinate her by the group known as Black September.

CHAPTER SIXTY-SEVEN

Elan had never been as happy since his marriage to Nina. It had been long since he'd allowed himself to feel anything. His emotions were like a volcano clogged up for years that had finally exploded. When Elan made love to Nina, he felt as if he were Moses treading on holy ground.

Although his vulnerability terrified him far more than a battlefield ever had, Elan adored his young wife and did everything he could to show her how much she meant to him. There was no doubt that Elan Amsel was not the same man he was ten years ago.

Every morning, he got up early to make breakfast while Nina slept, just so he could see her face when he brought her a tray with a rose from the garden in a small bud vase. Whenever he walked through the market, he bought her flowers or a box of chocolates. Instead of eating lunch, he often took the time out of his workday to search for and purchase small gifts of jewelry, mostly trinkets of gemstones and silver, to delight his young wife.

The two of them were inseparable. Friends would ask them if it was hard to work with a spouse, but neither Nina nor Elan ever felt that it was. They cherished every moment they spent together, always threatened by the underlying knowledge that in their line of work, either one of them could be killed at any time. They accepted the fact that this was what it meant to be an Israeli. They even took a trip to the Wailing Wall, where they stood to pray together.

But they never forgot to be aware, to keep watch of everything happening around them. Black September or the PLO could attack at any time. Elan and Nina knew that the enemies of the Jews were always just a step behind. Every night, as soon as they were alone, they fell into each other's arms. Like a cloak of safety in a mad and frightening world, Nina's tiny frame wrapped around Elan.

CHAPTER SIXTY-EIGHT

Nina longed to have a child, and although he felt he was too old for a baby, Elan agreed. However, no matter how hard they tried, she did not conceive. Several years passed, and they were happy, but Nina was missing something in her life.

Elan hated to see the disappointment in his young wife's beautiful eyes, so he tried to fulfill her dreams of becoming a mother. He accompanied her to every fertility clinic they could find, though it was out of character for him. They were both tested relentlessly. However, no doctor was able to uncover a single reason why Nina did not become pregnant.

She and Elan wanted a child even though they both realized that it was a selfish wish. Not only because of Elan's age, but the career they were committed to left them constantly at risk. Their child could easily become an orphan, and that wasn't fair.

So, in case they did conceive, Elan finally made peace with his brother, Aryeh, and his sister-in-law. Of course, Nina and Elan could not discuss their work in detail. So, one night, as they all shared a quiet meal, Elan asked Aryeh and his wife to answer an important question.

"I know this may sound crazy, but I need an honest answer,"

Elan said as they sat by the fireplace. "If Nina and I were ever to have a child and for some unfortunate reason we were both killed, would you take our child? Raise it as your own? Could I be sure that I could count on you?"

"Do you expect such a thing to happen?" Aryeh asked.

"We are Israelis, Aryeh, and we don't know what's going to happen."

"Are you still working with Mossad?"

"No," Elan lied. "But anything can happen at any time, and I need an honest answer from you, a true commitment."

Aryeh looked at Brenda. She nodded. "Can we expect the same thing from you for our child?" Aryeh asked.

"Of course," Nina said without hesitation.

Aryeh looked at his brother, then at Nina, and then his eyes went to those of his own wife. Brenda nodded in agreement.

"You are our family, our blood. If God forbid, something terrible happened, Brenda and I would raise your child like our own."

"Thank you," Elan said.

"Is Nina pregnant?" Aryeh asked.

"No," Nina said. "We were just asking for the future."

Later, Brenda and Nina were cleaning the dishes in the kitchen while the two brothers were in the living room, talking and drinking a shot of cognac. The women had become good friends over the years. Brenda never liked Janice, but she liked Nina.

"Brenda, I need someone to talk to."

"You know I'm here for you."

"Elan and I want a child, but I can't seem to get pregnant. The harder we try, the more impossible it seems to be."

Brenda nodded. "I think maybe you both work too hard. You've never just taken some time to relax and be together. Did you even have a honeymoon?"

Nina laughed. "Honeymoon? Are you kidding? We had a night, if you could call that a honeymoon, but we have never stopped working."

"Maybe that's what you need: a little rest and relaxation. Go away for a while, maybe go to Paris. They don't call it the city of love for nothing."

Nina laughed again. "Yes, I think that's a great idea. I'll talk to Elan tonight. We could use a little break. I'd love to go to Paris. We've been to France but only for work. I have always wanted to spend some romantic time in Paris, but I doubt we could afford that. Still, any vacation time alone together might be just what we need."

Elan thought it would be nice to be a father, to leave a small part of himself behind when he left this world. But at forty-three, he would be an old man when his child was a teenager. That was the only regret he had with marrying a woman of twenty-four. Nina was still young. She wanted a family of her own, and she deserved to be a mother.

Sometimes, he would think back and remember how he had felt that night when Janice told him she was pregnant. Looking back, he had to admit that he'd never really been in love with Janice. But in spite of everything that was wrong with his first marriage, something inside of him had been elated at the prospect of being a father. Then, when he received the letter from Janice asking for a divorce and informing him that she'd miscarried their baby, he felt a kind of emptiness inside of him.

Although he knew in his head that it was probably for the best. After all, a child without a father growing up with grandparents in America was not an optimal situation. It still felt like a loss to him.

Now, he decided that if Nina ever became pregnant, he would request that both of them be released from their services in Mossad and their commitment to Operation Wrath of God. Once they had a child, he felt it was only right to be as careful with their lives as possible. Even now, though she was not pregnant, he wished that Nina would quit.

The thought of something bad happening to her was unbearable to him. Yet he knew she was too devoted to Mossad to leave unless she had a very good reason. And he had known from the beginning of their relationship that she was a highly trained and invested agent. So, he could not ask her to give up the life she chose just because of his fears. He knew she would laugh at a request like that.

That night, after they'd showered and made love, Nina breathed deeply, lying in his arms. She reached up to take the hair out of his eyes. He took her face in his hands and gently kissed her. After the kiss, she broke away slightly, but her face was still very close to his, close enough that he could feel her soft, sweet breath on his skin.

"What do you think about taking a couple of weeks and going away? It would be deliciously lovely to spend all day doing nothing but making love, sightseeing, and eating too much." She giggled. "Seriously, Elan, I think maybe we need the rest," she said.

"I've never really given it much thought."

"We've never had a real honeymoon. What do you think about going somewhere?"

"Where would you like to go?"

"I'd love to go to Paris, but I know it's too much money. How do you feel about spending a week or two in Eilat? We could do some touristy things and spend plenty of time making love. It would be so much fun just to leave this all behind for a little while. What do you think?" She ran her fingers through his hair, and he felt an electric current of desire run through him.

"I think it would be a great idea," he said and meant it. He loved the idea of having her all to himself for two glorious weeks.

"We'll spend hours on the beach doing nothing, just being lazy. We'll take long showers together until our skin wrinkles like old people. Then we'll eat at fancy restaurants until we get sick from the rich food," she giggled.

He laughed. He loved to see her happy and excited. "I wish I could take you to Paris. You know I would give you the world if I could. So we'll go to Eilat, then."

"You do. You give me the world every day. Well, my darling, one thing you can count on is love on this trip. I am going to make love to you day and night until you are sick and tired of me…"

"That will never happen."

"What? The making love or you getting tired of me?"

"You know which one. You just want to hear it; that's all."

"You're right, I do."

"I love you, Elan. And I could never get tired of you or of making love to you."

CHAPTER SIXTY-NINE

Elan told his coworkers that he and Nina were going to Eilat for two weeks. They understood how badly their two friends needed to get away. Elan also said he wished he had saved enough money to take Nina to France, as that was where she really wanted to vacation.

There was no problem for either Nina or Elan to arrange time off. They had plenty of vacation time that they had never used. The trip was planned quickly. They were to stay at a romantic hotel located right on the water.

They were accustomed to packing quickly since they'd both traveled so much for work. It was early June, and the sun shone brightly as they loaded the car. Elan felt a sense of well-being come over him. Nina was so beautiful, her hair caught up in a high ponytail swinging behind her as she moved. So beautiful… He was so fortunate to have found her and even more fortunate that she actually loved him.

It was almost a four-hour drive to Eilat, but Elan never minded driving. He turned the radio on to the station that played the American music he loved and sang along. Nina read her book, occasionally looking up to smile at him.

The hotel was perfect. It looked just like it did in the brochure that Nina had picked up from a local travel agency. They had a room overlooking the pool. The bathroom had cotton robes, and the bed was large, clean, and comfortable. The salty fragrance of sea air drifted through the open door leading to a balcony.

They unpacked and made love until dinner. The following day, Nina insisted that they get up early and take a ride over to the Red Canyon. Elan would have preferred another day of making love, but he dragged himself out of bed and dressed.

They hiked the canyon. Elan found a small, private cave. He pulled Nina inside, took her into his arms, and kissed her passionately. As he kissed her neck, his hands traveled the length of her body. Both were breathing heavily, and sweat was beginning to form on Elan's forehead. He pushed her up against the wall and reached under her shirt. She moaned with longing for him. Their eyes were glued to each other. "I love you," he whispered, "more than the sun, more than the moon."

"I love you…"

His hands were under her tee shirt just as a group of tourists came around the corner. They were young teenagers with a guide. Elan and Nina saw the look on the faces of the hikers. They were shocked. Elan looked at Nina, and they both burst out laughing. Then, hand in hand, they ran away.

"Were you embarrassed?" he asked her, holding hands as they continued to walk.

"Yes, a little."

He kissed her forehead.

"But I'd do it again," she said.

He laughed.

By eleven that morning, the sun became too hot to continue hiking, so they returned to their hotel room, showered, and went out for lunch. After lunch, they took a nap by the pool and spent the rest of the afternoon in bed together.

The following afternoon, they heard a commotion outside the window of their room.

"Look, Elan. It's raining!!! It never rains in Eilat. I mean, once in a million years."

"It's not that rare, but pretty darn close. Come on, let's go get wet," he said.

They were wearing nothing but their robes. However, Elan grabbed Nina's hand and pulled her down the stairs and outside into the lightly falling rain. Elan took Nina into his arms and kissed her.

"Have you ever kissed in a rainstorm?" he asked.

"No, have you?"

"Actually, no," he said. "Let's kiss until we're drenched." And they did.

Every day was overflowing with joy, lovemaking, and romance. Nina had never been so at ease, so in love, and so happy. One day, they spent the entire day shopping in the stores in Eilat. Elan hated shopping but wanted to make Nina happy, so he wandered the stores with her for hours. On another day, they visited King Solomon's mines, where Elan bought Nina a sterling silver necklace made by a local artisan. It held a blue-green gemstone pendant which was supposed to have come from deep within the mine. They found a vendor on the street that sold the most delectable chocolate. Once Nina tasted the chocolate, she wanted to go and visit the chocolate stand every day, and Elan obliged.

Elan knew that Nina had always wanted to go to a very expensive steak house. They didn't go to extremely fancy places very often. But he knew how much Nina would enjoy going, so he decided to take this opportunity to splurge.

He left the room that afternoon while Nina was taking a nap, walked three blocks to the restaurant, and made a reservation. Then he raced back to the hotel and upstairs to his room. He hoped she would still be asleep, but she was standing at the window looking out.

"Where did you go? I was looking all over the place for you. I was getting worried," Nina said.

"I have a surprise for you. I went to make reservations at a very special place. You know the steak house we saw when we were coming into Eilat, which is a few blocks from the hotel? Well, that's where we are having dinner."

"Can we afford to spend so much money on one dinner?" she asked, but he could see that she was excited, and he knew how much she loved to get dressed up.

"Anything for my beautiful wife." He smiled at her and thought that he would spend any amount of money to see her so happy.

Nina spent an hour getting ready. She sat at the dressing table in the hotel room and studied herself.

"Elan, do you think I am pretty?"

"What? Of course, you're beautiful."

"No, I'm not. Not really. I mean, not in the classic sense."

"You are the most beautiful woman I've ever seen. What is bringing all of this on?"

"I don't know. I'm just feeling insecure all of a sudden. I mean, there are so many incredibly gorgeous women here in Eilat. I was just wondering if you ever fantasized about being with any of them."

He walked over to her and took both of her hands in his. Then he knelt beside her and looked directly into her eyes. "Nina, I love you. To me, there is no one as beautiful or as wonderful. But I not only love your lovely face and incredible body, but I love your kind heart and your brilliant mind."

"Now we both know who wants to get laid tonight." She laughed. "You know the old saying, flattery will get you everywhere."

He kissed her. "Too bad we have to be at the restaurant in ten minutes."

"Yes, too bad."

They arrived at the restaurant five minutes late and almost lost their reservation. Elan had to tip the maitre d' a fifty shekel bill to ensure he would still honor their time slot. The restaurant was filled with people, most of whom were tourists from around the world. Even with the reservation, they still had a fifteen-minute wait.

"Come, let's go have a drink," Elan said. He could easily have walked out. He would have loved to have told the maitre d' to take his restaurant and go to hell. The guy was an arrogant jerk. Elan wasn't impressed with all the pretentious BS. He would have been happy to have dinner in a quieter place. But he knew that Nina was looking forward to this dinner, so he shut his mouth and found them both seats at the bar.

"Whiskey, straight," Elan said.

"A glass of white wine," Nina told the bartender. She knew her husband was irritated, and she smiled knowingly at Elan. "It won't be too long before the table is ready. By the way, thank you for not telling him off."

"Who, the host?"

"Yes. Thank you for not starting a fight."

"I'm not that bad."

"I've seen you when you're mad, Elan."

"I'm not mad. I can swallow my pride and take a little crap if eating here makes you happy. You are my guilty pleasure. Everyone has something that they love and adore. You are my indulgence."

She laughed. "You say the craziest but sweetest things."

"Amsel, table for two."

"See, our table is ready," she said. "It took less time than we thought it would."

They sat at a round booth in the corner. Using the tablecloth as a privacy screen from the other guests, Elan slid his hand under the table and caressed her knee.

"My Nina," he whispered in her ear as they read the menu. Gently, he moved the hair away from her cheek and kissed her.

After they ordered, Elan looked around the dining room. "So many tourists here… I suppose we should have expected as much in Eilat."

"You don't like it here?"

"I do. It's just that, sometimes, when I see people from other countries who have come here to visit, I know they have no idea what it really means to be an Israeli. Israel is like no other country in the world. It's built on the blood of its people. The Sabras are the survivors. We know that if Israel falls, it is only a matter of time before the Jewish race will be wiped off the face of the earth. As you know, Nina, we Israelis go through life like everything is normal. But always in the back of our minds, we know that we can be called up to war at any time. And without question, we will go because we are Israelis."

"Yes, it's true. I don't think there is anywhere else in the world where people feel the way we do toward their country."

He felt his eyes well up with tears.

CHAPTER SEVENTY

As THE TWO weeks were nearing the end, Nina was sure that her period was late. As soon as she got home, she planned to make an appointment with her doctor to take a pregnancy test. It was probably too soon to tell, but she was keeping her fingers crossed, hoping and praying that it was true. Her cycle had always been regular. She'd missed her period, which was a good sign, but she didn't want to get Elan's hopes up until she was positive that she was pregnant.

On the final day, when they were to leave Eilat and return home to Tel Aviv, Elan had gone into the bathroom and was taking a shower. There was a knock at the door. Nina dropped the rest of her sundresses into the suitcase and went to see if it was the front desk bringing a copy of their bill.

As Nina opened the door, Elan came out of the shower with a white towel wrapped around him. His tan skin made a healthy contrast against the stark covering.

"Who is it?" Elan said, walking over to the door.

"I have a certified letter for Mr. and Mrs. Amsel."

Nina glanced over at Elan. He nodded his head. "It's okay. Sign it."

She signed the receipt and took the envelope.

"What do you think this is?"

"I have no idea. Here, give it to me. Let me open it." He shrugged his shoulders and then took the letter from her. If it contained bad news, he wanted to know first so that he could break it to her gently.

Elan closed the door to the hotel room and then opened the envelope. Nina was watching him.

"What is it?" she asked. "Tell me."

Elan read aloud:

"A very good day to both of you from your dear friends at Mossad! We all know how much the two of you wanted to go to Paris, and since you are our brother and sister, we decided to take up a collection to make that very dream come true. In this envelope, you will find two plane tickets to Paris. The tickets are for Air France flight 139, departing from Tel Aviv on June 27. You will also find hotel reservations for a room in Paris that has been paid in advance for one week. We know you must have spent a lot of money in Eilat, so we included a reasonable amount of French francs to pay for food. Your time off from work has been cleared. And it is with heartfelt love that we wish you both a wonderful time in France. L'Chiam. Your friends, your coworkers, your family, at Mossad."

CHAPTER SEVENTY-ONE

On the morning of June 27, 1976, Elan and Nina boarded Air France Flight 139 headed for Paris.

Elan and Nina decided it was best to be in disguise while traveling outside of Israel. She wore a blonde wig and dark sunglasses that almost covered her face completely. He had allowed his beard and mustache to grow and colored his hair all dark, washing away the salt and pepper color he'd had for several years.

They sat together on the plane, holding hands like newlyweds. In their missions with Mossad, they'd traveled a great deal. They were used to flying but never held hands or traveled as lovers.

A lovely young French stewardess brought them a nice lunch, and Nina looked out the window as they drifted through the clouds. For the first time, she did not feel afraid. They were traveling for pleasure rather than for Operation Wrath of God.

They were booked at a quaint hotel on the outskirts of Paris. According to the brochures, it was surrounded by a garden with an array of colorful flowers in fresh bloom.

"The weather is so beautiful in France in June," Nina said.

"Yes, I think the newspaper said it's about twenty-two degrees Celsius."

"I know, not too hot or too cold. I can't wait to arrive in Paris."

He leaned over and kissed her as she looked out the window of the Airbus at the clouds.

"I hate your beard," she said.

"I'm sorry."

"It scratches my skin."

"I know. So I won't kiss you."

"You can forget that idea, Mr. Amsel. You'd better kiss me. Paris is the city of love."

"Mmmm, and I never get enough of making love to you," he said into her ear.

After a few hours, Nina fell asleep. Elan watched her, and his heart was soft with love. She opened her eyes and looked at him.

"You know, I was thinking, maybe we should quit Mossad. Maybe we've tempted fate enough," Elan said.

"I've thought about that."

He was encouraged by her response. "We have enough money to live on if we are careful. It wouldn't be an extravagant life, but we could retire early and finally be at peace. And I will know that you are safe."

"You know, I agree with you, Elan. I've avenged my sister's death many times over. I am tired of fighting. I am tired of blood and death and risks…"

"Yes, me too. Now that I have you, life has so much more value, so much more meaning."

He reached over and took her hand in his and gently squeezed.

The stewardess brought around a cart with coffee. Elan and Nina sipped their cups of the steaming black liquid.

"This is good coffee, very strong, unlike in Israel, where it's that instant shit."

She laughed. "Yes, it is good. The food is fabulous, too."

"French sauces upset my stomach, but you're right. The food will be tasty…"

"It's a good thing we'll only be there for a week, or I'd get as fat as a cow."

"I won't let you get fat. Not that I wouldn't love you anyway, because it goes without saying that I would. But since you don't want to be fat, I'll make sure that we burn off all those extra calories."

"Elan, how crude." She giggled, shaking her head. "Paris is truly a beautiful city, and I can't wait to spend a week with you. But you know, as wonderful as France is, I could never live anywhere but Israel. My heart is in Israel."

"Yes, mine too. People who are not Israeli don't understand how much that tiny strip of land means to our people," he said.

"No, they don't, and they never will. How could they?" she agreed.

"Not even American Jews. Oh, they think they understand, but they don't. They might understand in an intellectual sense, but they don't feel it the way we do. They don't live it, the daily fear, the pride of our nation and all it has achieved, I mean, all of it," Elan said.

"Your first wife was an American. I'm assuming she was Jewish. I don't think I ever even asked you."

"Yes, she was an American Jew. She was a good girl. She was just not for me. And as much as she wanted to be a part of our country, in her heart, she was not an Israeli."

"Yes, it's a strange life we live. Outsiders will never be able to grasp it completely. Most of us Israelis are willing to die for our land. It's not like that in America or any other place in the world that I know of," she said.

He nodded. "When we get back home, let's put in for retirement. We'll explain that we want to have a family and all the danger… They'll understand," Elan said.

Nina was tired. The motion of the Airbus made her drowsy. She laid her head on Elan's shoulder and drifted off to sleep again. She slept until the plane stopped to refuel in Athens.

The air pressure during the landing hurt her ears. Her ears always popped during air travel. Elan knew this because of all the flying they'd done during their missions. So, without even asking, he placed a piece of bubble gum in her hand. She smiled and opened the gum, plopping it into her mouth and chewed hard, moving her jaw around, hoping her ears would finally pop and release the pressure.

"It's too bad there isn't enough time to get off the plane and see a little of Athens," she said. "I love spending time alone with you."

"We are going to retire and be alone together until you get sick of the sight of me."

"Yes, but we have so many friends and family in Israel. Here, it's just us…"

"We'll take a vacation again. Maybe next year, we can go to Athens or maybe America," he said.

"Not if we retire. We'll have to be very careful how we spend our savings."

"Do you want to see America after we retire?" he asked her.

"Do you?"

"I got married there."

"You never told me that," she said.

"You never asked."

"What was it like?"

"Excessive."

"What do you mean?"

"Wasteful. Lots of wasted food, I don't know. I mean, it has its good points, but it's not Israel. I would never trade living in Israel for America."

"Lots of Israelis do. They're moving there all the time."

"That's because it's easy to make money. Americans spend money like crazy and buy lots of junk they don't need."

She laughed. "I guess you don't really have a lot of nice things to say about your ex-wife."

"That's why she's my ex-wife, and you are my real wife."

"Did she buy a lot of things?"

"Her parents were rich, and they splurged on the wedding because she was an only child. She had no concept of money. But I have no bad feelings toward Janice anymore. We were young and far too different to be a couple. I guess I married her on the rebound."

"Rebound from what? You never told me about any other girls you were serious about."

"Yes, well, there was one, but it was a long time ago."

"Please fasten your seat belts and prepare to take off," the flight attendant said over the loudspeaker.

"Wait a minute. I want to know more about this girl."

"There is nothing to know. It was over a long time ago."

"Elan," she said, "we don't keep secrets from each other."

"All right, Miss Smarty-pants, did you have a serious boyfriend before me?"

"Never."

"Nobody?"

"No. I dated a guy I met in the IDF. We dated for a while. It was never serious. He wanted to go to bed with me, and I broke it off. That's it; that's all."

"She was a girl I met. We were very young. We fell in love… We got engaged, and it just didn't work out."

"Engaged! Oh no, wait a minute. I need to know all about this, Elan. This sounds like it was something that was an important part of your life."

"Not as important as you are, sweetheart."

"What was her name?"

"Who?"

"Elan, the girl who you were engaged to."

"Katja."

"Katja? That's not an Israeli name. Was she a Swede?"

"What difference does it make? It was a long time ago," he said, sounding more impatient with Nina than ever.

"To me, it makes a difference."

"I don't want to talk about it, please."

"Fine," she said, folding her arms across her chest and turning away from him to look out the window. "If you don't want to talk about it, that means it must have been pretty serious."

"Please, Nina, it was over long ago."

"You know, Elan, you never gave me a diamond engagement ring?" He could hear the anger in her voice.

"I didn't think you wanted one."

"Oh? And why is that?"

"I don't know. I didn't think so. That's all. Do you want one?"

"Every woman loves beautiful things. Just because I am not an American or a Swede, just because I am an Israeli Mossad agent like you, doesn't mean I'm not a woman. I'll bet she had a ring and your first wife, too."

"Why are you trying to pick a fight? I don't know what's wrong with you," Elan said.

"Nothing is wrong with *me*, Elan! I just didn't know we kept secrets in our pasts from each other; that's all. I thought I knew everything about you. Now, it seems like I don't. What else don't I know, Elan? What else have you kept from me?"

He glared at her. His first reaction was to be angry. But age had mellowed him, and he'd learned a thing or two over the years. Elan didn't say a word. He looked away and took a deep breath. Nina was not acting at all like herself. He wondered if she had gotten pregnant in Eilat. Perhaps her hormones were making her crazy? Well, no matter what the reason was that she was so edgy, he would stay calm and refuse to fight. Whatever she wanted to know, he would tell her.

A commotion at the front of the plane stirred Elan out of his thoughts. People were screaming. Several people had gotten out of their seats, and he could see them pushing each other from where he was. Elan got up and tried to look over the heads of the other passengers to get an idea of what was taking place, but he couldn't tell. Then, a woman in the back row of the aircraft let out a yelp of terror. Elan turned to look. He saw a man who looked Palestinian holding the woman in a tight grip with the blade of a knife at her throat.

"Nobody move from your seats," a nervous male voice with an Arabic accent came over the loudspeaker. "We are taking this plane hostage. You are now under the control of The Popular Front for the Liberation of Palestine."

Elan looked over at Nina. They were both in disguise, but he wondered if the Palestinian terrorists knew they were Mossad agents and if their presence on the plane might be the reason for the hijack. Elan wouldn't have been so terrified if he were alone, but

Nina was with him. His Nina. *Keep calm*, he told himself. *You can't do anything from a state of panic. If you lose control, you won't be able to save her. Keep your head, assess the situation, and look for a way to overtake them.*

From what he could see, he determined that there were seven of them. They'd positioned themselves all around the plane. There were too many to try to take them at this point. He'd have to keep his eyes open, watch, and wait like a panther, ready to spring at the opportune moment.

Nina took Elan's hand and squeezed it. They'd both forgotten the spat they were having before the terrorists had taken over the plane. His heart was pounding hard and fast. His mind was racing. There had to be something he could do. No matter what the cost, he must protect his wife. He had a gun, but it was only one, and there were seven of them. He knew that Nina carried a gun, too. It was all part of being an agent of Mossad. But he didn't want her to get involved.

He hoped for the best possible outcome: the terrorists would just take the plane and release the hostages. But Elan was an Israeli, and he knew better. They would make outrageous demands on Israel, and Elan was positive that Israel would not negotiate with terrorists.

"How many of you are Jews? Israelis?" the voice over the loudspeaker said. "Get your passports out now."

Elan felt the breath catch in his throat.

"Admit it, or we are going to find out anyway. And if we find out you're lying, we'll make sure it's the last lie you ever tell."

Elan looked at his wife. He could read the questions in her eyes.

"Jews on one side of the plane, the rest of the passengers get on the other side. When we get to Entebbe, those of you who are not filthy Jews will be released. The rest of you will be at the mercy of the decisions of your leaders in Israel. You'd better hope that they'll meet our demands."

Entebbe? That was in Uganda, Africa, where that insane dictator, Idi Amin, ruled. What did this have to do with Uganda? Think, Elan, think… Elan knew that Amin was working in conjunction with the Soviets. They had sold him planes. There was no doubt that Amin was insane and very dangerous. *God help us*. Elan worried as he looked at Nina. The chances of them surviving were slim.

A terrorist with a gun was coming through the aisles and sorting through the passengers. He demanded to see everyone's passports. Again, he repeated, "Jews to one side, everyone else to the other." When he got to Nina and Elan, the terrorist laughed and pointed the gun at Nina. "These two are Jews if I've ever seen them." He tore Nina's wig off.

Then he ran his hands over Nina and Elan and found their passports. His pistol hit Elan across the face, and blood squirted across the plane. A woman screamed, and then a baby began wailing. Elan was sure that he could kill this terrorist with one blow. However, he knew if he did that, one of the others would kill him. But more importantly, what would they do to Nina? There would be six of them left. She couldn't fight all six alone without him, and they would take their revenge on her. Elan tried to control the shudder that slinked up his spine.

"Sit down here," the terrorist said.

Nina was shaking. She wanted to reach up and touch Elan's face, but she dared not. If only she could feel the warmth of his skin, she could face death more easily.

Elan decided it was best not to retaliate in any way for the blow to his face. Instead, he took Nina's hand and went to the other side of the plane where the Jews were being kept. He had to exercise strong self-control. He must do nothing, no matter what happens, until he sees the perfect opportunity to take the terrorists. There was no doubt Nina was thinking the same thing.

CHAPTER SEVENTY-TWO

On the afternoon of June 27, 1976, a call came into the offices of Yitzhak Rabin, the prime minister of Israel. "The Popular Front for the Liberation of Palestine, with the help of the Red Army Faction, has taken hostage the passengers of a French Airbus on its way from Israel to Paris. They are planning to free the prisoners who are not Jewish or Israeli, but they say that unless we release fifty-three of their members and pay five million dollars, they will kill all the Jews."

"Oh my God," Rabin said, "who are the terrorists that they want to be released? Are they imprisoned here in Israel?"

"Some, yes, but some in other places, too."

"We have to think of something. How much time do we have?" Rabin asked.

"Forty-eight hours."

"Call for the minister of defense. Have him in my office within the hour."

"Yes, sir."

CHAPTER SEVENTY-THREE

LESS THAN A HALF hour had passed, and LTG Mordechai Gur arrived at the Office of the Prime Minister. "Shalom."

"Shalom, General, sit down, please," Prime Minister Rabin said. "Have you been briefed on the situation at hand?"

"Not completely."

"Here is what we know. A French Airbus has been taken hostage by a Palestinian terrorist group. They have released all non-Jewish and non-Israeli hostages. The rest are being held in Uganda at the airport. We have forty-eight hours to liberate fifty-three terrorists, or they will begin to kill the hostages."

LTG Gur took a deep breath. He rubbed his chin in thought. "Then the first thing we have to do is buy some time," he said. "Then we'll come up with a plan to rescue the hostages."

The Prime Minister nodded in agreement. "We will tell them that we will enter into negotiations with them. See if we can get a little time."

"It will be done," the general said.

LTG Gur was allowed to speak directly to the hostages and the terrorists at the same time. He told all of them that he was in the process of arranging the release of the prisoners and that Israel would meet the demands of the group known as The Popular Front for the Liberation of Palestine. But LTG Gur needed more time because only some of those the Palestinians wanted to be released were imprisoned in Israel. Others were in prisons all over the world. LTG Gur pleaded for time to speak to heads of the other governments who had control over the remaining prisoners.

The terrorists on the plane discussed the situation among themselves. They made a decision: LTG Gur was given until Sunday, July 4, to deliver the Palestinian captives.

CHAPTER SEVENTY-FOUR

"I'M sorry for everything I said before this began, all that stuff about secrets. And I'm really sorry for trying to pick a fight," Nina whispered to Elan as she sat against the wall in the tiny room at the airport in Uganda.

Elan nodded. "Me, too."

"In case we die here, I want you to know that I love you," Nina said, unconsciously rubbing her belly.

"I know. I love you, too, and there is no one else in my heart. You never have to worry about that," Elan said. He watched Nina rubbing her belly, and he knew. *She must be pregnant,* he thought. *God, why here, why now? Why this?* He felt helpless. The woman he loved was sitting beside him, along with about one hundred other hostages, and he could do nothing to help.

The terrorists had them at gunpoint. If he so much as moved, he was sure to be shot. It made him angry. He might have been foolish enough to fight back if he was not so in love with Nina. But instead, he sat quietly, burning inside with rage.

Nina had tears in her eyes. "Do you think they know who we are?" her voice was barely a whisper.

"No. If they knew, they'd be using us as bait to force Israel to bend to their will. They think we're just Israelis."

"Well, that's good, I suppose."

"Yes, let's hope so."

"Shut up over there, you two. There will be no talking," shouted one of the terrorists, a young man in his twenties with thick, black, wavy hair, wearing a green shirt and dark pants that were too big for his skinny frame.

Most of the women were crying. Some of the men were, too. Elan looked around him, and as always, he was reminded that this was why the Jews needed Israel. This was what it meant to be an Israeli.

CHAPTER SEVENTY-FIVE

ISRAEL'S PRIME Minister Rabin was awaiting the arrival of Lieutenant General Mordechai Gur, Major General Yekutiel "Kuti" Adam, Brigadier General Dan Shomron, and Minister of Defense Shimon Peres. He had received a call early that morning of July 1st, informing him that they worked without rest until they had devised a plan that they felt was feasible. Although he appeared calm, the Prime Minister was worried. He hadn't slept more than fifteen minutes since the hostages were taken, and now he drummed his fingers on the desk. No matter how genius the plan was, the Prime Minister knew it would be risky. However, as always, Israel was left with no choice but to take a monumental risk.

"Sir, everyone has arrived. May I show them in?" the prime minister's secretary asked.

"Yes, thank you, and bring in a pot of coffee. I expect this to be a long meeting."

"Shalom, gentlemen, and thank you for coming," the Prime Minister said. "General Gur, have you been successful in convincing Idi Amin to release the hostages?"

"Mr. Prime Minister, he will not help us."

"Then we have to seek a military solution."

"General Adam says that they have an idea," Defense Minister Peres said.

"Yes, we have. We think it will work," MG Adam said. "Since General Shomron put this all together, I will let him tell you."

"Go ahead, General."

BG Shomron cleared his throat. "Mr. Prime Minister, we have a great and unexpected advantage. The airport in Entebbe was built by an Israeli construction firm." He placed a stack of papers on the table. "Here are the blueprints. From these documents, we can find the locations of the entrances, and from there, we can determine the room where the hostages are being held."

The Prime Minister picked up the papers. "How can we be sure which room the Palestinians are holding them in?"

"Because we have already been in contact with the non-Jewish hostages who were released. They've told us everything. We know how many terrorists there are, what they look like, how many weapons they have, and how and where they and our people being held are positioned."

The Prime Minister took a deep breath. He lifted the papers and held them to his chest. "Praise God. We might have a chance of saving them."

"We will need four Hercules C130s, two of them to bring in the soldiers, one to destroy the MiGs stationed nearby, and the other to carry the jeeps and the Mercedes. Once we have landed, we will use the two jeeps to carry our soldiers and a black Mercedes that is an exact copy of the one owned by Idi Amin. This way, if we are spotted, the terrorists will think that Amin has arrived with his soldiers.

I will also need two Boeing 707s, one to act as a forward command post, the other we will land in Nairobi where it will wait, in case it is necessary to act as an airborne hospital after the rescue has taken place. I have already spoken to Colonel Yonatan Netanyahu, and he has agreed to lead the mission. Colonel Netanyahu will need two hundred of our best soldiers and plenty of arms and ammunition. It's not a guarantee by any means, but we have a shot," BG Shomron said.

Prime Minister Rabin furrowed his brow in thought. "Now, for us, our advantage is the element of surprise. The terrorists are expecting negotiations. I feel that it is best that until the mission is underway, we do not tell anyone other than those who absolutely must be informed. For this mission to work, it must remain top secret. In fact, I feel it is best that we do not even inform the Israeli cabinet until we've had a test run of the plan and are fairly sure it might work."

"I quite agree. Begin testing as quickly as possible. How long is the flight from Israel to Uganda?" Defense Minister Peres asked.

"Approximately seven hours, forty minutes, depending on the weather," BG Shomron answered.

"I think we should have the operation escorted by F-4 Phantoms for as long as possible," Prime Minister Rabin said.

"Yes, that is a good idea," the generals agreed. Defense Minister Shimon Peres was silent, absorbing the details. The Prime Minister studied his defense minister and sometimes political rival.

"Defense Minister Peres, do you concur?" asked Prime Minister Rabin.

"We certainly can't release any terrorists or pay any ransom. Yes, I concur." However, we should continue negotiating as long as possible so the terrorists and the Ugandans are not prepared.

"Agreed. Well, gentlemen, let's show them the Israelis are lions, not sheep."

By the following day, the plan was tested, and the timing was calculated. It looked promising.

CHAPTER SEVENTY-SIX

THE TERRORISTS TOOK turns guarding the prisoners, three at a time, while the others slept. Nina was sick to her stomach. She was thirsty, hungry, and exhausted but could not sleep. On the other hand, Elan was alert, his eyes darting around the room like a caged jungle cat. He did not speak, but his dark eyes closely watched everyone and everything.

Every hour, on the hour, the lead terrorist would remind the group of hostages of how many hours they had left to live if Israel did not comply with their demands. At one point, one of the older women had become hysterical and consequently had been pistol-whipped by a terrorist. Elan could hardly breathe as he watched the horror unfold. He had to continue to remind himself that if he acted rashly, all he would succeed in doing would be to get killed. Alone and unarmed, it would be impossible for anyone to overtake seven armed terrorists.

So, all Elan could do was lean against the wall with Nina's head on his shoulder and pray that Israel had a plan.

CHAPTER SEVENTY-SEVEN

As they flew through, thunderstorms erupted over Lake Victoria, but the Israeli pilots pressed on. Nothing could deter them from their mission, not even when the lights were turned on unexpectedly at the Uganda airport, blinding them.

LTC Yoni Netanyahu allowed his eyes to wander around the aircraft's interior and fall upon the young, courageous men and women who flew beside him on the C130 Hercules. He knew they were afraid. He, too, was afraid. But fear did not stop Israel. Israel did not have the luxury of turning back. He wondered how many of these young people would not be on the return flight. *How many lives would be lost? And how many mothers, fathers, husbands, or wives would mourn?*

He noticed a young soldier, a boy of around nineteen years old, watching him from the other side of the C130. Their eyes met. The boy reminded him of his younger brother, Bibi. Yoni loved his brother. They had grown up as the best of friends. Someone, somewhere, loved this boy who he was watching the same way that he loved Bibi.

LTC Netanyahu smiled confidently at the young man, who sat proudly wearing his newly pressed IDF uniform. The soldier returned Netanyahu's smile. He thought of how brave these young people were, and his heart swelled with admiration, pride, and perhaps even a touch of sadness.

The two C130s landed safely despite the glaring lights. Then, as quiet as cat burglars, the soldiers boarded the waiting jeeps and the black Mercedes. Now, in the dark of night, the caravan made its way into the interior of the airport.

When they arrived, the soldiers silently surrounded the area where they knew the hostages were being held. After they received the go-ahead from LTC Netanyahu, they burst into the rooms in an explosion of gunfire. The terrorists were caught completely unaware of the attack, but the Israelis were organized. As the fighting between the terrorists and the soldiers continued, a separate group of Israeli soldiers began loading the hostages into the jeeps.

Elan heard a scream and whipped around as he saw one of the hostages fall, shot and killed. A group of people were crying, but there was no time to stop. The crossfire continued all around them as the hostages were surrounded by sprays of bullets. Two more hostages were killed in the crossfire.

One of the soldiers stood pointing the way. Elan nodded as he passed, letting the soldier know he understood the command.

Then Elan put his arm over Nina's head, and they ran toward the jeep. His heart was pounding. At any moment, either of them could be shot. His Nina could be shot. He held her tighter and pulled her faster. They ran for what seemed like forever, but, in reality, it was only a few minutes. Then, finally, his legs shaking and his knees weak, Elan pushed Nina first and then followed.

Now he and Nina were in the jeep. Elan brushed the sweat from his brow with the back of his hand and allowed himself to look through the back mirror at the battle behind him. Almost all the hostages were on board, and from what he could see, he was pretty sure all the terrorists were dead. The hostages were safe. It was over. Thank God it was over.

Then Elan's heart was crushed when he looked back and saw LTC Netanyahu lying dead in a pool of blood on the tarmac. Israel had lost a good man, a very good man, and a good soldier, but he had not died in vain. His mission and bravery had saved all but three hostages from certain death. Elan felt tears well up in his eyes. *This was Israel!*

CHAPTER SEVENTY-EIGHT

ON THE WAY back to Israel, the plane had to stop for fuel; the passengers were given food and water and made as comfortable as possible. Nina and Elan slept for most of the ride back home. It had been a grueling experience for both of them.

Two weeks after they returned, Nina went to the doctor and discovered that she was pregnant. They decided that they both wanted to retire. They would move out to the countryside near the Golan Heights and live a quiet life. At least that was their dream, but of course, that was impossible: they were Israelis…

CHAPTER SEVENTY-NINE

ISRAEL 1981

IMA ZALTSTEIN SAT on a bench at the bus stop, waiting for the public bus. She'd missed the school bus, so she had to walk four blocks to catch the city bus that would take her close to the high school she attended. She carried her books in one hand and her purse in the other. Her long golden curls were caught in a high ponytail, and her long, shapely legs were crossed at the knee. How long would it take for this bus to get here? If she didn't hurry, she'd miss homeroom.

Maybe she should go back home and spend the day with her grandmother. Her mother would be mad that she missed school, but her grandmother never got mad. Ima considered the possibility of taking the day off. Her mother would not be home. Ima knew that her mother would be busy with the organization she'd founded for the widowed wives of soldiers.

Her mother was consumed with women who'd lost their husbands in service to Israel. It was the only thing that seemed to matter to her, and Ima resented everything about it. Ima's grandmother loved her; she knew that, but her grandmother was getting older, and Ima felt that she didn't understand what was happening in the world today.

Ima would have liked to go to Jennifer's house and read movie magazines and talk about boys and fashion. But first, she'd have to get to school to find Jen, and then they could skip out and return to Jen's house. Jennifer's mother was rarely home. She was one of the members of Katja's group of women who'd lost their husbands in the Six-Day War. However, unlike Katja, Ima's mother, Jen's mother had been left without much money. So, she was working two jobs to make ends meet. This made Jennifer's house the perfect place to go when they cut school. There were no adults.

Sometimes, Ima and Jen had boys they knew from school come over to Jen's house. They'd sit in the dark and neck, drink cheap wine, and play rock & roll. Ima had gone to second base but was scared to go any further, although she wondered what it would be like to do the real thing. There was so much talk about how wonderful it was, but whenever she came close, she was terrified.

If she cut school today, she would miss a math test. She'd have to make it up, but so what? Mr. Shelton had never called her mother when she missed his class, so she figured she could probably get away with skipping.

What the heck was going on, and where was the bus? It was ten minutes late, and she wanted to find Jen before homeroom. If they were both to skip, it was easier not to get caught if they took off before going to homeroom. If they were marked as present in homeroom and then did not attend their other classes, it could raise a red flag, and someone from the office might call the house to verify the absence. Then Ima would have to explain everything to her grandmother. She knew her grandmother, Zofia, wanted her to get a good education. "Make something of yourself," her grandmother always said. "Get yourself a career, something to fall back on, in case you need it later."

Grandma Zofia was a little weird. Grandma would never throw anything away. Even junk, like paper bags from the grocery store. She always had small stashes of trash stowed away in the most unlikely of places. Sometimes, Ima would find a block of cheese with mold on it and toss it into the garbage can. Then, later that day, Grandma Zofia would say, "Where is that cheese? What happened to that cheese?"

"I threw it out. It was moldy," Ima would tell her, trying not to lose patience.

"It was perfectly good cheese. All you had to do was cut off the mold. Don't be so wasteful," Grandma Zofia would say. "You never know what you are going to need."

Ima knew her grandmother had survived the Holocaust, and Katja had told her that Zofia had starved. Still, Ima was sure she was getting a little senile. After all, they had plenty of money. Her father had left them very well off. So Ima had no idea why Grandma Zofia was so strange about things.

Ima glanced down the street, but no bus was in sight. She sighed and plopped back down on the bench. Just then, a black automobile stopped by the side of the road. A man leaned over and opened the window. He was an older man, forty maybe, with a shiny bald head surrounded on all sides by thin, dark hair. From where she was sitting, Ima could see that he was a large man, tall, big-boned, and heavyset.

"Hi," the man said in a friendly enough voice. "Has anyone ever told you that you should be a model?"

Ima turned away. Her mother had told her not to talk to strangers since she was a child.

"I am an agent for fashion models, you know, for magazines? And I wouldn't have stopped and bothered you, except I have been searching for a girl to be the next top model, and you are just what I have been looking for. You're tall and blonde and very beautiful, like an American movie star." He smiled. "I would like you to consider doing a magazine shoot. It's for a new designer who has just come out with a clothing line. You would be the perfect girl to be the spokesmodel for this. I'm telling you, this designer would love you. And he would pay good money to have a girl like you representing his line."

Ima took a deep breath. She'd always wanted to be an actress or a model. She loved movie magazines and fashion. Was it really possible that this could be her chance to make all of her dreams come true?

A tiny voice in her head said; *don't pay any attention to him. You're in danger. Run home now*. She pushed the voice back as far as she could in her mind. This could be the opportunity of a lifetime. Everyone would be so envious.

"You really think I could be a model? In a magazine?"

"I know just by looking at you that you would make the cover," the man said confidently.

Ima smiled. "Really?"

"Of course. Do you think I stop every day at the corner of the street and talk to strange girls? I have better things to do, but you are something special. You have what it takes to make it really big in this business. By the way, what's your name?"

"Ima, Ima Zaltstein…"

"Ima," he repeated, "even your name is perfect for a top model. Get in, and I'll take you to the studio. You can see what we do and how we do it. There is a shoot going on today. I'm sure you would enjoy watching the other girls do their work. It would give you an idea of what is involved."

"I don't know," Ima said, feeling a chill run up the back of her spine. "I mean, I don't really know you."

"Of course, I understand. If you would rather not do this, that's fine. It won't be easy, but I'll keep looking until I can find another girl," he said, rolling up the window.

Ima could see the bus coming down the street. *Get on the bus*, a little voice inside her head said, *go to school.*

"Wait," Ima said to the man, "what's your name?"

"I'm Dan Hoffman. So do you want to come to the studio or not? I have to get going. I have a lot of work to do."

Ima hesitated, but only for a minute. Then she opened the car door and climbed inside.

The automobile sped away. Ima reached over to lock the door but found the locks missing. Then she looked down at the door handle and saw it had been removed. She felt a lightning bolt of fear shoot through her body. Then Ima looked over at the driver. He was smiling. She tried to roll down the window and scream for help, but the handle had also been removed. Who was this man? He'd prepared his entire automobile for a kidnapping. *Oh, my God, Mama, Grandma! Help me, please help me, God, someone, help me…*

CHAPTER EIGHTY

KATJA ZALTSTEIN SHOOK the rainwater from her newly styled, mid-length blonde bob. One of her best friends and the treasurer for her organization had convinced her to cut her hair like Princess Diana. Sometimes, she missed her long curls, but she had to admit that this hairdo was much easier to take care of. Katja had been shopping for food, and the bags she carried were wet. She began removing the groceries that she purchased for dinner. Then she got a towel and dried her hair as much as possible. Even though she'd had it straightened, her natural curls popped right back into place as soon as it got wet.

As usual, she was home late. Something had come up at the office. And even though her foundation was one hundred percent charitable, she still put all her time and effort into making it work. Katja figured her daughter, Ima, was probably in her room doing her homework, and her mother, Zofia, was probably taking a nap. She'd get dinner started before she went to their rooms to greet them. It was a little past seven o'clock, and she was sure everyone was starving.

Her foundation was her life. All the love she might have given to her husband had he survived, she now put into her work. The best part about being busy was that it kept her from thinking, kept the memories at bay, and gave her a sense of fulfillment and purpose. At least she was doing something worthwhile when she was giving comfort and financial support to other women who'd lost loved ones in the service of Israel.

Today, the fish looked very fresh in the market. The eyes were bright and clear, and the skin was smooth and shiny, so she'd bought three pounds. They would have plenty left over, and Ima could take the rest to school for lunch the following day. Opening the white paper package, she looked down at the fish. Fry or boil? Fried tasted better, but boiled was healthier. Katja bit her lower lip in contemplation. *Boil, I suppose,* she thought as she took out a bag of fresh carrots and another of celery.

After washing her hands, she began to peel and chop. At least the fish was quick to prepare. First, she would boil the vegetables, then add the fish, and everyone would eat in less than an hour. Once they'd finished eating and she'd cleaned up, she would have a little time to luxuriate in a hot bath and wash her hair. She placed the vegetables in the pot with boiling water and set the table, then went to the back of the house to let Ima and Zofia know that dinner would be ready soon.

"Mama," she whispered at Zofia's door, knocking softly to not startle her mother out of her sleep.

"Shalom," Zofia whispered, her voice groggy.

"I just started dinner. It should be ready in less than an hour."

"All right, I'll be right out to help you make the salad," Zofia said.

Then Katja knocked softly on the door to Ima's room. "Ima, sweetheart, dinner is almost ready."

No answer.

"Ima?"

No answer.

Katja opened the door. Ima's room was empty. The bed with its pink chiffon bedspread was perfectly made, just as Ima left it every morning. In the center sat the stuffed bear that Ima had won the previous year at a carnival. Her vanity table was cleared except for the three lipsticks she'd arranged in front of the mirror. On the wall were pictures of famous movie stars, both male and female. Tucked into the mirror were two different pictures of Ima and her girlfriends. But the room was deathly quiet. Ima was not there.

Katja felt a cold chill run up her spine. *I'm sure she must be at Jennifer's house*, Katja told herself, trying to stay calm. Ima never stayed out this late without calling first. Katja went into the kitchen, where the rotary phone sat on the countertop. She felt her hand begin to sweat as she picked up the receiver to place the call.

"Hi, Joan," Katja said to Jennifer's mother, "Is Ima there with Jen?"

"No, Kat. Jen's in her room alone."

"Can you please ask her if she has any idea where Ima might be?" Kat asked. Katja's hand was trembling, and she felt the hair on her arms raise with goosebumps. Something was not right.

As Katja stood there, frozen, with the phone in her hand, the pot of water and vegetables began to boil over. Katja watched it mindlessly as it spilled onto the stove.

Zofia walked into the room. She was wearing her housecoat over a nightgown. She saw the pot spilling over, so she took the top off and turned down the fire on the burner. Then Zofia studied Katja, who was still holding the telephone.

"Ima's not here. Do you know where she is?" Katja asked Zofia.

"No, she never said anything about being home late today," Zofia said.

Joan returned and picked up the phone. "Jen says she hasn't seen Ima all day and doesn't know where she is," Joan said.

"Thanks, Joan. I don't know where she is. If you hear anything, please call me right away." Kat felt her throat close as she put the receiver back on the phone.

"Jen has no idea where Ima is. She says Ima was not in school today."

"Oh my God," Zofia said.

"Mama." Katja turned to Zofia. "I can't believe this. Ima is missing. She wasn't in school today, and she's not home or at

Jennifer's house. What is happening? Where is my baby?" Katja was shaking.

Zofia's face had gone pale. "We have to call the police."

Katja picked up the phone. She felt her lungs closing. She could hardly breathe. "Mama, I can't talk. Would you please call for me?"

Zofia nodded. "Give me the phone," she said. When the dispatcher at the police station answered, Zofia said, "My granddaughter is missing. She did not show up at school today. We need help right away."

"We'll send out an officer."

The policewoman arrived within ten minutes. Her demeanor was calm and efficient, but it did nothing to keep Katja's hysteria at bay. The policewoman led Katja to the living room sofa, and then she motioned for Kat to sit down. Katja, in a zombie-like state, did as she was told. Then, the policewoman put her hand on Katja's shoulder. "We'll send out squads right away, and we'll find her."

"Oh my God, what could have happened to my daughter?"

"Did you have a fight with her earlier today? Do you think there is some possibility that she might have run away?"

Katja shook her head. "No, I didn't fight with her at all, did you, Mom?"

"No," Zofia said.

"Has she mentioned a boyfriend, perhaps, who she might be staying with?"

"No, nobody. There is no one that I know of. I called her best friend, and she had not seen her. She said that Ima was not at school all day."

"Give me the names of her friends, and I'll make sure that we get on this right away," the policewoman said.

CHAPTER EIGHTY-ONE

Katja could not sit still. She paced the room. Her skin had broken out into red blotches, and she felt the sweat pooling under her arms. Zofia sat on the sofa, twisting the hem of her housecoat and biting her lips. They waited with the phone on the coffee table right in front of them, wishing the police would call and fearing the news that the call might deliver.

A half-hour passed, and then the phone rang. Katja tripped on the carpet as she ran to pick it up with a trembling hand.

"Kat, did you find Ima?" It was Joan, Jennifer's mother.

"No, we called the police. I don't know what's happened to her." Katja was crying. "Oh my God, Joan…"

"I'm coming over," Joan said. "I'll be there in ten minutes."

"Bring Jen. Maybe she knows something, anything, a boy that Ima has been dating that we don't know about. Something, Joan, something…"

"I will."

Jennifer and her mother arrived. They sat on the sofa, Jennifer biting her nails and Joan with her arm around Katja.

"I'm sure she's fine," Joan said. "I'm sure she just went somewhere."

"Where? Where could she possibly have gone? It's dark outside. Ima wouldn't have gone anywhere and stayed this late without calling. It's not like her," Katja said, shaking her head. "Jen, do you know of any boys that she might be seeing? Do you know anything, anything at all, that can help? Please tell me if you do."

"Tell her, Jen. Whatever it is, you won't get in trouble. I promise you. This is serious. We have to find Ima."

"I'm sorry. I don't know anything at all. There was no boy that she was serious about. I mean, there were guys she liked, but she wasn't going with anyone."

"Please, Jen, tell me the names of all the boys so that the police can talk to them."

Jen took a deep breath and then looked at her mother. Joan gave her a dark stare. "I'll give you their names. Can I have a pencil and paper? I'll write them all down."

Joan had been at many meetings for Katja's foundation that had taken place at the Zaltstein home. She knew where Katja kept pencils and paper. "Sit, Kat, please, I'll get them for her," Joan said and went to the cabinet.

Jennifer left a list of boys' names, then she and her mother went home. There was nothing more they could do to help or comfort Katja and Zofia.

By ten o'clock, Katja was frantic. She'd called the police with the names of the boys almost two hours earlier when Jennifer had given them to her, but so far, she'd heard nothing. Zofia was quiet. She didn't say a word, but she looked pale, and the wrinkles in her brow were deepened. Katja called the police station again. And once again, there was nothing new to tell her. They were working on it, the dispatcher had said. They had squads out looking for a missing teenager.

Katja held her hand to her forehead. The clock ticked. She'd never noticed it before, but she could hear the incessant ticking in the silence. Every terrible possibility ran through Katja's mind. She excused herself and went to the bathroom to be alone, if only for a few minutes. After closing the door and locking it, she leaned her head on the cool wood and began to cry. "Mendel," she whispered.

"Mendel, our baby is missing." The faucet dripped. It had been dripping for several months now. She'd meant to get it fixed.

For a moment, she considered slashing her wrists. That way, if there was terrible news, she'd never have to face it. Then she heard the front door to the house slam. Someone had arrived. Oh God, what if it's the police? What if they have come to tell me that they found Ima, and she's…

CHAPTER EIGHTY-TWO

KATJA'S BODY trembled as if a bucket of ice water had fallen on her head and ran down her back. She whispered a prayer before she opened the bathroom door.

Then she heard Ima's voice.

Katja could hardly breathe. She ran toward the living room, tripping on the carpet and losing her footing. She righted herself by holding onto the wall in the main hallway. She could hear Zofia and a voice from where she was. Could it be? Could it be Ima?

"No, Grandma, I have nothing to tell you. I'm going to take a shower and go to bed."

"Ima? Ima, is that you?" Katja came running into the living room. She took Ima into her arms, but Ima was cold and stood there stick-straight and frozen. "Where were you? We were all worried sick," Katja said. Then she looked at her daughter and knew something terrible had happened. Ima was filthy. Her shirt was torn. There were scratches on her face and arms. Her clothes were spotted with dried blood. "Ima? Ima, what happened?" Katja asked, bending down to look into her daughter's eyes.

"Nothing. Please, let me go..." Ima ran into the bathroom and slammed the door. Katja heard her turn the lock. She ran to the door and started knocking.

"Ima, Ima, open the door," Katja yelled, although she didn't realize her voice was raised.

Zofia walked over to put her hand on Katja's hand. "Let her be for now. She needs to be alone," Zofia said.

Katja's eyes locked with her mother's, and she could see, in the depths of Zofia's eyes, the pain her mother had endured in her life.

"Mama… My Ima, what can I do for her?" Katja was crying. She'd fallen into Zofia's arms. Zofia held her and smoothed her hair.

"Let her be," she whispered. "She will come to us when she's ready. She needs some time to be alone." Zofia put her arm around Katja and led her to the sofa. "Sit here. I'll call the police and tell them to stop the search."

CHAPTER EIGHTY-THREE

Katja heard Ima run the water for a bath.

"I'm afraid she'll hurt herself. I am going to ask her to let me in," Katja said. "Something terrible happened. She needs to talk to someone."

"Yes, I can see that. But knocking on the door will only make things worse. Give her a chance to pull herself together. She's a strong girl. She'll be all right. Thanks be to God that she is alive."

"Thanks be to God," Katja repeated.

They waited. Ima finally came out of the bathroom and went to her room. She did not even look at her mother or her grandmother.

A couple of hours passed. Katja and Zofia listened, but no sound came from Ima's room. Quietly, Zofia opened the door and looked inside. Ima was asleep, or at least she appeared to be. "Get some rest," Zofia said to Katja. "She's sleeping. Perhaps she will be willing to talk to us in the morning. There is nothing we can do right now. Just thank God that she is home and she is alive. Believe it or not, everything else can be healed. I know this from personal experience."

Katja nodded. "Yes, Mama, thank God she's here and she's

alive. I have no idea what happened or where she was all night. But whatever she has to face, I will be there to help her."

"And so will I," Zofia said.

"Goodnight, Mama," Katja said, kissing Zofia's cheek.

"Goodnight, sunshine." Zofia rubbed Katja's shoulder, then turned and went to her room.

Katja heard the door to her mother's bedroom softly close. The house was so silent. Outside, an owl hooted. What was the next step? What was she to do now? But her mother was right. No matter what happened, they were blessed, and Ima was alive. Everything else would work itself out. Zofia was no stranger to suffering. Katja knew that for sure. She knew that Zofia had endured unspeakable things in the concentration camp. And with all she had endured, she'd gone on to live a life of gratitude to God.

Katja turned off all the lights in the house. Then she took off her clothes and put on her nightgown. She climbed into her bed, feeling alone and chilled. Her feet felt frozen under the covers, even though it was not cold in the room. She wished she could climb into bed with her mother like she'd done when she had a nightmare as a child. In her mother's arms, she might be able to escape from the dread of whatever had happened. As she lay there unable to sleep, her mind raced, imagining every possible horror that might have happened to Ima.

Finally, the sun began to rise. Katja gave up on trying to sleep. She got out of bed and went to the kitchen, where she found Zofia already awake and boiling water for coffee.

"She's still asleep," Zofia said, referring to Ima.

Katja glanced at Ima's door and nodded. "Did you check on her?"

"Of course. I checked to make sure she was breathing."

"You knew that was what I would do, didn't you?" Katja asked.

"Of course. I did it to you plenty. When you were sick or when you and Elan broke up, and you were so distraught."

"You checked to make sure I didn't kill myself?"

"I was worried, Katja. Of course, I checked."

"I never knew. I mean, I never heard you come into my room."

"I was quiet. I never wanted you to know. I just wanted to be sure you were okay."

"Oh, Mama, I'm so scared. I hope Ima will be all right. Do you think she took anything? Should we check on her again? I am worried that she could have overdosed on pills or done something else that was terrible."

"I just checked on her. She doesn't have anything narcotic to take. It's early. She'll be awake, and she'll come out of her room soon," Zofia said. "Sit down and have a cup of tea or coffee. Try to relax and stay calm. I'm here with you, sunshine."

Ima didn't come out of her room until the policewoman, who had been working on her case, arrived. She wanted to see Ima, to ask her where she was the previous night and if she was all right. Katja went to knock on Ima's door, but Zofia shook her head. "You're nervous and upset. Let me go and get her."

"Yes, Mom, you go into her room and talk to her. I think she would be more receptive to you."

Zofia walked into Ima's room and quietly closed the door.

It was several minutes, but Ima came out with Zofia behind her. She wore a black tee shirt and black jeans. Her beautiful golden curls had been cropped to less than an inch. Katja gasped when she saw her daughter. Zofia just bit her lower lip and shook her head at Katja, warning her not to mention that Ima had chopped off her hair. Ima plopped down in the corner of the sofa and wrapped her slender arms around her chest.

"Hi, Ima." The female police officer smiled. "You gave us quite a scare last night."

Ima shrugged. "I'm fine," she said, looking down at the floor as if there were something very interesting that she'd never seen there before.

"Yes, I can see that. Can you tell us where you were yesterday? Why you never went to school or came home on time? What happened?"

"Nothing happened. I was with some friends. That's it; that's all."

"Can you give us their names?"

"I don't remember. I met them yesterday. I don't want to talk about it. I'm fine."

"All right. But if you need help, you can call me, and I'll be happy to help you. We have someone on staff who you can talk to, a counselor. I mean, if you need to talk, she is a good listener…"

Ima nodded.

"Here is my card."

Ima took the card and put it down on the coffee table. The officer forced a smile at Ima, and then she got up and left.

"What happened to your hair?" Katja asked. She had to ask. She couldn't believe that her daughter had butchered her hair when she was in her room the previous night. She looked terrible, like one of the pictures Katja had seen of women in the concentration camps.

"I cut it. I got sick of it, sick of looking like a child."

Katja walked over and touched Ima's shorn locks. What was left of her hair looked like it had been shredded with a razor blade. "I would have taken you to the beauty salon to get it cut if you wanted a haircut…"

A deep line formed between Ima's brows.

"I think it looks very cute," Zofia said. "How about maybe you should eat something?" Zofia smiled at Ima.

"I'm not hungry. I'm not going to school today either."

"That's a good idea," Zofia said. "Let's spend the day together. Maybe we can watch a movie on the television. Huh? We always like to watch those old romantic movies, you and me?"

Ima shrugged.

"How about we'll see what's playing? I'll even let you pick what we're going to watch," Zofia said, and she got up to cut a slice of pita bread and put it into the oven to warm. "How about a biseleh pita or maybe a biseleh hummus? I just made this hummus yesterday, and not to brag or anything, but I think it's pretty good."

"I said I'm not hungry," Ima said.

"I know what you said. So I'm going to eat. You can watch me." Zofia sat down at the table and began to smooth the hummus slowly into the pita. Then she put it to her nose and took a deep breath in. "Mmm, it really smells wonderful."

Ima had not eaten since the previous morning. She began to realize that she was hungry, very hungry.

"I guess I'll have some."

"Here," Zofia handed her a large piece of the bread, then moved the plate of hummus and black olives toward her granddaughter.

Katja watched her amazing mother. Zofia always seemed to know what to do in a crisis. What wisdom, what patience. Of course, Katja knew that her mother had been to hell several times and had survived. In her life, Zofia had met the devil face-to-face in the form of a Nazi SS officer, and she'd come through stronger than ever. She'd lost the love of her life twice: once, when she'd believed that he perished during the war, then again when he died after they'd shared many years of deep love. Zofia had realized her dreams of a Jewish homeland. And though she'd endured terrible pain and loss in her life, she'd also experienced love and joy beyond words.

And now Katja knew that, for Zofia, her grandchild was the light of her life. Zofia hid it well, but Katja was sure it hurt her deeply to see Ima suffering. However, because of her own past, Zofia knew how to approach Ima. Unlike Katja, Zofia knew what to say and what not to say.

CHAPTER EIGHTY-FOUR

TWO WEEKS PASSED, and Ima still had not returned to school. Katja found the tubes of lipstick and mascara that Ima had cherished before her disappearance discarded in the trash can.

When Jennifer called, Ima would tell Katja or Zofia to tell Jen that she was asleep. Ima had completely withdrawn into herself. She hardly ate, and her already slender frame was becoming bony. With her short-cropped hair, she looked like a scarecrow. She didn't talk much, just "yes" or "no" answers to any questions posed to her. Ima spent most of her time alone in her room. Katja was beside herself with worry.

"What are we going to do with her, Mama? I think she needs to see a professional, a psychologist," Katja said to Zofia late one night, neither of them able to sleep.

"She wouldn't go, and it wouldn't help until she's ready to work with the doctor. All we can do is let her know that we are here for her and that we love her. Obviously, something terrible happened. Perhaps one of the boys at school forced her to do something…"

"But she won't tell us who it was or what happened. She won't tell us anything. How can we help her if we don't know anything? What can we do?" Katja said, her hands trembling. She had dark, puffy circles under her eyes. She'd always kept her hair perfectly styled in the past, but now it was flat and greasy from needing to be washed. She'd stopped coordinating meetings and fund drives for her organization. Instead, she stayed home all day and watched Ima, who moved through the house like a ghost. "I'm so afraid she will do something to hurt herself."

"I know. So am I. But if we try to force her to talk, she'll only withdraw more. All we can do is wait for her to come to us."

But Ima hardly ever left her bedroom. And when she did, she did not speak to her mother or her grandmother unless it was absolutely necessary. Even then, she said as little as possible.

One day, Ima came out of her room. She'd lined her eyes with thick black eyeliner and wore such heavy mascara that her lashes looked like giant black spiders against her pale face. She wore a short, tight, black skirt and a tight, black tee shirt without a bra. The nipples of her small breasts were almost completely visible through the fabric.

"Where did you get those clothes and that makeup?" Katja could not contain herself. She had never seen Ima looking so much like an angry hoodlum.

"I'm going out," Ima said.

"Where? Ima, please talk to me. Where are you going, and what's going on? Are you going with Jennifer?"

"I'm going to the bowling alley and not with Jennifer."

Katja shot a look at Zofia.

"So what's at the bowling alley?" Zofia asked, trying to sound calm. "You're going to go bowling in such a skirt as this? You won't be able to move."

"I'm not going to bowl, Grandma." Ima's tone was sarcastic.

"So, what else are you going to do at a bowling alley?" Katja asked.

"I won't know until I get there."

"I forbid you to go looking like that, and your tone with your grandmother is unacceptable. Please, Ima, sit down, and let's try to talk about this," Katja said.

"Bye, Mom. Bye, Gram." Ima walked out the door, slamming it behind her.

Katja put her fist to her open mouth to stifle a scream. "Oh my God, Mama, did you see her? I thought things couldn't get worse, but she's getting worse. I am sick with worry. What are we going to do?"

"Nothing. Right now, there is nothing we can do. If you go and follow her, she might run away from home. We can only wait."

That was the beginning of Ima's change from a shy, sweet, dreamy-eyed teenager to a promiscuous, lost girl. Sometimes, she stayed out all night. She went back to school, but she did not attend classes. The school counselor called Katja for a meeting and told her that Ima was out of control. The counselor said that Ima was flunking out and getting a bad reputation. She'd lost most of her close friends, and the high school boys swarmed around the house like wild dogs sniffing out a female dog in heat.

Katja and Zofia were at their wits' end. Without a father, there was no male support to lean on, and it was clear that Ima had lost all respect for herself. She had no permanent relationships. The boys came through like an assembly line. Jennifer had stopped calling and coming by. But worst of all, there was nothing Katja or Zofia could do to stop Ima's descent down the path of self-degradation.

CHAPTER EIGHTY-FIVE

IMA HATED HERSELF. She hated her body. If only one, just one of those boys she had sex with, made her feel worthwhile after they had their way with her, she might have felt better about herself. But the only time she felt loved, the only time she felt beautiful, was when she was in the arms of a lover. As soon as it was over, that terrible emptiness of abandonment set in again.

Worthless, that's what she was, worthless to anyone, even to herself. She considered suicide at least once a day, but she could not get past the fear of death, of the unknown. That was what stopped her. The sexual act itself meant nothing to her. In fact, she derived no pleasure from sex. It was the closeness she craved, and for a little while, she felt loved.

That horrible man had ruined her forever. He'd forced himself on her, then told her that she was good for nothing else but sex. He'd beaten her until she couldn't feel the pain anymore. Then, after he'd finished with her, he threatened to kill her family if she ever told anyone what happened. Ima's life had been shattered like a broken mirror in a single afternoon, leaving her empty.

She began drinking alcohol to numb the pain. It was easy for her to get a bottle of whiskey. All she had to do was trade sexual favors with older men she met outside the liquor store, and they were quite willing to buy the alcohol for her.

Then, one night, one of the men she met outside the liquor store offered her a pill. "Try it," he said, smiling, "it will make you feel beautiful."

Ima had become so reckless that she didn't hesitate. She took the pill and washed it down with a gulp of whiskey. Within a few minutes, she felt so tired that she could not open her eyes. She fell into the most restful, peaceful, blissful sleep she'd ever known.

When she awakened two days later, she found herself in a run-down motel room with the maid pounding on the door. She had no idea how she'd gotten there or what happened while she was asleep. All she knew was that she was alone, naked, and sick to her stomach. She felt dizzy when she got to her feet and vomited on the floor. The maid was still knocking. Ima's headache was blinding.

"Okay, go away. I'll be out of here in a few minutes," she yelled to the maid. Even as she said the words, the throbbing in her head worsened.

She arrived home that afternoon to a panicked mother and grandmother. They were nagging at her. Where was she for two days? They were looking everywhere. They called the police again. Why was she doing this? She wished they would just leave her alone. She felt sick and just wanted to lie down. Her mother was crying again. So, what else was new? She was always crying, always drowning in self-pity.

What the hell did her mother know about her suffering? She'd had a rich, adoring husband who gave her anything and everything she wanted. True, she'd lost him but then found her *cause*, and Katja's devotion to the women in her foundation made Ima sick. It got on Ima's nerves to see Katja always running around trying to do everything for everyone. Well, of course, that was before Ima was raped. Now Katja just sat at home weeping like the pathetic, clawing bitch she was.

Ima wasn't looking for a cause to rescue her, and there was no man she could claim as the love of her life. From her experiences with men, it grieved her to say that she didn't believe she would ever find anyone capable of loving her.

The next two years brought Katja to her knees. Zofia became ill. It began with a lump in her breast, followed by a visit to the doctor and a sobering diagnosis. Surgery followed, and then radiation therapy. Katja was with Zofia constantly, but Zofia was more worried about Ima than herself.

Even Zofia's illness had not cured Ima's internal rage. Instead, Ima began to exchange, regularly, sexual favors for the pills she'd come to love, very addictive pills called Quaaludes.

Katja felt as if she'd aged a thousand years. She was losing the two people she loved the most: her dear mother and her baby girl. But despite the vomiting and inability to keep food down due to the radiation, Zofia never complained. She joked with Katja while she waited for her radiation sessions.

In the waiting room, Katja kept a light attitude, sitting beside Zofia, who looked frail and old in her hospital gown. But as soon as her mother went in for therapy, Katja fell into tears. It seemed as if her life had fallen apart. Sometimes, she thought of Helga, her birth mother. Sometimes, she even wanted to write a letter to Helga to apologize for not understanding.

Zofia pulled through, but she was weak. For now, the doctor said the cancer was in remission. Katja hugged Zofia, but inside, she was riddled with fear. At any time, the cancer could return and claim her mother. Then she would be alone with her daughter, who was out of her reach, a girl who had experienced something terrible and then completely disconnected from her family.

Every morning, Katja and Zofia took short walks. Katja watched as Zofia forced herself to eat, never complaining and always smiling. *Dear God, that woman was strong*, Katja thought.

Finally, Ima turned eighteen. All Israelis were obliged to serve in the IDF, and she was no exception. It was strange to Katja to think that once, long ago, she would have dreaded this day. She would have felt lost to have her daughter go off to serve in the army for two years. Now, because of all that Ima had become, Katja welcomed it. Ima would go for training. If anyone or anything could straighten that girl out, it would be the IDF.

Ima didn't want to go, but there was no refusing. So, with Katja's help, Ima packed as she was told, and Katja drove her to the bus station. They waited together silently until the bus came. Then, clumsily, Katja took Ima in her arms. "I love you, Ima. You be careful and safe, please. Maybe you'll call or write to me?"

"Bye, Mom," Ima said, her eyes blank, dark, and dead as she climbed the stairs and disappeared into the back of the long bus.

CHAPTER EIGHTY-SIX

How can I endure an entire month of this basic training? Ima thought as she was lying on her bunk after the first three days of it. The constant demands of exercise and participation were overwhelming. In fact, this very morning, she'd not been on time for roll call, so her commanding officer had punished her entire group. They were forced to do one hundred pushups and run two miles.

Everyone was angry with her, and she wished she could just get up and leave. There was no way out of this prison. She was convicted of being an Israeli and sentenced to hell. The room was dark. She could hear the steady breathing of all the other recruits, and she began to cry into her pillow.

Damn, if she only had a 'lude—just one pill. That would help. But where the hell could she get a Quaalude in this hellhole? Her body shook. She knew she wouldn't be able to get through the physical training. She needed a pill, just one. Since that day when her innocence had been stolen, she'd felt alone, but never as alone as she felt here and now in the IDF. *I'll get those pills. I'll find a way, no matter what I have to do.*

CHAPTER EIGHTY-SEVEN

SGT Rivka Berkovitz was Ima's squad leader, and she was meeting with her commanding officer, LT Dov, in his office.

"So, how are the new recruits?"

"Most of them will be all right, but I do have one that I am worried about. It's Ima Zaltstein. I think we should give her a dishonorable discharge. She's got mental problems."

"Ah," LT Dov said, rubbing his chin, "so is that how we treat our fellow Israelis? A girl is damaged in her mind, so we just toss her away like a used tissue. Is that how we do it, Sergeant?"

"She's a lot of work, and I'm not sure she will ever be up to standard."

"Yes, there are some of our recruits that take more work than others. But getting her up to standard, Sergeant, is your job. If you think she needs mental help, then see to it that she gets it. Work her hard, clean her up, and make her into a soldier, an Israeli soldier. That's what we do, Sergeant. We don't just throw our own people away."

SGT Berkovitz nodded her head, but she had a frown on her pretty, sun-kissed face. "Yes, sir," she said, anticipating the job ahead of her. This one would take extra time, but LT Dov was right. This was what she was there for, and she would do whatever was necessary to turn this girl into an Israeli soldier.

CHAPTER EIGHTY-EIGHT

The harder SGT Berkovitz was on Ima, the more Ima fought her. SGT Berkovitz put Ima into the hospital to detoxify her body from the drugs. Ima was like an animal. She screamed and fought, but SGT Berkovitz persisted. Ima lay on a cot for three weeks, kicking, screaming, and begging for drugs until she fell asleep, only to awaken in an hour or so crying and shaking.

One afternoon, Ima was so bad that she hit her head against the wall. The doctors called SGT Berkovitz and told her they were forced to put Ima into a straightjacket.

I cannot give up on her, SGT Berkovitz thought. *It would be a waste of Jewish life, and I must not allow that to happen.* SGT Berkovitz heard the young girl's screams in her dreams every night. It would be so easy just to tell LT Dov that she couldn't help Ima. But then, every morning, SGT Berkovitz tried again. She put her heart and soul into rehabilitating this lost girl. It was not as if she didn't have enough to train the other new recruits, but every day, SGT Berkovitz found time to go to the hospital and check on Ima.

When Ima was finally discharged from the hospital, she was weak and tired, but she was clean and detoxed. SGT Berkovitz knew that Ima needed to be watched very closely, or she would find a way to get her hands on drugs again. So, SGT Berkovitz assigned one of the other recruits, Noam, to help take care of Ima. Noam was a short but solid young man with thick muscles that stretched across his body and a thick mane of black hair that reminded SGT Berkovitz of a picture of a black lion she'd seen once.

"Make sure she stays clean. Make sure that she eats, and if you have any trouble with her, let me know," SGT Berkovitz instructed.

"I will," Noam said.

"Report to me and keep me updated on her progress," SGT Berkovitz said, glad to have someone else to help her with this problematic girl.

Noam had no patience. He yelled at Ima to get out of bed. But Ima just laid there and sobbed. Noam would demand that she stop crying, but Ima would still lie there, weeping softly.

"Come on, Ima. Let's get up and get moving."

"Go to hell," she said.

"Get up, now!" he commanded.

"Fuck you." She turned over to face the wall.

It was a week later that Noam gave up. He could not work with this troubled girl and went to SGT Berkovitz to tell her.

SGT Berkovitz was not surprised. Ima was unwilling to try to better herself, making it almost impossible to help her. So SGT Berkovitz, at her wit's end, went back to LT Dov and asked him what to do about Ima's situation.

LT Dov rubbed his chin with his hand as he looked across the desk at SGT Berkovitz. They'd had people like this before in the IDF. There were special squad leaders who were better trained to work with them. SGT Berkovitz had tried. She'd given it her best shot. That was all that LT Dov could expect. He took a deep breath. "I think we should send her to another squad. I know an officer who is very good with people with problems. It's his specialty. I'll contact him today. You prepare the papers."

"Yes, sir," SGT Berkovitz said, glad to be rid of Ima.

CHAPTER EIGHTY-NINE

IMA KNEW that there was no way out of the IDF. She would have to serve her two years; if she continued to be uncooperative, they would keep her in boot camp even longer. It was terrible. Every day, someone was bothering her to exercise, yelling at her to pull herself together when all she really longed for was a Quaalude and some peace. If she had a bottle of Quaaludes, she would have taken all of them and ended her miserable life.

Rivka told her they planned to transfer her to another squad as if that might make a difference. As far as Ima was concerned, it was just Noam and SGT Berkovitz's way of getting rid of her, pawning her off on someone else. *So, who cares? What difference did it make?* Rivka told her that the squad where she was being sent was for troubled people. Well, that might be good after all. If there were other people who took drugs, some of them might have connections and be able to smuggle some good stuff into the barracks.

CHAPTER NINETY

STAFF SERGEANT IDO HADAR sat at his desk and swatted a fly buzzing around his ear. He had looked twice at the files on Ima that he'd been sent on Ima. He still held the papers in his hand and shook his head. There was more to this girl. Something had to have happened to her to make her so angry. It was just a matter of finding out what that was, and then he would be able to work with her.

Ima Zaltstein, he thought—my project for the next six months at least. She would be arriving in a few hours. LT Dov had sent a personal letter asking Ido to see what he could do to rehabilitate this one. Well, Ido had never lost one, at least not yet. He refused to surrender a single Israeli as a lost cause. Every person counted, and he was prepared to do whatever he had to save this girl. Not one Jewish life, not one could be lost. Israel is a small country, Ido thought, and she desperately needs the support of every single one of her citizens.

Ido watched out his office window as Ima got out of the car that had brought her. Her hair had grown back and was hanging uncombed over her shoulders. She was as skinny as a corpse. And even from where he sat, he could see Ima's large eyes surrounded by dark, bruised-looking skin. He knew it wasn't from bruising, though. It was from lack of proper sleep and nutrition.

The guard who brought Ima knocked on Ido's door.

"Come in," Ido said.

"This is Private Ima Zaltstein."

"Hello, Ima, have a seat," Ido said. Then, turning to the guard, he said, "You may go. I have her from here. Thank you."

Ima, who felt she could see through men all the way to their disgusting souls, could not help but look at this tall, handsome Israeli with his strong, honest face and feel a twinge of attraction. *I'm sure he's just like all the others, just out for sex, and that's all.* But somehow, his eyes conveyed a different message.

"Welcome, Ima. My name is SSG Hadar," his voice was warm, comforting, and gentle.

She nodded her head and looked away from him. His eyes were too honest, and that scared her.

"I know you don't want to be here. But I am here to help you, and I am going to help you."

"If you want to help me, then just let me out of here. Or better yet, just give me a bottle of sleeping pills and let me get out of this miserable world."

He smiled. "Well, I have no plans to do either of those things, but I am going to help you."

"Yes, I'm sure you are. You're another one who has my best interest at heart, right?"

She was bold. She should not talk to her squad leader that way. Ido wanted to correct her, but he knew he had to reach her first, and alienating her was not the way.

"Believe it or not, Ima, I do have your best interest at heart."

"Hmm, I'll bet," she said.

SSG Hadar came to Ima's bunk every morning and personally forced her out of bed. At first, she complained, cursing at him and calling him names. But SSG Hadar persisted by pouring cold water over her head and dragging her out of bed. She tore at him with her nails, but he was quick and avoided her attacks. "You might as well try to work with me because I'm not giving up," he said.

She stuck her tongue out at him. Surprising her, he laughed. The next day, he came to drag her out of bed with a handful of hard candy.

"Look what I have for you," he said, pulling the colorfully wrapped candy from his pocket.

"I don't want candy. What do you think I am? A child?"

"Well, you are acting like one, aren't you?" he asked.

She glared at him and then laughed. "Oh shit, just give me a piece of candy. I could use a little sugar right now."

He laughed, too, and handed her the pile of sweets. She opened one and put it into her mouth. "It's good."

"Yeah," he said, "they're my favorite. Have you ever had raspberry hard candy before?"

"Actually, no."

"It's rare. And you see, Ima, I care enough about you to share my rare candy with you."

She couldn't help but smile.

"Come on now. Let me help you," he said. "If you have to be here in the IDF anyway, let's make this whole thing easier on both of us."

"I don't want to be here. I want to go home. Don't you think it's unfair that people are forced to serve Israel when they don't want to?"

"No, I don't. I think that Israel needs its people. In turn, our country gives us its all, its everything."

"Well, I think it's unfair. I think that people should have the right to choose whether they want to be here or not, and I don't. I don't see the point. I want to go home."

"I have a very special day planned for you today, Ima."

"Hmm, I'll bet. More exercise, more torture," she grunted.

"We'll see. Give me a chance."

That morning, Ido took Ima to a building that was newly constructed. They walked inside. The young woman at the desk knew Ido by name.

"Hello, SSG Hadar. You've come to do some volunteer work again?"

"Yes, I brought a new soldier with me."

The woman at the desk smiled at Ima. "Welcome," she said, "I'm Tamar. If you two need anything, just let me know. The kids will be glad to see you again, SSG Hadar."

"I'm glad to be here." He smiled. "Is it possible that the kids could have the day off from studying so we can visit them?"

"I'm sure it will be fine. I know that they are at recess right now. Let me see what I can arrange to give them the day off from class," Tamar said.

"Thanks." Ido smiled at Tamar and then turned to Ima. "Follow me."

They walked down a long hall and passed several rooms where children were sitting at desks in class with a teacher at the front of the room. Then, they came to an indoor area where children were playing. Each of them seemed to have a physical handicap. Some were missing limbs, and others had trauma to their faces. But as soon as they saw SSG Hadar, they called out his name and came toward him as quickly as their disabilities would allow them to move.

He walked to each of them and gave them a handful of candy as he emptied his pockets. Ima watched without saying a word.

"What's wrong with them? This isn't a hospital. It looks like a school," she whispered to SSG Hadar.

"It's an orphanage. All the kids in this room came from another orphanage that was bombed in a terrorist attack. They get special treatment here because of their physical and psychological disabilities. They still take classes, though. The fact that they have been damaged does not mean they no longer have any worth. Israel will find a way to bring out their personal talents. But today, they will not study. Today is an exception because we are here."

All afternoon, the children played with SSG Hadar. Ima was amazed at his ability to charm them. But she was also astonished that the kids didn't seem bitter or angry. They were orphans, and they'd been hurt in a bombing, but still, they laughed and played. It seemed they didn't know how bad things were for them.

Ima began playing with the children as the day progressed, and as she did, she forgot her own misery. They were smart and alert. It was obvious that they were not being ignored. Instead, each was being trained and educated according to his or her abilities. They knew they were treasured, and because of this, they had self-respect and self-esteem.

In the car on the way back to the base, Ima turned to look at SSG Hadar. His profile as he drove was strong and righteous.

"They're an amazing bunch of kids."

"Yes, they are. Do you know why?"

"No, actually, I don't. I cannot believe they aren't angry because of everything that's happened to them."

"I brought you here for a reason. What you saw today, Ima, that's Israel! We don't give up on our own. We work with our people. We help them, and we never discard them, no matter what. Every single person here is taught to fit in and become a productive member of our society. That's why, no matter what you say or what you do, I will never give up on you."

She could not look at him. She turned her face toward the car window and felt a tear form in the corner of her eye. How could this man still have faith in her when she did not even have faith in herself?

SSG Hadar used light exercise to free her from her depression. He did not push her as hard as he might have pushed another soldier who was more adjusted. She needed tender, loving care, so he began to work with her slowly. He sat beside her at breakfast and talked with her while they ate. However, his real goal was to make sure that she ate. He knew this would take time, so he waited and waited.

SSG Hadar had done this before. In fact, he was well-known in the IDF for fixing the toughest cases. His work with misfits had earned him a hero's reputation amongst the other officers. It was a status that embarrassed him. He knew from experience that she would eventually talk. Once she felt she could trust him, she would tell him what had happened to make her this way. And after she began to open up to him, he knew instinctively that he would be able to help her.

To Ima, SSG Hadar was funny. Things that would have irritated her in the past now amused her. Looking at life through SSG Hadar's eyes, Ima could not help but laugh at herself. He actually had a way of making the training tolerable, sometimes even fun. She even began to feel that she might be able to live without drugs. Maybe.

Ima jumped back and fell on her rump the first time she fired a gun at target practice. SSG Hadar laughed, but not at her, with her. He extended his hand to her and helped her to her feet, and she laughed, too.

"I never realized it would be so loud or intense," she said.

"You have a good eye. I can tell." SSG Hadar stood close and helped her hold the rifle properly. "Now aim," he said, both of them looking straight at the target. But he felt her hair brush against his face, and his heart beat like a triphammer. "Ready?" he asked.

"I think so." She fired and hit the target, not the bullseye but the target.

"Great job!" he said. "You're going to put the others to shame. You have the natural talent of a marksman."

She laughed. "I hope I'll never have to go to battle."

"Don't worry. I'm training you for office work," he said. "You're far too pretty to go to battle. You're going to have to get married and make some beautiful Jewish babies someday. We need more Israelis," Ido said. But he didn't tell her that he still wasn't quite sure he could trust her, and he would not let her have access to a gun when he wasn't around—at least not yet.

Why did he say that about making babies? Was he trying to seduce her? Not another one of those men who wanted one thing from her. She thought SSG Hadar was different. She hoped she wasn't wrong about him. That would be so disappointing.

But he did not try to touch her or kiss her. He was just kind and easy with her, letting her work through her insecurities one by one.

When the others gathered to talk or play cards in the evening,

SSG Hadar took Ima walking. In the first several weeks, neither of them spoke much. Then he began telling Ima a little about his past.

"So I was born here in Haifa. My mother is a school teacher; my father is an electrical engineer. They met and got married very young."

"Were both of them native to Israel?"

"Yes. They had two more children. I have a sister who is older than me, and I had a brother, but unfortunately, he died at birth. My parents have always worked hard. They believe in this country. They believe in the power of a Jewish homeland. And that's where I got my values, I guess because Israel is the most important thing in my life."

"Every Israeli says that. Every Israeli except me," she said.

"You're so cynical, Ima. Why?"

"Well, you really want to know?"

"Of course. I wouldn't ask if I didn't want to know."

"My father was killed in the Six-Day War. He was a lawyer. I don't remember him at all. My mom and grandma raised me. My grandmother was a Holocaust survivor, and apparently, she adopted my mother. They don't talk much about it, and my mom gets flustered when I ask questions. I'd really like to know more about my background, like who my mom's birth parents were. You know, just so that I could know if I have any genetic predisposition to any diseases. But when I ask my mother, she avoids the questions.

"Anyway, my mom was never much of a mother. She was too caught up in this foundation she created for the widowed wives of Israeli soldiers. Yep, everyone loves my mother. She will do anything for anybody as long as they aren't in her family. And I mean anything. She was always ready to help—anyone but me, that is. I was ignored most of the time. She was always on the phone with one of her friends or members. And if she wasn't on the phone, she was out.

"My gram is okay, but she's old. She hoards things. It's kind of strange. No matter what it is, Gram will find a use for it. She keeps old string and pieces of fabric. What can I say? She's a little odd. I wish I'd known my dad, but I was raised by two women."

"Women are just as strong as men," he said.

"Stronger, I think. Women can control themselves. Men are controlled by their dicks."

"You have such a foul mouth, Ima. Not all men are controlled by their sexual desires. Some men actually care about their character and their integrity."

"Oh, sure. I'm sure men like that are in storybooks. Not in real life. I've never met one."

"Well, you have now. I am not controlled by my urges. I find you to be a beautiful woman, yet I would never think of taking advantage of your position. You see, Ima, how I see myself is more important to me than how the world sees me. I am responsible to myself for my actions. And when I go to sleep at night, I sleep with a good conscience because I believe that I am acting in the right way. Do you understand?"

She nodded but twisted her mouth as she struggled to believe him. It was true. He'd always acted with honor. In fact, he'd never used bad language like she did. She smiled to herself quietly. Ima knew that she used vulgar language to get a rise out of people, to have an effect, to offend, to get their full attention. And somehow, she knew that SSG Hadar understood her fully, the way no one had ever understood her before.

They walked quietly for a few minutes. Then she turned to face him. "Do you want to sleep with me tonight?" she asked.

"Yes," he said, "but I won't. I'm your squad leader."

"So?"

"So I don't think it's appropriate that we engage in that sort of thing, you know?"

"No, I don't know."

"Well, then, I am telling you."

"You don't find me attractive."

"I just told you a few minutes ago that I think you are beautiful. But I will control my urges, my friend Ima. I will help you, not take advantage of you."

The evening walks SSG Hadar and Ima shared became a daily ritual that Ima anticipated with pleasure. He was the first man she'd ever felt she could trust entirely. And as the weeks flew by, she felt closer to him than she'd ever felt to anyone.

Because she was happy, Ima began to see the world through different eyes. She even began to feel more kindly toward her mother and grandmother. She wrote them long letters as she lay on her bunk at night, telling them about how new life felt and about Ido. However, she could not bring herself to mail them, not yet. It felt strange to write about him. In fact, writing brought all of her feelings to the surface, and as she held the pen in her trembling hand, she felt tears form in her eyes.

Could she be falling in love? Ima? The girl who didn't believe in love? The girl who used sex to manipulate men against their own sick nature? But SSG Hadar Ido was different. He was unlike any other man she'd ever known. And Ima believed in her heart that something inside of her, something crucial, had changed. In fact, she hardly knew herself as she continued to write the letter. When she finished, she folded it and placed it in her footlocker at the head of her bed. Someday, she would send them, but not today.

It had been a long time since Ima had given any thought to her appearance. She'd hacked her hair off in the bathroom when it got too long, and she failed to comb it so often that it was always a mess of knots. Sometimes, she drew thick black eyeliner around her eyes just for shock value. On other days, she wore no makeup at all. Now she looked in the mirror, really looked at herself. She was unkempt, sloppy, a frightened child who took no pride in herself. This look of the walking dead no longer served her. In fact, it became important to Ima that Ido think she was pretty. And as she gazed at her reflection, she doubted that even an angel would find it possible to see her as attractive.

So she asked one of the other girls, who was a hairdresser before joining the IDF, to cut her hair. Because of the uneven length, Ima's hair had to be cut to her shoulders. But, after the fresh cut and shampoo, her hair fell into golden curls, just like her mother's had at her age.

Then she went to the commissary and purchased a pale pink lipstick and matching rouge. She abandoned the heavy black eyeliner and replaced it with a light coat of mascara. When Ima looked into the mirror, she saw a surprisingly young, beautiful girl with an air of innocence. *How could this be? Innocent? Hardly.*

But that night, when Ima and Ido went walking, Ima felt excitement travel through her as she saw the look on Ido's face. There was no doubt in her mind that he noticed the difference. However, unlike any of the men in her past, Ido did nothing about his attraction. When Ido didn't try to kiss Ima, she became angry for allowing herself to be vulnerable.

In fact, she decided that she would put a stop, here and now, to any feelings she might be developing for Ido. She would ruin this before it started, and she knew just how to do it. She would just tell him about her past. She would tell him everything. Then he would see her for what she was, and she could go back to being comfortable and safe as a person without feelings.

"Ido…"

"Yes?"

"You don't really know much about me."

"That's true," he said, looking up at the stars. "It's a beautiful night, yes?"

"Yes, I suppose. Do you want to know more about me?"

"I want to know only what you want to tell me."

"I'm ugly, Ido. I'm damaged, and I'm ugly inside," she said, hating herself for wanting him to love her and feeling undeserving of his love. She wanted to look into his eyes and see that he felt disgust and disdain toward her. Only then would she be free of these feelings.

"I was raped. Beaten and raped by an old, disgusting pig-of-a-man. He beat me and threatened me." She was crying, and her nose was running.

Once she'd said the word 'rape,' the rest spewed from her mouth like vomit. She told him how terrified she'd felt when she got into the car and found that the door and window handles had been removed. The man's words came rushing back to her. He'd called her a whore, a slut. His hands, his terrible, thick hands, were covered in black, curly, pubic-like hair, forcing themselves inside her innocent body.

She wept now as she'd never wept before, with sorrow so heartfelt that the sound tore through the night like the pain of a dying creature. The shame she felt after it was over, her disgust and hatred for her own body. She told Ido. She told him all of it. How painful it was when she'd gotten up and tried to run away, only to be caught and punched in the face until she fell to the ground.

She choked on her sobs, but she could not stop the flow of the words. Ima told Ido of the terrible agony and how her body had ceased to be her own when this horrific devil-of-a-man had parted her and invaded the deepest, most sacred place inside her. Then she told him how she'd despised her femininity and used her own body as a tool to get the drugs that blocked all of her emotions and made her numb.

Suddenly, Ima began to vomit, purging the deepest, darkest memories from the depths of her soul. Ima fell to the ground when she finished, covering her face with her hands. "So now you know. Now you know what I am."

Ido knelt beside her, gently pushing her vomit-soiled hair away from her face and behind her ear. Then he took his hand and lifted her chin, forcing her to see his eyes.

"It wasn't your fault, Ima," he said.

The kindness and sincerity of his voice drove the pain deeper inside of her, and she winced at the tenderness.

"Yes, but what came after the rape was my fault," she said, the anguish clearly seen on her face. A deep wrinkle had formed between her eyes. Her skin was blotchy with tears, but still, she continued. It was as if she could not control the words. They had taken power over her. Now, she would put an end to the silly dreams she'd been having about a future with Ido. It would all stop right here, right now. He would know the truth.

"Maybe you do not understand what I am telling you. After the rape, I wasn't the same after that day anymore. I was a whore, a slut. I was trading sex with anyone who would give me money for drugs. I watched how easily men could be manipulated by their sick desires. Because I was nothing but a tramp, men never hid what they really were from me the way they did from other girls. Decent girls. I saw them as the pigs that they were. And because of that, I decided I would never fall in love."

She was crying so hard now that she began coughing. "I hated my body. I hated my mother for being busy with the organization she formed. Too busy for me. I hated my father for not being there to protect me, for dying and leaving me vulnerable and alone. I hated men for the urges that made them hurt and use women. But most of all, I hated myself. I know that something inside me made that man do what he did to me."

"I understand how you feel. But it was nothing you did. It was him. He was a perverted man. No normal person would want to have sex with someone who did not want him. Only someone very sick could rape."

She looked away from him.

"You have to believe me, Ima. It was nothing you did. It was all him. I promise you that it was all him. There was a missing piece in his head. You can't blame yourself. You can't allow this to destroy your precious life. You're young. You have so much ahead of you."

"Ido, when I first met you, I hated you, too. But now, I don't hate you. In fact, I don't hate you at all. But the worst part of all this is that I don't deserve you. You're too good for me. I'm a whore."

"Shh, Ima. You're not a whore. You're a deeply hurt girl, and you lashed out in anger, mostly at yourself. I understand you."

Neither of them spoke for several minutes. The crickets chirped in the trees.

"I think I love you, Ido."

"I know," he said. "I've known for a while."

"You knew how I felt before I did?"

"Maybe I knew. Maybe it was wishful thinking," he said.

"You don't love me, do you?" her voice was so soft he could hardly hear her.

He sighed and looked away. "Ima, I have very strong feelings for you, very strong. In a week, you will be out of basic training and relocated to a base. I am proud of the strong, healthy woman that you have become. But I honor the IDF because every day, the Israeli Army puts its all into rehabilitating those who need it.

"So, out of respect, as long as I am your squad leader, it is inappropriate for us to have a relationship. I am your superior, and I must behave in the proper way. But I am going to ask for a transfer to the base where you are stationed. I do not want to be in charge of your squad. That way, it will be all right if we are dating. The reason I am asking for this transfer is because of you. I think I am in love with you, too."

She could not believe what she'd just heard. Was this real? Was it really possible? Ima felt like whirling around in circles as she did when she was a little girl pretending to be a ballerina. But instead, she was crying again. Did this wonderful, kind, gentle, strong man really love her? She bit her knuckle just to be sure she was not dreaming. Then she fell into his arms, and he held her there for a long time but did not kiss her. He would not kiss her until he was no longer her superior officer.

CHAPTER NINETY-ONE

BARI no longer needed private training. When she turned eleven, she began attending classes. By the time she was seventeen, she was studying at the studio with a class of teenagers. That was where she met Marilyn Goldstein, a quiet girl whom Bari found easy to befriend.

During the week, the two girls attended after-school classes at the karate studio. Then, on weekends, they went shopping or out to lunch. Lucas was glad to see Bari had finally made a friend.

Janice was too busy with her career to notice. She'd gotten a promotion and was now president of the art department. It took up a great deal of her time. However, even though she hardly knew her daughter, she was still controlling and overprotective of her. Lucas tried to talk Janice into allowing Bari to go to popular teenage nightclubs with Marilyn, but Janice would not give her permission.

One afternoon, Marilyn was sick and didn't show up for karate class. Afterward, Lucas asked Bari if she'd like to go and get a cup of tea at the diner down the street.

"Sure, Dad."

They sat across from each other, sipping the tea.

"You know, I'm really proud of you," Lucas said as he stirred honey into his tea.

"You mean because I'm up to test for my brown belt next week?"

"Yep, that's quite an accomplishment."

"I know. I could never have done it without you."

Lucas smiled. "It was all you. I was only the instructor."

She shrugged and smiled at him. "And a great dad."

He laughed. "I try."

"Dad, can I ask you a question?"

"Sure, Bari."

Bari looked away. "Dad, do you think I'll ever meet someone? I mean, do you think I'll ever have a boyfriend?"

Bari had never been on a date. In fact, she'd never been to a school dance or had a boy call her on the phone.

"Of course, you will," Lucas said. He was concerned because he knew that Janice kept Bari under such a tight rein that it was hard for her to behave like the other teenagers.

"Even Marilyn has been out on a date with a guy, but I never have."

Lucas nodded. He wasn't sure what to say. It was time for Bari to start dating. Again, he was going to have to talk to Janice. He dreaded it. Janice could be so difficult sometimes.

That night, he talked to Janice. She was appalled at the idea.

"Janice, she has to grow up sometime. She's seventeen."

"I remember what boys were like when I was seventeen."

"If you don't let her have some freedom, she will rebel. And then you won't be able to reach her at all," Lucas said.

"Oh, Lucas, it's just that she's still my baby. You know?"

"Yes, sweetheart, I understand. But do you know what a mama bird does when her babies are old enough to fly?"

"No, Lucas, I don't." Janice's voice was rocky with frustration.

"The mama bird throws them out of the nest. She forces them to fly because she knows that they will never fly if they don't fly now. And if they don't ever fly, they will die."

"I get your point, Lucas. I'll try to let go a little."

"Thank you, love." He kissed her.

CHAPTER NINETY-TWO

THAT SAME YEAR, Lucas planted his feet firmly, and with the strength of an oak tree, he held his wife and stepdaughter as they grieved when Janice's father passed away.

Ronald Lichtenstein died quietly in his sleep. When the phone rang in the wee hours of the morning, Lucas knew that something wasn't right. Janice took the call. Lucas could see by the look on her face that something bad had happened. Janice told Lucas and Bari that her father had died. Then she became hysterical, and Bari Lynn followed suit. Lucas helped the two women get themselves together, and then they went to the Lichtenstein home. There, Janice comforted her mother while Lucas took care of the funeral arrangements.

After the funeral, Janice asked Lucas if he wanted to move the family into the Lichtenstein home. It was much bigger than theirs, and they could rent their home to a young couple. The money they could charge for rent would easily be able to pay their mortgage. Janice said it would mean a lot to her to know that her mother would not be alone. Lucas considered the situation. He would have preferred to stay in his own house.

"Are you sure you want to move in with your mom?"

"I don't know if you can understand, Lucas, but I caused her and my dad so much aggravation over the years. I feel so guilty for everything that I put them through. And now, she's all alone, and we don't really have room for her to move into our house. I mean, my parents' house is so much bigger."

He nodded with understanding. Lucas had lived with Janice long enough to know how she felt just by looking into her eyes. Over the last year, she'd told him several times just how sorry she was for having run off to Israel when she was younger. She felt guilty for shaming her parents by her divorce and having to raise a child alone, without a husband. She had said that she knew her parents had suffered the chatter of the neighbors who had quietly questioned whether Janice had ever truly been married or if Bari was born out of wedlock.

It hadn't mattered what the Lichtensteins told their friends; the community had always leaned toward the juiciest gossip, which meant they had believed the worst. People never considered who could be hurt by their casual words.

Since Bari was born, Lucas knew his wife had gained more respect for her parents, knowing how hard they'd tried to raise her. In truth, Lucas had never really had a problem with his mother-in-law. She could be opinionated, holding the views of her husband, but Lucas was so easygoing and so forgiving that it had never really bothered him. Now, Frances Lichtenstein was a lonely woman with no one else to turn to but her daughter.

"Okay, we can move in with your mom if it's what you want."

"We'll just rent the house out. That way, if you ever feel that you can't take living with my mom anymore, we can move back in."

So Bari, Lucas, Janice, and Harry, their cat, moved in with Bari's grandmother.

Sometimes, if he allowed himself to think about it, Lucas still missed living in the back of the karate studio. Often late at night or on a Sunday afternoon when the studio was closed, he would go there alone to meditate, burn candles and incense, or read the *I Ching*. Mostly, he just liked to take some time to clear his energy.

CHAPTER NINETY-THREE

Chicago 1984

When Bari Lynn was eighteen, her best and only friend, Marilyn Goldstein, was going on a trip to Israel with the young adult group from her synagogue, Temple Beth Israel. Bari Lynn had not attended Temple since her grandfather died. But when Marilyn asked her to join her on the trip, Bari was excited. She wanted to go. This would be her first time going anywhere without her parents or grandparents.

Bari had grown up to be an attractive young woman, if not beautiful. She had thick auburn hair that fell to her shoulders, strong cheekbones, deep brown eyes, and a warm olive complexion. Unlike her mother, she was tall, and because of the years she'd spent training with Lucas, she'd shed the excess weight of her youth and now had a lean, muscular build. Bari knew that her mother wouldn't approve of her traveling halfway across the world with Marilyn and her Temple, so she knew the best thing to do was talk to Lucas. Lucas had a way of getting to her mother. He was the only one who could sway her.

"Dad." Bari found Lucas sitting outside on the porch, sipping a cup of herbal tea and reading a book. "Can we talk?"

"Sure, sit down." Lucas smiled at Bari and indicated a chair. Bari sat down across from Lucas.

"You want some tea?" he asked.

She shook her head. "No, thanks."

"What's the matter?" Lucas laid the book on the table, giving Bari Lynn his attention. He seemed to have a sixth sense. Perhaps it was intuition, or maybe he was just very sensitive. But Lucas was immediately aware that something was going on with Bari.

"I want to go on a trip with Marilyn. I don't think Mom is going to let me go. She's so overprotective, and well, she's ruining my life."

Lucas raised his eyebrows in thought.

"It wouldn't be just the two of us going on this trip. A whole group of people in their late teens will be going, and I was invited to join them."

Lucas knew how hard it was for Bari to make friends. Even though she'd come a long way from the chubby little child sitting on the sidelines, she was still shy and not outgoing. So he was surprised that she even wanted to go on a trip with a youth group, but he thought it would be good for her.

As much as he loved Janice, he knew she could be overbearing when it came to Bari. Janice had a difficult time allowing Bari to grow up. Bari was fighting to overcome the insecurities that had been set in motion when she was just a child, but Janice constantly reinforced the fear. Lucas did what he could to foster Bari's independence. He watched as she tried to break free, and he was afraid that if Janice didn't loosen the reins on her daughter, she might rebel, and then she could get into trouble.

So, a trip with a youth group seemed like an ideal way for Bari to come out of her shell.

"Where are they going?" Lucas asked.

"To Israel. Didn't Mom go to Israel at my age?"

The words hit Lucas in the stomach. He knew that Janice wouldn't want Bari anywhere near Israel after what had happened to her there. Worse yet, it drove Lucas crazy that Janice had lied to

Bari and told her that her father was dead. He hated lies, and this one had always bothered him.

"Israel?" Lucas sighed.

"Yes, I'd like to see Israel. Marilyn and her parents are active in the synagogue, and Marilyn always talks about how her parents feel that having a Jewish homeland is important. Truthfully, Dad, I don't know about all that. For me, it would just be great to spend a little time on a vacation with a friend, away from Mom."

"When is this trip taking place?"

"In the beginning of February. They want to go in the winter because the summers in Israel are too hot."

"Well, I guess I'll have to figure out a way to talk to your mother."

"Thanks, Dad." Bari was glowing. "I knew you'd help me."

Lucas bit the inside of his cheek. Israel. Couldn't it be Paris, or Texas, or anywhere but Israel?

CHAPTER NINETY-FOUR

JANICE, Lucas, and Bari met at the house later that night when Janice had finished work and Lucas had finished classes.

"I'm tired. Let's order a pizza," Janice said.

"Okay with me. How about you, Bari?" Lucas asked.

"Sure."

They sat at the table and ate while Janice talked about one of the students who was giving a teacher in her department lots of problems. Janice was angry, and the more she rambled about the situation, the more livid she became.

Lucas and Bari cast glances at each other.

"Why don't you just let go of all that for tonight? Let me get you a glass of wine," Lucas said.

"You're right. I don't know why I bring all of this home with me."

Lucas got up and poured a glass of merlot for Janice and one for himself. She took a sip.

"That's better," she said.

Lucas turned on some soft rock on the radio. "Karma Chameleon" was playing.

"I love this song," Janice said.

"Yeah, I like it too," Lucas said.

Janice emptied her glass, and Lucas refilled it.

Lucas cleared his throat. "Jan, listen, we need to talk about something."

"Sure." Janice put her slice of pizza down. She was much more relaxed.

"Bari talked to me. She wants to go on a trip with a youth group. I think it's a good idea."

"What youth group? Bari doesn't belong to any group," Janice said.

"Marilyn does. And she invited Bari to join her."

Janice took a bite of pizza. "Sounds cool. Where are they going?"

Lucas was surprised to get such a positive reaction but knew the tough part was yet to come. He bit his lower lip. "Israel."

"What? Absolutely not." Janice threw the slice of pizza back onto her paper plate. "There are a million places in this world that you could go. You're not going there."

"But, Mom, you did…"

"Exactly. And that's why I forbid you to go there. Wars break out there all the time. There is always trouble there, and you have no business going. Besides, it's probably expensive."

"I'll work. I'll get a part-time job and pay for it myself."

"No. I said no!"

"Why, Mom? Why do you have to be like this?"

"Because I said no, and that's the end of it."

Bari started crying. She pushed the chair out from the table and ran to her room.

Lucas didn't say a word. He just looked at Janice.

"Not Israel, Lucas. I don't want her going there. Not after what I went through in that country."

"Jan, you can't hold on to her forever."

"There is just too much shit in the past for me to allow this. I just can't."

Lucas nodded. He knew his wife. He had to let her digest the news and wait until later, after she'd settled down, to bring it up again.

Bari stayed in her room, and Janice went into the bedroom she shared with Lucas. He left her alone and cleaned up after dinner. He'd wait an hour or so and bring her a soothing cup of lemon balm and chamomile tea.

Lucas sat in the living room reading, but he couldn't concentrate. He hated the television. He felt it was a media people used to escape from using their minds. Bari should be told the truth. It was not fair to lie to her, and he felt conflicted. He'd promised Janice to keep the secret, but he hated how the deception made him feel.

Finally, he decided that he must break his promise and tell Bari about her father. Janice would be angry, he knew, but he could not go on lying to Bari. It wasn't fair. After all, Bari had no idea why her mother forbade her from going on this trip, and he didn't want to see her turn against them. He was well-acquainted with rebellion.

He had been an angry teenager because of all the lies he'd been told as he was shuffled from one terrible home to another while in foster care. He'd questioned his caseworker, Miss Parkson, about his background. But she always told him tall tales, lies she believed would make life easier for him to endure. It took years for him to find out the truth about his birth, and he'd never really learned everything, but he knew enough.

When he was sixteen, he'd broken into the main office of Children and Family Services and found his files. It wasn't hard. He knew where his case worker sat. It was just a matter of breaking the lock on the file cabinet at her desk. Then he stole what he believed belonged to him–his files–and took them to the park, where he sat under a street light alone and began to read.

Lucas had been born to a girl of fifteen somewhere in the slums of St. Louis, Missouri. His hand had trembled as he held the paper, but he could not stop. He had to go on reading. It was time he knew the truth.

That night, Lucas learned he had a twin brother who died at birth. The caseworker had written in smeared, blue ink that his mother had given birth prematurely, and the doctor believed that his twin died because of violence inflicted upon his mother during her pregnancy. She noted that she had reason to believe that his mother was a prostitute.

After that night, his own rebellion had begun. Lucas dropped out of high school and was arrested for stealing. He carried a switchblade and wore a black leather jacket. If it had not been for a friend introducing him to the martial arts, Lucas was sure he would be dead or serving life in prison.

Once he found the martial arts studio, his life changed. He found a purpose and answers to questions that burned in his soul. Questions like: Why had he been born? Was there a God? Why would God let him be born into such a bleak existence?

The answers he had found were through meditation and the study of the Eastern ways. They were not cut and dry by any means, but they were enough to help Lucas find inner peace. He became close friends with his teacher, his sensei. Studying hard, he advanced quickly to the black belt. Sensei became the father that he needed so desperately, enlightening him not only with the wisdom of the Far East traditions but also sharing friendship and understanding, something Lucas had never had.

With the confidence he'd gained from working with his sensei, Lucas studied on his own for his GED. He passed the first time he took the test and got his high school diploma. Then Lucas had enrolled in junior college, taking courses in philosophy, but mostly he worked at the studio alongside his sensei, teaching the martial arts.

Material things meant very little to him, so he hardly spent the money he had earned. Once, when he was older, he'd looked for his birth parents but never found them. In the file he'd stolen, he had a last known address for his birth mother, but when he went to that location, he found nothing. Nobody in the area had ever heard of her.

When his sensei died in a car accident, Lucas no longer wanted to stay in the city. He could not bear to go to the studio without his sensei. It was best that he start his life over in a new place. Over the years that he'd worked at the studio, Lucas had saved a nice sum of money, so he took what he had and left St. Louis on the bus. As soon as he arrived in Chicago, he opened his own studio.

Lucas hoped that he'd done for Bari what his sensei did for him. And one thing he remembered that he could count on was that his sensei would always tell him the truth. No matter how harsh that reality might be. Perhaps that was why the lie that Janice had told Bari about her father bothered Lucas as much as it did. In keeping his wife's secret, he felt he was a part of the lie. Bari deserved to know the truth. If she chose to contact her father, for whatever reason, so be it.

Janice hated Elan. Lucas did not believe in holding a grudge, but he understood why Janice felt the way she did, and he would not judge her for her feelings. Elan had hurt her deeply, and even though many years had passed, she still could not find it in her heart to forgive him.

But Lucas' conscience was bothering him. There were no accidents. Everything happened for a reason. And for some reason, Bari was being drawn to go to Israel. Perhaps it was to learn the truth in spite of Janice. Lucas loved his wife, but he knew what he must do.

CHAPTER NINETY-FIVE

JANICE CAME HOME CARRYING her briefcase and a pile of papers. She threw her jacket on the dining room chair. Lucas watched her and could tell by the way that she moved that she'd had another challenging day. Lucas took a deep breath. He dreaded the talk they were about to have.

"Can I get you a drink, Jan?"

"Yeah, vodka and cranberry."

"Sure." Lucas got up and began making the beverage. When he was finished, he handed her the glass.

Janice stepped out of her black high-heeled pumps and sat on the couch. "That bastard, Neilson. He's pushing me far too hard on the budget. They want to cut funding for the arts again! Why is it always the arts? When there is a cut, they always take it from the arts! I don't know what the hell he expects me to do, but he's making me look like an asshole in front of my whole department!"

Lucas sat quietly, breathing deeply, listening, and waiting for her to finish. He'd heard variations of this rant for the past two weeks. It was tedious, but he wanted to be as supportive as possible, so he continued to sit quietly and allowed her to vent. It took over half an hour and an entire drink before she quieted down from her day. When she did, Lucas got up and rubbed her shoulders.

"You have always been so good at massaging," she said, looking up at him.

He smiled. "Your muscles are tight."

"I know. I feel on edge."

"Why don't you take a hot shower, and then we can have dinner?"

"That's a good idea. And maybe after dinner, some alone time?"

"Of course," he said. "I look forward to it."

After they made love, she lay calmly in his arms. Now Lucas began to speak.

"Jan, I want to talk to you about Bari."

"Bari?"

"Yes. You know that Bari wants to go to Israel with Marilyn and the youth group from Marilyn's synagogue. I think it would be good for her."

"I don't want her going to Israel. I told you that before. There is too much shit in my past from Israel. I am not going to allow her to go there. That's all there is to it."

"Jan, be reasonable."

"I am being as reasonable as I can. When I think of Israel, I want to scream. I am trying to stay calm. But I said no, and it's no."

"She needs friends. Marilyn is her only friend. She needs to be with kids her own age. This would be good for her."

"Why Israel? Her father is there. She thinks he's dead. What happens if she finds out he's not? He's such a bastard, Lucas. I refuse to allow this to happen." Her face was red with anger.

"Janice, I know you're not going to agree with me, but I think you're wrong for lying to Bari about her father. It's unfair of you. You should tell her the truth. Let the cards fall where they may, but she deserves to know the truth."

"What the hell do you care, Lucas? She's not your kid," Janice said, turning away from him in the bed.

"That's not fair. I've raised her like she was my own like she was my blood. Don't be this way, Janice. Let her know that her father is alive. If she wants to meet him, let her meet him. You just can't control everything."

"Fuck you, Lucas." Janice sat up and crossed her arms over her chest. "You don't know him. You don't know anything about him."

"I know he hurt you. I love you, and I'm sorry for anything you went through, but you need to tell Bari the truth. If you don't tell her, Janice, I will."

"Lucas! Who the hell do you think you are?"

"I'm sorry. But this lie has been eating at me for years. It's time she knew."

Janice glared at him in the dark room, lit only by a streak of light from the moon. "You had better not."

"I'm sorry, Jan, but I'm going to tell her. Then I am going to give her the money to go to Israel."

"You wouldn't dare. I won't sign the papers allowing her to go."

"Please, Janice. Please don't do this. She's eighteen. I think she can travel without your consent."

"Lucas, I forbid her."

"You don't want her to go because of your own feelings about what happened to you in Israel. I know you are afraid she will meet someone, fall in love, and stay there like you did. But Jan, you have to let her live her life. You can't let what happened to you ruin things for Bari. She needs this. I don't know if she needs a signature, but if she does and you don't sign the release forms, I will."

Janice was angry, and she began to cry. Lucas leaned over and took her into his arms. At first, she tried to push him away, but he held her tightly until her body grew limp in his arms. Then he knew that she was ready to listen.

"I'm just so afraid for her. I'm afraid of what she'll do when she finds out I've lied to her all these years."

"Then I'll tell her. I will make the peace between you for both your sakes."

"You always help me, Lucas." She laid her head on his chest, and he stroked her hair.

"That's because I love you, my little red-headed, stubborn brat."

She laughed. "I love you, too, Lucas. How did I get so lucky to marry a man like you?"

He kissed her. They sat for a while in each other's arms. Then Lucas whispered in Janice's ear, "I'll go and tell her now."

Janice nodded. "I suppose you will have to tell her his name, too. Do you know that she doesn't even know his real name?"

Lucas shook his head. "It'll be okay," he said. He wasn't about to reprimand Janice.

Lucas put on his sweatpants. From the look on Janice's face, Lucas could see that she was worried. He gave her a smile of encouragement and hugged her shoulder.

"By the way, I've never asked before. What is his name, Janice?"

"Elan Amsel."

CHAPTER NINETY-SIX

LUCAS WENT into Bari Lynn's room. They sat down on her bed and waited for a few minutes. Bari Lynn watched him. "So, did you talk to Mom? Did you ask her if I could go with Marilyn to Israel?"

"Yes," Lucas breathed. "And you will go with your friend. But first, Bari, there is something I have to tell you. Something you should know."

"Okay, Dad."

"Your mother made a mistake. She kept something from you that she thought would hurt you. She never wanted to lie to you, but she couldn't tell you."

"Tell me what, Dad?"

"Bari, your father is alive. His name is Elan Amsel. He lives in Israel. I am assuming you might want to see him. I don't know what you will find if you look him up. But what I do know is that you deserve to know the truth. Then whatever you decide to do about it should be your decision, not mine or your mother's," Lucas said.

"Oh my God," Bari said, staring at Lucas in disbelief. She was quiet for several minutes. Lucas gave her time to digest what he'd just told her.

"You're my dad. You'll always be my dad, but I'm stunned."

"It's understandable."

"I thought my birth father was dead, that he died in the Vietnam War. I never even knew he was an Israeli. I can't help it, but I want to know who this Elan Amsel is and why he left my mom. I want to see him, to look at him, and to know where I came from. Does that make any sense at all?" Bari asked.

"Yes, of course it does. I understand completely. Please, Bari, don't be too hard on your mom. For me."

She nodded. Her face was pale. "My mom is so damn controlling. I should have known this all of my life. She thinks it's her right to keep things from me. It's not fair."

"It's only because she loves you, Bari."

CHAPTER NINETY-SEVEN

THE FIRST TIME Ido kissed Ima, she felt like she was flying. It was as if she'd never been kissed before. All the men and all the memories of the horrors from her past dissipated like snow on a warm day. The first time they made love, Ima trembled with fear. She felt like a virgin, and in many ways, she was.

Ido did not rush. He was careful, letting her set the pace. He felt her body trembling in his arms, and he knew she was terrified of her own emotions. So he stopped making love to her and just held her for a long time, whispering softly into her ear. He told her an old story that he'd once heard about a man who lived in ancient times, a man whose love for a woman had conquered all her fears and made her whole again.

As his quiet words soothed her nerves, Ima began to relax again, to breathe more slowly.

"Are you sure you want to do this?" he asked.

She nodded. "Yes."

Ima and Ido were married on the base. Ima finally felt she could write a letter to her mom and grandma that she could send.

Dear Mom and Bubbie,

I just signed up for a second term in the IDF. The army has been a great experience for me. I met someone. He is the love of my life. His name is Ido, and I know you will both love him. This is going to sound a little strange, but we got married in a civil ceremony. Believe me, I know it was the right thing to do. I've messed up a lot of things in my life, but this isn't one of them. Ido has helped me to realize how much I've hurt both of you over the years, and I am really sorry. I hope you can forgive me.

Ido and I are coming to see both of you next week. We will only have a week to spend with you because although we have a longer leave, we've signed up for an extra assignment. The assignment pays well, and we could use the extra money since we want to buy a small house. The assignment seems like fun, actually. We are going to be escorting a group of American teenagers from a synagogue in the U.S. all around Israel. This should be interesting! Anyway, Ido and I look forward to seeing you both. By the way, my new name is Ima Hadar! Can you believe it?

Love to you both,
Ima

CHAPTER NINETY-EIGHT

KATJA HAD to admit that Ima sounded much more mature and happier. But married? Just like that? Katja knew she must be thankful. After all, they had almost lost Ima forever. Before Ima went to serve in the IDF, her mother and grandmother were afraid that someday they might find Ima dead from suicide or an overdose of drugs. Katja was pleasantly surprised at the outcome of everything.

Her friends, the other women who were a part of her organization, had told her to expect that Ima would come back from the IDF as a different person. "They'll help her in the army, you'll see," one of Katja's friends said. Katja had been hopeful when Ima left. She hadn't known what to expect. And now Ima was married? Katja's mind whirled. Married? To whom? How did it happen?

When Katja told Zofia, somehow, Zofia was not surprised.

"This was what Ima needed. She needed to grow up, and the IDF does that. It makes them grow up," Zofia said.

"But married?" Katja said. "I can't say I expected that…"

"Listen, they'll be here next week. Then we'll meet the boy, and we can get a better grasp on everything. Young love can happen very quickly, Kat. You forget, my sunshine."

"Yes, I suppose. That's what age does to you, Mama."

Zofia laughed. She didn't need to say anything. She understood. She was still young at heart. Even after all this time, she still remembered how it felt to be in Isaac's arms. Even though they lived in the worst possible conditions when they first met, hiding in the forest from the Nazi persecution, she'd still felt such joy at his touch. So she understood young love, even now—maybe especially now.

Although Zofia would never tell her daughter, when she was so terribly sick with the radiation treatment, she'd wanted to die because she wanted to be in Isaac's embrace again. When she couldn't eat because of the horrible way the treatments left her feeling, she remembered the time back in the forest when Isaac helped her eat raw fish. She'd almost vomited, but as he put the food into her mouth, he began talking about the bread his mother baked. His voice was so calm and comforting that she could almost taste the warm, sweet dough. And somehow, he had managed to help her to swallow the food. He saved her life.

Oh, Isaac, I miss you so much.

CHAPTER NINETY-NINE

THE WIND SEEMED to jitterbug through the trees as Ima opened the door to her mother's house.

"So come in. This is where I live." She smiled at Ido.

"If I had known you were rich, I would have married you sooner." He laughed.

"That's why I never told you." She winked at him.

"You know it doesn't matter, don't you?" he asked.

"Of course, I know," she said. "Mom, Grandma, we're here," Ima called out.

Katja came rushing down the stairs and stopped short as she gazed down at her daughter, whose arm was hooked into the arm of a strong young Israeli man. Katja felt her heart sink as she remembered long ago when she'd become engaged to Elan. She had looked so much like Ima that it caused her to shudder. Zofia came out of her bedroom, still in her housecoat. They had not expected Ima and her new husband until much later in the day.

"Mom, Grandma, this is Ido."

"It's a pleasure to meet you," Zofia said, coming over and engulfing Ima first and then Ido in an embrace.

Katja just stood frozen like an ice sculpture on the stairs.

"Mom?" Ima said.

Katja could not release her gaze. Ido reminded her of Elan, strong and so incredibly sexy. What would he think if he knew the truth? What if he knew that Ima was the daughter of a child born under Nazi direction into the Lebensborn? Elan had left her. Would Ido leave Ima? Even now, Katja's past haunted her.

Katja still stood, unable to move, and watched her daughter as if watching a movie. She closed her eyes tightly, trying to push the memory of Elan out of her mind. Instead, she saw Helga's face appear in her mind's eye. Helga, her birth mother, was crying, and then the image of the helmet of an SS officer shot through her brain, and Katja's knees buckled.

"Mom, what's wrong with you?" Ima asked.

Katja tried to shake off the visions she was having and tried to come back to the present moment. She cleared her throat and started down the stairs but was dizzy. She tripped and fell. Ido was there in an instant to lift her.

"Are you all right, Mrs. Zaltstein?"

"Yes." Katja could hardly breathe. At that very moment, as Katja looked at her daughter, she was so happy and so changed by the love of this strong Israeli that Katja decided she would never tell either of them the truth. She'd made that mistake long ago with Elan, and he'd walked out on her.

If this man walked out on Ima, it might kill her daughter. Katja knew that Ima was not stable on her own. It was only through the strength of this man, who now stood beside her, that she had, by some miracle, returned from the living dead. No, Katja would take her secret to her grave. Katja glanced at her mother, who seemed to be reading her mind. Zofia nodded as if she agreed.

"Sorry, I can be so clumsy sometimes." Katja tried to laugh, but her voice was several octaves higher than normal.

"Are you all right?" Ido asked again.

"Yes, of course. It's so nice to meet you. Welcome to Ima's home. As you've probably already guessed, I'm her mother, and this is her grandmother." Katja was usually so gracious. And she was trying to be that way now, but she was stiff and nervous.

Zofia knew what Katja was thinking. How could she not? Zofia remembered how happy Katja was with Elan until he learned the truth. Zofia trembled slightly. She would never speak of the past. For Ima's sake, neither Ima nor Ido must ever know who Katja's birth parents were. It was best if they never learned that Katja was born in the home of the Lebensborn.

Zofia could not be sure of Ido's reaction, and Ima had been through far too much to risk Ido leaving her the way Elan had left her mother. There was no reason for them ever to find out that Zofia was not Katja's birth mother. The truth would remain a secret buried in Zofia's heart forever. Right then, Zofia swore a vow of silence to God and herself. But in the back of her mind, she knew from experience that the truth always had a wicked way of coming to the surface. She prayed for the sake of her daughter and her granddaughter that somehow, someway, this time, the truth would remain buried in the archives of the horrors of Nazi Germany.

Katja could not believe how much Ima had changed. Her hair was no longer chopped. She had lost all the edge and anger that used to shoot off her like the bullets from a machine gun. Ima smiled, laughed, and even talked to Katja and Zofia the way she had before that horrible day when their lives had changed.

It was beyond wonderful to have a man in the house again. The water in the bathroom sink had been leaking for over a year. Katja had meant to call a plumber but never did. In less than fifteen minutes, Ido fixed the leak. He was a true gem, adjusting closet doors that had fallen off their hinges and just doing little things that had gone undone. It was not because she couldn't afford the repairs; she could. It was simply because the heart had gone out of her the day Ima first came back home with torn clothes and a bruised face. Now, her Ima was restored, and her husband was fixing her house.

Now Katja remembered what it was like to have a man in the house. It made her miss her father and husband, but more importantly, deep in the depths of her soul, she feared for her daughter.

Katja could not help but recall how happy she'd been at the beginning with Elan before he found out the truth.

What if, by some terrible twist of fate, Ido learned that Ima's mother was not of Jewish blood and even worse? This tugged at the rope of Katja's intestines, and she could not bring herself to eat. "I'm trying to lose some weight," she said. Zofia studied her daughter. She had not mentioned dieting before and suspected she was trying to deal with *her secret.*

Ido took them all out for dinner one night. They sat outside at an outdoor restaurant. Katja had convinced the couple to have a small ceremony to celebrate their marriage, and they were all making plans for the celebration.

As they sat outside talking and laughing in the warm breeze, Zofia tried to join in, but she was tired. She knew something was not right. She'd been more lethargic lately. When they were leaving, Zofia stood up too fast and felt dizzy. She tripped on a stone on the sidewalk. Ido caught her before she could fall and helped her into the car. He helped her out of the car and back to her room when they arrived home.

After everyone left and Zofia lay in bed alone, she knew the cancer was back. She'd felt this way before. *At least Ima will be all right now*. She should talk to Katja. Tell her how she felt. Zofia took a deep breath and felt a twinge of that old pain. Katja would need her if Ido found out the truth about everything and left Ima. Ima would need her, too. And she wished she could be there for them. But she could not live forever. The time would come when Katja and Ima must stand alone without her help.

Zofia would think about Isaac when she was alone in her bed at night. She missed him. Quietly, she would whisper to him in the silence of the room and tell him how much she wished she could come home to him and once again lie safely in his arms. There was no doubt Zofia was getting old. The cancer and the treatments had weakened her, and the bones in her hips and shoulders ached. And now that Ima and Katja were okay, she was ready to leave this world and go to Isaac.

The only reason she took those horrible treatments in the first place was that Katja and Ima needed her. Now, she would let nature take its course and prepare to join her beloved husband, Isaac. She would spend her last days writing memoirs about the Holocaust so that future generations of Jews would never forget.

So she whispered softly into the darkness in the empty room, "Isaac, my darling, my love, it won't be long. Our Katja and Ima will be okay. I will come to you and once again rest in your sweet embrace."

That night, Zofia dreamed of Isaac. They were young again, back in the forest in Poland, hiding from the Nazis. It was a terrible time but a wonderful time, too. They were young and in love, and although she had never been so terrified, she'd never felt such joy. "Even in the darkest hour," she heard Isaac whisper in her ear, "there is always a flicker of light."

CHAPTER ONE HUNDRED

KATJA HELPED Ima pack her duffel bag. They were alone in Ima's room. Ido and Zofia were in the dining room having breakfast.

"You like him, Mom?"

"Yes, I do," Katja said. She was longing to tell Ima the truth. It hung on her tongue, choking her, but she dared not speak the words.

"He makes me so happy, Mom."

"Do you really have to leave so soon? Stay another week," Katja said. Maybe, just maybe, she was wrong about Ido. Perhaps she was just projecting her fears onto him. She had no concrete reason to believe that he was anything like Elan. The only thing that she was sure that Ido and Elan shared was their confidence, their overwhelming attractiveness, and their love for Israel.

"We can't. We have an assignment. We're escorting a group of American tourists who are coming to visit Israel with their synagogue. We are going to tour with the teenagers in the group. You know, show them around their homeland, but more importantly, it is our responsibility to see that they return safely to America. That's why they are being accompanied by five members of the IDF. Ido and I are part of the group going with them."

"Do they have a tour guide, too?"

"Yes, but we are not supposed to let the Americans know that we are with them as protection. We have to act as if we are just there to help show them around. It's a fine line we've been instructed to walk. Because we're close to them in age, we can be like friends instead of soldiers.

"We want to encourage more Americans to travel to Israel, so we want to be sure that nothing happens to them while they're here. Even though we will be in uniform, we don't want to be a constant reminder of the dangers that Israel faces every day." Ima zipped the side of her duffel bag, then turned to her mother and smiled. "Unless you live here in this country, you can't possibly understand what this land means to our people and the sacrifices we Israelis are willing to make to protect it."

Katja nodded. She knew exactly what Ima meant. She'd lost her husband for Israel.

"Are you ready, sweetheart?" Ido called Ima. "We have to get moving. I want to get back a day early so we can have time to settle in before we meet the group at the airport."

"I'm coming. I'll be right there," Ima said. Then she turned and kissed Katja on the cheek and hugged her hard. It had been so long since Katja had seen that much affection from her daughter.

"I love you, Ima," Katja said, a tear running down her cheek. "Be safe."

"I love you, too, Mom. We'll return in six months to begin putting the party together."

"How long will this group from the synagogue be in Israel?"

"Two weeks."

"Be careful, be safe. I love you."

"Thanks, Mom. I'm so glad that you like Ido. You think Bubbie likes him?"

"I know she does."

Ima smiled.

Katja's heart swelled as she looked at her beautiful daughter. Ima had grown up, and somehow, she seemed healed of her previous anger. *Praise God, I was so worried…*

. . .

The End

AUTHORS NOTE

I always enjoy hearing from my readers, and your thoughts about my work are very important to me. If you enjoyed my novel, please consider telling your friends and posting a short review on Amazon. Word of mouth is an author's best friend.

Also, it would be my honor to have you join my mailing list. As my gift to you for joining, you will receive 3 **free** short stories and my USA Today award-winning novella complimentary in your email! To sign up, just go to my website at www.RobertaKagan.com

I send blessings to each and every one of you,

Roberta

Email: roberta@robertakagan.com

ABOUT THE AUTHOR

I wanted to take a moment to introduce myself. My name is Roberta, and I am an author of Historical Fiction, mainly based on World War 2 and the Holocaust. While I never discount the horrors of the Holocaust and the Nazis, my novels are constantly inspired by love, kindness, and the small special moments that make life worth living.

I always knew I wanted to reach people through art when I was younger. I just always thought I would be an actress. That dream died in my late 20's, after many attempts and failures. For the next several years, I tried so many different professions. I worked as a hairstylist and a wedding coordinator, amongst many other jobs. But I was never satisfied. Finally, in my 50's, I worked for a hospital on the PBX board. Every day I would drive to work, I would dread clocking in. I would count the hours until I clocked out. And, the next day, I would do it all over again. I couldn't see a way out, but I prayed, and I prayed, and then I prayed some more. Until one morning at 4 am, I woke up with a voice in my head, and you might know that voice as Detrick. He told me to write his story, and together we sat at the computer; we wrote the novel that is now known as All My Love, Detrick. I now have over 30 books published, and I have had the honor of being a USA Today Best-Selling Author. I have met such incredible people in this industry, and I am so blessed to be meeting you.

I tell this story a lot. And a lot of people think I am crazy, but it is true. I always found solace in books growing up but didn't start writing until I was in my late 50s. I try to tell this story to as many people as possible to inspire them. No matter where you are in your life, remember there is always a flicker of light no matter how dark it seems.

I send you many blessings, and I hope you enjoy my novels. They are all written with love.

Roberta

MORE BOOKS BY ROBERTA KAGAN

AVAILABLE ON AMAZON

Margot's Secret Series

The Secret They Hid

An Innocent Child

The Blood Sisters Series

The Pact

My Sister's Betrayal

When Forever Ends

The Auschwitz Twins Series

The Children's Dream

Mengele's Apprentice

The Auschwitz Twins

Jews, The Third Reich, and a Web of Secrets

My Son's Secret

The Stolen Child

A Web of Secrets

A Jewish Family Saga

Not In America

They Never Saw It Coming

When The Dust Settled

The Syndrome That Saved Us

A Holocaust Story Series

The Smallest Crack

The Darkest Canyon

Millions Of Pebbles

Sarah and Solomon

All My Love, Detrick Series

All My Love, Detrick

You Are My Sunshine

The Promised Land

To Be An Israeli

Forever My Homeland

Michal's Destiny Series

Michal's Destiny

A Family Shattered

Watch Over My Child

Another Breath, Another Sunrise

Eidel's Story Series

And . . . Who Is The Real Mother?

Secrets Revealed

New Life, New Land

Another Generation

The Wrath of Eden Series

The Wrath Of Eden

The Angels Song

Stand Alone Novels

One Last Hope

A Flicker Of Light

The Heart Of A Gypsy

Made in the USA
Middletown, DE
23 September 2024

61363452R00227